RAGE AND RUIN

**Books by Jennifer L. Armentrout
available from Inkyard Press**

**The Harbinger★
(in reading order)**

Storm and Fury
Rage and Ruin

**The Dark Elements
(in reading order)**

Bitter Sweet Love★★
White Hot Kiss
Stone Cold Touch
Every Last Breath

Stand-alone titles

The Problem with Forever
If There's No Tomorrow

★Set in the world of The Dark Elements
★★Ebook prequel companion novella; does not need to be read to enjoy
the full-length novels

JENNIFER L. ARMENTROUT

RAGE
AND
RUIN

inkyard
press

inkyard
press™

Recycling programs
for this product may
not exist in your area.

ISBN-13: 978-1-335-01825-0

Rage and Ruin

This edition published by arrangement with Harlequin Books S.A.

For questions and comments about the quality of this book, please contact us at CustomerService@Harlequin.com.

Inkyard Press
22 Adelaide St. West, 40th Floor
Toronto, Ontario M5H 4E3, Canada
www.InkyardPress.com

Printed in U.S.A.

To Loki, who was by my side while I wrote *Rage and Ruin*, and to Apollo, who is with me now while I edit this book.

I miss you.

I love you.

1

I blinked open achy, swollen eyes and stared straight at the pale, translucent face of a ghost.

Gasping, I jerked upright. Strands of dark hair fell across my face. "Peanut!" I pressed the heel of one palm against my chest, where my poor heart pounded like a steel drum. "What in the Hell, dude?"

The ghost, who'd been sort of a roommate of mine for the past decade, grinned at me from where he floated midair, several inches above the bed. He was stretched out on his side, cheek resting on his palm. "Just making sure you're still alive."

"Oh my God." Exhaling raggedly, I lowered my hand to the soft dove-gray comforter. "I've told you a million times to stop doing that."

"I'm kind of surprised you still think I listen to you half the time."

Peanut had a point.

He had an aversion to following my rules, which were only, like, two rules.

Knock before entering the room.

Don't watch me while I sleep.

I thought they were quite reasonable rules.

Peanut looked like he had the night he died, way back in the '80s. His Whitesnake concert T-shirt was legit, as were his dark jeans and red Chuck Taylors. On his seventeenth birthday, for some idiotic reason, he'd climbed one of those massive speaker towers and subsequently fallen to his death, proving natural selection was a thing.

Peanut hadn't crossed over into that shiny bright white light, and a few years ago, I stopped trying to convince him when he said to me, quite clearly, it was not his time. It was far past his time, but whatever. I liked having him around... except when he did creepy crap like this.

Pushing the hair out of my face, I looked around my bedroom—no, not my bedroom. This wasn't even my bed. All of this belonged to Zayne. My gaze flicked from the heavy sunlight-blocking curtains to the bedroom door—the closed bedroom door that I'd left unlocked the night before, just in case...

I shook my head.

"What time is it?" I leaned back against the headboard, keeping the blanket close to my chin. Since Wardens' body temps ran higher than humans' and it was July, so it was most likely hot and sticky as a circle of Hell outside, Zayne's apartment was like an icebox.

"It's almost three in the afternoon," Peanut answered. "And that's why I thought you were dead."

Damn, I thought, scrubbing my hand across my face. "We got back pretty late last night."

"I know. I was here. You didn't see me, but I saw you. Both of you. I was watching."

I frowned. *That* didn't sound creepy at all.

"You looked like you'd been through a wind tunnel." Peanut's gaze flickered over my head. "You still do."

I'd felt like I'd been in a wind tunnel. A mental, emotional and physical wind tunnel. Last night, after I'd had a complete and utter breakdown by the old treehouse at the Warden compound, Zayne had taken me *flying*.

It had been magical, up there with the cool night wind, where the stars that always looked so faint to me became bright. I hadn't wanted it to end, even when my face went numb and my lungs began to strain with the effort to breathe. I'd wanted to stay up there, because nothing could touch me in the wind and the night sky, but Zayne had brought me back down to Earth and to reality.

That was only a handful of hours ago, but it felt like a lifetime. I barely remembered coming back to Zayne's apartment. We hadn't talked about what had happened with…Misha, or about what had happened to Zayne. We hadn't talked at all, really, other than Zayne asking if I needed anything and me mumbling no. I'd gotten undressed and climbed into bed, and Zayne had stayed in the living room, sleeping on the couch.

"You know," Peanut said, drawing me from my thoughts, "I might be dead and all, but you look way worse than me."

"I do?" I murmured, even though I wasn't surprised to hear that. Based on the way my face felt, I probably looked like I'd face-planted a brick wall.

He nodded. "You've been crying."

I had been.

"A lot," he added.

That was true.

"And when you didn't come back yesterday, I was worried." Peanut floated upright and sat on the edge of the bed. His legs and hips disappeared a few inches into the mattress. "I thought something happened to you. I was panicking. I couldn't even finish watching *Stranger Things* I was so worried. Who's going to take care of me if you die?"

"You're dead, Peanut. No one needs to take care of you."

"I still need to be loved and cherished and thought of. I'm like Santa Claus. If no one alive is here to want and believe in me, then I'll cease to exist."

Ghosts and spirits didn't work that way. At all. But he was so wonderfully overdramatic. A grin tugged at the corners of my lips until I remembered I wasn't the only one who could see Peanut. A girl who lived in this apartment complex could also see him. She must have watered-down angelic blood kicking around in her veins, like all humans who were able to see ghosts or displayed other psychic abilities. Enough to make her…different from everyone else. There weren't many humans in existence with traces of angelic blood, so it was a shock to learn that there was one so close to where I was staying.

"Thought you made a new friend?" I reminded him.

"Gena? She's cool, but it wouldn't be the same if you ended up as dead as a doornail, and her parents aren't choice, you know?" Before I could confirm that *choice* meant *good* in '80s speak, he asked, "Where were you last night?"

My gaze shifted to that closed, *unlocked* door. "I was at the compound with Zayne."

Peanut inched closer and lifted a wispy hand. He patted my knee, but I felt nothing through the blanket, not even the cold air that usually accompanied Peanut's touch. "What happened, Trinnie?"

Trinnie.

Only Peanut called me that, while everyone else called me Trin or Trinity.

I closed my sore eyes as realization sank in. Peanut didn't know, and I wasn't sure how to tell him when the wounds left by Misha's actions hadn't scabbed over yet. If anything, I'd just slapped a weak-as-Hell bandage over them.

I was holding it together. Barely. So, the last thing I wanted to do was talk about it with *anyone*, but Peanut deserved to know. He knew Misha. He liked him, even though Misha could never see or communicate with Peanut, and he'd come to DC with me to find Misha instead of staying behind in the Potomac Highlands Warden community.

Granted, I was the only one who could see and communicate with Peanut, but he'd felt comfortable in the community. It was a big deal for him to travel with me.

Keeping my eyes closed, I drew in a long shuddering breath. "So, yeah, we…we found Misha, and it wasn't…it wasn't good, Peanut. He's gone."

"No," he whispered. And then louder, he repeated, *"No."*

I nodded.

"God. I'm sorry, Trinnie. I'm so damn sorry."

Swallowing around the hard lump in my throat, I met his gaze.

"The demons—"

"It wasn't the demons," I interrupted. "I mean, they didn't kill him. They didn't want him dead. He was actually working with them."

"What?" The shock in his voice, the way the one word pitched to near glass-breaking levels, would've been funny in any other situation. "He was your *Protector.*"

"He set it up—his abduction and everything." I pulled my knees up under the blanket, pressing them to my chest. "Even made it so Ryker saw me that day using my *grace.*"

"But Ryker killed…"

My mom. I shut my eyes again and felt them burn, as if there could possibly be more tears left inside me. "I don't know what was wrong with Misha. If he's always…hated me, or if it was the Protector bond. I found out that he was never supposed to be bonded to me. It was always supposed to be Zayne, but there was a mistake."

A mistake that my father had known about, and not only had he done nothing to fix it, he hadn't seemed to care about it at all. When I'd asked why he hadn't done anything, he'd said he wanted to see what would happen.

How freaking messed up was that?

"The bond could've twisted him. Made him turn…bad," I continued, voice thick. "I don't know. I won't ever know, but the *why* doesn't change the fact that he was working with Bael and this other demon. He even said that the Harbinger had chosen him." I flinched as Misha's face formed in my thoughts. "That the Harbinger told him he was special, too."

"Isn't that who's been killing Wardens and demons?"

"Yeah." I opened my eyes once I was sure I wasn't going to cry. "I had to…"

"Oh, no." Peanut seemed to know without me even saying it.

But I had to say it, because it was the reality. It was the truth I would live with for the rest of my days.

"I had to kill him." Each word felt like a kick to the chest. I kept seeing Misha. Not the Misha in the clearing outside the senator's house, but the one who'd waited for me while I talked to ghosts. Who'd napped in his Warden form while I sat beside him. The Misha who had been my best friend. "I did it. I killed him."

Peanut shook his head, his dark brown hair fading in and out as he became more corporeal for a moment and then lost his hold. "I don't know what to say. I really don't."

"There's nothing to be said. It is what it is." Exhaling, I stretched out my legs. "Zayne is now my Protector, and I'm going to be staying here. We need to find the Harbinger."

"Well, that part is good, right?" Peanut rose from the bed, still in a sitting position. "Zayne being your Protector?"

It was.

And it wasn't.

Becoming my Protector had saved Zayne's life, so that was a good thing—a *great* thing. Zayne hadn't hesitated to take the bond, and that was before he'd found out it was always supposed to have been him. But it also meant Zayne and I… Well, we could never be more than what we were now, and it didn't matter how badly I wanted to be more or how much I liked him. It didn't matter that he was the first guy I was ever seriously into.

I tipped my head back instead of suffocating myself with the pillow. Peanut became a blur as he drifted toward the curtain, though that had nothing to do with his ghostly form. "Is Zayne up?"

"He is, but he's not here. He left you a note in the kitchen. I read it while he wrote it." Peanut sounded rather proud. "It says he went to see someone named Nic. I think that was one of the guys who came with him to the community? Anyway, he left maybe a half hour ago."

Nic was short for Nicolai, the Washington, DC, clan leader. Zayne probably had unfinished business with him since he'd left whatever meeting they'd been having last night to come find me.

Zayne had *felt* my emotions through the bond. That strange new connection had led him right to the treehouse. I wasn't sure if I was amazed by that, annoyed or really weirded out. Probably a mixture of all three.

"Wonder why he didn't wake me." Pushing the cover aside, I scooted to the edge of the bed.

"He actually came in here and checked on you."

I froze, praying I hadn't been drooling on myself or doing anything weird. "He did?"

"Yep. I thought he was going to wake you. Looked like he was debating it, but all he did was pull the blanket over your shoulders. I thought it was totally bodacious of him."

I wasn't sure what *bodacious* meant, but I thought it was... God, it was sweet of him.

It was so like Zayne.

I might have known him for only a few weeks, but I knew

enough to be able to picture him carefully pulling the comforter over me, and doing it so gently that he didn't wake me.

My chest squeezed as if my heart had fallen into a meat grinder. "I need to shower." I stood on legs I expected to be shaky but that were surprisingly strong and stable.

"Yeah, you do."

Ignoring the comment, I checked my phone. I'd missed a call from Jada. My stomach tumbled. I placed the phone down and padded on bare feet to the bathroom, flipped on the light and winced at the sudden brightness. My eyes did not care for bright light of any kind. Or dark or shadowy areas, either. Actually, my eyes pretty much just sucked 95.7 percent of the time.

"Trinnie?"

Fingers lingering on the light switch, I looked over my shoulder at Peanut, who'd moved closer to the bathroom. "Yeah?"

He cocked his head, and when he looked at me, I felt stripped bare. "I know how much Misha meant to you. I know it has to hurt something bad."

Ending Misha's life hadn't hurt me. It quite possibly had *killed* a part of me, replacing it with a seemingly bottomless pit of sour bitterness and raw anger.

But Peanut didn't need to know that. No one did.

"Thank you," I whispered, turning away and closing the door as the burn hit the back of my throat.

I will not cry. I will not cry.

In the shower, with its multiple jets and stall large enough to fit two fully grown Wardens, I used the minutes under the hot, stinging spray to get my head straight.

Or, in other words, compartmentalize.

I'd had my much-needed breakdown last night. I had given myself time to cry it all out, and now was the time to put it away, because I had a job to do. After years of waiting, it had finally happened.

My father had called on me to fulfill my duty.

Find the Harbinger and stop it.

So, there was a lot to sift through and file away in my mental cabinet so that I could do what I was born for. I started with the most critical. Misha. I shoved what he'd done and what I'd had to do all the way to the bottom of the cabinet, tucked under my mother's death and my failure to stop that. That drawer was labeled EPIC FAIL. The next drawer was where I sent the cause of the blackish-blue bruises covering my left hip and the length of my thigh. Another bruise colored the right side of my ribs, where Misha had delivered a nasty kick. He'd kicked my butt and then some, but I'd still beaten him.

The usual feeling of smugness or pride over having bested someone who was well trained didn't surge through me.

There was nothing good to feel about any of that.

The bruises, the aches and all the pain went into the drawer I called BUCKET FULL OF NIGHTMARES, because the reason Misha had managed to land so many brutal hits was because he knew I had limited peripheral vision. He'd used it against me. That was my one weakness when fighting, something I needed to improve on, like, yesterday, because if this Harbinger discovered just how poor my vision was, it would exploit it.

Just like I would if the shoes were on other feet.

And yeah, that would be a nightmare, because not only would I die, so would Zayne. A tremor coursed through me as I slowly turned under the spray of water. I couldn't cave to that fear—couldn't dwell on it for one second. Fear made you do reckless, stupid things, and I already did enough of those for no good reason.

The top drawer had been empty and unlabeled until now, but I knew what I was filing there. That was where I was putting everything that had happened with Zayne. The kiss I'd stolen when we'd been back in the Potomac Highlands, the growing attraction and all the *want*, and that night, before we were bonded, when Zayne had kissed me and it had been everything I'd read about in the romance novels my mom had loved. When Zayne kissed me, when we'd gone as far as we could go without going all the way, the world had truly ceased to exist outside us.

I took all of that, along with the raw need for his touch, his attention and his heart—which most likely still belonged to someone else—and closed the file.

Relationships between Protectors and Trueborns were strictly forbidden. Why? I had no idea, and I guessed the reason the explanation was unknown was that I was the only Trueborn left.

I closed that drawer, which I simply labeled ZAYNE, and stepped out of the shower into the steam-filled bathroom. After wrapping a towel around myself, I leaned forward and wiped a palm over the mist-covered mirror.

My reflection came into view. As close as I was, my features were only a little fuzzy. My normally olive skin, courtesy of my mom's Sicilian roots, was paler than usual, which made my brown eyes seem darker and larger. The skin around them was puffy and shadowed. My nose still tilted to the side, and my mouth still seemed almost too large for my face.

I looked exactly as I had the evening Zayne and I left this apartment to go to Senator Fisher's house in hopes we'd find Misha or evidence of where he was being held.

I didn't feel the same.

How could there not be a more noticeable physical manifestation of everything that had changed?

My reflection didn't have an answer, but as I turned away from it, I said the only thing that mattered.

"I got this," I whispered, and then repeated louder, "I got this."

2

Hair damp and most likely looking like a complete mess, I sat at the kitchen island, bare feet tapping, staring at bare walls as I nursed a glass of OJ.

Zayne's apartment was so incredibly *empty*, reminding me of a staged home.

Other than my black combat-style boots, which were by the elevator door, there were no personal belongings scattered about. Unless I counted the punching bag hanging in the corner and the blue mats tucked against the wall as personal belongings. I didn't.

A soft cream-colored blanket was folded neatly, draped over the gray couch, picture ready. Not even a stray glass had been left on the kitchen counter, or a dish in the sink. The only room that remotely appeared as if someone lived here was the bedroom, and that was because my suitcases had thrown up my clothes all over the place.

Maybe it was the industrial design that added to the coldness. The cement floors and large metal fans that churned quietly from the exposed metal beams didn't add any warmth to the open and airy space. Neither did the floor-to-ceiling windows, which had to be tinted, because the sunlight seeping through them didn't make me want to poke my eyeballs out.

I would go stir-crazy if I was the only person who lived here.

That was what I was thinking about—real important stuff—when I felt the sudden burst of warmth in my chest.

"What in the world?" I whispered to the empty space. The warmth flared.

Was I having a heart attack? Okay. That was stupid for a multitude of reasons. I rubbed my chest. Maybe it was indigestion or the beginnings of an ulce—

Wait.

I lowered the glass. What I felt was an echo of my own heart, and I suddenly knew what it was. Holy granola bar, it was the bond—it was Zayne, and he was close.

I now had Zayne radar, and that was a little—or a lot—super freaking weird.

I started to bite on my thumbnail, but picked up my OJ instead, finishing it off with two loud, obnoxious gulps. My heart rate kicked up at the ding of the elevator arriving, and my gaze swung toward the steel elevator doors as I filled with nervous energy. I put the glass down before I dropped it. Every time I saw Zayne, it was like seeing him for the first time all over again, but it wasn't just that.

I'd cried all over Zayne last night—like, *all* over him.

Heat crept up the back of my neck. I wasn't a crier, and

until the night before, I'd been starting to believe that I had faulty tear ducts. Unfortunately those tear ducts were fully functioning. There'd been a lot of ugly, snotty sobs.

The door slid open, and the anxious energy exploded in my stomach as Zayne walked in.

Damn.

He made a plain white T-shirt and dark denim jeans look like they were tailor-made for him and only him. The material stretched across his wide shoulders and chest yet was fitted to his narrow, tapered waist. All Wardens were large in their human form, but Zayne was one of the largest I'd ever seen, coming in around six and a half feet.

Zayne had beautiful thick blond hair with the kind of natural wave I couldn't recreate with hours to spare, a YouTube tutorial and a dozen curling irons. Today it was tucked back in a knot at the nape of his neck, and I hoped to God that he never cut his hair.

He saw me immediately, and even though I couldn't see his eyes from where I sat, I could feel his gaze on me. It was somehow heavy and gentle, and sent a fine shiver of awareness dancing down my arms, making me grateful that I wasn't holding on to the glass any longer.

"Hey, sleepyhead," he said as the elevator door slid shut behind him. "Glad to see you up and moving about."

"Sorry I slept so late." I lifted my hands and then dropped them back to my lap, unsure what to do with them. He was carrying some kind of paper rolled up and tucked under one arm and a brown paper sack in his other hand. "Do you need help with any of that?" I asked, even though that was a dumb question considering Zayne could lift a Ford Explorer with one hand.

"Nah. And don't apologize. You needed the rest." His features were blurry to me, even with my glasses on, but they became clearer and sharper with every step he took toward me.

My gaze skittered away, but that didn't stop me from knowing what he looked like.

Which was utterly, breathtakingly, brutally beautiful. I could come up with more adjectives to describe him, but in all honesty, none would do him justice.

His skin was a golden hue that had nothing to do with being in the sun. High, broad cheekbones matched a wide, expressive mouth that was finished off with a jaw that could've been carved from granite.

I wished he was less attractive—or that I was less shallow—but even if both were the case, it would make little difference at the end of the day. Zayne wasn't just a pretty package that hid an ugly interior or a vapid personality. He was wicked smart, with a keen intelligence that was as sharp as his wit. I found him funny and entertaining, even when he was getting on my nerves and being overprotective. Most important, though, Zayne was genuinely *kind*, and God, kindness was so underrated by most.

He had a good heart, a big and gracious one, even though he was missing a part of his soul.

There was a saying that the eyes were the window to the soul, and it was true. At least for Wardens it was and, because of what happened to him, his eyes were a pale, frosty shade of blue.

He'd been dating Layla, the half demon, half Warden he'd

grown up with, who also happened to be the daughter of Lilith. She and Zayne had kissed and, because of the way Lilith's abilities had manifested in Layla, she'd taken a part of his soul.

My hands curled into fists. The whole soul-sucking thing had been accidental, and Zayne had known the risks involved, but that didn't stop the flash of anger and something far more sour that shot through me. Zayne had wanted her bad enough—loved her enough—to take that risk. To put himself and his life beyond this one into jeopardy just to kiss her.

That was hard-core, because I doubted a less-than-whole soul was looked upon favorably when one got to the Pearly Gates, no matter how good someone's heart was.

That kind of love couldn't just die, not in seven months, and something I didn't want to acknowledge—something I had filed away in that cabinet—wilted a little in my chest.

"You doing okay?" Zayne asked as he placed the bag and rolled-up paper on the island. The scent coming from the brown bag reminded me of grilled meat.

Wondering if he was picking up anything through the bond, I kept my eyes trained on the paper bag as I nodded. "Yeah. So, um, about last night."

"What about it?"

"I'm sorry for, you know, blubbering all over you." Heat swept over my cheeks.

"You don't need to apologize, Trin. You've been through a lot—"

"So have you." I stared at my fingers and my chipped, blunt nails.

"You needed me, and I needed to be there." Zayne made it sound so simple, as if that was the way it always had been.

"You said that last night."

"Still holds true today."

Pressing my lips together, I nodded again as I drew in a long breath and then let it out slowly. I felt the warmth of his hand before his fingers pressed under my chin. The moment his skin touched mine, an odd shock of electricity, of awareness, coursed through me, and I had no idea if that was due to the bond or if it was just him. That unique scent of his, which reminded me of wintermint, teased my senses. He tipped my head up, lifting my gaze to his.

Zayne was leaning across the island, his arm stretched over the rolled paper. That pale gaze flickered over my face, and one side of his lips curled up. "You're wearing your glasses."

"I am."

That half grin grew. "You don't wear them often."

I didn't, and not because of some lame vanity reason. Other than reading or being on the laptop, they didn't help much other than to make some things a little less blurry.

"I like them. I like them on you."

My glasses were just plain square black rims, no cool color or pattern, but I suddenly felt like I should wear them more often.

And then I wasn't thinking about my glasses, because the fingers on my chin shifted and I felt his thumb slide along the skin just under my lip. A fine shiver danced over my skin, followed by a wholly different kind of flush, one that was heady and exhilarating.

You want to kiss me again, don't you?

I could hear him speak those words as if he'd said them out loud, like he had after I'd helped remove an imp's claw from his chest. I'd said yes then, without hesitation, even though it hadn't exactly been a wise idea.

Unwise ideas have always been fun—a lot of fun.

His gaze lowered, lashes shielding his eyes, and I thought that he might be staring at my mouth, and that… I wanted that too much.

I pulled back, just out of his reach.

Zayne dropped his hand, clearing his throat. "How did you sleep?"

"Good." I found my voice as the warmth eased and my pulse slowed. "You?"

The glance he sent me as he straightened said he wasn't sure if he believed me or not. "Slept only because I was exhausted, but it could've been better."

"The couch can't be all that comfortable."

His gaze met mine again, and my breath caught. I knew better than to offer him the bed, but it was big enough to share and we were both mature adults. Sort of. We'd shared before without shenanigans going down, but shenanigans of the fun and forbidden kind had definitely gone down the last time we'd shared that bed.

Zayne shrugged. "You got my note?"

Relieved at the change of subject, I shook my head. "Peanut saw you writing it and told me all about it. Said you went to see Nicolai."

He froze, fingers in the process of opening the bag. I pressed my lips together to stop my smile as he glanced behind him. "Is he here now?"

I looked around the empty apartment. "Not that I know

of. Why? Are you creeped out that he was with you and you had no idea?" I teased. "Scared of little old Peanut?"

"I am confident enough in my badassery to fully acknowledge that having a ghost hanging around gives me the heebie-jeebies."

"Heebie-jeebies?" I laughed. "What are you? Twelve?"

He snorted as he unrolled the bag and the scent of grilled meat increased. "Watch it, or I'll eat this hamburger I got for you right in front of you and enjoy it."

My stomach grumbled as he pulled out a white carton. "I would drop-kick you into a wall if you did that."

Zayne chuckled as he placed the carton in front of me and then pulled out another. "Want something to drink?" He turned to the fridge. "I think there might be a Coke in here, since you refuse to drink water."

"Water is for people concerned about their health, and I'm not about that kind of life."

Shaking his head again, he pulled out a can of carbonated goodness and a bottle of water. He slid the first over the island toward me.

"Did you know drinking eight eight-ounce glasses of water a day is about as helpful as the whole 'an apple a day keeps the doctor away' for most healthy people?" I asked. "That you really only need to drink water when you're thirsty, because duh, that's why you experience thirst, especially because you get water from other beverages, like my beautiful calorie-ridden soda, and from foods? That the studies that came up with the whole eight eight-ounce stuff also stated that you can get most of your water in the foods you eat, but when the reports were made public, they conveniently left that out?"

Zayne arched a brow as he screwed the lid off his water.

"Fact-check me. There's no scientific evidence whatsoever that supports the whole eight-by-eight rule, and I'm not someone who needs to drown themselves in water." I popped open my soda. "So, let me live my life."

He downed half the bottle in one impressive gulp. "Thanks for the health lesson."

"You're welcome." I grinned at him as I opened the carton. My stomach did a happy dance when I got an eyeful of the grilled hamburger smack-dab between a toasted sesame bun and a side order of curly fries. "And thank you for the food. You're a keeper."

"Good. I want to be kept."

My gaze flew to him. He wasn't looking at me as he got busy opening his food, which was a good thing, because my imagination had taken those five words and gone to town with them.

Sensation burst in the center of my chest, and it reminded me oddly of how pepper smelled. It felt like frustration, and I thought it might be coming from Zayne.

That was weird.

"But you really can't get rid of me at this point, can you?" He looked up through thick lashes. "You're stuck with me."

"Yeah." I blinked and finished unwrapping my burger. I didn't think of it that way, though. He was my bonded Protector. I was the Trueborn he guarded. Together, we were a force to be reckoned with because we were built for one another, and the only thing that could separate us was death.

Deep down, did he look at us as if we were *stuck* with one another, even though he hadn't hesitated when he'd been offered the bond? Wasn't that what had happened with Misha? Besides the fact that we never should've been bonded, I had sensed a growing unrest in him, but I'd been so wrapped up in myself that I hadn't paid attention.

Not until it was too late.

Zayne had learned that my mother was supposed to have brought me to his father, and because she hadn't done that, his father thought Zayne was supposed to take in Layla, somehow mistaking me, a Trueborn who rocked a whole lot of angelic blood, for a half demon, half Warden.

Which was kind of a big *oops*.

I had no idea how Zayne felt about any of that. Or if it mattered to him that it should've been me he'd grown up with.

I picked up the bun and removed the thick tomato slice as I opened my mouth to speak. But I made the mistake of actually looking at his carton of food. He'd gotten a grilled-chicken sandwich. My lip curled, because it looked about as appetizing as an unseasoned chicken breast could look. While I smacked my bun back onto my burger, Zayne took his top bun off.

"You're a monster," I whispered.

Zayne chuckled. "You going to eat that?" He pointed to the tomato that I had gotten rid of. I shook my head. "Of course not. You don't like vegetables or water."

"Not true. I like onions and pickles."

"Only if they're on hamburgers." He carried his box of food around the island and dropped onto the stool beside me, plucked up the tomato, then plopped it on his poor grilled-chicken sandwich. "Eat, and then I'll show you what I got when I met with Nic."

We ate side by side, exchanging napkins, and there was no

urge to fill the silence with idle words. There was an intimacy in it that was quite surprising. When we were finished, I volunteered for cleanup, since he'd gotten the food and I'd done nothing but sleep. Once I'd finished wiping down the island, I returned to the stool beside Zayne.

"Before we look at what you got, I have a favor to ask." I took a shallow breath.

"Done," he replied.

My brows lifted. "I haven't told you what the favor is."

He lifted one large shoulder in a shrug. "Whatever it is, you got it."

I stared at him. "What if I was asking for you to trade in your vintage Impala for a minivan from the '80s?"

Zayne looked over at me, his brows furrowed. "That would be a seriously weird request."

"Exactly, and you just agreed to it!"

His head tilted. "You're weird, Trin, but I don't think you're that weird."

"I feel like I should be offended by that statement."

Zayne grinned. "What's your favor?"

"I need help...with training." I squared my shoulders. "Misha and I trained every day. I don't need that, but I do need to practice in a certain area."

That got his full attention. "What area?"

"You know I don't have much peripheral vision." I shifted my feet from the floor to the bar on the stool. "It's literally a blind spot for me, so when I fight, I try to keep enough distance between me and my opponent so they stay in my central vision."

He nodded. "Makes sense."

"Well, Misha knew my weakness and he exploited it, which is why he landed so many hits. I would do the same thing in a fight. Anything goes."

"Same," he murmured.

"And I doubt Misha kept that to himself. He could've told Bael. Maybe even this Harbinger," I explained. "I need to get better. I don't know how, but I need…"

"To learn not to rely on your vision?" he suggested.

Exhaling, I nodded. "Yes."

Zayne's lips pursed. "Working on that is a great idea and training is always smart. I didn't think of that."

"Well, the whole bonding thing did just happen, so…"

He shot me a brief grin. "Let me think of some ways to work on what you're asking."

Relieved, I smiled. "I'll do the same. So, what did you want to show me?"

He unrolled the paper, spreading it across the island. "I got Gideon to print the plans from Senator Fisher's house that Layla took pictures of. I figured you'd want to see them."

I hadn't been able to see them that night, so this was incredibly…thoughtful of him. Leaning over the document that ended up being half the size of the island, I scanned the designs while Zayne rose from the bar stool. I didn't have experience looking at construction plans, but within a few moments, I knew that their assumptions had been on point. "These really are plans for a school, aren't they? These boxes are classrooms. This is a cafeteria, and those are dorm rooms."

"Yep." Zayne returned to the island with a laptop. "Gideon did a quick records search and he couldn't find any permits linked to the senator and a school, but I want to see if I can find anything online referencing it while he's still searching through different databases."

"Sounds good," I murmured, staring at the plans.

"Listen to this," Zayne said after a few minutes. "We know that Fisher is the majority leader and that he's known to be a God-loving and wholesome man, all about 1950s-era family values."

"How ironic," I muttered.

"I can't even tell you how many websites are coming up, dedicated to him from religious folks. Even ones from the Children of God."

I rolled my eyes. "Well, that right there should tell you something."

He snickered. "According to their website, they believe he's some kind of prophet or a savior who is destined to save America. From what, I have no idea." Fingers moving over the touch pad, he shook his head. "Luckily these people seem to be a very, very small minority."

Thank God. There was a twisted irony to the situation with the senator. The man was definitely not a fan of God, considering he was hanging out with an ancient Upper Level demon and going to witches to get enchantments that turned humans into walking cannon fodder—the very same coven that had betrayed us by telling the demon Aym, who was super dead. Thankfully.

Man, I wished I could cast spells, because I'd curse the coven with a pox and then some. "I doubt whatever he's planning is anything good."

"Agreed." Zayne's fingers tapped away on the keyboard. "Looks like the fire made the news." He tilted the laptop so that I could see a picture of a gutted, charred house with the headline "Overnight Fire Destroys Senate Majority Leader Fisher's Home." "It doesn't say much beyond blaming faulty wiring."

I snorted. "I may not be an arson specialist, but I seriously doubt anything about that fire would make anyone think it was due to electrical failure…" I trailed off as I saw the unholy red flames in my mind, saw Zayne, who in his Warden form was almost indestructible, burned and near death—

"Fisher probably has people working with him in the fire department," Zayne explained, snapping me out of my thoughts. "When demons infiltrate human circles, it becomes an epidemic, with the demon as the disease. The first human they corrupt becomes the carrier and brings others into it. Like a virus that spreads from contact to contact, and the farther the source gets from the carrier, the more the humans don't realize what or who they're truly working for."

"But the senator knows he's working with a demon. He went to the coven and got that enchantment." I frowned. "And he also promised parts of a Trueborn—of me—in return. Jerk."

A low snarling sound raised the tiny hairs all over my body, and I looked around the kitchen to see where the sound was coming from. I'd never seen a hellhound, and I imagined that was the kind of noise they made, but that sound was coming from Zayne.

My eyes widened.

"That's not going to happen." His eyes flashed an intense pale blue. "Ever. I can promise you that."

I found myself nodding slowly. "It won't."

He held my gaze and then went back to his internet search. Muscles stiffened as a burst of fear spiked me in the chest, followed by the sudden clarity that Zayne…he would die for me. He already almost had, and that was before we were bonded. He'd pushed me out of the way when Aym had made a run at me, and nearly paid for that with his life. Aym had been horrifically talented with Hellfire, which could burn anything in its path, including a Warden.

As my Protector, giving his life for mine was in Zayne's job description. If I died, so would Zayne, and if he died protecting me, I would live on, and I guessed another would replace him—another like Misha, who was never supposed to have been bonded to me.

"You don't need to be afraid," he said, staring at the laptop screen.

My gaze shot to him. The glow from the screen lit his profile. "What?"

"I can feel it." He placed his left palm against his chest, and my shoulders tensed. "It's like an icicle in my chest. And I know you're not afraid of me or for yourself. You're too much of a badass. You're afraid *for* me, and you don't need to be. You know why?"

"Why?" I whispered.

Zayne looked at me then, his gaze unflinching. "You're strong, and you're a damn good warrior. I might be your Protector in some instances, but when we fight, I'm your partner. I know you're not going to put my ass in a sling because you're not holding your own. There's no way I can fall with you beside me, and no one will best you with me beside you. So, get those fears out of your head."

Air lodged in my throat. That was possibly the nicest thing anyone had ever said about me. I sort of wanted to hug him. I didn't, though, managing to keep my hands and arms to myself. "I like it when you say I'm a badass."

That got a grin. "Not remotely surprised to hear that."

"Does this mean you're finally going to admit I beat you and won that day in the training room back at the Community?" I asked.

"Come on now. I'm not going to lie to make you feel better about yourself."

I laughed as I gathered up my hair, twisting the thick length. "Are we going patrolling tonight?"

Patrolling was what Wardens did to keep the demon populace in check, but that wasn't the kind I was talking about. We were looking for a certain demon and a creature we had no idea what to call other than the Harbinger.

He paused. "I was thinking we could just chill for the night. Take it easy."

Take it *easy* with Zayne? A huge part of me jumped at that, but the fact I wanted to do it as badly as I did was a clear indication it should be the last thing I did.

"I think we should look for the Harbinger," I said. "We need to find it."

"We do, but is one night going to make a difference?"

"Knowing our luck? Yes."

A quick grin appeared and then disappeared. "You sure you're up for it? Yesterday…"

I tensed. "Yesterday was yesterday. I'm up for it. Are you?"

"Always," he murmured. Then louder he said, "We'll patrol tonight."

"Good."

He refocused on the screen. "Found something. It's an article dated back in January in the *Washington Post* where Fisher talks about acquiring funding for a school for chronically ill children. I quote, 'This school will become a place of joy and learning, where sickness does not define the individual and disease does not determine the future.' And then he talks about how there will be medical staff on-site, along with counselors and a state-of-the-art rehab facility."

"It can't be real, right? That he's building a school for sick kids? Like a demonic St. Jude's?" Sickened, all I could do was stare at the words I couldn't see clearly enough to read. "Using ill children as a cover? Man, that is like a whole new level of evilness."

"Well, wait until you hear this." Zayne sat back, crossing his arms. "He says the entire proposal and plan are in honor of his wife, who passed away after a long battle with cancer."

"God. I'm not sure which part of that is worse."

"They're equally terrible." He glanced at me. "It says he's already acquired the land for this school, so it's interesting that Gideon hasn't found a record of it yet. Makes you wonder why that's not easily findable public information."

I took a drink of my Coke. "I can't believe this is real. That he really is building a school. Like, why, because I sincerely doubt it's for the betterment of anyone."

"Agreed. Most messed-up part? People could use a school like this, and there will be no shortage of people willing to be involved." That was a terrifying truth. "My imagination can come up with a million different terrible motives behind this, especially since he's linked to Bael and the Harbinger."

And all of them—Bael, Aym, the Harbinger—led back to Misha.

Which was why I needed to get out there and find Bael and this Harbinger. That was imperative. Not just because the Harbinger was hunting Wardens and demons, or because my father had warned us that the Harbinger was a sign of the end times, but also because it was personal.

Misha had said that the Harbinger had chosen him, and I needed to know why...why he'd been chosen, why he'd gone along with it all. I needed to know why he'd done what he had.

I *needed* to understand.

Looking down, I realized I was clenching my fists so tightly that my blunt nails were digging into my palms.

Tonight couldn't come fast enough.

3

"Stay here, Trin. I'll be right back."

"What—" I turned to where Zayne had been standing, but it was too late.

The mofo had already disappeared into the throng of people out enjoying the balmy evening in Washington, DC, moving faster than my vision could track.

My mouth dropped open as I stared at the blur of unfamiliar faces. Had Zayne seriously just left me on the sidewalk while he went off after the Upper Level demon that I had sensed, like I was third-string or something?

Stunned, I blinked stupidly, as if Zayne would somehow reappear in front of me.

Yep.

He'd done exactly that.

"You have got to be freaking kidding me!" I exclaimed. A man on his cell phone frowned in my direction. Whatever he saw on my face caused him to not only take a healthy step away from me, but to then cross the street.

Probably a good thing, because I was armed and irritated enough to launch an iron dagger at some random person.

I couldn't believe Zayne had just left me, especially when seeing an Upper Level demon was kind of important. They were the most dangerous demons to walk this Earth, cloaking themselves by appearing human so that they could move in circles that contained some of the most powerful, influential people in the world. With their ability to manipulate people, they used humans' God-given free will against them. Upper Level demons were the most formidable adversaries in the never-ending battle to maintain the balance of good and evil in the world, but they'd been scarce since the creature known as the Harbinger had appeared on the scene, months before I'd arrived in the city.

Seeing or sensing an Upper Level demon was huge, but it was even a bigger deal than normal because of *where* we'd seen it. Zayne and I were patrolling the area of town where the demon Bael had been seen with Senator Fisher.

There was a chance that this demon might lead us to Bael, or that we could use it to find out what the Hell the senator truly planned to do with the school. And if this demon had nothing to do with the Harbinger, I'd still be able to work out some of my aggression. But instead of joining Zayne on the hunt, I was standing here like a leftover thought, and that was not cool.

Zayne obviously didn't comprehend that being my bonded Protector wasn't code for leaving me—*his* Trueborn—behind while he went off to track down demons. Granted, our bond was new, so I was going to give Zayne this one get-out-of-jail-free card, but still.

I was *not* a happy camper.

A horn blew in the street and someone shouted. I plopped down on a bench, letting out an aggravated sigh as I looked around. Because my vision was so damn blurry, it was hard for me to tell if the people walking past me were ordinary humans or the dead.

Ghosts and spirits—and there was a world of difference between the two—often not only sensed me but knew that I could see and communicate with them before I even realized they were there. Since no one was bothering me, I was guessing those around me belonged to Team Alive and Breathing.

I kicked one leg over the other and jabbed an elbow into my knee and jammed my chin into my palm. Over the scent of exhaust, I smelled cooking meat, making me hungry even though Zayne and I had grabbed a bite to eat only an hour or so ago. The ever-present warm tingle at the nape of my neck told me there were demons nearby, probably low level ones like Fiends, so I wasn't going to do anything about them as long as they weren't actively harming humans.

I wasn't familiar with the city, and with my poor vision, roaming around wouldn't be the brightest of ideas, but sitting here like a dog given an order kicked my irritation into overdrive.

The chance of me throat punching Zayne when he reappeared was currently somewhere between 60 and 70 percent. Although that was probably far smarter than what I normally wanted to do when I saw Zayne.

I focused on the little ball of pulsing warmth in the center of my chest. I'd never felt it with Misha, but since there were no other Trueborns for me to compare notes with, the lack of sensation hadn't been a red flag.

But it wasn't like others hadn't started to guess that something wasn't right between Misha and I. Thierry, the duke who oversaw the Wardens in the Potomac Highlands region, and his husband, Matthew, had begun to suspect that there'd been a mistake once Zayne had arrived. If I was being honest with myself, I'd known something was up. From the moment I'd laid eyes on Zayne, there'd been *something* there. Right now, I could feel that little ball of warmth, but I couldn't sense emotion through it like I had yesterday, when I'd felt his frustration as if it were my own. Maybe distance had something to do with that.

We needed to explore all of that.

My gaze flickered over the crowd to the restaurant across from me. I couldn't make out the name of the place, but it was definitely a burger joint. If I had to wait here, I might as well indulge in some fried yumminess. A grumble from my stomach told me it was way on board with that idea.

I had no idea why I was always hungry. Maybe it was all the walking. I was burning a lot of calories and—

My phone vibrated in my pocket and I fished it out. Pressure clamped down on my chest as I saw my best friend's pretty face staring back at me. Jada was calling once more.

My finger hovered over the answer button. I needed to answer, because I knew she probably had more questions about what had happened with Misha, but I wasn't—

Heat exploded along the nape of my neck, jerking my head

up. The hot, tingly pressure was a warning system coded into
my DNA.

There was a demon very close.

Letting Jada's call go to voice mail, I slid my phone back
into my pocket as I scanned the busy sidewalk. Demons that
looked human easily blended with the populace. The only
thing that stood out was their eyes, which reflected light like
a cat's. Picking a demon out of a crowd of humans wasn't easy
for someone with two normally functioning eyeballs, and for
me, it was an exercise in frustration. I squinted and willed my
vision to come in a little more clearly.

That didn't help.

I didn't see anyone who was obviously not human and hail-
ing Lucifer, but the pressure was still there, settling between
my shoulder blades. The demon had to be—

There.

My gaze stopped on a fair-haired man dressed in a dark
suit walking down the sidewalk, hands in the pockets of his
pants. Everything about him seemed normal, and he wasn't
close enough for me to make out his eyes, but some inherent
sense told me that he was the demon.

And not only that, an Upper Level demon.

Certainty filled me as I planted booted feet on the ground.
Before I came to DC to find Misha, I'd seen only a hand-
ful of demons, and never in a situation like this, but I knew
I was right.

And if he was the second Upper Level demon spotted in the
same area where Bael had been, that had to mean something.

I was on my feet before I realized I was standing. Soon he

would be at the intersection, and I wouldn't be able to keep track of him. If I waited for Zayne to return, I'd lose him.

Zayne had told me to stay here, but I was thinking that was more of a suggestion than an order.

Mind made up, I hurried around a group of people who were waiting to cross the street and hung back from Suit Demon. I stuck close to the buildings so that I wouldn't run into anyone, hoping that Suit Demon stayed under the glow of the streetlamps.

When the pedestrian light turned green, he crossed to the next block. A non-jaywalking demon. How unexpected.

I had no plan as I followed him past a shuttered bank and several closed administrative offices, but that didn't stop me.

Suit Demon hung a sharp right, disappearing from my view. Cursing, I picked up my pace and realized he'd entered a dimly lit, narrow alley between two buildings that were dozens of floors tall. I hesitated at the mouth, scanning the relatively clean breezeway. It was empty—

My gaze lifted. "Holy crap."

I caught a glimpse of a blurry shape pulling a Spider-Man, scurrying up the side of the building. I looked over my shoulder, but no one was pointing with their mouth hanging open.

That was a good thing. Even though the general public was aware of Wardens, the vast majority had no idea that demons were real. Due to a whole set of celestial rules about free will and blind faith, humans weren't supposed to know that there were most definitely consequences in the afterlife for deeds committed while alive.

People thought Wardens were some kind of genetic cross-breed between humans and who knew what. I had no idea how they convinced themselves any of that was even remotely possible, but human nature demanded logical answers, even if the answer was, in fact, illogical.

To humans, Wardens were like legends and stone come to life, superheroes who often helped law enforcement. But Wardens weren't out there hunting criminals.

I entered the alley, stumbling over uneven pavers I couldn't see. Halfway down, I spotted a fire escape several feet off the ground.

"Ugh," I muttered, glancing back at the mouth of the alley and then to the fire escape, judging the distance between the ground and the bottom landing.

Smart Trinity demanded that I head back to where Zayne had told me to wait. I didn't have a plan, and if someone saw what I was considering doing, it would be hard to explain.

Impatient Trinity screamed DO IT like a battle cry.

"Double ugh," I growled as the latter won out.

I ran across the alley and launched myself into air with a prayer that I didn't face-plant the building, because that was sure to sting.

My palms smacked onto the metal rung. I swung forward, muscles in my arms stretching. I planted my feet on the side of the building and pushed off *hard*. Swinging back, I twisted as I let go, springing over the railing.

I winced at the sound of rattling metal as I landed on the base of the fire escape. I stayed still for a moment, waiting to see if anyone started yelling, and when there was nothing but silence, I was kind of disappointed that no one had witnessed my gymnastic feat of awesomeness.

Story of my life.

I quickly climbed the fire escape, which had to have about a hundred different code violations. With only the moonlight to guide me, instinct took over, and I didn't let myself think about how I couldn't really see where my hands or feet were going. If I let doubt creep in, I could fall, and I was high enough I would end up with a couple of broken bones.

A warm, sticky wind caught the loose strands of hair that had escaped my bun as I reached the rooftop. Placing both palms on the cement ledge, I scanned the area. Luckily, bright floodlights shone from three different maintenance sheds, each complete with its own massive antenna. I didn't see Suit Demon, but I knew he had to be up here. I could feel him.

I pulled myself over the ledge. The breeze was more of a wind up here, which I welcomed as it rolled over my sweat-slickened skin. Daggers secured to my hips, my fingers twitched with the desire to unsheathe them as I walked across the roof.

Near the second shed, I caught sight of Suit Demon. He was on the ledge opposite the area I'd climbed up, crouched in a manner that was so Warden-like, I frowned. He'd gotten rid of his suit jacket at some point, and his white dress shirt billowed in the wind. The demon appeared to be watching the world down below. Was he waiting for someone? Maybe he was up here waiting for the demon Zayne had followed.

Maybe even Bael.

A plan quickly formed, thank God. Catch the demon off guard, gain the upper hand and make him talk.

Sounded legit and well-thought-out.

I stepped from behind the shed, keeping my hands open at my sides. "Hi!"

Suit Demon whipped around, rising with unearthly fluidity. He was on the narrow ledge and then one heartbeat later, he was a few feet from me.

A rational person would've experienced some level of fear at that point, but that wasn't what I was feeling.

He was close enough that I could tell he was handsome, which wasn't surprising. Demons rarely appeared as anything other than someone who would be viewed as universally attractive. What hid pure, unadulterated evil better than a comely face?

Cocking his head, the demon frowned. He stared at me as if he'd ordered a tender marinated filet, but instead had ended up with a cheap flat beef patty. I was sort of offended.

I was 100 percent organic Angus beef, thank you very much.

But the demon didn't realize that because to him, I appeared like any ordinary human who'd foolishly stumbled into his path...on a rooftop.

The frown smoothed out, and while I couldn't see his eyes, I could feel his gaze drift over me, as if he were sizing me up. I felt the exact moment he dismissed me.

Big mistake.

Suit Demon smiled. "What are you doing up here, girl?"

Surprised that he hadn't tacked on *little* in front of *girl*, I shrugged. "Was about to ask you the same question."

"Were you?" He chuckled, and the sound grated on my nerves. It was patronizing. "You look a little young to belong to the official roof police."

"And you look old enough to not say words like *official roof police*."

The humor vanished as a blast of hot air streamed over the roof. "Well, you're obviously not smart enough to sense when to watch your mouth."

"Funny you would insult my intelligence when you had no idea I was following you."

His upper lip peeled back in a snarl that would've impressed a cougar. "Following me? If that's true, then you've made the stupidest mistake of your life."

"Well." I drew the word out, taking a small step back. I was careful to keep some distance between us so that he didn't get outside my center vision. "I don't think this would even make the top *ten* stupidest mistakes I've made."

He hissed, and yep, he no longer sounded like a cougar, but like a very ticked-off lion. "You're going to beg for my forgiveness." He sunk into a crouch, hands clawing. "And pray for your death."

I tensed but planted a smile on my face. "So unoriginal. I'm experiencing secondhand embarrassment on your behalf. Why not get a little more creative?"

Suit Demon stared at me.

"Like how about 'you're going to beg me to stop chewing on your entrails' and 'pray that I toss you off the roof'? Now that paints a not-so-pretty picture, don't you think?"

Suit Demon blinked.

"Why don't you give that a try?" I suggested helpfully. "And let's see if I move this encounter to the top twenty on my stupid list?"

The demon let out a keening growl, a cross between a wailing infant and rabid hyena. Tiny hairs all over my body rose at what had to be one of the most obnoxious sounds ever.

"I'm going to rip out your tongue," he promised. "And then shove it back *through* your throat."

"There you go!" I clapped excitedly. "That's so much better—"

Suit Demon launched into the air, just as I'd expected, and I bet he thought he looked fearsome enough for me to wet myself. I wished I could see his expression when I rushed into the attack, but alas, I was just going to have to pretend he had an *oh snap* look on his face.

Dipping down, I slid under him as I reached up and grabbed ahold of his legs. The demon's momentum and strength worked in my favor as I yanked his legs down. Hard. Harder than I realized. Letting go, I popped up as he slammed belly down onto the roof several feet away, the impact rattling the door on the nearby shed and causing the lights to flicker. Inky liquid sprayed out across the rooftop—from his face.

Damn.

I didn't realize I was *that* strong.

Unsheathing the daggers, I stalked toward the demon. I had a different weapon—a far better one. My *grace*. But it was too risky to whip out here, in the heart of the city, even though it was burning through my stomach like acid, demanding I let it out.

That I use it.

The demon flipped onto his back, leaving the facade of his human form behind. The fair hair disappeared as his skin shifted to a burnt orange marbled with swirling streams of black. He lifted his hand, and the inky substance on his skin flowed to his palm, forming a shadowy ball.

Oh, Hell to the no.

I fell forward, slamming my knee into his midsection as I leveled the business end of one of the daggers to his throat and the other above his heart. Either area would be fatal.

"These are iron daggers," I warned him. "Whatever you're about to do with the little ball of nightmares, think twice. You will not be as fast as I will be."

His pitch-black pupilless eyes widened, and I guessed he was shocked by my strength and general awesomeness. He had no idea what I was, but if he did, he would be trying to devour me the way I'd happily dig into a hamburger. Consuming my *grace* would not only give the demon untold power and strength, it would be the closest it would ever get to Heaven.

I was a Trueborn, and in the giant pecking order of things, this Upper Level demon was a declawed cat compared to me.

The shadow ball pulsed and then collapsed into a fine dust of unspent power. "What are you?" he gasped.

"The official roof police," I retorted. "And you and I are going to have a little chat."

4

"You foolish, idiotic human," the demon sneered. "I'm—"

"Not very observant and uncreative? We've already established that and it's time to move on." I pressed the throat-level dagger against his skin, and I think the demon stopped breathing. "Answer my questions, and maybe I won't impale you to the roof through *your* throat."

The demon glared at me, silent.

I smiled back at him. "Are you working with Bael?"

There was a slight flaring of the demon's nostrils, but he remained quiet.

"You're going to want to play along and do so quickly, because I have the patience of a hungry toddler and a severe problem with impulsivity. I don't think before I act. Are you working with Bael?"

His lips peeled back in a snarl, revealing jagged sharklike teeth, and I wondered if he had a little Nightcrawler in him. "Bael isn't topside."

"Bull. Poopy. Yeah, he is. I've seen him with my own two eyeballs, and he's been spotted in this very area of town. Try again."

He growled.

I rolled my eyes. "You do realize that unless you have helpful information, you're going to be dead before you can find a breath mint." I paused. "And you need one. Stat. Because your breath is kicking."

"Aren't you a cute little thing," he snapped back. "Well, not so little. I think your ass is crushing my diaphragm."

"That's my knee, you idiot, and that's not going to be the only thing that gets crushed." To drive home the point, I slid my knee down his stomach, stopping just below the belt. "Tell me where Bael is."

The demon stared up at me for a moment and then he laughed—deep belly laughs that shook me. "You stupid cow—"

I flipped the dagger at his throat so that it was handle down and swung my fist into the side of his head, cutting off his words. Wet warmth sprayed against my palm. "Didn't your mommy demon teach you if you don't have anything nice to say, shut the Hell up?"

He cursed as I pressed the other dagger harder into his chest, tearing the fine material of his shirt. "You're…obviously out of…your mind if you think…I'm going to say crap about Bael. I'm not afraid of death."

"But you're afraid of Bael?"

"If you know anything about Bael, then you know that was about seven different levels of a stupid question."

"Do you think he can do worse to you than I can?" Anger

flared, and the need to dominate got the best of me as I leaned down so that we were eye level. I knew I shouldn't do it. It was wrong for a hundred different reasons, but I let just the tiniest bit of my *grace* spark. The corners of my vision, which were usually shadowy and dark, flipped bright white. "Because I'm here to tell you that he *can't*."

His eyes widened, and when he spoke, there was a mixture of horror and awe in his voice. "You're it. You're the nephilim."

I reigned the *grace* back in, and the white light faded. "First off, the term *nephilim* is so outdated, and second, you *have* been talking to Bael, because—"

"If it was common knowledge that one of your kind was in the city, you'd already be dead." His eyes went half-mast, and a lazy smile crossed his swirling orange-and-black face. "Or worse. Right? Is it true? What they say about your kind and mine?"

My lip curled as I stared at him. He looked near orgasmic, and that was more than a little disturbing. "Is what true?"

"That if a demon *eats* you—"

I shifted, digging my knee into his groin. He shouted in pain, withering under me. "Yeah, I'm just going to stop you right there. Tell me where—"

"It wasn't Bael that…" He dragged in a deep breath, gasping through the pain. "It wasn't Bael who told me about you, you stupid cu—"

Punching him again, this time in the jaw, I made sure the dagger handle got in on the action. "That better have been the word *cutie* that was about to come out of your mouth."

After spitting out blood and possibly a tooth, the demon straightened his head. "It was him."

Coldness seeped into me even as I became aware of the increased pulsing warmth in my chest. "Who?"

"The one who sold you out. What was his name?" The demon laughed, spit and blood leaking from the corners of his mouth as his arms fell limp to his sides. "Ah, yeah. *Misha.* Funny thing is, I haven't seen him in a couple of days. Wonder what's going on with him? Other than being dead."

"You spoke to Misha?" A tremor coursed through me. "What did he say to you? What did you—"

"You killed him. Right? Sent his soul to Hell. That's where he is now, because he was just as evil as I am."

A shudder rocked me. "You're lying."

"Why would I lie?"

"I can think of a lot of reasons," I seethed, but even as I said the words, they rang untrue. "Tell me what he said or—"

"Or what? You'll kill me? You're the nephilim. I'm already dead," he said, and I had no idea what that meant. The demon lifted his head off the roof, thick tendons standing out of his neck. "You killed him, and it's already too late. You have no idea what kind of storm is coming your way."

I slammed his head back down. "Tell me what you did to him!"

"He was chosen." He laughed, chilling me to my very core. "The Harbinger is finally here, and there's no stopping what is coming. Rivers will run red. End times, baby, and there's no way you can stop the Harbinger. You're going to be a part of it all."

I opened my mouth, but the demon suddenly moved. Not to roll me off or to attack. He gripped the wrist of my hand that held the dagger to his heart, and then he thrust up as he pulled me down.

Impaling himself.

"What the—" I shouted, jumping up and stumbling back as flames spilled from the hole in his chest and licked over his body.

Within seconds, he was nothing more than a scorch mark on the roof.

I looked at my dagger, then at the spot, and then back to my dagger. "What in the ever loving—"

The warm ball in my chest next to my heart pulsed, and a moment later, a ginormous thing dropped out of the sky and landed nimbly on the ledge like a Trinity-seeking missile of pissed-off-ness.

Oh, crap.

The Warden rose to his full height. Wings fanned out as wide as the body was tall and then some. Under the silvery moonlight, golden hair stirred between two proud, thick horns.

Zayne was a fearsome sight as he stepped onto the roof and stalked toward me, chin dipped low. Some people might think Wardens in their true form were grotesque, but not me. I thought he was beautiful in a raw, primitive way, like a coiling cobra moments before it struck.

In Warden form, Zayne's skin was slate gray, and those two horns could puncture steel and stone, as could those wickedly sharp claws, and I thought for probably the hundredth time that it was a damn good thing Wardens were on Team Good.

As he drew closer, I realized his fangs were out. Those things were enormous, and I knew him well enough to know that they meant he was very, very angry. But even if I hadn't seen his fangs, I'd have known. I could *feel* his anger right next to my heart. It felt like how cold medicine smelled, and it was further confirmation that this bond was a two-way street, feeding feelings to each other.

Slowly, I sheathed my daggers and then clasped my hands. A few seconds passed, and then I blurted out the first thing that came to my mind. "Do you know I love fireworks?"

Wow. That was random, even for me.

"This would be an amazing place to view them," I tacked on. "Wish I'd known about this building before the Fourth of July."

Zayne ignored that. "You're not where I left you."

I glanced around the empty rooftop. "I'm not."

"What part of 'stay where you are' wasn't clear?"

"The part where you thought I'd actually listen to you?" I suggested.

Zayne stopped a few feet from me. "Trin—"

"Don't." I cut him off with a wave of my hand. "You left me."

"I left you for a handful of minutes so that I could see who this demon was before involving you. That's my job—"

"Your job is not to leave me on the sidewalk like a dog that can't go into a restaurant."

"What?" Wind caught his shoulder-length golden hair, tossing several strands over his horns. "A dog—"

"You left me behind, and I get that this whole Protector thing is new to you, but leaving me behind—"

"Is apparently not the smart thing to do, because when I turn my back on you for five minutes, you end up on a rooftop several blocks away from where I left you," he interrupted. "How did you even get up here? Better yet, *why* are you up here?"

I folded my arms over my chest. "I ran and jumped."

"Really?" he replied dryly, tucking his wings back.

"Onto a fire escape," I added. "No one saw me, and I'm here—"

"What in the Hell?" Zayne was suddenly next to me, staring down at the scorched patch of cement. Very slowly, he lifted his head. "Please tell me you did not follow a demon up here."

"I hate that you asked so nicely when I'm going to have to tell you what you don't want to hear."

"Trinity." He angled his body toward me. "You engaged with a demon?"

"Yes, just like you ran off to do," I pointed out. "I spotted him while I was waiting for you, and since I thought it was probably a big deal that two Upper Level demons were in the same area that Bael had been in, I decided it would be smart of me to see what was up."

He opened his mouth.

"You know damn well I can take care of myself. You said so yourself. Or was that a lie?" I cut him off before he could say something that would remind me I'd planned to throat punch him. "I'm a fighter. This is what I was trained for, and you know I can defend myself, with or without you. Just like

I know you can defend yourself without me. You don't put me on the sidelines, because not only is that not cool, it's a waste of time. I will not stay there."

Zayne's chin lifted and a long, terse moment passed. "You're right."

Surprise shuttled through me. "I know I am."

"But you're also wrong."

I blinked. "Excuse me?"

"What I said earlier stands. I don't doubt your ability to defend yourself. I've seen you in action. Asking you to stay behind while I checked out the demon wasn't about me putting you in a timeout because I thought you couldn't handle yourself."

"Then what was it about?"

"It was about what happened with Misha," he said, and I recoiled, actually taking a step back as my arms dropped to my side. *"That,"* Zayne said. "That right there. Your reaction. You just went through something horrible, Trin, and—"

"I'm fine."

"Bullshit," he snapped, and I swallowed the irrational urge to giggle that always accompanied him cussing. "You and I both know that's not true, and that's okay. No one in their right mind would expect you to be okay."

But I *had* to be okay.

Didn't he understand that? What had happened with Misha sucked donkey butt, but everything I felt surrounding that was filed and tucked away, and it was going to stay that way forever and a day. It had to be that way. I had a job to do, a duty to fulfill.

Zayne sighed. "I think it was pretty obvious I didn't want to patrol tonight. That I thought we should stay in." He paused. "But I also get why you want to be out here, doing something, so I relented."

Irritation flared. "As my Protector, you don't get to *relent* or not when it comes to—"

"As your *friend* I sure as Hell get to step in when I think something is a bad idea." Zayne's jaw hardened. "That's what friends do, Trin. They don't just let you do whatever the Hell you want, and if they do, then they're not your friends."

I thought of Jada. I knew that she would've suggested the same thing. Take some time. Deal with what happened and process it as best as I could.

But there really was no processing any of this.

Zayne's wings twitched but remained tucked. "I wanted you to sit it out, because I thought it was a good idea for you to take it easy, because you had to end the life of someone you cared about deeply."

I sucked in a sharp, scorching breath.

"And if you think that's wrong, so be it. I'm sorry if I made you think I doubted you, but I am not sorry that I'm thinking of what you've been through."

I swallowed hard, wanting to fire back at him, but...what he was saying made sense. Looking away, I gave a little shake of my head. "I'm ready to be out here."

Zayne said nothing.

"I'm okay. I wasn't distracted or in danger. Obviously." I turned and promptly tripped over something, because, of course, God hated me. Catching myself, I lifted my gaze to Zayne.

He threw his arms up in frustration. "Seriously?"

I looked down and saw what happened to be a cable. "I didn't see it. Whatever." It was time to change the subject. "Did you find the demon?"

He muttered what sounded like a curse under his breath. "I tracked him, but he rounded a corner onto First Street and disappeared."

First Street meant nothing to me.

Zayne must've sensed that, because he explained, "First Street can lead you toward several of the Senate buildings. Doesn't mean that's where the demon was heading. What happened here?"

I twisted at the waist and looked down at the charred patch. "Well, the demon sort of decided to end things himself."

"Come again?" His head jerked in my direction, gray-tone lips pressed in a thin line.

"He impaled himself on my dagger." I shrugged. "He was all smart mouth and threats until I got him on his back. I wanted to make him talk, you know? See if he knew anything about Bael or the Harbinger."

"Make him talk?"

I nodded, deciding it was a good idea to keep to myself the fact I'd showed the demon what I was. "I've learned I can be very convincing."

Zayne opened his mouth.

I rushed on. "Anyway, he wouldn't tell me anything about Bael, but he knew him...and Misha."

He moved closer as I returned to staring at the spot. "How can you be sure?"

A knot formed in my stomach. "He mentioned Misha, and he must've figured out who I was based on the questions I was asking." That wasn't exactly a lie. "He knew that I'd killed him."

"Trin." Zayne reached for me, and I felt the brush of his warm fingers against my arm.

An immediate rush of raw, pounding emotion swirled through me, and I stepped out of his reach. "He also knew about the Harbinger. Said roughly the same thing my father did. Rivers were going to run red and it was the end time." I left out the part about Misha's soul, and me being a part of it all, because I couldn't believe the first part and the latter made no sense. "Didn't really say anything helpful before literally impaling himself on my dagger. It was bizarre, but I think..."

"Think what?"

"I don't know. He said he was already dead because I was the nephilim." I folded my arms. "Like killing himself was the only option."

Zayne seemed to mull that over. "Like he feared that either Bael or the Harbinger would know he'd been in contact with you, and that was it for him?"

I nodded slowly. "Doesn't really make sense."

"But it does if the demon was that afraid of what the Harbinger would do if it believed he'd talked." His wings unfurled, creating his own gust of wind. "Or the demon understood once it figured out what you were that there was no escape. You'd kill him, anyway."

True.

I would've totally killed him just because he made really lame threats, but I didn't think it was that. The demon was more afraid of the Harbinger than me, and that didn't bode well.

Not at all.

5

The rest of the evening was pretty uneventful. No more demons, just human-on-human violence. It ended with a shooting at a club we'd walked past that was apparently over a drink being spilled on someone's girlfriend.

One thing was for sure, humans didn't need demons to prompt them to do terrible things.

I thought about that after we got back to Zayne's apartment and parted ways, him to the living room, me to the bedroom. Sometimes I wondered why God made such an effort to save humans and their souls when humans were so quick to throw it all away.

There had to be a balance of good and evil. That was why some demons, like Fiends, were allowed topside. They were a test, working humans' every last nerve by destroying random things around them to see if they'd snap. One outburst of anger wasn't a ticket to Hell, but everything a human did or thought was tallied up, and since the invention of social media, I could only imagine how long those tallies were becoming. Even some Upper Level demons had a purpose, interacting with humans to tempt them into using free will for sin and deviant behavior. It became a problem only when the demons crossed the line by actively manipulating humans or harming them. Of course, demons that didn't look human—and there were a lot of them—weren't allowed near humans, and that was when the Wardens stepped in.

Then again, most Wardens killed all demons on sight, even Fiends, and had since, well, the beginning.

But God had created Wardens to look after people, to risk their lives to help stack the odds in favor of eternal glory instead of eternal damnation, and people just... They still sought to destroy one another and themselves, as if it was innate. Some would say it stemmed from the self-destructive nature of Adam and Eve and the apple, that the battle played out every day, in every person, and that was the serpent's greatest accomplishment—or curse—but at the end of the day, humans chose their own paths.

There was a whole lot of losing going on these days. Murders and assaults, robberies and greed, racism and bigotry, hatred and intolerance—all of it increasing instead of getting better, as if a boiling point was coming. Were these things symptoms of demons doing a damn good job, or were humans bound and determined to do the demons' job for them?

Kind of made you wonder what the Hell the point was some days.

"God," I muttered as I wiggled my arms. "That's dark."

Annoyed with my thoughts, I rolled onto my side and shut my eyes. I missed those tacky stars that had adorned my bedroom ceiling. They glowed a soft luminous white in the dark and made me feel…comforted. I knew that sounded strange.

I was strange.

I had no idea when my brain clicked off and I fell asleep, but it felt like only minutes before I opened my eyes and saw that the darkness had lifted from the room.

Feeling like I hadn't slept at all, I dragged myself out of bed and got down to the morning routine. Letting my hair air-dry, I dressed with the same speed as I'd showered, and I was ready to leave the bedroom, glasses perched on my face, within fifteen minutes of waking.

I hesitated before I opened the bedroom door, preparing myself to see a sleepy, disheveled Zayne. I'd left the door unlocked again, and I refused to think about why. It took a moment for my eyes to adjust to the brighter room. Zayne wasn't at the island, so that meant…

My gaze coasted toward the coach, and yep, there he was, sitting up and…

Muscles flexed under golden skin and rippled across bare shoulders as he lifted his arms over his head, stretching. His back bowed, and I didn't know if I should be grateful or disappointed that the couch blocked most of my view.

"I can't look away, even though I need to," Peanut said, and I jumped about a foot off the floor as he appeared out of thin air beside me. "He makes me feel like I need to spend more time at the gym."

My brows inched up my forehead.

Zayne twisted toward where I stood. "Hey," he said, voice rough with sleep as he thrust one hand through his messy hair.

"Morning," I mumbled, thankful when Peanut blinked out of existence. I lifted my hand and bit down on a nail.

"Sleep well?" he asked, and I nodded, even though that was a lie.

When Zayne rose, I looked away and hurried toward the kitchen, all the while hoping my face didn't look as red as it felt. I didn't need an eyeful of the glory of Zayne's chest. "Want anything to drink?"

"I'm good but thanks," he replied. "Be back in a few."

Zayne wasn't talkative when he first woke up, something I was learning. After grabbing a glass of OJ, I took a sip and then placed it on the island next to the plans for the school. The paper was still unrolled.

I heard the shower turn on and hoped Peanut wasn't in the bathroom being a creep. I went to the couch and turned on the TV, settling on a news station, and then folded the soft gray quilt and draped it over the back of the couch before going back to the island. I finished off my OJ and had moved on to a can of soda when Zayne finally stepped out of the bedroom. Nervous energy had me chewing on my thumbnail again as I wondered why it took him double the time it took me to shower. His hair was wet and slicked back and he was, thankfully, fully clothed in a pair of navy blue nylon pants and another plain white shirt. His feet were bare.

He had nice feet.

"Soda for breakfast?" he commented as he strolled past me, catching my hand and gently tugging it away from my mouth.

I sighed. "This is dessert."

"Nice." He made his way to the fridge. The wintery scent that always clung to Zayne lingered. Was it some kind of bath wash? I didn't think so, because I'd already scoped out the bottles in the shower.

I swiveled around. "Do I need to remind you of our water conversation yesterday?"

"Please, God, no." He opened the fridge. "Want some eggs?"

"Sure. Can I help?"

He looked up as he placed a carton of eggs and a tub of butter on the island. "Aren't you the person who almost burned down Thierry's house trying to make fried chicken?"

I snorted. "Aren't you the person who said you'd teach me to make grilled cheese?"

"You know, you're right." He picked up an egg and pointed it at me. "But I need to feed myself first."

"Priorities."

"And I really don't want you to do the eggs. Even though they're hard to mess up, I have a suspicion you might do just that, and then I'll be embarrassed for you."

"Really?" I muttered dryly.

He grinned, and I was sure I got a little goofy in the face as I watched him. "Scrambled okay?"

"Sure thing, Chef Zayne."

That got me a low chuckle. "You know, you can sit on the couch. Got to be more comfortable than the stool."

"I know." And it probably was, but Zayne slept there, and for some reason, I felt like that was his space.

How long could we keep this up? Zayne sleeping on the couch, us sharing a shower? Where would we go, though?

We had to stay in the city. There was his clan's compound, which had room for us, but besides Nicolai and Dez, his clan didn't know what I was, and it had to stay that way. Also, I had a feeling Zayne wouldn't be down with that idea.

"I figured after breakfast we could do some training," Zayne said, drawing my attention back to him. "I haven't come up with anything in particular to help with the vision thing, but if you and Misha practiced daily, we should be doing that."

I glanced down at myself. My leggings and loose shirt were perfect for training.

"Unless you got anything better planned?"

I pinned him with a dry look. "Yeah, I made plans with that demon who impaled himself on my dagger. He's coming back to life and we're going to hang out."

Zayne grinned. "Then how about you unroll the mats." A pause. "If you can handle it?"

"I can *handle* it," I mimicked, hopping off the stool, "if you can handle the epic ass kicking you're going to receive."

He laughed at that, so loudly that I turned to look at him.

"You're so going to regret that laugh," I muttered, and stalked to the mats.

As Zayne got down to scrambling, I hefted the surprisingly heavy mats and dropped them to the floor with a loud *thunk*. After unrolling them and pushing the two large sections together, I wiped the sweat off my forehead and joined Zayne back at the island. Once we'd finished the buttery eggs, I felt a lot more energized, as if I actually had gotten some real rest last night.

We cleaned up, and then I followed Zayne to the mats, stretching out my arms.

"Normally I'd do some warm-ups first." As he stepped onto the mat, Zayne tugged an elastic hair tie off his wrist, scooped up his hair and secured it in a half-finished ponytail that looked a thousand times better on him than when I tried to do it. "Definitely run a bit at least."

I frowned as I grabbed my bent elbow and pulled it across my chest until I felt the stretch in my shoulder. "I don't like running."

Zayne faced me. "That's a shocker."

"Ha. Ha."

"I figured we'd start with block techniques and take-downs." Standing there, arms crossed and feet planted with his hips lined up with his shoulders, he reminded me so much of Misha that I had to look away. "Then move on to defensive—"

"So, the basics?" Mimicking Zayne, I crossed my arms. "The stuff I learned when I first begin training?"

He nodded. "Stuff that can always be improved, no matter how much training you have."

"Huh. And you continue to practice basic blocking techniques?" I raised my brows.

Zayne said nothing.

"I'm going to take that as a no. What makes you think I need to?" I asked.

He tilted his head. "Because I have way more in-field experience than you do."

"That's true." I uncrossed my arms.

Zayne straightened his head, features marked with confusion as if he'd expected more of an argument.

I smiled.

And then I made my move. Shooting forward, I slid down like I was coming in to home base, planting my palms on the mat as I twisted and kicked out one leg. I swept his legs from underneath him, and he went down like a tree, landing on his side with a grunt and then rolling onto his back. Pushing up, I spun and dropped my knees on either side of his hips just as he started to sit up. I shoved my hands onto his shoulders, straddling his stomach as I held him down, tapping into my strength—and the strength borrowed from him. I could feel the strain on my muscles, but he wasn't moving.

I took a second to soak in his look of surprise and my feeling of pure, unadulterated pleasure in having bested him. "I don't think I'm the one who needs to practice defensive techniques."

Zayne's eyes drifted halfway shut. "Touché."

"Is that all you have to say?" I asked, feeling his chest rise.

One side of his lips quirked up. "What did you and Misha do during training?"

"We fought."

His brows lifted. "That's it?"

I nodded. "We fought, and we didn't hold back." I shifted my hands to his chest, ignoring how warm it felt under the thin shirt. "Well, maybe Misha did hold back a little, but we fought each other and then I practiced with daggers."

"The dagger thing is going to be hard to practice in here," he commented, and I nodded. "But I think we could do that at the compound. There's a lot of land and a lot of trees to stab."

"I'm not sure I like stabbing trees, but that will work."

"What about your eyes? The sunlight won't be a problem?"

I shrugged. "The sunlight could be an issue. So could a too-cloudy day, but it's not like I'll always have the perfect ambient lighting when fighting, so it's probably smarter to do it under uncomfortable circumstances."

"Good point." Zayne looked rather comfy under me, like he was taking a break.

"Are you going to be able to really fight me? Not take it easy?" I asked. "Because I don't need you to pull punches or kicks."

"Why do you think I can't do that?"

"Well, maybe because you wanted to start with the basics? And you're a nice guy. The last time we fought, you didn't really come at me. Not as hard as you could've."

"Which is why you were able to get the best of me?"

My lips thinned. "Whatever. I need to know if you can do this instead of just lying there, like you're doing right now, because like I said, you're a nice guy."

That half grin grew. "Maybe I'm just lying here because I'm enjoying myself."

I blinked. "What—"

Zayne's hands landed on my hips, and a burst of shock left me unbalanced. A heartbeat later, I was on my back and Zayne was over me, his knees digging into the mats on either side of my hips. I started to sit up, but he caught my wrists and pinned them to the mat.

My heart jumped and my pulse kicked up as he leaned

down then stopped when his mouth was within a few inches of mine. The weight of his hands on my wrists and the warmth of his body had my imagination leaping happily into the gutter.

"I don't like the idea of causing you pain, and that's going to happen when we train. It's inevitable." A strand of hair came loose from his ponytail and fell across his cheek. My fingers itched to tuck it back. Thankfully I couldn't move my hands. "But I also know that pulling back isn't going to help you. It's not going to help me. I know what I need to do as your Protector."

As your Protector.

For some reason, those words repeated over and over until he said, "And I was telling the truth. I was lying there because I was enjoying myself, not because I'm a *nice* guy."

My lips parted as a heady burst of exhilaration swept through me, banging on that file cabinet drawer labeled ZAYNE. I didn't know how to respond, or even if I should, because it was probably best that I didn't.

Zayne let go of my wrists and rocked back onto his feet. He extended his hand toward me. "Ready?"

Well then…

Exhaling a ragged breath, I sat up and placed my hand against his palm. His hand curled around mine, the grip warm and firm as he hauled me to my feet with minimal effort on my part.

"Ready." I gave myself a good mental slap in the face.

We squared off in the center of the mats, and I thought I would have to begin, but I was wrong. Zayne came at me first. I got over the initial shock and darted under his arm. I was quick and light on my feet, but so was Zayne. I came back at him, but he feinted in one direction only to spin, kicking out his leg. I blocked the kick, and at that moment I knew Zayne wasn't holding back because the blow echoed up my arm, forcing me to take a step back.

And that brought a smile to my face.

Kind of twisted, but whatever.

I spun out to avoid a sharp thrust that would've surely hurt and delivered a rather brutal sideways kick to his back.

Zayne grunted but stayed on the balls of his feet as he faced me. "Ouch."

"Sorry. Not sorry." I shot toward him, losing the distance that kept him in my central vision, and Zayne must have realized that because he darted right. My breath caught and then exploded from my chest. I couldn't move fast enough. His fist caught my shoulder, spinning me around. I stumbled back, stuck between irritation and respect. He'd done what he needed to do. Found my weakness and gone for it.

We kept at it, blow after blow. Most I deflected. Some I missed because we were fighting too close and he was too quick for me to gain any distance. Sweat dampened my brow, and my heart pounded from the exertion.

"I've taken you down five times," I told him, dragging my arm over my forehead as we broke apart.

"And I've gotten you on those mats six times," he replied. "Not that I'm counting."

"Uh-huh." I charged at him, dipping low and going for his legs, something I was learning was *his* weakness.

Zayne saw it coming and swung his fist again, but this

time I was fast enough, moving to the side so I could see the punch. I caught his fist and twisted.

Zayne *tsk*ed and broke the hold all too easily, but I was prepared. I turned on my heel, moving behind him. Planting my weight on one foot, I swung my arms in a low arch to pick up momentum as I jumped off my left foot and spun in the air with my right leg out lower than usual, delivering a butterfly kick to Zayne's kneecaps.

He went down onto his back as I landed and rose to stand over him.

"We're tied now." I grinned despite the ache in my forearms and legs.

Zayne picked himself up. "You're enjoying this," he said, knocking the strand of hair out of his face.

"I am," I chirped.

"A little too much."

Laughing, I started toward him but skidded to a halt when I saw that he'd lowered his hands and was staring at me with a rather strange look on his face. "What?"

He pulled his lower lip between his teeth. "Your laugh."

"What about it?"

A smile formed and then vanished as he gave a shake of his head. "It's nothing."

"No. It's something. Was it weird? Did I cackle? Peanut says I cackle. Like a witch."

"No." Half of that smile returned. "It wasn't a cackle. It was nice. Actually, it was a great laugh. You just... I haven't heard you laugh like that a lot."

I shifted from one foot to the next. "You haven't?"

"No." He pushed the hair out of his face again. "I think the last time I heard you laugh like that was when you jumped those rooftops and nearly gave me a heart attack."

I smiled. I had scared the bejesus out of him, and he'd come at me, angry and… Well, anger hadn't been the only thing he'd been feeling that night. My smile faded. That had been the night the imps had attacked and I had taken the claw out of his chest and…

I looked away, letting out a breath and pumping the brakes on that train of thought. "Maybe I'll jump off some rooftops again so you can hear the laugh."

"As much as I love the sound, that would be entirely unnecessary."

"I don't think so." I padded to where I'd left my Coke and took a drink, wishing it was fresher. "I think I'm going to need another shower."

"Ditto." Zayne stepped off the mats.

My skin flushed as I thought about the fact that there was only one shower, we both were sweaty and conserving water was good for the environment.

He stopped by the couch and propped a hip against the back. "You know what I think?"

Hopefully what I was thinking. Or maybe not hopefully.

"You don't give yourself enough credit."

I opened my mouth.

"Yeah, I know that's shocking to hear, since you give yourself all kinds of credit." He smirked when I snapped my mouth shut. "But I was purposely getting into your blind spots, and you were handling it well."

Trying not to be too pleased, I put on my glasses and sat

on a bar stool. Zayne's face became a little clearer. "But not perfect, and I need to be perfect."

"No one can be perfect," he corrected. "But you could improve and I think…" Zayne trailed off as his phone beeped. He picked it up, and then his brows slammed down and his jaw became so hard that I thought he'd cracked a molar. "Dammit."

I stiffened. "What?"

"It's Roth," he bit out. "He's here, and he brought friends."

6

Roth.

Also known as Astaroth, who just happened to be the actual Crown Prince of Hell.

"He knows where you live?" I asked.

"Apparently," Zayne grumbled. "There goes the neighborhood."

I squelched my laugh as Zayne strode across the floor and placed the cell on the island. I wasn't all that concerned that Roth knew where Zayne lived or that he was here. Yes, Roth was a demon—a very powerful Upper Level demon—but he wasn't the enemy.

At least, not ours.

Zayne and Roth had a weird relationship.

A lot of it had to do with the fact that Wardens and demons being remotely friendly toward one another was unheard of, because, well, duh. One represented Heaven. The other represented Hell. Wardens hunted demons. Demons hunted Wardens. That was the circle of life right there, and it was quite understandable that they were natural-born enemies.

Except it wasn't.

Zayne was the first Warden I'd met who didn't view all demons as if they were evil incarnate. Like all Wardens, I was raised to believe that there was no question when it came to their evilness, but because of Zayne, I was learning that demons were…complex, and some seemed to be able to exercise free will, just like humans and Wardens.

Not all demons were irrationally evil. Though, I wasn't sure if *rationally* evil was any better, but I was learning that good and evil weren't cut and dry. That no one, not even Wardens or demons, was born one way and stayed stagnate in their choices and deeds. Demons were capable of great goodness, and Wardens could accomplish great evil.

Look at…look at Misha. Although Wardens were born with pure souls—and if there was a list of all that was good and holy in the world, they'd be damn near the top—Misha had done horrible things. He'd been evil. There was no denying that.

But it wasn't only what Zayne and Roth each were that made it strange that they were sort of friendly with one another. It was what they had in common.

Layla.

Anyway, I guessed Zayne and Roth were sort of frenemies.

Roth had helped Zayne and I meet with the coven of witches who'd been responsible for placing an enchantment spell on humans, and that was something he hadn't needed to do. Another oddly undemonic thing he'd done was, when we'd been ambushed by Upper Level demons and nearly died at Senator Fisher's house, Roth had come back to help Zayne after he'd gotten Layla to safety. Maybe he'd done it because of Layla's complicated history with Zayne, but he had come back and that meant something.

"Wait," I said. "You said he's bringing friends?"

He nodded. "Yeah."

Every muscle in my body tensed as Zayne went to the console beside the door and hit a button just as a buzzing sound came from the intercom.

"Come on up," he said into the speaker, his voice full of exasperation.

When Roth said *friends*, did he mean Layla? Would he really bring her here, knowing all that had gone down between her and Zayne? It was the demon who had told me about Zayne and Layla's messy history. I'd had no clue about it until Roth had broken the news.

Although if he had brought her, I didn't have a problem with her being here. Layla had been nothing but nice to me— well, she hadn't exactly rolled out the welcome mat when I'd first met her. I still thought there was a good chance she wanted to eat me, but she seemed okay and she was obviously so very deeply in love with Roth.

Maybe Roth was bringing Cayman, a demon broker who bartered souls and other valuable possessions for a whole range of things that humans were willing to give up. He even made deals with other demons, so he was an equal opportunity player right there. I hoped it was Cayman, because I knew I was a sweaty, hot mess, and my hair was a ratted—

I felt the sudden hot pressure along the nape of my neck,

and a heartbeat later, the door glided open. The first person I saw was the demon prince.

Roth was death and sin wrapped in one really gorgeous package. Dark spiky hair. High, angular cheekbones. Lush mouth. His face alone could launch a thousand magazine covers and probably start a few wars.

"You look so thrilled to see me," Roth said, his tone light and those lips curved into a half smile as he looked at Zayne. The demon was a little taller than the Warden, but not as broad.

"I'm just bursting with excitement. I can barely contain myself." Zayne remained by the door, his tone dry as a piece of burnt toast. "Didn't realize you knew where I lived."

"I always knew," the demon replied.

"Well, that is…great."

"I didn't know." A familiar voice spoke from behind Roth. "He never told me he knew where you lived."

My gaze zeroed in on the elevator bay. Roth wasn't alone, and he definitely hadn't brought Cayman.

The one who spoke was *her*. Layla. And God, seeing her, it was easy to understand why Zayne had fallen for her so hard. Why even a demon like Roth would fall in love. She was a paradox. With white-blond hair, big eyes and a bow-shaped mouth, she had a startling blend of doll-like innocence and raw seduction etched into every feature. She was the embodiment of good and evil, the daughter of a Warden and one of the most powerful demons in the world, who luckily was caged in Hell.

I knew there was more to her than the fact she was interesting to look at. There had to be for Zayne to have loved her. He was measurably less shallow than me.

"Kind of surprised he kept that secret," Zayne said, clearly amused and maybe even a little happy. "I see someone tagged along with you guys."

"Couldn't shake her." Roth turned toward me just as someone else darted out of the elevator and all but launched herself at Zayne.

He easily caught the tall, thin girl in dark jeans and a violet-blue tank top. Her arms circled his shoulders, and his went around her narrow waist.

Who in the holy hot water was that?

My insides felt weird, chilled to the bone, as I watched Zayne dip his head and say something to the girl that earned a muffled laugh from her. What had he said? Better yet, why was he still holding her like they were long-lost best friends who didn't care that one of them was super sweaty?

"Hi there."

It took me a second to realize Roth was talking to me. I glanced at the demon and then went back to staring at Zayne and the girl. "Hi."

Roth sidled up to where I sat. "Layla was worried about Zayne and wanted—"

"—to see for myself that he was really okay," Layla jumped in. "Roth would tell me that Zayne was okay even if he wasn't, just so I wouldn't get upset."

"True," Roth agreed, and there wasn't an ounce of shame there.

"Which is one of the reasons we're here," Layla finished. Her voice was low and filled with so much relief, I had to look away from Zayne and the girl, who were still playing octopus. Layla was looking at me, her blue eyes nearly the same shade as Zayne's, which was odd. "He's really okay, right? He looks okay."

Blinking as if I was coming out of a trance, I nodded. "He's…he's perfect."

Layla's head tilted slightly as a set of light brown brows snapped together.

I realized what I'd said. "I mean, he's totally okay. In perfect health and all. Just fine."

Roth chuckled as Layla nodded slowly.

Finally, after about twenty years, the happy reunion by the door broke apart. I knew that Zayne was smiling, even though I couldn't see his face clearly.

I knew this because I could *feel* the smile through the warmth in my chest. Happiness. It felt like basking in sunshine, and *I* sure wasn't feeling that at the moment.

Zayne was genuinely happy to see this girl, even more than he was to see Layla.

"That's Stacey." Layla filled me in. "She's a friend of ours, and she's known Zayne for—God, for years."

Stacey.

I knew that name.

This was Stacey—the girl Roth had told me about the same night he'd dropped the Layla bomb. I didn't know *all* about her, but I knew enough to know that she'd been there for Zayne after he'd lost his father and Layla, and he'd been there for her after she, too, had suffered a loss.

They'd been friends…but more. That was the impression

I'd gotten from Roth, and even Zayne. Based on that greeting, they could still be more.

An uncomfortable feeling rippled through me, and I desperately tried to make it go away as I planted a smile on my face I hoped didn't look as bizarre as it felt. My stomach was jumping all over. Maybe the eggs had been bad, because I thought I might vomit.

Zayne's head swung in my direction, and I stiffened, realizing he was picking up on my emotions through the bond.

Dammit.

I started thinking about...llamas and alpacas, how they looked so alike, like a cross between fluffy sheep and ponies. Alpacas were like cats and llamas were like dogs, that was—

"When I heard you were injured, I had to come see you." Stacey stepped back, but then punched him on the arm with the weakest fist I'd ever seen. I stopped thinking about llamas and alpacas. "Especially since I haven't heard from you in forever. Like *forever*."

"Sorry about that." He turned back to her. "Things have been crazy busy lately."

Stacey cocked her head. "No one in this world is so busy they don't have five seconds to send a text that says *Hi, I'm still alive*."

She might have a weak punch, but she also had a point, and that made me think of Jada. What excuse was I going to give her for not returning her calls?

"You're right." Zayne led Stacey to the rest of us. "That's a lame excuse. I won't make it again."

"You better not." Stacey reached the end of the island, and she was now close enough I could see her features. Chin-length brown hair framed a pretty face, and then she was staring at me in the way I imagined I was staring at her. Not with outright hostility, but definitely with a healthy amount of suspicion. "So, this is her."

I jerked and my tongue came unglued from the roof of my mouth. "Depends on who you think *her* is."

"Yes, this is Trinity." Layla stepped in. "She's the girl we told you about. She lived in one of the larger Warden communities in West Virginia and came here to find a friend of hers."

My gaze swung to Roth as I wondered what else they'd told Stacey. Like what I was. If so, we were about to have a big problem. Maybe I'd have to silence Stacey. I started to smile.

Roth winked one amber-hued eye at me.

My smile faded into a frown. I looked back at Stacey. "Yep, that's me."

"Sorry to hear about your friend," Stacey said after a few seconds, and there was a genuineness in her tone. "That really sucks."

Uncomfortable because I was just plotting her death and smiling about it, I muttered, "Thank you."

"They told me that you're trained to fight like this big guy." She lifted an elbow at Zayne. "That's pretty cool. I didn't know Wardens trained humans."

"Or raised them," Roth added. "Like pets."

My narrowed gaze landed on the demon. "I wasn't raised like a pet, you ass."

He grinned.

"And Wardens don't normally train humans." My gaze flashed to Zayne's. His chin dipped, and it looked like he, too, was fighting laughter. Besides the fact that Roth had compared me to a pet, this was good news. Roth and Layla hadn't shared everything. I drew in a shallow breath. "I'm a...fluke."

"Fluke," Roth repeated under his breath as he looked over at me. "That you are."

I was probably fifteen seconds away from showing him exactly what I'd been trained to do. "Lots of flukes around these days."

Roth's grin kicked up a notch.

"So, when are you going back home?" Stacey asked.

What she asked wasn't so much a question as it was a dismissal. Like, *nice to meet you, but it's time for you to leave.*

Rude.

"She's not," Zayne answered, leaning against the island. "She's staying with me for the foreseeable future."

The room went so quiet that you could've heard a cricket sneeze. If crickets actually sneezed. I had no idea if they had sinuses or sinus problems.

"Oh," Stacey responded. Her face didn't fall in disappointment or flush with anger. She didn't show *any* emotion, and normally I was good at reading people.

I started to look away from her, but something strange caught my eye. There was a...shadow behind Stacey, in the shape of a...person? The same height as her, maybe slightly taller and a little broader. My eyes squinted as I refocused on her and saw...nothing. No shadow at all.

Stacey was starting to frown...

...because I was staring at her.

Warmth crept into my cheeks as I got busy checking out my empty soda can, dismissing the weird shadow. Sometimes my eyes did that—made me think I saw things when there was nothing there.

"Well, since that's out of the way, did you guys really come over here just to make sure I'm alive?" Zayne broke the awkward silence. "Not that I'm not happy to see you all—"

"You should be thrilled to see us," Roth cut in.

"We know you're not thrilled to see *him*." Stacey's lips eased into a smile.

"But you better be damn happy to see me," Roth said.

"Of course I'm happy to see you," he said, and that was with a grin. "But as you guys can see, I'm fine. You didn't need to worry."

"I just needed to see it. *We* needed to see it." Layla was beside Roth, one arm curled around his as she leaned into him. Roth dressed all in black and Layla with that white-blond hair and cute pale-pink-and-blue maxi dress—they were such a contrast of light and dark. "I hope you're not mad that we came by."

I waited with bated breath for Zayne's answer, because I honest to God wasn't picking up much through the bond except for that momentary flash of happiness when he'd hugged Stacey. I didn't know if that meant he wasn't feeling anything powerful enough for me to sense, or if he was better than I at controlling his emotions. Probably the latter, but I did know that when Zayne and Layla had talked while Roth and I had met with the witches, he hadn't seemed all that relieved by the conversation. If anything, he'd been morose and...*confused* that night.

Zayne looked at Layla, and I thought it might be the first time he'd actually looked directly at her since they'd arrived.

"No, I'm not mad," he said, and I believed him. "Just surprised. That's all."

Layla couldn't hide her surprise, and I wondered if she'd expected Zayne to say the opposite. A tiny, decent part of me actually felt bad for her as a small, hesitant smile began to appear. "Good," she whispered, blinking rapidly.

Roth dipped his head, pressing his lips to her temple, and my gaze shot to Zayne. There was no reaction. No blast of jealousy or envy through the bond or on his face.

Zayne only smiled faintly and then asked, "How are you feeling?"

"Good." She cleared her throat as she patted her stomach. "Just a little sore. I think that damn Nightcrawler was trying to disembowel me."

The low growl that came from Roth was startlingly similar to the sound Zayne had made.

"I think I'm glad I've never seen a Nightcrawler," Stacey mused, lips pursed. "That name alone doesn't bring the warm fuzzies."

"There was a whole horde of them incubating in the old locker rooms at school." Layla tossed it out there like it was no big deal. "It was a while ago, and Roth and I killed them all, but man, those things are mean."

I had so many questions about why a horde of incubating Nightcrawlers would be in the locker rooms of a human school.

"I really didn't need to know that." Stacey shuddered. "At all."

"Hey, you've only got a couple of weeks of summer school, and then you'll get your diploma." Layla smiled at her friend.

"Then you won't have to worry about our little version of a *Buffy* Hellgate."

"I think we have more demonic activity at that school than *Buffy* did in all the seasons," Stacey commented.

I had to wonder how many demons beyond Roth and maybe Cayman she'd seen. Only humans who were accidentally introduced to the world of things that went bump in the night and somehow survived and those who were entrusted to keep the truth safe knew.

Stacey probably thought I was one of those exceptions.

"Summer school?" I had no idea if that was normal in the human world, and also not all that sure I knew what it even meant.

"I ended up missing a lot of school at the beginning of the year." Stacey tucked a short strand of hair behind her ear and folded her other arm across her stomach. "Too much for me to make up, so I'm stuck in school for the next couple of weeks."

"But they let her walk with her class during graduation," Layla told me. "These classes are more like a technicality."

"A technicality?" Stacey laughed softly. "I wish. It feels like some kind of cosmic punishment. Do you know what that school smells like during the summer?"

"That I do not," Roth answered. "But I am dying to hear."

Stacey pinned him with a look. "It smells like hopelessness, unfairness and a pair of old, wet sneakers that have been worn through all the back alleys of the city without any socks on."

Ew.

"You know, I used to think I was missing out on the whole public school thing, but I was wrong." Zayne closed his eyes briefly. "So wrong."

"I kind of miss that smell," Layla murmured, and everyone shot her a dubious look. She shrugged.

"Well, no one else will get to know that smell and love it like you." Stacey smiled.

"Oh, right. The school's getting remodeled or something in the fall. It's about time. Pretty sure both the lockers and the air-conditioning system are vintage."

"As was the food," Roth chimed in.

Confusion flickered through me. "How do you know what the food was like?"

Roth's smile was like smoke. "I was a recipient of public education for a very short period of time."

I almost laughed at the absurdity of the Crown Prince of Hell attending public school.

"Anyway…" Layla faced me. "You saved my ass a couple of nights ago. Twice."

I stiffened. "Not really. I mean, I was just doing what I… needed to do."

Her pale gaze held mine. "You know it wasn't nothing. It was a big deal, and things could've gone south worse than they already had."

That was true. I'd purposely cut myself to draw the demons that had been surrounding Roth and Layla. The moment they'd scented my blood, the whole mass of them had bum-rushed me like I was an all-you-can-eat demon buffet, allowing Roth to get Layla out of there.

"You have my thanks," she finished.

I started to argue, but realized there was no point, so I just nodded.

"Are those the building plans we found at the senator's

house?" Layla changed the subject, slipping free of Roth and coming to the island to look at the paper.

"Yep," Zayne answered.

As he filled them in on what we knew, which wasn't much, I sat back and listened. Well, I pretended to listen while I snuck glances at Zayne…and Stacey.

They ended up side by side as Zayne began to show everyone the articles he'd found on Senator Fisher. She asked a lot of questions, as if discussing powerful senators who were involved with demons was a conversation she had once a week. And that wasn't all she did.

Stacey was *touchy*.

Very much so.

It seemed playful. A teasing punch or a smack on the arm, as if it were something she did quite often. A hip bump broke up the punches every so often, and Zayne responded with a quick grin or a shake of his head. Even if I hadn't known that they'd been intimate before, and even with my relationship experience being pretty much limited to the bleachers, I still would've picked up on it. There was a comfortableness between them, an ease that said they knew each other very well.

The bitter burn in my throat tasted a whole lot like envy, so I cracked open the ZAYNE drawer and shoved that feeling inside, then slammed the drawer shut.

It remained cracked open, just a sliver.

Resting my elbow on the island and my chin in my hand, I watched the four of them huddle around the building plans. Now I knew how Peanut felt in a room full of people with no one paying a lick of attention to him. Did he throw himself a pity party like I was? Probably.

I dragged my gaze away from the group and stared at the gray cement floor. Zayne was telling them about the demons from last night but leaving out details, maybe so that Stacey wouldn't have questions.

My glasses slipped down my nose, and I squinted. There was a small crack in the cement, and I wondered if it had been made on purpose. Too much perfection was considered a bad thing nowadays, a flaw itself. How ironic was that?

Why in the world was I thinking about cracks in the floor? My mind was normally one continuous nonsensical thought after another, but this was ridiculous. Still, it was better than—

"Hey." Zayne's voice was followed by the weight of his hand on my shoulder.

I jerked my head up so fast that my glasses started to take flight. Zayne's reflexes were on point. He caught them before they left my face, straightening them.

"You okay?" he asked, voice low.

"Yeah. Totally." I smiled as I realized we had an audience. "Just zoned out. Did I miss something?"

His gaze searched mine as a slight frown appeared between his brow. "They're getting ready to head out."

How long had I been staring at the crack? Good Lord.

"But first, you're going to take me on a tour of your place," Layla said.

Zayne lifted a shoulder. "Well, there's not much more than what you're looking at now."

Layla turned toward the closed doors. "There has to be more." She started walking toward them. "Show me."

Zayne wasn't given much of a choice. He caught up with

Layla just as she opened the door to the linen closet. Roth was only a few steps behind them, and that meant…

I looked to my right and found Stacey smiling tightly at me. "Hi," I said, because I had no idea what else to say. "You're not joining them on the tour?"

She shook her head. "No. I've been here before."

Keeping my face blank was an Oscar-worthy effort. "And you didn't tell Layla?"

"Nope. Zayne didn't want her to know, and yeah, I thought that was ridiculous, but I learned a long time ago not to get between them and their functional dysfunction." Angling her body toward me, she propped her hip against the island. "You know that I know."

"You know what?" I glanced over to see Zayne and crew disappearing into the bedroom.

"That there's only one bedroom."

I turned back to her. "You're correct."

Her brown eyes stared into mine. "Zayne is a great guy."

A prickly heat invaded my skin. "He's an amazing guy."

"And I don't know what's really going on here, but I have a feeling Layla and Roth aren't being completely honest about you."

"Whatever is going on here is none of your business," I told her, voice low.

"We're going to have to disagree on that, because Zayne's my friend and I care about him a lot, so it is my business."

"You're right. We're going to have to disagree on that."

She lifted a brow. "Just know, if you hurt him in any way, you'll have to deal with me."

I would've laughed in her face, but I actually respected that threat. I really did. I was glad Zayne had a friend like this. A little annoyed, too, but mostly glad.

So, I said, "You have nothing to worry about, Stacey. Seriously."

"We'll see." Her gaze flicked past me as she pushed off the island. "How was the tour?"

"Short," Roth said. "Really short."

"Yeah." Layla looked a little concerned. "It's a nice place. The bathroom is amazing."

I wondered if she was thinking the same thing about the bedroom as Stacey had. Neither needed to waste time on the idea of anything of interest happening on that bed any longer.

Unfortunately.

There was a quick succession of goodbyes, and I hopped off the stool, my poor butt feeling numb.

Zayne followed the girls to the elevator doors, but Roth hung back. I didn't realize he was so close to me until he stepped into my central vision. Those eerie tawny eyes met mine, and when he spoke, his words were meant for my ears only. "I'll be seeing you again, real soon."

7

"You tried to eat the puppy!"

My shout was drowned out by horns blaring from a nearby congested street as I raced down a narrow foul-smelling alley.

Not that it would do any good, but I tried not to breathe too deeply. The rancid smell was most likely coming from overflowing dumpsters, and the stench was seeping into my clothing and soaking my skin.

Sometimes I thought the entire city of Washington, DC, smelled like this—like forgotten humanity and despair mixed with exhaust and faint undertones of decay and rot. I almost couldn't remember the clean mountain air of the Potomac Highlands at this point, and part of me wondered if I ever would smell it again.

A bigger part of me wondered if I even wanted to, because the Community would no longer feel like home without…

Without Misha.

My heart squeezed as if someone had reached inside and caught it in a fist. I couldn't let myself think about that. I *wouldn't*. Everything with Misha was filed away under EPIC FAIL, and that drawer was nice and secure.

Instead, as I raced down the stinkiest alley in the entire country, I focused on how my night had gone from boring to *this*. After Roth's cryptic parting message, Zayne and I had puttered around the apartment all afternoon and then headed out to look for the Harbinger.

We'd spent the evening patrolling the area where we'd spotted the two demons, with no luck. The streets were dead, with the exception of a few Fiends messing with traffic lights, which, for some reason, had actually made me want to laugh. Other than causing a minor fender bender that had backed up traffic, it was rather harmless.

Granted, if I'd been either of the two drivers or those stuck behind the two men yelling that both their lights were green, I probably wouldn't have thought it was all that funny.

While Fiends were testing the nerves of humans, Zayne was testing mine by asking if I was okay about five hundred million times. Like I was a fragile glass flower seconds away from shattering, and I hated feeling that way, because I was *fine*. Totally okay with everything. I wasn't pestering him with questions about Stacey and their previous more-than-just-friends status. Even if he'd picked up on something through the bond while Stacey had been at his place, it had been a momentary lapse of control. I was acting normal, so I wasn't sure why he was so worried.

By the time we'd spotted the Raver demons, I was happy for the distraction. Until I'd smelled this alley.

Stringing together a slew of curse words, I focused on the task at hand. With my narrow, blurry vision and the dim flickering glow of the lone alley light, I couldn't afford any distractions when it came to the puppy-eating jerk that looked kind of like a rat.

If rats were six feet tall, walked on two legs and had a mouthful of razor-sharp teeth.

The long-tailed bastard and its pack of ugly low level demons had just tried to snatch up a dog that reminded me of the blue alien from *Lilo and Stitch*.

What kind of dog was that? A French bulldog? Maybe? I had no idea, but the Raver had made a grab for the so-ugly-it-was-cute puppy and its fedora-wearing owner, who'd wandered too close to the alley the horde of Ravers had been scavenging in.

Luckily Fedora Guy hadn't seen the Raver. I wouldn't even begin to know how to explain what it was to a human. A mutated sewer rat? Not likely.

The demon had scared the poor puppy, causing it to yelp and topple onto its side with its little legs rigid. And that flipped me straight into Bitch Got to Die mode.

Trying to eat humans was bad enough, even if it was the result of cosmic karma for the human wearing a fedora in the humidity of July, but trying to munch on cute Frenchie pups?

Completely unacceptable.

I'd nailed the sucker with a dagger, scaring it off and scattering the pack, and now it was booking it on two muscular hind legs while Zayne went after the rest. It stopped and crouched. Before it could jump, I launched off the cement and went airborne.

For about two seconds.

I landed on the Raver's hairless back, my arms circling its thick neck as it let out a squeak that sounded an awful lot like a dog's chew toy.

The demon pitched forward and hit the alley hard, the impact jarring me to the bone. It reared, but I held on as it tried to buck me off.

"That puppy did nothing to you!" I yelled as I rocked backward, planting my knees in the ground—the suspiciously wet ground. I was so not going to think about that. I tightened my arm around its neck. "A puppy! How dare you!"

The thing chattered and clicked its jaw as it snapped at the air.

I yanked free the dagger jutting out of its side. "You're gonna regret—"

The Raver face-planted the alley and went limp. Unprepared for the tactic, I flipped over its head, landing on my back in what had better be a puddle caused by the late-afternoon thunderstorm.

"Ugh." Sprawled out, I caught a whiff of what was definitely not rain.

I was *so* going to spend ten hours in the shower after this.

Hot, fetid breath blasted my face, causing me to gag as the Raver stumbled to its feet and hovered over me. My stomach churned. I shouldn't have eaten those two hot dogs or those fries...or half of that falafel. For once, I was grateful for my poor eyesight. In the dim light of the alley, the finer details of the Raver's features were nothing more than a blur of teeth and fur.

I lurched up and grabbed the Raver by the shoulders before it could get me with its teeth or claws. Its fur was patchy and rough, its skin slippery and all around repulsive. I yanked it backward, tapping into my Trueborn strength as I felt the little ball of warmth and light in my chest burn brighter as Zayne drew near.

The Raver slammed into the ground, arms and legs flailing. I fell forward, straddling the demon as I planted a hand on its chest and held it down.

Something clicked off in my head. Or maybe it turned on. I didn't know and I wasn't thinking. I was just *acting*. My fist slammed into the demon's jaw. A tooth clinked on the alley floor as pain flared along my knuckles. I landed the next blow, and another tooth went flying, bouncing off my chest, and...

My perfectly sealed mental file cabinet split wide open, files bursting in every direction. Primal rage poured into me, lighting up every cell and fiber of my being much like the *grace* did when I tapped into it. Fury roared through me like a tornado as I gripped the demon by the throat and lifted it off the ground, and then connected my fist with its face once more.

Anger wasn't the only thing coursing through my veins, causing my blood to feel like it was tainted with battery acid. Raw grief was there, tearing through the fury. A helpless sorrow that I wasn't sure would ever lessen.

The alley, the sounds of cars and people, the wretched smell, the entire world constricted, until it was just me, this puppy-eating demon and this…this *anger*, and a continuous stream of images flashing through my mind.

My mom, dying on the side of a dirty road, killed by Ryker. Two-headed Aym, taunting me. Me, blindly and *stupidly* rushing outside the senator's house, just like Aym had known I would—just like Misha had known I would. Zayne, burned and dying, still trying to fight. My father, arriving, showing no remorse for the mistake that had been made.

The images whirled together, each one powerful and consuming, but the one that stood out the most, the one I couldn't unsee, was the look on Misha's face. The flicker of surprise in those beautiful blue eyes, as if, for one second, he couldn't believe that I would do what I'd needed to do.

What I'd *had* to do.

How could Misha have done this? To me? To himself? To *us*?

My fist connected with the Raver's snout as sorrow and rage gave way to guilt and dug its nasty, bitter claws into my very soul. I couldn't get it out of me. How had I not seen Misha for what he really was? How could I have been so wrapped up in my own woes that I hadn't seen this *evil* festering in him, hadn't noticed—

"Trin."

I heard the familiar voice, but I didn't stop. I couldn't. My fist slammed into the Raver's snout again and again. Something warm and foul-smelling sprayed my chest.

"You need to stop."

"It tried to eat a puppy." My voice trembled on a shaky, frail breath. "A cute puppy."

"But it didn't."

"Only because we stopped it." I hit the demon again. "That doesn't make it okay."

"Didn't say that it was." The voice was closer, and the warmth in my chest was reaching out, beating back the dark, oily feelings that had spread like a noxious weed. "But it's time to end this."

I knew that.

My fist slammed into the Raver's jaw yet again, and a few more teeth hit the ground.

"*Trinity.*"

I raised my fist again, vaguely aware that the shape of the Raver's head looked wrong in the gloom of the alley, like half its skull might be indented. The demon wasn't fighting back. Its arms were limp at its sides, its mouth hanging—

The scent of wintermint overshadowed the stench of the alley a moment before a warm, strong arm circled my waist. Zayne hauled me off the prone demon. From the amount of heat he was throwing off, I knew he was still in Warden form.

My hands unfurled on reflex as I reached down, clasping his arm. I fully intended to force him to let me go, but the skin-to-skin contact was jarring, like a static charge passing between us, shorting out my senses. The sense of familiarity, of many moving pieces finally clicking into place as the warmth in my chest beat in tandem with my heart, taking over. My grip on his arm loosened, and my fingers seemed to have a mind of their own. They trailed down his granite-like skin to the tips of his claws.

I focused on that, on the feeling of him, as I took short, shallow breaths. I needed to get ahold of myself. Had to gather up those files and shove them back away. And I did just that, picturing myself running through the alley, snatching up files of memories and emotions. I gathered them to my chest and then forced them back into that cabinet in the recesses of my soul.

"Trin?" Concern rasped in his voice.

"I'm okay." I struggled to catch my breath. "I'm fine. I'm all right."

"You sure about that?"

"Yes." I nodded for extra emphasis.

"If I put you down, will you make me a promise?" Zayne turned us away from the Raver, his large wings stirring the air around us. "You won't run back and start hitting the demon like it's your own personal punching bag?"

"I promise." I wriggled against his hold and immediately felt a burn that spiked in my chest, right next to my heart. That burn dropped lower...and simmered below my navel. I stilled as my senses tried to sort out what I was feeling. It was like razor-sharp frustration that tasted of dark chocolate. A mix of desperation and indulgence.

Desire.

Forbidden desire, to be exact.

And I was pretty sure those potent sensations weren't originating only from me.

Surprise rippled through me as I sucked in a heady breath. I hadn't picked up on *this* through the bond before. My fingers pressed into Zayne's hard skin as my eyes drifted shut. Even though we were pretending the night we'd kissed had never happened, the memory consumed my thoughts at record speed.

The ZAYNE drawer rattled insistently, cracking open the sliver I'd left before into a tiny fissure, and my heart went full throttle with it.

There was no stopping it.

I let myself *feel*.

8

The tumultuous thunder of emotions sent my heart racing and thoughts scattering. Anticipation and yearning took root, spreading through me like a flower seeking sun, and the feeling of *this* is *right* beat back the tiny bursts of fear.

What would Zayne do if I turned in his embrace, stretched up and wrapped my arms around his neck? Would he resist me? Or would he meet me halfway? Lower his mouth to mine and kiss me, no matter that it was forbidden? Right here, right now, with a dying Raver a few feet from us, while we stood in a stinky alley surrounded by piles of garbage.

Super romantic.

But a tremor still curled its way down my spine, causing my breath to hitch. I was hot. So incredibly hot, and suddenly the world around us didn't matter. Nothing mattered beyond the heat and the pounding of my heart.

Zayne's arm tightened around my waist, drawing me impossibly close, until there was no space between us. I felt him move behind me, the soft edges of his hair tickling the side of my neck, and then the impossible featherlight graze of his lips just below my ear. Every muscle in my body tightened almost painfully in want.

It was the wake-up call I needed for a multitude of reasons. If this consuming, unspent desire really was coming from him, it was just a by-product of mutual attraction. Obviously, that existed between us, but it wasn't—it *couldn't*—be anything more than skin-deep.

It took more than a moment to calm that stupid organ of mine, to pump the brakes on this train wreck of desires… but I did it.

I did it.

I opened my eyes and tapped on his arm. "Are you going to put me down or do you plan on carrying me around the rest of the night like an overstuffed handbag?"

"Do you promise to not start beating the Raver again?" He cleared his throat, and when he spoke again, the thickness was absent. "Because you haven't agreed."

I rolled my eyes. "Just to make sure we're on the same page—you're saying I'm *not* supposed to be chasing after puppy-eating demons?"

"You can chase them, as long as you promise to kill them the moment you catch them."

"I honestly don't know what the big deal is."

"Seriously?" He dipped his head again, and this time, those soft strands of hair glided over my cheek. "What you were doing was a little aggressive."

"Hunting demons requires aggression."

"Not like that. Not that kind of violence."

Zayne was being logical, and that was annoying. "Put me down."

His sigh rattled through me once again. "Stay put."

My head whipped in his direction as my brows lifted, but before I could address the whole *stay put* thing, he deposited me ever so gently on my feet.

Zayne slid his arm away from my waist, leaving a series of shivers in its wake. I jolted as I felt the barest brush of his palm along my hip.

He lifted his hand, revealing he'd snatched one of my daggers.

Sneaky Warden.

Tucking in his wings, he stalked to the Raver. Surprisingly, the thing was still alive—moaning, but breathing.

Not for long.

One quick downward stab later, and the demon was nothing but a pile of glowing crimson ashes that faded quickly.

When Zayne rose, he was facing me, and I could see the glow of his pale blue eyes. "That's what you should've done the moment you got the Raver cornered and down."

I figured it wouldn't be in my favor to mention that I'd jumped on the Raver's back like a rabid cat. "Thanks for the fighting lesson I didn't need."

"Apparently you do need it."

I extended my hand and wiggled my fingers. A few seconds passed, and I exhaled heavily. "Dagger."

He approached me slowly, shifting into his human form as he did so. The black shirt he wore had ripped along the back and shoulders when he'd shifted and now looked like it had seen better days.

Wardens sure went through a lot of shirts.

His wings folded into the backs of his shoulders, tucking into thin slits that wouldn't be visible to human eyes, as his horns retracted so fast it was like they'd never parted his shoulder-length blond hair.

God, he was gorgeous.

And that annoyed me—him and his…pretty hair and eyes…and mouth and whatever.

Ugh.

I wiggled my fingers again.

He stopped in front of me, still holding my dagger. "I know you're not used to patrolling, Trin, so I'm not going to stand here and lecture you."

"You're not?" I asked. "It sure sounds like you're gearing up for a lecture."

Zayne apparently had selective hearing. "One of the reasons we dispatch demons quickly is so they're not seen by humans."

I looked around, seeing nothing but the dark shapes of dumpsters and the lumpy shadows of garbage bags. "No one saw."

"Someone could have, Trin. We're near the street. Anyone could've come back here."

"This *really* sounds like a lecture," I pointed out, swallowing a groan.

"You need to be careful." He placed the dagger handle down in my palm. "*We* need to be careful."

"Yeah, I know." I sheathed the dagger, making sure it was

hidden once again under the hem of my shirt. "I was being übercareful."

"You were being übercareful while you were pummeling the Raver into oblivion?"

I nodded as my phone vibrated against my thigh. When I pulled it from the pocket of my jeans, Jada's face smiled from the screen. My stomach turned over as I quickly slid the phone back into my pocket. For once, I actually had a reason to not answer, because I seriously doubted Zayne would appreciate it if I took a call in the middle of his nonlecture lecture.

Zayne's head was cocked when I looked back at him again. "Not to point out the obvious—"

"But you're going to."

"There is no way in holy Hell you would've seen a human walk down this alley. I don't think you would've heard Godzilla coming down the alley."

My lips thinned with annoyance, partly because the first thing he'd said was true while the second part was ridiculous, but mostly because this seriously was a lecture.

"Besides the risk of exposure, we also kill quickly because it's the humane thing to do," he continued. "It's the decent thing, Trin."

A muscle tensed along my jaw as I averted my gaze. He was right. Killing quickly was decent and humane. Considering all the angel blood coursing through my veins, being decent and humane should be second nature to me. Hell, first nature to me.

Apparently the violent, destructive human side of me was in control.

"You can't get caught up in the *why*s of the hunt. Even

if the demon wanted to snack on a puppy," he said, and my gaze flew back to his. "Doing so leaves you distracted and vulnerable, more prone to mistakes and open to attack. What if it wasn't me who came up behind you? What if it was an Upper Level demon?"

"I would have sensed it and punched it, too," I snapped. "And then you would've been pulling me off that one."

He stepped forward. "You might be as badass as they come, but if an Upper Level demon comes up behind you and you're unprepared, you're in for a world of hurt."

Annoyance gave way to anger as I stared at him. "You're my Protector, Zayne, but you sound like you're my keeper. You're not my father."

"Thank God for that," he retorted, sounding disturbed.

Heat crept into my cheeks, and I snapped my mouth shut.

"I know you didn't have any official training, not like I and other Wardens, but I know you understand the basics of what to do when you come across demons. You've proven that."

"Thierry and Matthew did teach me the basics." So had Misha, but none of them had prepared me for patrolling, because no one thought I'd end up doing that. But I knew the rules. Mainly because the rules were kind of common sense. "They talked about…stuff."

"Did you listen to them?"

"Of course," I said, affronted.

A deep, raspy chuckle radiated from him. "Yeah, not to sound like a lie detector, but I'm going to have to say that's false."

"Okay. I had a wee bit of a hard time paying attention, because I'm easily distracted and suffer from chronic boredom.

Like right now. I'm bored. With this conversation," I tacked on. "So, I'm suffering."

"Not as much as I'm suffering right now."

My frown grew until I felt like my face was going to be stuck like that. "Do I even want to know what that means?"

"Probably not." He was closer now, no more than a foot away. "I get it."

"Get what?"

Zayne's pale gaze caught mine. "I get why it takes hours for you to fall asleep."

I wasn't sure I wanted to know how he was aware of that.

"And I get why you're so angry."

Drawing in a sharp breath, I took a step back from Zayne, as if I could put physical distance between what he was saying and me. "I'm not…" I shook my head, not wanting to get into this conversation with him. "I'm not angry. I'm actually hungry."

"Really?" he replied dryly.

I arched an eyebrow. "Why do you sound like you don't believe me?"

"Maybe because you ate two hot dogs from a street vendor less than an hour ago."

"Hot dogs aren't very filling. Everyone knows that."

"You also ate fries and half of my falafel."

"I did not eat half of it! I had, like, a bite of it," I argued, even though I'd had two…or three bites. "I'd never had a falafel before and I was curious. Not like you can find them in the hills of West Virginia."

"Trin."

"And beating the crap out of the Raver in an *inhumane* and

indecent manner burns a lot of calories. Whatever I ate has been used up and I'm now in a caloric deficiency. I'm starving."

He crossed his arms. "I don't think that's how calories work."

I ignored that. "We can go back to that place and get you another falafel," I said, starting past him. "I might get one myself. Then we can falafel together."

Zayne caught my arm, stopping me. The warmth from his hand and the jolt of the contact was unnerving. "You know you can talk to me, right? About anything, anytime. I'm here for you. Always."

A lump formed in my throat, and I didn't dare look at him as I felt the drawers start to rattle again.

Talk to him?

About anything?

Like how I hadn't really known Misha? Hadn't known that a man I'd loved like a brother had not only hated my guts but had orchestrated my mother's murder? Tell him how I hated Misha for all he'd done, but somehow still missed him? How I wanted desperately to believe that the bond had been responsible, or that it had been the demon Aym or this Harbinger creature that had caused Misha to do such horrible things? Did Zayne think I could tell him that what I feared most was that maybe the darkness in Misha had always existed and I'd never seen it, because I'd always, *always* been so wrapped up in myself?

Or I could tell him how eternally grateful I was that the bond had saved his life, but that I hated what that meant for us—that there could be no us—and how guilty I felt that I could be selfish enough to wish he wasn't my Protector. Tell him how much I missed Jada and her boyfriend, Ty, but that I was avoiding her calls, because I didn't want to talk about Misha. Or how I had no idea what was expected of me. How I was supposed to find and fight a creature when I didn't know what it looked like or what its motives were, in a city that was completely unfamiliar to me. Confide in him that I was afraid my failing vision would continue to worsen to the point that I could lose my ability to fight, to survive and to be…to be independent.

Should I share with him that I was terrified that he would die because of me, like he almost had that night at the senator's house?

Pulse racing like I'd been running a mile, I shook my head. "There's nothing to say."

"There's a whole Hell of a lot to say," he countered. "I've been giving you space. You needed that, but you have to talk about this. Trust me, Trin. I've lost people. Some to death. Some to life. I *know* what happens when you don't get the grief and the rage out."

"There's nothing to talk about," I repeated, my voice barely above a whisper. I turned toward him then, stomach churning. "I'm fine. You're fine. We could be so much closer to eating a falafel, and you're delaying the deep-fried feast."

Something fierce flared in those pale wolf eyes, making them momentarily luminous, but then he let go of my arm and whatever it was…was gone.

A heartbeat passed and then he said, "We're going to need to stop by my place first."

A breath of relief punched out of me. The cabinet in my head stopped shaking. "Why? To get you another shirt?" I started walking toward the street. "We should start packing extras."

"I need a new shirt, but we need to head back because you smell and you need a shower."

"Wow." I looked at him as he fell in step beside me. I could make out a half grin on his face. "Way to make me feel self-conscious."

As we reached the sidewalk, I looked both ways before stepping out, so I didn't get run over by someone in a hurry. I blinked rapidly, trying to get my eyes to adjust to the brighter streetlamps, headlights and lit storefronts.

Didn't really help.

"Smelling you is making me all too conscious."

"Jesus," I muttered.

"What does He have to do with your stench?" he teased.

"You didn't seem to have a problem with the way I smelled back in the alley," I pointed out. "You know, when you picked me up and held me like I was in one of those things people use to carry babies around."

"The smell clouded my judgment."

A laugh burst out of me, and under the brighter streetlights, I could now see that there was definitely a grin on his face. "If that's what you need to tell yourself."

"It is."

I pressed my lips together, deciding it was best to ignore that altogether. Zayne stuck close to me as we walked toward his apartment, him on the side closest to the road and me within arm's reach of the buildings. Walking this way made it easier for me to keep track of people so that I didn't walk into them. I'd never told Zayne that, but he'd seemed to pick up pretty quickly on my preference.

"By the way, what did you roll around in back there?" he asked.

"A puddle of bad life choices."

"Huh. I always wondered what that smelled like."

"Now you know."

Despite the fact I smelled rank, another laugh tickled the back of my throat as I looked at him again. The black shirt he had on was a mess, but his leather pants held up under the constant shifting from human to Warden and back again, which must be why he wore them when he patrolled.

And I was not complaining about them. At all.

I imagined that, between my smell and his half-shirtless appearance, we were drawing a fair amount of attention. Then again, I was sure people had seen stranger things in this city and had definitely smelled worse. I wondered if anyone realized what he was.

"Do people recognize what you are?" I asked, keeping my voice low.

"Not sure, but no one's ever seen me in my human form and asked if I was Warden," he answered. "Why?"

"Because you don't look like other humans." I knew that Wardens rarely shifted in public. It was for privacy and security, since there were people out there, like those Children of God fanatics, who believed Wardens, ironically, were demons and should be slaughtered.

He tucked a strand of hair back from his face. "Not sure if that's a compliment."

"It's not an insult." I thought I saw a smirk before he turned to scan the street.

"How do I not look like other humans?" he asked. "I think I blend in."

I snorted. Like a piglet.

Hot.

"You couldn't blend in if you covered your body with a paper sack," I said.

"Well, I definitely wouldn't blend in then," he replied, and I heard the grin in his tone. "Walking around in a paper sack would be kind of noticeable."

The image of Zayne in nothing but a paper sack immediately formed in my thoughts, and I felt my cheeks flush. I hated myself for even putting that into the universe.

"You don't blend in, either," he said, and my chin jerked in his direction.

"Because I reek like I imagine a moldy butt smells?"

Zayne laughed, a deep rumbling sound that created interesting little flutters in the pit of my stomach. "No," he said, stopping at a busy intersection. "Because you're beautiful, Trin. You have this *thing*. It's this spark from within. A light. There isn't a single person out here that can't see that."

9

I was waiting for Zayne in the center of the mats, sitting cross-legged, and, instead of stretching, I was daydreaming about a different life where it was okay for Zayne to tell me I was beautiful. Granted, this spark or light he was claiming everyone and their mother could see probably was my *grace* and not my stunning physical attributes.

"I have an idea," Zayne announced as he strolled out of the bedroom.

My gaze dropped to Zayne's hand. He held a strip of black material. I raised my brows. "Should I be worried?"

"Only a little." He grinned, lifting the material.

When I realized he was holding a tie, I started to ask for more detail, but the buzzer on the intercom went off. "Expecting anyone?"

"No." Zayne jogged to the doors. "Hello?"

"It's me, your new best friend forever." The all-too-familiar voice floated through the speaker.

"What in the Hell?" Zayne muttered.

"Is that who I think it is?" I rose onto my knees.

"If you're thinking it's Roth," he replied with a sigh, "then you'd be correct."

"Are you ignoring me?" Roth's voice came through the speaker once more. "If so, I'm going to have a sads."

My lips twitched at that. I guessed Roth's parting words the day before exemplified the demonic talent of making a normal statement sound like something a serial killer would utter.

A moment later, I felt the warning of Roth's arrival, and then the elevator doors opened.

"Yo," I heard Roth say, but from where I was sitting, I couldn't see much of him.

"Two days in a row?" Zayne said. "To what do we owe the honor?"

Roth chuckled. "I'm bored. That's the honor."

"And you decided to come here?"

"I was in the neighborhood, so, yep." The Crown Prince strolled through Zayne's living room like it was a common, everyday occurrence. As he drew closer, I saw that he was slurping something from a white foam cup. There were red letters on the drink, but I couldn't make them out. Roth spotted me and grinned. "Hey there, Angel Face, you look like you're praying. I hope I'm interrupting."

Angel Face? "Sorry to disappoint but no."

"We were about to do some training." Zayne followed the demon, his expression a cross between exasperation and reluctant amusement. "We're kind of busy."

"Don't let me stop you." Roth winked at me as he lifted his free hand and twisted it around. Next to the couch, the oversize chair I'd never seen Zayne use slid around so that it was facing the mats.

Well, wasn't that a neat ability I was only a little jealous of.

Roth plopped down in the chair and hooked one denim-clad leg over the other. He took another drink.

Zayne stared at him as if he didn't know quite what to say. I imagine I had the same look on my face.

"Where's Layla?" Zayne finally asked.

"Girls' day with Stacey since it's Saturday," he answered, and Hell, I'd had no idea it was the weekend. "They're going to lunch and then out to some shops. Or something. Whatever girls do."

A tiny ball of jealousy formed in the center of my chest. *Whatever girls do.* We hung out. We shared desserts and appetizers. We talked about stupid things and we shared our deepest, darkest moments. We reminded each other that we were never truly alone. That's what girls did.

I missed Jada.

"You know, Layla and Stacey would love for you to join them," Roth continued, almost as if he were reading my mind. "As long as Stony would let you out of his sight for a few hours."

Yeah, well, I wasn't sure hanging out with not one, but two girls Zayne had messed around with was my idea of fun times.

"Trinity can come and go as she pleases," Zayne replied dryly. "I'm guessing Cayman isn't around, either?"

"Nope. He's working. You know, trading pieces of human souls for frivolous things." Roth waggled his brows at me. "Does that offend your angelic senses?"

I lifted a shoulder. "Not like he's out there persuading humans to do it. They're making their own bed, so they get to roll around in it."

Roth tipped his cup at me. "Not a very angelic thing to say. You should care. You should be *affronted*."

"I'm affronted," Zayne muttered. "By this unexpected visit."

"The lies we tell ourselves." Roth looked between us. "Lucky me. I get to see a Trueborn and a Warden fight—well, play fight, if you two are actually going to do anything other than stare at me like you've been blessed by my appearance."

I bit down on my lip to stop from laughing, because I had a feeling it would only antagonize the demon and annoy Zayne.

To be honest, I was glad to see Roth. Zayne and Roth might be stuck in a weird rivalry and have fundamental differences, but they were still friends, and since I'd been here, other than yesterday, no one had come to see Zayne. Not even members of his own clan. Everyone needed a friend, even if said friend was the Crown Prince of Hell.

Popping to my feet, I turned to Zayne. "I have no problem with him watching us train."

Zayne looked like he wanted to say that he did, but he simply shook his head and stepped onto the mat.

"So, what's up with the tie?" I asked, and Zayne stared down at it like he'd forgotten he'd been holding it.

"Now that is a question I was dying to ask," Roth commented. "BDSM, Stony? I am shooketh."

My cheeks flushed as Zayne shot Roth a withering glare before refocusing on me. "Remember when you wanted to learn not to rely on your vision during a fight?"

"Why would you want to do that?" Roth asked.

"Trueborns' eyesight isn't like a Warden's or a demon's at night," Zayne explained. "Since most of our patrolling is done at night, you can fill in the blanks."

I had no idea if Roth believed him, but I picked up on what Zayne was saying without giving too much away. I nodded.

"I figured the best way to practice is to force you not to use your vision, which is why I have the tie." Zayne dangled the material. "Sorry to disappoint, Roth."

"Blindfolded training. Not nearly as sexy as I was thinking, but still vastly entertaining" came the comment from the one-man peanut gallery.

"That is a good idea." Anticipation swirled in my chest. "Let's go."

"This should be fun to watch," Roth declared.

"Can you not talk?" Zayne snapped as he walked to where I stood.

"I don't think that is a promise I can make."

I pressed my lips together as I reached for the tie, but Zayne stepped behind me.

"I got it," he said. "Let me know when you're ready."

In other words, let him know when I was prepared to be completely blind. I wondered if he remembered how I'd freaked out the night the Community had been attacked and he'd folded his wings around me, blocking out all sources of light.

I hoped I didn't freak out like that again, especially considering we had an audience.

Drawing in a shallow breath, I shook out my arms. "Ready."

A heartbeat later, I felt the heat of Zayne at my back. I held still as the tie appeared in my vision. As it drew close to my face, already blocking out most of the light, my heart started pounding.

I didn't like this.

I didn't like this at all.

Which made it hard not to stop this whole thing as the tie touched my face and blackness settled over my eyes. By some kind of super willpower, I allowed Zayne to secure the tie.

The material was surprisingly soft and not completely opaque. I could see vague shapes in front of me, and the longer I stared, the more clearly I could see a tiny dot of light.

Was this how it would be once the disease had taken its toll? Nothing but shapes and a pinprick of light?

Panic exploded in my gut and I reached for the tie, wanting to rip it from my face and burn the material.

This is what you wanted.

Telling myself that was the only thing that stopped me from tearing it off. I could deal with this. I had to. I just needed my heart to stop pounding like it was going to throw itself out of my chest, and for the choking feeling in my throat to ease up.

Zayne's hands landed on my shoulders, causing me to jerk. "Are you okay?" His voice was soft, and I had no idea if Roth could hear him. "We can try this another day."

Another day as in *never again* sounded like a wonderful idea, but another day meant I was one day closer to doing this all over again. I was eventually going to run out of days.

I took another breath and focused, breathing in and breathing out—

Oh my God.

All at once I realized why Zayne wanted to put the blindfold on. He'd cut two minuscule holes in the tie, and somehow he'd lined them up perfectly with my pupils, and I'd just been too panicky to notice. I couldn't see much with such restricted vision, but if I focused, there was still a tiny amount of light, like there'd most likely be once retinitis pigmentosa ran its course. Zayne must've done some research on that laptop of his, and that meant the world to me.

Emotion clogged my throat, but those nearly insignificant holes helped me breathe easier. "I'm fine."

Zayne squeezed my shoulders. "Let me know if that changes."

I nodded.

"I stand corrected," Roth said from the sidelines. "This is sexy."

Zayne sighed from behind me. "I wonder what Layla would think about that."

Roth snorted. "She'd probably want to try it out."

"Thanks for sharing," I muttered.

"You're very welcome," Roth replied. "Angel Face is way more polite than you, Stony."

"Call me Angel Face one more time, and I'll show you how polite I am," I warned as I felt Zayne move from behind me.

"That would be scarier if you weren't standing there blindfolded."

Zayne snickered. "I'm in front of you."

Before I could tell him that I could vaguely see that, Roth spoke up. Again. "Doesn't telling her where you are defeat the purpose of this?"

"Shut up," Zayne and I said in unison.

A laugh came from the general direction of where Roth sat. "You two are on such the same page."

Proving just that, we both ignored him and got down to business. "Without your vision, you have to rely on your other senses. They're just as important in hand-to-hand combat."

I wasn't so sure that was true, but I nodded nonetheless.

"Hearing. Smell. Touch," Zayne went on. "All of those things will give away your opponent's next move."

"Especially if they smell bad," Roth added. "Or they're loud and clumsy."

I grinned at that.

"You're going to need to concentrate really hard to do this," Zayne went on. "And I mean *really* hard."

The corners of my lips started to turn down. "Okay."

"You cannot allow yourself to become distracted. Everything in this room, especially the uninvited third wheel, needs to fade away."

"Hey," Roth scuffed. "That's offensive."

"This is my I-don't-care face," Zayne replied.

I planted my hands on my hips. "I think I know how to concentrate, Zayne."

"And I think I've been around you enough to know that you have the concentration level of a puppy on its first car ride."

Roth laughed.

I opened my mouth and then closed it. Could not argue with that observation. "I feel personally attacked by that statement."

There was a low rumble of a chuckle from Zayne. "Once you concentrate, you'll notice things you haven't before. Okay? Let me know when you're there."

I stood there for a few seconds. "Ready."

"You sure?" Zayne sounded doubtful.

"Yes." I shifted into my stance, bracing myself as I waited for—

Zayne's hand hit my forearm, startling me. I reached out and ended up brushing my hand over his chest, which meant he'd made his move. We tried again, breaking apart, and then he was on me once more. Again and again he moved, and I… I just stood there, missing his every move and virtually blocking air. Worse part was, he was pulling his punches and kicks.

"I can't see you," I said, dropping my arms. "At all."

"That's the point," he reminded me.

"Well, yeah, but…" I trailed off, shaking my head as I opened and closed my hands.

"You can't get frustrated already." Zayne stayed close this time, not backing off.

"I'm not."

"Sounds like it," Roth chimed in.

"Am not." I jerked my head in his direction.

Fingers curled around my chin, guiding my head back toward Zayne. "*Yes*, you are."

I wanted to argue, but it was pointless, because I knew he was picking up on it. "I just… I don't think I can do this."

"You can," he said, and I thought he'd stepped back. "And you will."

I reached out, my hands feeling empty air. I'd been right.

"You knew he wasn't there," Roth said. "Right?"

Closing my hand around nothing, I nodded.

"How?" the demon persisted.

"I… I couldn't feel his warmth," I admitted, pulling my hand back and hoping that didn't sound as weird as I thought it did.

"Demons are the same way," Roth said. "We give off a

lot of heat. If you can feel that, then you know one is close enough to touch. Too close. How about—"

Warmth danced along my skin. I lifted my hand before Roth could even finish. My fingers brushed against something hard and warm. Zayne's chest. "I felt him get close."

"Good." This time it was Zayne who spoke, and I could feel the rumble of his words through my palm.

Without warning, Zayne grasped my arm and spun me around. "Get back into your stance."

I did just that, spreading my legs and rooting my feet into the mats as I lifted my hands.

"Is he near you?" Roth asked.

I gauged the temperature of the air around me. "No."

"Correct," Zayne confirmed. "Concentrate."

I inhaled deeply and then exhaled slowly, focusing on the space around me. Not just for the temperature, but for any movement. There was nothing—and then I felt the slight change in movement around me. A stir of warm air, and this time I didn't just stand there.

I struck out, hitting nothing. "Dammit!"

"Almost had me," Zayne said, and my left ear tingled. I spun, kicking out, but he was suddenly at my back, his breath along the nape of my neck. "Almost."

Spinning, I jabbed out my elbow, but with a whoosh of air, I felt him move to—to my *right*. I whirled, finding the space empty once more. God, this was making me a little nauseous. I thrust my hand out, and my palm glanced off him.

"Ha!" I shouted, having made contact—weak contact, but contact.

"Almost," Zayne repeated.

Following the sound of his voice, I stepped forward and found nothing. Frustration piqued, I jumped when I felt the stir of air and landed unbalanced on the balls of my feet.

"Nice," murmured Roth. "That would've been a kick to the legs."

I smiled.

"Don't get cocky," Zayne warned.

The next second proved exactly why I shouldn't, because I missed Zayne by a mile on the next swing. The next punch I threw was just another glancing blow, as was the one after that and after that.

"Almost." Zayne danced around me, and I played pin the freaking fist on the Warden.

A game I sucked at.

And I was really beginning to hate the word *almost*.

"You're losing your concentration," he told me. "Take a breath and refocus, Trin."

"I'm *concentrating*." I whipped out a leg, and this time I didn't come anywhere near him. Anger turned my blood to acid as I moved, seeking Zayne through the pinprick holes.

"Trin." Zayne's voice was a low warning, and I knew what he was saying.

Air stirred around me again, and I lashed out with my arm. I went a little wild with the punch, but it was too late to pull back. Going too far, I lost my balance. Zayne must've seen that, because I felt his hands on my shoulders. Neither of us could regain our footing, so when I fell, he went down with me. I landed on my back with a grunt, Zayne on top of me.

I swung at him again, since I knew exactly where he was

now, but Zayne caught my wrists and pinned them above my head before I could make contact.

"You lost your focus," Zayne said.

Fury roared through me as I lifted my hips, managing to get one leg free. "No, I didn't!"

"Yes," he said softly. He pressed down, and when he inhaled, his chest pressed against mine. In the darkness of the blindfold, all I could feel was him and his warm breath against my lips. I stopped fighting and didn't dare move. Not a fraction of an inch. "You did lose focus."

My hands opened and closed fruitlessly against the mat. "How do you know?"

"Because you got frustrated." His voice was low, still incredibly soft and gentle considering he was pinning me down. "And that got the best of you."

I pressed my lips together to stop the denial.

Zayne's grip on my wrists slackened. His hand slid down the length of my arm, over my shoulder. He cupped my cheek. "You were doing really well."

"No, I wasn't." Sweat dampened my brow. "I was barely able to get near you."

"But you did get near me." He shifted slightly, and his thumb grazed my lower lip. "This is the first time you've tried this. You're not going to be perfect right off the bat." His chest rose against mine again, sending a prickle of heat down my spine. "You have to give yourself time."

"I don't know if I can do this," I admitted in a whisper.

"I know you can," he insisted, and my next breath came out shaky. "I don't have a single doubt in my mind."

I wished I could see him. His eyes. His face. See how he

was looking at me, because if I could see that faith he had in me, then maybe I could feel it.

Zayne's thumb moved again, this time sweeping across my bottom lip. My breath hitched as a sweet rush of unwanted anticipation surged. "Okay?"

I had no idea what he was asking, but I nodded, and then neither of us moved beyond our rising and falling chests. My arms were still stretched above my head. I could move them, but I didn't, and I knew his mouth was still close to mine because his breath teased my lips. I would have given just about anything to know what he was thinking right then. If he felt that anticipation, if he was brimming with yearning for what couldn't be.

Maybe there *was* something to other senses heightening when you couldn't see, because I swore there was a tension to the air that hadn't been there before. I could feel it.

"Question?" Roth's voice broke the silence, and holy crap, I'd forgotten he was there. Zayne had, too, based on the way his muscles tensed against me. When Roth spoke again, amusement practically dripped from each word. "And I'm asking for a friend. Exactly what kind of training are you guys doing right now?"

10

Training while blindfolded could not have ended more quickly. Zayne had rolled off me and helped me up. The tie had come off next, and I sort of wished it hadn't, because I'd rather not have seen Roth's oddly smug, grinning face.

We hadn't stopped training, though. We'd moved on to fighting without the blindfold, and out of what I guessed was boredom, Roth had gotten in on the action. The demon was actually helpful, for the most part. Then Layla had called, and he'd poofed out of the apartment.

Just blinked right out of existence.

Yet another ability I wished I had.

Patrolling that night hadn't turned up anything remotely exciting, and I was wondering how long we were going to roam around aimlessly before we found something—anything—that would lead us to the Harbinger.

The following morning, I'd just finished pulling my hair

up in a ponytail and was about to join Zayne on the mats for more blindfolded training when my phone rang from the nightstand. The moment I saw Thierry's name, I almost let it go to voice mail. But I couldn't ignore his call.

Stomach twisting, I answered with a greeting that sounded like I'd been punched in the stomach at the exact moment I said *hello.*

"Trinity?" Thierry's deep voice tugged at my heart hard. "You okay?"

"Yes. Totally." I cleared my throat. "What's up?"

"What's up?" he repeated the words slowly. "I think a lot of things are *up* right now."

Closing my eyes, I plopped down on the bed, knowing what he meant. Misha. Jada's missed calls. My overall mental and emotional well-being. "Yeah, a lot is up right now."

His sigh was heavy and so familiar that it caused a pang in my chest. I missed him. I missed Matthew and Jada and Ty and— I cut that thought off as Thierry spoke. "I know you're busy, but I need to talk to you. There's been a development regarding your future."

I opened my eyes. "I am half-afraid to ask what that is."

"It's a good thing."

"Really?"

"Really," he confirmed with a soft laugh. "As you know, serving as a Warden is financially lucrative for those who Ascend training and commit their lives to battling those who seek to harm," Thierry said, and I knew that. It paid really, really well. Where Wardens got their money, I had no idea, but I liked picturing Alphas doing flybys, randomly dropping off loads of cash. "Until you were summoned by your father, we cared for you and your mother, providing you with whatever financial stability you needed."

I was starting to feel like I was being cut off, but he'd said this was good news, so I kept my mouth shut.

"That is no longer necessary," he continued. "I will be sending you a screenshot of the bank account that has been established in your name that will have all the necessary information for you to access the account in a few days, once the transfer clears—"

"Wait. What?"

"You're being paid for the services you're rendering," he explained, and the way he said that made me feel like I needed a shower. "And I think you will be pleased with what you'll see."

"I don't understand. I've never had money. Or even a bank account. It's a shock that I even know how to use a credit card," I replied. "How do I have money now?"

"You father wants to make sure you're provided for and that your focus will not be distracted by—how did he say it—'frivolous human concepts such as money.'"

Okay. That sounded like something my father would say. "Did you see him?"

"Unfortunately."

An inappropriate giggle swelled in my throat. "When? I haven't seen him since…"

"I know." All humor had vanished from his tone. "He was here this morning, in all his glory. He wanted to make sure funds were set up and that, in the meantime, you were covered. He said to tell you to check what you hold most dear, and yes, he was as vague as angelically possible."

Check what I held most dear? Immediately, my gaze swiveled to the worn Johanna Lindsey paperback that had been Mom's favorite book. Did it…look thicker than normal?

"You're still there?" Thierry's voice snagged my attention.

"Yeah. Yes." I cleared my throat. "Sorry. This has just caught me off guard."

"As it did Matthew and I. We weren't expecting your father to consider things like you needing money to buy food." I could almost picture him pinching his brow. "Actually, we were planning to wire you some money ourselves, but that won't be necessary."

"Thanks," I murmured, unsure how to respond. At the Community, money wasn't something I'd had to worry about. I'd been privileged in a lot of ways, and realizing that now, as I stared at the book, made me a little uncomfortable in my own skin.

"Trinity," Thierry began, and I tensed, recognizing that tone. "I'm not going to ask how you're doing. I already know, but… I'm sorry. I should have known that Misha wasn't your—"

"It's okay." I swallowed hard. "You all did what you thought you were supposed to, and I…did what I had to. Everything is going to be okay."

Thierry was silent. Too silent.

I rubbed my fingers over my temple. "How…how is Jada?"

"Upset. Confused." A pause. "She misses you."

"I miss her," I whispered. "I miss all of you."

"We know. She knows," he replied. "And she knows you need time to process everything. Just don't forget that she's here. That we are all here, and we miss you."

"I know."

Thierry didn't keep me on the phone much longer. I hung up, feeling a little heartsick and a little happy to have heard his voice.

Slowly becoming aware that I wasn't alone, I placed my phone aside and looked up.

Zayne stood in the doorway. "Everything okay?"

I nodded, smiling a little. "It was Thierry. He was calling to say that my...that my father had come by to make sure I was financially set."

"That's good news, then."

In other words, he was probably wondering why he was picking up on sadness through the bond, but I wasn't up to offering that information as I leaned over and picked up the book. It felt different, and as I turned it around, I saw that there were gaps between several of the pages.

"I think...my father was here," I said, glancing at him.

"Seriously?" Zayne leaned against the door frame. "When?"

"Maybe last night?" I hadn't paid attention to the book then. Giving it a little shake, I wasn't all that surprised when I saw green paper flutter to the comforter in a never-ending stream of money.

Zayne made a choking sound. "Holy..."

"Hundred-dollar bills," I said, eyes wide as I stared at the dozens and dozens of them. There was a chance that one had been tucked between every page. I looked up with a smile. "I guess I'm covering dinner tonight."

I did buy dinner, but that turned out to be a little embarrassing, because he'd picked Subway and I had to break a hundred-dollar bill on two footlongs.

Not long after I'd gotten off the phone with Thierry, the screenshot he'd promised came through as a text with all the necessary information. I'd never seen so many zeroes after a number before, and I had no idea what my father thought food and shelter cost, but he might have overdone it by a couple hundred thousand or so.

"I. Am. So. Bored," I whined, hours into roaming the streets.

"Most would consider that a good thing," Zayne replied.

I glanced at him, able to make out just enough of his profile in the low light as he stared into the city park. His hair was back in that tucked ponytail. He was in his human form, and I imagined those who saw us thought we were a young couple or friends out enjoying the night.

I doubted the fact that we were both dressed in head-to-toe black like old-school cat burglars was all that noteworthy.

Though, Zayne in black leather pants was very noteworthy to me.

For the last hour or so, we'd been scoping out the area where we'd spotted the Upper Level demons the other night. But other than a handful of Fiends, we hadn't come across any.

"If we were out here keeping the streets clear of demons and the humans safe, then I guess being bored would be a good thing," I mused. "But we're looking for the Harbinger, so a dull night seems like a bad thing. We're no closer to finding him than we were yesterday."

Zayne stopped under a streetlamp just outside the park entry. "You know what I think?"

"No, but I bet you're going to tell me." I went to hop up on the two- or three-foot-high limestone retaining wall that flanked the entryway, but as soon as my booted foot hit the ledge, I realized I'd misjudged the height. I started to topple backward—

Zayne caught me by the hips, steadying me until my feet were planted on the ledge. "I have no idea how you can leap from one roof to another and scale a fire escape, but nearly crack your skull open on a three-foot retaining wall."

"Skills," I muttered, turning so that I was facing him. For once, I was the one looking down at him. "Thanks."

"No problem. I got you." His hands lingered on my hips, his grip light just above the iron daggers I wore hidden under my shirt. "You good?"

I nodded. "I think so."

"I want you to be sure." His tone was light, even teasing, as he looked up at me. "I wouldn't be a very good Protector if you ended up breaking an arm my first couple of weeks on the job."

My lips twitched. "Yeah, that would mean you kind of suck, but I think you're forgetting one important factoid."

"And what's that?" The weight of his hands on my hips shifted, somehow becoming...heavier.

"It's going to take more than a three-foot fall to crack open my skull."

"I don't know," he replied as a group of what sounded like teenagers crossed the street, heading away from us as they shouted at one another. "Stranger things have happened."

"Not that strange."

His head tilted. "When I was younger and just learning to fly, I misjudged a landing and fell. Broke my arm. It was only a couple of feet."

It was rare for Wardens to suffer broken bones from something even a human would likely survive. "How old were you?"

"Six."

I laughed. "Yeah, well, I'm not six. I'm fairly confident that I'm not going to break anything if I fall."

"So, you're positive, if I let go, you're not going to come tumbling down?" he asked, and I became aware of his thumbs moving. They were slowly sliding up and down, just inside each hip bone, and I wasn't even sure if he was aware of that.

But I was.

Totally engrossed, actually, and my pulse kicked up. A heady flush swept through me, and I did feel a little unsteady. It had nothing to do with my balance and everything to do with the way he was touching me.

"How about I make you a deal?"

"Depends on the deal." I wasn't aware of what I was doing until I did it. My hands landed on his. Not to pull them away, but to keep them there.

Zayne stepped in, as close as he could with me being on a wall. Our bodies weren't touching, but the entire front of my body warmed as if we were. "If you can keep your feet on the ground—both feet," he added, "I'll stock the fridge with as much soda as you can drink."

"Really?"

"Really," he repeated, his voice deeper, thicker.

"Including Coke?"

"I'll even throw in a couple of cases of root beer."

"Mmm. Root beer. People who don't like root beer are monsters. That's a great deal." I lowered my head, stopping a few inches from his. In the soft buttery glow of the lamp, I saw his eyes go half-mast, and the look he gave me, even if he was unaware of it, even if it meant nothing, melted me. "But I can do that all by myself and still keep both my feet off the ground and then some. I refuse your deal."

Zayne chuckled. "Then I'm going to have to come up with a better deal."

"Yeah, you are."

His lower lip slipped between his teeth as his grip on my hips tightened, both actions eliciting a deep, clenching sensation inside me. I felt the tension in the tendons of his hands, the power in his arms, and the flex of his muscles in his forearms and biceps. He was going to lift me up. Maybe settle me on my feet. Or maybe settle me against him.

I knew I shouldn't allow it, because that ZAYNE drawer was still cracked open, but I didn't step back and put distance between us. Those pale wolf eyes met mine, and our gazes connected. *We* connected. He didn't move. Neither did I. Nothing was spoken between us.

A car horn blared. Zayne dropped his hands as if his palms were burned. I froze, stuck between damning the car horn to Hell and being thankful for the interruption. Then I turned sideways and dragged in deep breaths of exhaust and the sweet, lemony scent of a nearby magnolia tree. I reined in my hormones and latched on desperately to my common sense.

Zayne walked a few feet ahead, hands fisted at his sides. He stayed close to the wall, within reach, probably in case I decided to throw myself off, which sounded great at the moment. Though, I'd been right earlier. A fall from this height would damage only my ego.

Silence ticked by, and I tried to sense through the connection what he was feeling, but I couldn't get past what was going on with me.

Looking up at the dark sky, I exhaled long and slow. Time to get back on track and move on. Moving on was something I could pretend to be good at. "So…you were about to tell me what you thought?"

He looked over his shoulder, watching me slowly place one foot in front of the other as if I were on a balance beam. "I was thinking about how long the Harbinger has been here, on these streets, hunting Wardens and demons, and none of us have caught one glimpse of it, as far as we know. Makes me think we could spend every night out here, searching, and not find it."

I stopped, one foot in the air. "Why don't you think we'll find it?"

"Because I don't think we'll find the Harbinger until it wants to be found."

Just before midnight, hot tingles erupted between my shoulder blades.

We'd moved on from the park to roam an area of Capitol Hill that Zayne called Eastern Market, which was a mecca of yummy-smelling restaurants that had my stomach grumbling. I made a mental note to start our next patrol here so that I could taste something from each place.

I stopped walking and looked behind me. "I feel a demon."

Zayne halted, head tilted to the side and chin up. Turning toward the wide street, I propped my hands on my hips. There were still people out and an ever-present racket of sirens coming from all different directions, but it was nowhere near as busy as earlier in the night.

"Kind of jealous over how quickly you can sense them," Zayne commented as he stepped toward the curb.

"Yeah, well, you can fly, so..." I followed him, squinting but seeing nothing beyond the streetlamps. "See anything?"

He shook his head. "It's nearby. Probably a Fiend, but let's check it out."

Letting Zayne's awesome eyeballs lead the way, I followed him across the street. I had no idea where we were going, and I couldn't read the street signs, but the farther we walked, the darker the sidewalks became. Hoping they were in good condition, I stayed close to him as my tunnel-like vision became worse with each step.

"Where are we?" I whispered as we crossed onto another tree-lined street. It was freakishly quiet.

"We're on Ninth Street," he answered. "Southeast. We're not too far from the naval yard. Normally don't see a whole lot of demon activity down here."

I guessed demons didn't like sailors.

There were a lot of dark buildings and lighted windows surrounding us. They looked like apartment buildings or condos.

"By the way, I'm going to have to push back training tomorrow until later in the afternoon," Zayne said. "Unless you want to get up early."

"Yeah, I'll pass." Leaves stirred above us as what I hoped was a bird took flight. "What are you doing?"

"Got some stuff— Wait." Zayne lifted an arm, and I plowed right into it. Lowering his arm, Zayne stalked forward down the street past a narrow alley and then stopped. He knelt. "Look at this."

My boots crunched over the gravel as I joined him, kneeling down. Zayne's fingers were on part of a busted chain-link fence. "I see…nothing but your fingers."

Zayne cursed under his breath. "Sorry. Didn't think—"

"It's okay." I waved him off. "What is it?"

"Blood. Fresh. Well, kind of."

I rose, looking around. "What does that mean?"

"It's wet, but really thick. Weird." He tipped his head up, staring at the trees on the other side of the fence, and then he stood. Going back to the sidewalk, he glanced down the street and then turned back. "I think I know what's beyond this fence."

My brows rose. "A big slice of pizza? Hopefully?"

He snickered as he strode forward. "Not quite. It's an old manufacturing building that was supposed to be converted into apartments, but the funding fell through several years ago."

"An abandoned building?"

"If you don't consider bleeding demons occupants, then yes." Kneeling again, he grabbed the broken section of the fence and peeled it back. "Let's check it out."

"Sure. Why not?" I dipped through the opening and wisely waited for Zayne to join me, since I legit could see nothing due to the tree branches blocking out any and all light.

My steps slowed and then stopped. The absence of light was disorienting, causing my heart to start jumping. This was as bad as the blindfold. Maybe worse. My stomach turned cold as I stared at the different shades of nothingness.

"Careful," Zayne warned, moving ahead. "The branches are really low in here. I need to move them out of the way."

"Thanks. I…" Drawing in a deep breath, I told myself to get over it and just ask for what I needed. "Can I put my hand on your back? Is that—"

Before I could even finish, Zayne's hand wrapped around mine, and a second later my palm was flat against his back. With a ragged exhale, I curled my fingers around his shirt and whispered, "Thank you."

"No problem." There was a pause. "Ready?"

"Ready."

My still-in-training Guide Gargoyle led me around trees and low-hanging branches that would've surely knocked me out. I counted my steps and noted when Zayne slowed to announce a large rock or fallen tree limb. It took fifty-two footsteps before the thickness of the darkness shifted and shapes began to form in the silvery moonlight.

We stepped onto a lawn that hadn't been tended in years, the grass reaching my knees. Bushes and weeds choked a driveway that was cut off by the chain-link fence. I took a step and realized sticker bushes had latched on to my leggings.

Ugh.

Letting go of Zayne's shirt, I reached down and brushed off the little buggers and then straightened, getting my first look at the building.

It was… Um, it might have been lovely in its heyday.

Now the monstrous building looked like something straight out of a horror film. Several stories tall, it had two wings and a whole lot of boarded-up windows. I couldn't even tell what color it was supposed to be. Gray? Beige? Dusty?

"Well…" I drew the word out. "That definitely looks haunted."

"Then you'll come in handy, won't you?"

I shot him a look behind his back as he made his way through the jungle of a yard to the side of the building. Stopping at a boarded and chained door, he looked back at me. "You still feel the demon, right?"

"Yeppers peppers."

"Yeppers peppers," he repeated, shaking his head as he moved to the nearest window. He grabbed one of the boards and yanked. Wood cracked and gave way. He propped the board against the side of the building.

I stepped in and gripped the next board and then pulled. The old wood broke free, and I started to toss it.

Zayne stopped me. "The boards have nails still attached. If we come back out the way we came, I don't want you stepping on one."

"Oh." Chagrined, I gently placed the board against the wall. "Good point."

"I'm useful like that." Zayne pulled down the last board, and it joined its friends against the wall. Stretching up, he leaned through the window. "All clear."

I was happy to hear him speak, because I kept picturing something straight out of an '80s horror movie. The kind Peanut loved to watch that involved a lot of bizarre decapitations.

Zayne pulled himself up and disappeared through the window. A nanosecond later, his hand shot out. He wiggled his fingers. "Come on."

I rolled my eyes. "Back up."

There was a sigh, and then his hand disappeared. I planted

my palms on the dusty windowpane, then jumped through the window and landed nimbly on floorboards that groaned under my weight. I straightened, finding Zayne standing a few feet in front of me.

"Show off," he muttered.

I smirked as I looked around. A good part of the ceiling was missing, as apparently was either the roof or an interior wall, because a decent amount of moonlight filtered in. There was a maze of broken, toppled chairs, and graffiti marked the walls.

We left the room in silence, entering a hallway where less of the moonlight could penetrate. "Damn," Zayne muttered. "Looks like a lot of this floor is rotted out."

Without asking this time, I gripped the back of his shirt. "Lead the way, wherever that may be."

We passed several rooms with doors broken off their hinges but found no sign of the demon except for the blood that Zayne could see.

We entered another wider hall with windows, which allowed more light through. I let go of his shirt and peered around to get a better grasp of my surroundings. There were several more open rooms, and the musty smell was starting—

A vision in white burst from a wall—well, actually not a vision. It was a person in a…white uniform. White pants. White top. Even a strange little white hat. A nurse. It was a nurse.

Who ran through another wall without looking in our direction, as if she were in a hurry.

I stopped walking. "Uh, you didn't see that?"

Zayne looked over his shoulder at me. "No."

"Oh." I stared at the empty hall. "What did you say this place used to be?"

"An old manufacturing building," he answered. "Why? Wait. Do I even want to know?"

I slowly shook my head. "Probably not, but I think we should go in that direction," I said, pointing to the left.

We made our way to where I'd seen the ghost nurse disappear and came to a set of rusted yellow double doors. Zayne carefully opened the doors as quietly as possible. Every muscle in my body tensed as I prepared to see the demon.

But that's not what we found.

It was a ledge, about twelve feet by twelve feet. Only a railing separated us from wide, open emptiness below.

"I'm so confused," I said, looking back and then up, just to confirm that we were still on the first floor. "We didn't go up any stairs, right?"

"No." Zayne kept his voice low as he crept to the railing and looked down. "It's an old pool. Emptied out, but it must've been in the basement or a lower level than where we entered. Probably used for rehab."

I joined him, placing my hands on the metal bar, surprised to find that it was sturdy. This definitely wasn't a normal basement, because the whole west wall was full of unbroken windows, allowing light to spread across the bleached cement pool.

Was this where the ghost nurse had come from? There weren't any rooms between where I'd seen her and here, but that didn't mean much. She could've come from anywhere, but—

Footsteps echoed through the open space. Zayne suddenly grabbed my hand and pulled me onto my knees. My head spun toward him, but he placed a finger over his lips and then jerked his chin toward the pool.

I followed his gaze, not seeing much at first, and then someone shuffled toward the steps leading into the shallow end of the pool. It must be the demon, but...

Something seemed wrong with the way it shuffled, taking a few steps and then twitching uncontrollably, the head jerking left once and then twice.

Pulling my hand free of Zayne's, I grasped the bars of the railing and leaned forward as far as I could. My eyes were bad, but I could still see enough to know something looked really, really off about this demon.

Then it stepped into a ray of moonlight, and while its features were nothing but a fuzzy blur, I could tell it was missing a nose.

And when it jerked its head again, something flapped out from its cheek. Loose skin, I realized. Loose, partially unattached skin. What we were looking at was definitely not a Fiend or an Upper Level demon. It was something...

Something that used to be human.

11

My palms sweated as I watched the creature stop in the center of the pool. "Is that...is that what I think it is?"

Zayne leaned in, his arm pressing against mine, and when he spoke, his voice was nearly a whisper. "If you think that's what happens when a Poser bites a human, you'd be correct."

"Jesus." My grip tightened. Now I knew why that poor ghost nurse was hauling butt. That thing down there even freaked out ghosts.

Posers were demons that looked and acted human with the exception of their insatiable appetite, crazy strength and nasty habit of biting people. Their infectious saliva transferred via one nip of their teeth, and three days later, the poor sucker who was snacked on turned into a potential extra for *The Walking Dead*, complete with a tendency to eat everything, including other people, and with a healthy dose of rabid rage. We called them zombies. Not very creative, but the word *zombie* and its meaning had existed long before pop culture got ahold of it.

"Never seen one before, have you?" he asked.

I shook my head. "I haven't even seen a Poser. At least, I don't think I have."

"They're rare." Zayne's breath stirred the tendrils of hair around my ear. "And as you can see, their bite is bad news, but they don't chomp on humans often."

My gaze flickered over his face. "Because they can only bite seven times before they die?"

He nodded as he turned back to the pool below. "What is this zombie doing here, in an abandoned building?"

"Urban sightseeing?" I suggested.

His chuckle was low. "When a human first gets bitten, they'll go to familiar places. Home. Places of employment. But the guy down there is way past his expiration date of it being a fresh bite. At this point, he should be chasing after anything that's alive."

Which was why it was important to put down Posers when they were found. All they had to do to cause chaos was bite one human. Just like in the movies, the infected human then spread the demonic virus to another human through a bite, saliva…any bodily fluid. It had happened in the past, probably more often than I knew. As the demonic infection spread, zombies lost their ability for cognitive function beyond walking and eating.

"I'm guessing the game plan is to take it out."

"Yeah, but I want to see what it's up to. There has to be a reason it's here, when—"

A door at the other end of the room swung open, and the

sound of feet shuffling over tile rose until it was a loud hum. My mouth dropped opened.

Zayne stiffened. "Holy…"

"…zombie apocalypse," I finished for him, staring down at the limping, twitching mess. They weren't groaning, more like barking harsh, clipped snarls in between snapping their teeth together. "There have to be a dozen down there."

"And then some."

I took a deep breath and immediately regretted it. The stench was overwhelming, a mix of sulfur and rotting meat left out in the sun, and it triggered my gag reflex.

"Remind me never to say I'm bored again."

"Oh, trust me, I will never allow you to say that again." He angled his body toward me. "Something is up. They don't flock together like this, especially where there's no food service."

That was something pop culture got wrong about zombies. They didn't travel in groups. The reason could be seen here, as they snapped and snarled at each other below while they stumbled forward and into the empty pool.

"It's like they're waiting on something," Zayne continued. "But that doesn't make sense."

Very little of this made sense. Like, how did we just happen to sense a demon and end up here, where an assembly of the dead was waiting and the demon we'd sensed was MIA? Unease stirred. Could we have been led here? "Zayne—"

Cold air blasted the nape of my neck. My head cranked around. The frigid temperature reminded me of when I'd accidentally walked through a ghost, but this wasn't a full-body blast. This chilly sensation settled in the same spot that burned when I felt a demon, along the bottom of my neck and between my shoulder blades.

"What?" Zayne touched my arm.

I rubbed the back of my neck. The skin felt normal, but the chill was still there, tingling. "Do you feel anything strange?"

"No. Do you?"

My gaze found his as I dropped my hand. "It's weird. Like a cold—"

A guttural howl whipped our heads toward the pool. One of the zombies had stepped forward, its head thrown back as it screamed. I had a sinking suspicion we'd been spotted.

"Um, I think they want to say hi," I murmured.

"Dammit," he growled. "Well, no more waiting around to see what they're here for. We can't let them leave."

"You know, I'm beginning to think they don't plan to leave," I said, not even bothering to keep my voice low as another screamed. "I think we're the reason they're here, but since they don't have the capacity to plan, I'm thinking that demon led us here."

"I think you're onto something." Zayne rose. "But *why* would be the question."

"I don't know. Maybe they think we can't take them." I peered over the railing. "How high up do you think we are?"

"About twelve feet from here to the pool deck. Why?"

"Perfect." I sent him a grin. "Beat you down there."

Zayne spun toward me, my name a shout from his lips, but I was fast. I vaulted over the railing and dropped into nothingness. Musty air seemed to pull me down. The fall took seconds, but I landed on both feet. The impact was jarring, shooting a dull burst of pain along my ankles and up my knees into my hips, but it faded quickly enough. I rose, unsheathing my daggers.

"Dinnertime," I called.

Several zombies turned to me, and the fresher ones scrambled for the pool wall, clamoring up its smooth sides. I caught glimpses of flayed skin and gaping throat wounds. One came over the side onto the deck and blocked most of the moonlight.

Probably should've anticipated that, but oh well. I'd seen enough to know where to aim. The zombie lurched forward with startling speed, and I struck even faster, thrusting the dagger into the center of the head-shaped blob. Sticky, foul smelling liquid hit the air as I yanked the dagger back. The zombie folded like a paper sack but was quickly replaced by another.

I snapped forward as Zayne landed in the deep end of the pool, wings unfurled. He'd shifted, which was good, because I didn't think zombie teeth could break his Warden skin.

Me on the other hand? I had no idea what would happen if I got bit. Didn't want to find out, either. I shoved the dagger in, under the throat this time, because this zombie was super tall.

"I swear to God, Trinity," Zayne growled as he snatched up a zombie by the head. There was a wet, ripping sound, and all I could see was a body falling, minus an important part. Zayne threw the head, and it went *splat* against the side of the pool.

That was one way to go about destroying the brain.

"You shouldn't swear to God." I hopped into the shallow end of the pool, figuring that Zayne was worried I was going to start pummeling zombies like I'd done with the Raver. "Baby Jesus wouldn't approve."

Zayne swore as he flung another headless zombie aside. "I think you have a death wish."

"Nah. I just wanted to beat you." I grabbed the hair of a zombie shambling toward the deep end and pulled it backward, but that didn't quite work out. There was a weird mushy tearing sensation, and the zombie kept going without its hair and most of its scalp. "Ew!"

I dropped the hair, gagging. "I'm never going to forget how that felt. Never. Ever."

"You jumped down here, so stop being a wimp."

Shaking my hand, I shuddered and swallowed the taste of bile. "I had its scalp in my hand, Zayne. It's *scalp*."

He lifted into the air, catching the scalpless zombie. "Behind you!" he shouted.

I spun as I jumped back. My foot slipped in gunk and my leg went out from under me. I tried to catch myself, but I was too close to the slanted drop in the deep end. When my foot came down, there was nothing there. I hit the cement with a loud *oomph* and rolled like a log down the pool. When I came to a stop, I was prone on my back, arms and legs widespread.

A body crashed onto me, and based on the funk I was inhaling through my nostrils, I knew it was the zombie. A second later, teeth snapped an inch from my face. As close as the creature was, I got a good look at an exposed jaw and one eye hanging, attached by a pinkish jellylike cable of tissue.

"Oh God," I groaned, catching it by the throat. I cringed as my fingers sank into tissue and muscle. Swinging my other arm around, I slammed the dagger into the side of its head.

Liquid sprayed my face and chest as the reanimated pain in my ass slumped.

"I hate zombies," I muttered, shoving the corpse off me.

"Are you okay?" Zayne shouted.

"Yeah." I sat up, squinting as I twisted toward the shallow end. I saw Zayne, but there were four zombies still on their feet between us. Three of them were coming straight for me.

Groaning, I popped up and got down to business. The zombies weren't hard to take down. They weren't born fighters, and coordination was definitely not something that reanimated along with them, but they sure were messy. By the time I was done, I was standing among a whole lot of gore and funk.

"You done up there?" I called out, eyes searching the beams of moonlight.

Zayne appeared where the pool began to dip. "You okay?" he repeated.

I assumed that meant there were no more zombies. "I'm fine. Not a scratch or a bite."

He turned sideways. "There had to be at least two dozen."

"That's bizarre, isn't it? There's no way that many zombies just moseyed on over here. People would be freaking so badly, we'd hear them in here."

"Yeah," Zayne agreed, wings lifting and then lowering. "I got twelve. How many did you get?"

I frowned. "I wasn't counting."

He scoffed. "Amateur."

I flipped him off.

"No need to be hateful." The humor had faded from his voice when he spoke again. "I need to call this in."

That made sense. This many zombies gathered in some random abandoned building was highly abnormal and created a whole lot of questions that needed answers.

I stared down at what was left of the zombies, and for the first time in probably my entire life, I wasn't hungry. Lifting my gaze as Zayne pulled his cell from his pocket, I thought of something. "What do I say when the rest of the clan gets here? They're going to have questions. Hell, they probably already have questions."

"I'm calling Dez," he answered, referencing the only other Warden besides Nicolai who knew what I was. He'd accompanied Zayne and the clan leader to the Community. "Get him to take you back to my place before the rest get here."

"What if more zombies show up while you wait for the others to arrive?" I asked.

"I can handle them." He put the phone to his ear. "And the others will be here fast."

I nodded, even though I hated having to cut and run. Sheathing my daggers while he talked to Dez, I looked around the pool. It looked like a butcher shop.

"Dez is on his way," Zayne said, sliding the phone into his pocket. "Something's up, though."

"What do you mean?"

"He sounded off." Zayne looked down. "Let me get you out of here."

"I can get myself—"

"There are bodies and gore covering just about every square inch of the pool. You're going to walk in it and slip." Zayne's wings spread out and he lifted in the air. "And I doubt Dez would be happy with you getting brains all over the car seat."

I frowned. "Brains are already on me."

"Even more reason to not get more on you." He hovered above me, extending his arms. "Let me just get you out of the pool."

Zayne had a point, but I hesitated, feeling as if I needed to prove that I could do this without help. I'd already needed his help once tonight. Frustration burned as I took a step and felt something sticky under my boot.

"What is it?" Zayne's wings moved soundlessly. When I didn't answer, he moved to my other side. "Talk to me, Trin."

"It's just that… I already had to rely on you tonight when I couldn't see, and I *can* get out of here. It might be messy, but I just…" My hands opened and closed, and I thought about how badly I'd performed while training blindfolded. "I need to be independent."

"What?" Confusion filled his voice.

Staring at what I thought might be exposed ribs, I struggled to find the words to explain. "I don't want you or anyone to think that I can't be…independent, or that I need to rely on others all the time."

"I don't for one second think that you accepting help when you need it means you're not independent."

"Yeah, well, other people won't agree with you."

Zayne landed next to me, probably in the only clear spot. He tucked his wings back. "Who are these people?"

I coughed out a dry laugh. "Everyone? Have you seen how people talk about others who have…" I swallowed hard. "Who have disabilities?"

God, saying that was harder than I'd realized. *Disability*. What a loaded word, one I wasn't sure I'd spoken aloud before. Maybe I'd never said it because of what it implied, that there was something different about me, something that had to be accommodated.

But disability *wasn't* a bad word, and it didn't mean that. It just meant what it meant. I was a Trueborn. And a kick-ass fighter. But I was still disabled at the end of the night. And I knew that didn't define me. It wasn't the sum of who I was. It was just a part of me.

Still, it was a hard word to say.

And I felt bad for feeling that it was a hard word to say. Like I was betraying others with disabilities by finding it hard to admit I, too, had a disability.

Didn't change that I felt like I had to prove myself.

"Trin?" Zayne's voice was soft.

I shook my head. "People expect you to be self-sufficient and strong all the time. Like you're supposed to be a shining example of rising above the suckage handed to you, or you're there to serve some freaking purpose of proving how anyone can overcome odds if they're just *positive* enough. Even people who have the same damn problems sometimes think that way."

"Has Thierry or Matthew said anything like that to you?" he demanded in a way that made me worried for them.

"Not really. I mean, they taught me to not let it hold me back. So did my mom, but…" I started to scrub my hands over my face then realized they were caked in zombie blood. "I belonged to this vision support group a few years back. It was this online thing, and I wanted to know what others thought, you know, who were dealing with something similar. Most were great, but there were some who were so caught up in making sure everyone heard their opinions and how they dealt with things, that they never listened to anyone else. They were so busy telling everyone in the group how we should adapt or feel, or even how we should talk about how we're feeling, or the challenges and—" I threw up my hands. "I don't even know why I'm talking about this right now. We're surrounded by dead stinky zombies."

"There's no more perfect time than now," he said.

"Oh, I can think of *many* more perfect times that don't involve brain matter." I planted my hands on my hips. "Look, I just don't want to be…"

A burden. A victim. A challenge. Someone to pity and coddle and worry about. Someone treated *less* than, even with the best intentions.

I took a breath. "I don't know what to say. It's late. I'm tired, and I have brains on me."

"That's okay. I know exactly what to say."

"Goody," I muttered.

"First off, I don't give a crap about what some random person on the internet who appointed themselves the mouthpiece of everything thinks. You've proven a hundred times over that you're independent and strong. You just jumped off that—" he gestured at the railing "—and didn't think twice about it. Still wish you hadn't done that, but whatever. You needing my help once or twice or five times in one night isn't an indication of losing your independence."

"Then what is it?"

His chest rose and then fell. "You're doing the best that you can, Trinity."

I sucked in a sharp breath. Those were the words I'd spoken to him when I'd told him about my eye condition. *I'm doing the best that I can.* I'd said that.

"You're so damn amazing, and you don't even know it."

My wide eyes met his.

"And you're also so freaking frustrating," he added. The corners of my lips turned down. "You know, there've been plenty of times that I've forgotten you can't see well and when I remember, I'm actually kind of shocked that you don't need more help, and you have no idea how…how in *awe* of you I am, that you do what you do under these circumstances. That you're carrying out your duty and not holding back or letting your vision limit you. So, dammit, Trinity, don't let what others think or say or even what you fear hold you back when you need help. Don't waste a damn second worrying about it. Let me help you—let anyone help you when you need it, and that'll make you even stronger."

"You…you're in awe of me?" I asked, my voice sounding too small.

"Is that the only part of what I just said that you heard?"

"Well, no." I rocked back on my heels. "I heard everything."

Zayne leaned forward, his wings spreading out to balance him, and even though I couldn't see his eyes, I felt the intensity of his stare. "You never cease to amaze me, Trinity. I don't think there'll ever be a time that you do. So, yes, I'm in awe of you."

I opened my mouth and closed it. In my chest, there was a swell of emotion so powerful that I thought it might float me right up to the ceiling.

"But I still think you should drink more water."

A shaky laugh left me. "That is all…really nice. Not the water part, but what you said. Thank you." My cheeks flushed as I held out my hands. "Okay. You can take me out of here."

Zayne stared at me, his face half-hidden in the shadows. "You drive me crazy."

"Sorry?"

"No, you're not." Zayne sighed.

He didn't take my hands. Instead, he folded an arm around my waist and pulled me against him as he lifted into the air, much like he had the night we flew as high as we could. On instinct, my hands landed on his shoulders. The full-body contact was as jarring as the landing I'd made earlier, because he was too warm and felt too good.

The trip to the pool deck was quick and when he landed, I took my hands from his shoulders. He didn't let go, at least not immediately. He held me to him, and I didn't dare lift my head to see if he was looking down at me. I also didn't concentrate on the bond to see if I could pick up what he was feeling beyond my own suddenly pounding heart.

His chest rose against mine, and his chin grazed the top of my head. "Make me a promise."

"Anything," I responded, unintentionally parroting what he'd said when I'd asked for a favor.

Zayne's arm tightened. "Promise me that whenever you need help, no matter what, you'll ask for it."

I closed my eyes, shaken, and the words left me without much effort. "I promise."

"Good," he replied, and then I felt his lips against my forehead.

A kiss so chaste, so sweet that it shouldn't have undone me, but it did. The kiss rattled me to my core, just as his words had. I *almost* wanted him to take back what he'd said, and the kiss, too, because it was easier that way. So much easier. But I cherished it all, probably too much.

He turned suddenly, and then his grip around my waist loosened and I slid down onto my feet. The friction was a blast to my senses, and I took a step back.

"Sorry," he said, voice raspy. "There was…stuff on the deck."

"It's okay." I looked around, avoiding eye contact. Blowing out a long breath, I wiped my hands on my outer thighs. Time to get back to what was important. "I have a bad feeling about all of this."

"As do I. A demon led us right to this place where a horde of zombies were conveniently waiting."

I crossed my arms, glancing at Zayne. He was still in his Warden form. "Are there demons out there that can control zombies?"

"Not that I know of, but all you'd need is to have a Poser bite one human and then bring more to be infected."

"Some of them looked like they were a second away from being nothing but a skeleton."

"They decompose fast. The rough-looking ones could've just been here for a few days," Zayne explained.

That sounded terrible. People snatched off the streets to be turned into the walking dead, left here where there wasn't even something to eat. Well, unless there'd been any homeless in here, seeking shelter from the heat and the storms.

And that sucked more.

"Dez is here," Zayne announced.

I turned just as a part of the wall swung open, a hidden door screeching on its rusty hinges.

The dark-haired Warden was in his human form, and I could tell the moment he saw the mess in the pool and on the deck, because he drew to a sudden halt. "You weren't exaggerating."

"Unfortunately not." Zayne moved to stand beside me.

"Hi." I waved a bloodied hand at Dez. "Ever seen anything like this?" I gestured behind me…and around me.

"I've only seen five zombies in my life, and each sighting was years apart." He lifted a hand and thrust it through his dark hair. "You said you sensed a demon and it led you here, where these poor SOBs were waiting?"

"Yes," Zayne answered. "We're thinking it—"

"—was a setup?" Dez cut in, and the unease resurfaced with a vengeance. "You didn't see the demon?"

"We didn't." I stepped forward. "Why do you think it was a setup? Because we were starting to think the same thing."

When Dez spoke, his voice was as tired as any battle-weary solider. "Because about ten minutes ago, Greene was found dead. Eviscerated and hanging inside the damn Eastern Market."

"Where?" Zayne asked as my stomach dropped.

"Eastern Market Metro platform," Dez confirmed. "Only a few blocks from here."

Based on the way Dez was eyeing me as I climbed into the passenger seat of the SUV, I figured he wanted to crack open a fire hydrant and hose me down but was resisting.

As Dez jogged around the front of the vehicle, I stared out

the window. All I saw were the vague shapes of trees, but I knew Zayne was still in the building and within minutes, other Wardens would be arriving to help clean up the mess and scour the rest of the building to make sure there were no zombies left.

I hated to leave Zayne there by himself after learning that one of his clan had been murdered, and right where we'd just been.

The demon leading us to this abandoned building couldn't have been a coincidence. Had the Harbinger been out there, stalking Greene, and we'd had no idea? Or had Greene been in another area of the city and was brought there as a twisted message to let us know that we'd been seen?

That we'd been played.

The SUV rocked as Dez folded his long body into the driver's seat. I looked at him, able to make out his profile in the streetlamp. Dez was young, only a handful of years older than Zayne, and he was already mated, with two adorable twins who were just learning to shift.

A lot of Wardens grew up parentless, having lost either their mother during childbirth or to demon raids and their father to the never-ending war. The statistics weren't in the twins' favor, but I hoped Izzy and Drake didn't meet that same fate as so many others.

"I'm sorry about what happened to the Warden," I said as Dez hit the ignition button.

He glanced at me, expression hidden in the shadowy interior as he pulled away from the curb. "Thank you."

I wanted to ask if Zayne had known him well, but that seemed insensitive. "Had he been with the clan long?"

"Yeah, he's been here for several years," he answered, and my heart squeezed. "He wasn't mated, and I guess that's a blessing."

How sad that had to be tacked on, as if the reminder that it could've been worse needed to be spoken. "But he'll still be missed."

"Of course. He was a damn good fighter and an even better friend. Greene didn't deserve to go out that way." He sighed. "None of the ones who were killed before you got here did."

A knot filled in my throat as I turned back to the window, unsure what I could say or if anything other than *I'm sorry* could be said. I went to chew on my fingernail but stopped when I remembered my hands were caked with zombie blood. "We were right there, no more than thirty minutes ago. That part of town was virtually empty, and we didn't sense anything other than the demon. If we had, or had known what we were looking for..."

"But you didn't know," Dez finished. "You're in the dark as much as we are, and I don't mean that as a criticism. Whatever this thing is, it's clever. It waited until you and Zayne had moved on."

I nodded as unease unfolded in the pit of my stomach, spreading like a poisonous weed. The Harbinger wasn't just clever. I had a sinking suspicion that, even though we had no idea who or what it was, it knew exactly who and what Zayne and I were.

My entire body jerked upright as I gulped in air, blood pounding so fast, I could hear the rushing in my ears as disorientation swept through me. It took me a moment to realize I'd fallen asleep after showering.

Dammit, I hadn't meant to pass out. I wanted to be up when Zayne returned. I had no idea how long I'd been asleep or if Zayne—

"Trinity!" Peanut's ghostly face was suddenly mere inches from mine, illuminated by the glow of the bedside lamp I'd left on.

"Jesus," I sputtered, pressing my hand against my chest. "Why would you do that?"

"Trin—"

"Sometimes I think you're trying to give me a heart attack." I twisted away from Peanut, irritation buzzing through my veins like a nest of hornets as my eyes adjusted. I realized that the bedroom door I'd left open so that I could hear Zayne return was closed, meaning Zayne most likely had returned and closed it, because I seriously doubted Peanut would've done that. "Peanut, I'm being serious. The next time you do this—"

"Listen to me, Trin, there's—"

"—I'm going to exorcise your ass right into the afterlife," I snapped. "It's not okay, Peanut. Not at all."

"I wasn't watching you sleep or trying to scare you!" Peanut flickered.

"Whatever," I muttered and reached for my phone to check the time.

"Listen to me!" Peanut shouted so loudly that if he could be heard by other people, he would've woken up half the apartment building.

I'd never heard him yell before. Ever. I focused on him, really looked at him, and for a ghost, he looked freaked-out. "What?"

Peanut drifted back a foot. "There's something here—something in the apartment."

12

I shot off the bed like a rocket was attached to my butt. "What?"

Peanut nodded. "There's something here."

"You need to give me more detail." I snatched up a dagger from the nightstand. "Stat."

"I saw it in the other room, near the kitchen island," he said. "It doesn't belong here."

Oh my God, Zayne was out there.

What if the Harbinger had followed us? It was possible, especially if it had known we'd been in the Eastern Market. We hadn't sensed it, so it could be here undetected. Racing forward, I threw open the door and stepped into the common room, which was lit by the moonlight and the soft glow of the under-cabinet kitchen lighting. My gaze darted over the kitchen island to the couch— Wait. Something was behind the island. It was blocking out a section of the light.

I took a step forward, my hand gripping the dagger as I squinted. The shape was that of a…person, but it wasn't solid. Every other second, I saw the lights from the cabinet blinking through, as if the shape was flickering…

"You see him?" Peanut questioned from behind me. "He's not supposed to be here."

I saw him.

Slowly, I lowered my dagger.

"He was looking around and stuff, checking out Zayne," Peanut continued, staying behind me as if I was his personal shield. I inched toward the couch. "I asked him what he was doing, but he wouldn't answer. He ignored me like he can't see me, but that's totes not the case."

I spared a glance down when I reached the couch, and relief punched me center in the chest. Zayne *was* there, asleep. One arm was thrust behind his head, the other resting across his stomach. His face was turned toward me, and a sliver of moonlight kissed his cheek.

I jerked my gaze back to the kitchen, blood pressure settling. Zayne was okay, but the shadowy shape was still in the kitchen, and it wasn't the Harbinger or a demon that had somehow gotten through my internal radar system.

It was a ghost…or a spirit.

Which would've been good for Peanut to have mentioned when he'd woken me up, instead of giving me a minor heart attack.

Ghosts and spirits, for the most part, were benevolent, even the ones who could interact with their surroundings, like Peanut. There were a few who became stuck and unwilling to acknowledge that they were dead, and their anger festered, rotting their souls. They became wraiths. You had to watch out for them, as they could be dangerous and violent.

I guessed this ghost had seen me somewhere and followed me here. Wouldn't be the first time a ghost had sensed me and then found me later.

"Make it leave," whispered Peanut.

I shot him a look and then refocused on the unexpected visitor. I might be here to find the Harbinger, but helping ghosts and spirits was important to me. For many of them, I was their only chance to impart a message or to get aid in crossing over.

Out of everything I was capable of, helping the deceased move on or communicating a spirit's message was the most amazing gift I had in my arsenal. At least, I thought so.

As I neared the island, the shape changed without warning. Clothing appeared. A black-and-white flannel shirt thrown over a T-shirt with words on it was suddenly filled out by a chest and arms. Features formed. A roundish, almost boyish face. Messy brown hair that looked slept on. Glasses perched on a straight nose. He was around my age, give or take a year or two.

And he was a spirit.

I knew this immediately, because his skin carried an ethereal glow that told me he'd seen the light and gone into it. But I'd never seen a spirit do what he had just done—change from a black, shadowy form into a full-bodied apparition.

"I don't like him," Peanut whispered. "I don't want him here."

The spirit focused on Peanut. "You're not very friendly for a ghost."

Peanut gasped. "I am not Casper, you insolent fool."

"Funny you mention Casper," the spirit replied, head tilted. "Did you know that when Casper was first created, he was a ghost of a little boy who died, but then the creators worried that a dead child was too dark, so they changed him to where he was always a ghost and gave him ghost parents, because in their minds, ghosts having ghost babies was less hard to explain?"

I blinked.

"What?" Peanut vocalized my confusion.

"Exactly." The spirit nodded. "I mean, if you ask me, the idea that ghosts are born and capable of procreating is way more disturbing, but what do I know?"

Okay.

I had no idea what time it was, but I could safely say that it was way too late or too early for this nonsense. Holding up my hand, I waved the dagger. "Hi. How can I help you?"

The spirit's eyes widened behind his glasses. "You can see me?"

"Dumb question," Peanut muttered. "Because duh."

If I could smack Peanut, I would have. "Uh. Yeah. I can see and hear you. Isn't that why you're here?"

"Holy crap," the spirit whispered, and then flickered out.

My brows lifted as I lowered my dagger. The spirit didn't blink back into existence.

Peanut drifted over to where the spirit had been standing. Hovering a few feet off the ground, he stared down. "He's not hiding back here."

"You've got to be kidding me," I muttered.

"Trin?" Zayne's sleep-rough voice called out, and I spun

around. He was sitting up and peering over the back of the couch. "Is everything okay?"

Two choices presented to me. Tell Zayne there'd been a spirit in his apartment, but not be able to tell him who the spirit was or why he'd been here. Or tell him nothing at all, because already having one ghost hanging out at his place was one dead person too many.

"I was waiting up for you, but I must've fallen asleep," I blurted out, my mouth making up my mind for me as I deftly hid the dagger behind my thigh. "I came out to see if you were awake, and when I saw you weren't, I got something to drink."

"Liar," Peanut retorted. "Liar, liar, pants on fire."

"I'm sorry to wake you," I added, stepping sideways.

"It's okay." He dragged a hand through his hair. The moment he lowered his arm, those thick strands fell back into place. "You get something to drink?"

"Uh-huh." I also nodded, and when Peanut didn't comment, I glanced behind me to see that he was gone.

"You were waiting up for me?" he asked, resting his arm on the back of the couch.

"Yeah. I wanted to see how you were doing." I stepped closer, keeping my hands behind my back. "If you were okay."

"Always."

"Always?" I repeated. "Dez told me that Greene was with the clan for several years. You knew him, and he's…"

"He's dead." He pushed the hair back from his face again. "There's nothing more to say."

"There's a lot more to say." I felt a tinge of grief through the bond. "You knew—"

"There's really not, Trin." He swiped a hand down his face. "It is what it is."

He wasn't being dismissive or heartless. He was avoiding the loss and the pain that followed. I could understand that. "I'm sorry, Zayne. I really am." I swallowed the knot in my throat. "I wish I could do something."

I couldn't see his face clearly, but I thought I saw a brief smile. "You going back to bed?"

"I guess so."

"Really? You sound wide-awake," he said, and boy, wasn't that the truth. "Are you really going back to sleep, or will you lie there, staring at the ceiling?"

"Are you psychic?" I joked. Kind of.

Zayne chuckled as he turned back around. "I'm awake now. We could keep each other company. You know? Until one or both of us passes back out."

The offer stole my breath a little, and how lame was that? I should yawn loudly and obnoxiously, but he'd just lost someone and I would do anything to make that better for him.

"Sure." The dagger all but burned my palm. "Uh, I'll be right back."

Not waiting for a response, I darted into the bedroom, my bare feet sliding over the cool cement floors. I placed the dagger on the nightstand and then sprinted back into the living room. I skidded to a stop when I didn't see Zayne at the couch. Glancing at the kitchen, I didn't see him there, either. Or Peanut. Or a random spirit.

Was I even awake, or was this some kind of bizarre dream?

"Zayne?"

"I'm here" came the immediate response.

I turned to the couch with a frown and inched around the side, and he was there, lying on his side with his cheek resting on the curl of his arm. There was a vacant pillow beside his elbow.

He patted the space beside him.

I glanced from him to the space and then back to him again, my throat suddenly making me wish I had gotten a drink. My skin felt heavy, and I really needed to get it together. He was inviting me to lie with him and not to *lie* with him.

"There's enough room," he said. "I promise."

There was enough room on the couch to fit a T. rex, but I still stood there, hands opening and closing at my sides. I didn't know why I was being so weird. This wouldn't be the first time we'd lain side by side while we'd been unable to sleep. It had been a brief habit until...until the night we'd done more than talking and sleeping.

"Trin?" Zayne started to rise. "You okay?"

"Yeah, I'm fine." I plopped down on the couch beside him, landing on my back with the gracefulness of a cow falling over.

"Wow," he murmured.

"What?" I clasped my hands together, over my stomach. There were a few inches between us, but I could still feel the warmth of his body.

"Just surprised you didn't break your back with that move."

"Shut up," I muttered.

Zayne chuckled.

I wiggled my toes and then my butt, sinking an inch into the cushion. "You know...this couch is more comfortable than I thought."

"It's not bad."

But still not as comfortable as his bed. "I feel terrible about taking over your apartment—your bathroom." I paused. "Your kitchen. Your *bed*."

"Don't worry about it."

My brows knitted as I turned my head toward him. I couldn't tell if his eyes were open or not. "Kind of hard not to. I could sleep out here and—"

"That would go against every code I have. Not going to happen," he replied. "What woke you up?"

The spirit I'd seen formed in my thoughts. Shivering, I wondered if or when he would come back and what he had wanted. Sometimes they never returned.

"Cold?" Zayne reached down and snatched the blanket pooled at his waist. With a flick of his hand, the soft material floated out and then fell over my legs.

"Thanks," I murmured. "I just woke up. Not sure why. I really am sorry for waking you."

"It's okay." He paused. "I thought I heard you talking to someone when I woke up."

"You must've been hearing things."

"Uh-huh."

My lips twitched. "It was Peanut." That wasn't exactly a lie.

Zayne shifted beside me. "Is he still here?"

When I opened my eyes, I could see enough to know he was looking around. My smile grew. "He's not here right now."

"Huh." His head tilted toward mine. When he spoke, I felt his breath on my forehead. "Where does he go…when he's not here?"

"That's a good question. I hope he's not bothering that girl who lives somewhere in this building. Which reminds me, I really need to check on that." I sighed, mentally re-adding that to my list of things I needed to do yesterday. "Any time I ask him where he goes, he gives me a ridiculous answer. Like once he said he went to the moon."

"Maybe he did. Maybe ghosts can travel to the moon."

I laughed as I shifted my gaze back to the ceiling. "Yeah, I don't know about that."

"Would be kind of cool, though."

"Yeah, it would." My eyes drifted shut. "I really did try to wait up for you, because of…of Greene, and also because I wanted to know if you found any more zombies."

Zayne was quiet for a moment. "I checked on you when I got back. You were out cold. Didn't even hear me take a shower," he said. "We didn't find more zombies. After cleanup, I went to the Eastern Market platform. Greene had already been taken down. A cop found him. He was still there."

"Did you talk to him?"

"Yeah, but he didn't see anything." Zayne curled his knees just the slightest. "There were no signs of a struggle or traces of blood, and the cop was in the area the whole time. He would've heard a fight. Greene was killed elsewhere and then brought there for a reason."

I processed that. "I've been thinking about that. Greene was…displayed like the other Wardens and demons have been—left to be found. I don't think it takes a leap of logic to say that the Harbinger is behind all of it."

"Agreed."

"Were the bodies of the other Wardens ever found where others had been minutes before but hadn't seen anything?"

Zayne was quiet for a moment. "Not that I know of. Most of them were found in extremely busy public places. That platform is deserted at that time of night."

"So, this was a message." I paused. "To *us*. The Harbinger killed Greene and brought him to a place we'd just been, and the demon has to be working with it."

"I know where you're going with this thought. That it's possible that either the demon or the Harbinger know who we are—know what you are."

I rolled onto my side, facing him. Hair fell across my face, but I left it alone, keeping my arms folded between us. "Do you think that?"

"I think it's possible."

"That means the Harbinger has the upper hand," I whispered. "A very big upper hand."

"It's an upper hand, but that just means we need to be more aware," he said, and I felt him move. "Hold still. My hand is going to come close to your face."

A heartbeat later, I felt his fingertips brush my cheek. The touch didn't startle me. He caught the strands of hair and brushed them back, tucking them behind my ear. His fingers lingered, his thumb grazing the line of my cheekbone. After a second, he dropped his hand.

"Thanks," I murmured.

"No problem."

"I'm only a little jealous of Warden eyesight," I added. "Then again, if I had fully functioning eyeballs, I'd still be jealous."

"Yeah, being able to see in the dark does have its benefits," he said.

Silence fell between us as we lay there, face-to-face. I don't know why my next thought came to mind, but it did, and for some reason, asking things in the middle of the night wasn't so hard. "I have a random question."

"You? Never…"

I smiled. "How often do you do the, uh, deep-sleep thing? You know, the stone-sleeping thing. Misha used—" My chest squeezed as I inhaled sharply. "He used to nap a lot in that form, but I haven't seen you do it yet."

"I do it when I need to," he answered. "Used to grab a couple of hours here and there. Napping like…yeah, like him, if I was feeling worn down or had been injured, but ever since the whole bonding thing, I haven't had to do it."

"Oh. That's kind of interesting."

"It's a lot interesting, and I wish I knew why, but unless your father is going to reappear with a Protector handbook, I guess I won't know."

"Yeah, I wouldn't hold your breath for that."

"Does it ever…" He exhaled. "The way it is with your father—does it bother you?"

"No one's ever asked me that," I said as the realization hit. "Wow. I don't even know how to answer that."

"Try," he said softly.

"I… I don't know. I don't even think of *him* as my father. Thierry and Matthew helped raised me. They're my dads. But does it irritate me that he hasn't been around? Yeah. And it pisses me off that he knew Misha was the wrong choice and did nothing. Didn't even seem to freaking care. Like he has no emotions or—" I cut myself off as the anger surfaced. "It doesn't matter."

Zayne tapped my arm. "I think it does."

"No, it doesn't. Anyway, it's probably a good thing you haven't needed to do the deep-sleep thing. I have an overwhelming urge to annoy the living crap out of any Warden when they're in that form."

"Good to know, but your father—"

"I *really* don't want to talk about him. Besides, I have another question."

"I wish you could see my surprised face."

I grinned at that. "Why does your apartment look like no one lives here?"

"What?" He laughed.

"You know what I mean." Unclasping my hands, I lifted one. "There's nothing here. No photos or anything personal. No clutter—"

"How is not having clutter a bad thing?"

"It's not, but it's like…"

"It's like what?" Zayne shifted again, and I felt his fingers brush my bare arm.

It was hard to ignore the jolt of awareness that followed his touch. "It's like *you* don't really live here. More like you're… staying here."

Zayne didn't respond. Not for a long time. I thought that maybe he'd fallen asleep, but then he said, "It's just a place to rest my head, Trin."

I thought about that. "That's…kind of sad."

"Why?"

I wiggled my shoulders in a shrug. "I don't know. You should think of it as a home."

"Do you miss your home?" he asked.

My lips pursed. Yes. No? Both. And yet neither? "Some days," I said, settling in the middle.

"Strange answer."

It was, but… "I miss my stars," I said. "But we're not talking about me. We're talking about you."

There was a quiet laugh. "Then ask me a different question."

I blinked at that. "Okaaay." I drew the word out as another question I had no business asking filled my thoughts.

"You want to ask another question."

My head cut toward his. "How do you know that?"

"The bond."

"What?" I started to sit up.

"I'm kidding." He laughed, catching my arm and stilling me. "I can see it on your face."

"My face?" I settled back.

"You wrinkle your nose whenever you're thinking about something you want to say and trying not to say it."

"Really?" I had no idea if that was true. The nose part, that is. Everything else was, as Peanut would say, totes true.

"Really. I'm observant like that." Zayne's hand slipped into the space between us. His knuckles rested against my arm. "What do you want to ask? I have a feeling this is going to be a good one."

I arched a brow. Then I told myself not to ask it. My brain did not listen. "You seemed really happy to see Stacey."

The moment that came out of my mouth, I wondered how

fast I could roll off the couch and run headfirst into a nearby wall. There were so many more important things we could talk about besides his less-than-cozy apartment and friends with benefits.

"You sure that was a question?" he asked. "Because it sounded like a statement, but yeah, I was happy. I hadn't seen her in a while."

I pressed my lips together, thinking about her warning. "She seemed happy to see you."

"I guess so." Zayne pulled his hand back as he settled into the cushion. "Stacey and I are just friends."

The snort that left me sounded vaguely like a wild boar running from hunters. "Yeah, I don't think you can say you're just friends. Not that I care or anything. Or that it's any of my business."

"Okay. You're right. We were more than friends," he replied. "Not that you don't know that already. Or care."

Shifting onto my back, I crossed my arms. "I totally don't care."

"Then why did you bring it up?"

"Because I'm nosy," I admitted. Then I forced myself to say, "She seems pretty cool."

"She is. I hope you get to know her. I think you'd like her."

I wasn't so sure about that. "I didn't know she'd been here."

Zayne was quiet for a moment. "There's a lot you don't know, Trin."

"What's that supposed to mean?"

"Exactly what it sounds like."

I stiffened. His tone wasn't cold or anything, but there was something off about it, and he was totally closing a door on that conversation. Which was his right, but it made me feel like I...like I'd crossed a line, and maybe I had.

And boy, didn't that shine a huge glaring light on the awkwardness of our relationship? There was almost a professional aspect to us, with the whole Protector and Trueborn bond. We were friends, but we'd briefly been more, and a part of me felt like we were still tiptoeing around that line despite the fact that the line was actually a wall. And even though I'd filed away what I felt for Zayne, I was still a jealous little monster when it came to Layla and Stacey. I had no right to those feelings, and Zayne was...well, he was Zayne, and I had no idea how he felt about *any* of this.

"How do you feel, knowing that it was supposed to be me that Abbot raised?" I blurted out. "That if my mom had done what she was supposed to do, you might never have met Layla?"

"That's..." Zayne shifted as if he were trying to get comfortable. "That's a hard question to answer. I don't know what to think, or if thinking about it even matters, because that's not what happened. The past is the past, and what should've been doesn't change that, but if you're asking if I regret these series of mistakes that led to this moment?"

My breath hitched. "I'm not asking that. Of course you don't regret it. I wouldn't—"

"I don't," he cut in. "And I do."

I stilled.

"If what was supposed to have happened had, we would've had years of training and preparing together. We wouldn't be playing catch-up, and maybe I wouldn't—" He stopped and then drew in an audible breath. "We would be more ready than we are now, and everything that happened with Misha wouldn't have."

I flinched, heart dropping a little.

"But I can't regret that my father took Layla in," he continued. "Even with how all of that turned out, I can't regret it. I don't."

I let that sink in. "I understand." And I did. I got it, and I was glad he didn't seem to be dwelling on it.

Zayne didn't respond, and I decided I'd asked enough random questions for at least the next couple of hours.

I should probably get up, but I was comfortable and I... I missed this.

I missed having someone to talk to.

I thought about the calls from Jada. I really needed to call her.

"You miss your stars." Zayne spoke into the darkness. "The ones back home, on the ceiling. Took me a bit to realize what you were talking about, but I remember."

"Yeah," I whispered. "Those stars."

"Got a question for you. A quick one."

I turned my head toward him. "What?"

"If you were coming out here to see if I was still awake, why did you have your dagger with you?"

Dammit.

"You know..." I started.

"No, I don't."

I rolled my eyes. "You know, I don't know why I grabbed it. Habit, I guess."

"Strange habit."

"Yeah, I guess so."

"After a night like this, grabbing a dagger wasn't a bad idea," he tacked on, and I wasn't entirely convinced that meant he believed me. He chuckled under his breath.

"What?" I asked.

"It's nothing. I was just thinking about... I was thinking about Greene." He cleared his throat. "He wasn't a good sleeper, awake in the mornings and up in the afternoons, which may be normal for humans but not us. I saw him a lot since I kept the same hours because of Layla and her school schedule. Anyway, both of us had trouble staying asleep, so we'd end up watching soap operas."

"Really?" I shifted back onto my side.

"Yep. *Days of Our Lives*."

"You're joking."

"No." He laughed. "We were pretty invested in the Deveraux and Brady drama."

"Wow." I laughed, but it was heavy. "I really am sorry about what happened to him."

"So am I." He exhaled heavily. "Greene was quiet, and other than *Days of Our Lives*, he kept to himself, but he was someone any of us could count on. He even went against my father about everything that went down with Layla. What happened to him is sad. It's wrong. His life shouldn't have ended that way. Worst part is that his name is now another on this list that just keeps growing longer. Greene will be mourned. He will be missed. And then his name will become the next person we've lost. Then the third and the fourth, and we'll have to stop mourning him to allow room for someone else, because after a while, you don't have enough room. You just can't."

Zayne dragged a hand down his face. "I know that sounds callous. Maybe like I don't even care, but…you get used to the death. Too used to it. No need for the seven stages. You go right from shock to acceptance."

Sadness filled me as I lay there. I knew firsthand what loss felt like, but I was also far removed from the almost weekly losses some clans experienced. The sorrow I felt in my chest wasn't coming just from me. It was also flowing from him, a grief tinged in anger and acceptance, and I wanted to comfort him. I wanted to ease what he was feeling, and I didn't know how to do that.

So, I did the only thing I could think of.

Wiggling toward him, I unfolded my arms and threw one over his shoulder. He stilled, but I kept squirming, weaseling my way against his chest. Once I was there, I squeezed.

Zayne didn't move.

"I'm hugging you," I told him, voice muffled against his chest. "Just in case you have no idea what I'm doing."

"I figured it was that." His voice sounded like it had when he'd first woken up. "Or you were pretending to be a seal."

I let out a short laugh, but Zayne remained as stiff as a wall. Realizing my awkward hug was a bit of a failure, I started to pull back.

Zayne moved then, folding an arm over my waist. His fingers curled around the back of my shirt as he held me there. Then, after a few seconds, I felt his body relax against mine, but the grip on my shirt was still there.

His chest rose against mine. "Thank you."

13

As I floated through waking up, everything smelled like fresh snow and winter. Yet I was toasty, almost too warm. It reminded me of a time I'd dozed off on the roof beside Misha while he slept in his Warden form. It had been early summer, so the sun hadn't been too strong and the warmth had been surprisingly relaxing.

But I'd ended up with a nasty sunburn.

I was pretty sure I hadn't fallen asleep on a roof. I started to move, but could only wiggle about an inch. Was I wrapped in a blanket cocoon? I've done that before, tossing and turning until blankets ended up wrapping around me like cellophane.

Stretching my legs, I froze when I felt another set of legs against mine.

Last night.

I'd fallen asleep on the couch with Zayne. I hadn't meant to do that. Had he fallen asleep before me? Or had I passed out plastered against him like I was at this moment? I'd hugged him and he'd thanked me and then… Neither of us had said anything after that.

God, I hoped I hadn't passed out and trapped him against the back of the couch like a—

The arm around me tightened, and Zayne made a deep rumbling sound that I felt all the way to the tips of my toes.

My eyes flew open, and I found myself staring at a chest covered by a white shirt. That was just about when I realized my cheek was not on a pillow but on rather firm biceps.

Oh my.

There were few things in life stranger than unexpectedly waking up in the arms of someone. Or more wonderful than when it was in the arms of someone like Z—

Stop.

Cutting off those thoughts, I focused on what to do from this point. Slowly, I tilted my head back and lifted my gaze.

Zayne was still asleep.

Thick lashes fanned his cheeks and his lips were slightly parted. He looked so…relaxed. Vulnerable, even. My gaze roamed his face. I should probably stop staring at him while he slept, because that was more than just notably creepy, but it was so rare I was this close to him and had such an unobstructed view.

He had a freckle. Three of them, actually, under his right eye. They were faint, but I could… I could see them, and they formed a little triangle. Did he have others? I scanned his face. I didn't see more, but there was a faint shadow along his jaw and chin. I'd never seen him with facial hair, and I wondered what he'd look like if he let it grow.

Probably hotter. Sounded impossible, considering he was beautiful enough that it bordered on obscene.

For a moment, I did something so stupid and I let myself…dream.

I closed my eyes, imagining what it would be like if I woke up in his arms and he was mine and I was his. I'd kiss him and then snuggle closer, and if that didn't wake him, I would do something annoying to get him to wake up. My imagination filled in what would come next. Zayne, because of who he was, wouldn't be annoyed that I'd stolen minutes or even hours of his sleep. He'd laugh and then give me that sleepy, sexy smile of his. Then he'd roll me under him and kiss me. And of course, in my perfect fantasy, there'd be no such thing as morning breath. So that kiss would be deep and long, a languid caress that would lead to more kissing. I pressed my lips together, squirming as my skin heated. Zayne's shirt would come off, so would mine and then there'd be nothing—

The arm around me curled again, and suddenly we were chest to chest, hip to hip. My eyes popped open and I looked up at Zayne. He was still asleep, but his body—well, a certain part of him was definitely awake.

Oh, goodness.

Could he pick up on what I was feeling even though he was asleep? If so, that would be really, just completely, annoying.

Time for me to get up. Definitely well past time, because if I didn't, things were going to get awkward and I was already at peak awkward, so I needed to avoid that. I lifted my gaze, drawing in a breath.

Pale blue eyes met mine.

Too late.

"Morning," I mumbled.

Those lashes swept down and then back up. "Morning."

My pulse was thrumming. His arm was still around me, more relaxed, but there. "I didn't mean to fall asleep out here."

"I didn't mind." Those eyes were half-open now, and the fingers along my back were moving up and down in short, slow strokes.

"Really?"

"Not at all. It was nice."

My heart was now pitter-pattering like a happy little fool. "I liked it, too. I think I got the best sleep I've had in days."

"Same." He turned his head, yawning like a lion. "It's good having a sleeping buddy."

Sleeping buddy? Like a stuffed animal?

That tripped the pitter-patter. My heart fell on its stupid face, and a part of me was happy. Because it should know better.

Why was I thinking of my heart as something outside me that I had no control over?

I needed help.

I also needed to get up. "I'm thirsty," I announced, because why not?

Pulling back, I rolled onto my side just as Zayne lifted his arm and started to sit up. He shifted, and the sudden change of weight on the cushion sent me tumbling into him. Zayne froze as our bodies lined up in all the very interesting parts that emphasized the vast difference between the soft and hard areas.

My entire face flushed as I attempted to roll away from him. My hip brushed a *very* sensitive area. "I'll just—" I jerked and, somehow, that just made it worse, because Zayne groaned "—get up and—"

"Can you just stop moving for a second?" Zayne's hand landed on my hip, his voice raspy. "Just be still. Okay?"

I squeezed my eyes shut, cursing under my breath, and did as he suggested. I took a breath and then rocketed to my feet without rubbing myself all over him like an alley cat on ecstasy. Face burning, I stepped away from the couch.

"Sorry about that," Zayne muttered. "Especially if it made you uncomfortable."

"No, it's okay." *Uncomfortable* was *not* a word I'd use. At least not in the way he was insinuating. I glanced over my shoulder at him. He was sitting up, and I kept my gaze north of his shoulders. "I mean, it's no big deal. I know how guys get in the morning."

Zayne looked at me, brows raised as his lips twitched. "You do?"

"Of course." I forced a laugh. "You don't need to be a part of the dick brigade to know that."

"Dick brigade?" He bit down on his lower lip. "All right then."

Feeling like I could've kept that to myself, I smiled tightly and crossed my arms. "I'll get changed and we can get started on training." I was proud of how steady and unaffected my voice sounded. "Unless you want to eat something first?"

Zayne picked up his phone, swearing under his breath. "I have to hop in the shower and get out of here in, like, thirty minutes or I'm going to be late."

"Late…?" I trailed off.

"I told you yesterday I have some things to take care of

today." He rose and started around the couch, his movements somewhat stiff. "Remember?"

Now that he mentioned it, I did. "I forgot. What do you have to do?"

"Just a few things." He headed for the bedroom, keeping his back to me. "It'll probably take a couple of hours, but I should be back in time for us to work in some training."

My arms unfolded slowly. Why was he being so vague? I took a step forward as I opened my mouth, but snapped it shut as I remembered what Zayne had said last night.

There's a lot you don't know.

If Zayne wanted me to know, he'd tell me, and if he didn't, then I needed to engage in a little mind your own business.

I hated minding my own business.

"But what are you—" I heard the bathroom door click shut. "Okay. I'll just wait out here while you take your ten-year-long shower and then I'll just wait here all afternoon until you're done doing whatever it is that you're doing."

There was no response.

Obviously.

I let my head fall back and groaned, "Ugh."

"Yeah."

Squeaking, I whipped around and saw Peanut by the kitchen island. He nodded.

"You guys are as awkward as getting caught picking your nose. You should work on that."

I sighed. "Thanks for the advice I didn't ask for."

"You're welcome." He gave me a thumbs-up with half his arm transparent. "And by the way—a dude in the shower for that long, after waking up in the morning? What do you think he's doing? Washing his hair twice and deep condition-ing with Herbal Essences? Uh, no."

"I…" My eyes widened. "Oh. *Oh*."

"Let him live his best life." Peanut vanished.

My gaze flew to the bedroom, and my imagination ran *wiiild* for about 10.3 seconds. Then, because there was noth-ing else to do, I walked to the couch and face-planted it.

"'When you was young, you never needed anyone,'" Pea-nut sang from somewhere in the apartment.

I needed to do laundry. I guessed I could do that this af-ternoon since I was—

"'All by yourself.'" Peanut came through the bedroom wall and continued singing about me—or *someone*—being alone and insecure and unable to see love.

I blinked slowly. "You're a jerk."

"'But you're all by yourself!'" he sang back to me, disap-pearing through the wall.

I'd been all by myself since Zayne left about thirty minutes ago, off to do *stuff*, and I had no idea what to do with my af-ternoon. It was the first free time I'd had since I'd come here.

Twisting my hair into a topknot, I turned toward the open bedroom door. "Hey, Peanut, you still here?"

"Yeah," he called back. "What's up, buttercup?"

"That spirit last night—did he say anything to you?"

"Besides referring to me as Casper?" Peanut blinked into existence in the doorway. "No. He was just poking around the apartment like he belonged here."

"That's weird." I glanced at the messy bed, frowning. "I guess he saw me outside and followed me here."

"Then why did he freak out when he realized you could see him?"

That was a good question, but even if ghosts and spirits could sense I could communicate with them, they were often surprised when I confirmed it. When ghosts and spirits experienced acute emotion, they tended to lose their connection with the consciousness that allowed them to take shape and be seen.

Well, there was nothing I could do now about last night's strange visitation. Instead, I checked the washer, which was stacked above the dryer in one of the linen closets. After switching my clothes to dry, I looked around the room, my gaze settling on the tinted windows.

I wanted to go outside. To roam. To explore. To be out there with *people*. To watch and see, before...

Before I couldn't see anymore.

I crossed my arms as indecisiveness filled me. I'd been out there enough times with Zayne that I was pretty confident I could find my way around without getting seriously lost, but considering my eyeballs, getting lost was a scary thing to think about. I'd have to rely on strangers to help me read street signs or my phone, if I used one of those map apps, and people were, well, not always helpful to those in need.

But I could walk at least a couple of blocks, if not a little more. I could do it.

My stomach dropped precariously the moment that thought finished. I started nibbling on my thumbnail. Just last night I'd told Zayne that I wanted to be independent, needed to be, and yet here I was, afraid to go out by myself.

Maybe I should check out that girl Peanut had been visiting.

That seemed a more important and easier thing to do. But I needed to get ready first. Whipping around, I headed for the bathroom and took a ten-year-long shower. As I wrapped a towel around me, a text alert pinged from my phone. I shuffled back into the bedroom, where it was charging on the nightstand, and picked it up. Not recognizing the number, I opened the text.

It's me, your friendly neighborhood Demon Prince. I'm about to call you.

My lips parted in surprise. Roth, the actual Crown Prince of Hell, had texted me.

Was there some kind of universal Hell and Heaven phone book? Because I doubted Zayne had given him my number.

Obviously, I didn't have a problem with Roth, but tiny knots filled my stomach with uncertainty as I stared at the phone.

It suddenly rang in my hand, startling me. I answered with a cautious "Hello?"

"Zayne's not there, right?" was Roth's greeting.

My brows pinched as I moseyed back into the bathroom. "No, he's not here. Are you trying to get ahold of him?"

"No."

Then why had he asked about Zayne?

"You busy?" he asked.

"Uh…" I looked around as if I'd find my answer there while I clutched the two halves of the towel together. Were Stacey and Layla hanging out again, and Roth was once more bored and in need of company? "Not particularly. You?"

There was a deep, rasping chuckle. "About to be. So are you."

"I am?"

"Yes. I'm coming to pick you up. We now have plans."

"We do?" I blinked once and then twice at my fuzzy reflection in the bathroom mirror. "I just got out of the shower."

"Well, you're going to need to put some clothes on, because I doubt Layla will be thrilled if I pick you up and you're naked as the day you were hatched out of a little Trueborn egg."

I was so not hatched from an egg, and he knew that.

"Is…?" I trailed off, suddenly unable to say her name as I stared into the mirror. I squeezed my eyes shut tight.

Layla.

Layla.

Layla.

A flash of envy mixed with anger in my chest, and I hated that I felt that way. That I was being so dumb about her past with Zayne.

When I reopened my eyes, she hadn't appeared like some new, updated and totally personalized version of Bloody Mary.

I wrinkled my nose at my reflection. There was something seriously wrong with me. I knew what it was. The green-eyed monster. Jealousy. And why was jealousy a green-eyed monster? Why did people say "green with envy"? What was wrong with the color green? Was it because some money was green? I really needed to google this, as—

"You still there?" Roth's voice snagged me from my thoughts, thank God. "Or did you hang up on me? That wouldn't be nice. My feelings would be hurt."

"I'm still here. Is Layla with you?" I asked.

"No," he answered. "She can't be a part of this."

I turned from the mirror, hand tightening around the phone. Peanut reappeared suddenly through the wall, pirouetting like a ballerina across the bedroom and through the bed.

"What makes you think I want to be a part of whatever this is?" I demanded.

"Because you owe me a favor, and it's time I collect."

When I'd thought about exploring the city, this wasn't what I'd had in mind.

But here I was.

Leaning against a wall, I squinted from behind my dark sunglasses. While I waited for Roth, a steady stream of people passed me, each one seeming in a hurry to get wherever they were going. Since I had no idea what Roth was up to, I'd decided curbside pickup was the best.

A huge part of me was regretting it, because I'd been outside for only a handful of minutes, and I felt like I was melting.

Sweat dotted my brow while I stood in the shadow of Zayne's building. Even though my tank top and jeans were thin and my heavy, still-wet hair was pulled up in a knot, I was about a minute from stripping off all my clothes.

It got hot back in the Potomac Highlands, but with the mountain air and open fields, there was always a cool breeze. Here there were only smoggy, hot and stinky drafts passing between the tall buildings.

Nervous energy buzzed through my veins as I shifted my gaze from the sidewalks to the congested street full of yellow cabs and black cars. The warm tingle along the back of my neck alerted me to the presence of demons, but none seemed close.

But I was about to get all up and personal with one.

For a favor.

A favor I owed the Crown Prince of Hell.

Crap.

I hadn't exactly forgotten that Roth had said he'd help Zayne and I find Misha because he wanted a Trueborn to owe him a favor, but it hadn't been at the forefront of my thoughts.

I had no idea what I could do for Roth that the demon prince couldn't do for himself. He had all kinds of nifty abilities I was envious of, and whatever it was, I doubted Zayne would be happy to hear about it. I should text him, in case he got back before I did and found me MIA, but if I did, then Zayne would have questions. Questions I obviously couldn't answer. Not only that, he'd probably intervene and stop whatever favor Roth needed from me, and admittedly, I was more than just a little curious.

Distraction and avoidance were the two best coping mechanisms out there. I didn't care what therapists across the world claimed.

Plus, Zayne was busy doing top secret *stuff*, so, whatever.

I just hoped whatever Roth wanted didn't involve anything too…evil.

Shifting my weight from one foot to the other, I crossed my arms as a hot whirl of wind caught the hem of my long shirt, playing with the edges. The slim, lightweight iron daggers currently attached to my hips stayed hidden. Roth might be a cool demon 99 percent of the time, but I wasn't stupid. Not that I needed the daggers when I had my *grace*, but I wouldn't just whip out my *grace* willy-nilly and start a party with it.

I'd *end* a party with it.

The blur of vehicles slowed down as a sleek fancy-looking car stopped at the curb and the shivery heat along my neck and shoulders increased. One tinted window rolled down and I heard, "Hey, Angel Face, want a ride?"

My eyes rolled. I peeled myself away from the side of the building and inched forward, careful to not get flattened by the humans in a hurry. I started to bend down to peer into the window but the car door opened without either of us touching it.

Again. Nifty abilities.

"Get in." Roth's voice floated from the shadowy interior.

I hesitated. "How about 'please'?"

A dark chuckle was my answer. "That word is not in my vocabulary."

Groaning, I got in and was blasted with cold air. Roth was behind the wheel, dressed in all black and looking very much like anyone would imagine a demon prince would look.

One ring-adorned finger tapped the steering wheel. His rings were sliver and had some kind of markings on them, but I couldn't make them out.

My gaze drifted over the interior of the car. Even with the tinted windows, I needed my sunglasses but the glare wasn't as bad as usual. I could see a gold emblem on the steering wheel.

Was this a...Porsche? Good God, why were there so many buttons in a *car*? "Being a demon must pay well."

"Being the Crown Prince does." Roth grinned at me as he eased away from the curb.

"So, what's Layla doing?"

"Currently marathoning *Doctor Who* with Cayman," he answered. "And I want no part of that life."

A tiny ball of melancholy formed in my chest. Marathoning movies and shows. I used to do that with friends.

I missed Jada.

"Sounds like a good time. What's your favor?"

"Not into small talk, are you?" The Porsche came to a stop at the light. "Did you tell Zayne you were heading out with me?"

"No." I laughed. "Doubt he'd be cool with whatever this is."

"Why? You think he doesn't trust me?"

I folded my arms and said nothing.

Roth chuckled. "He knows I'm a bad influence."

"So, your favor is something that's going to fall under you being a bad influence?"

"Oh, most definitely." The car started moving again. Outside the windows, the buildings were beige blurs. "I need your help."

"I figured that much." I looked over at him.

A faint grin reappeared. "Remember Bambi?"

Immediately, I thought of the Hummer-size snake that had acted like an abandoned puppy in need of cuddling when she'd seen Roth. Familiars often resided as tattoos on the body of the demon that controlled them, but Bambi was now with that damn coven of witches that I hoped soon found themselves unexpectedly in the middle of a bonfire. I nodded. "The giant snake that's with Faye, the witch."

He inclined his head. "Bambi has been with me for a long time. Not that I have favorites, but she is…special to me." Roth's gaze was fixed on the road. "When Layla was hurt by her clan, I couldn't fix her. She was so bad off and she was…" His jaw clenched. "She was dying, and that meant I would do anything to save her."

I stayed silent, letting him speak even though Zayne had already told me most of this.

"There are good witches and there are bad ones. Faye's coven worships Layla's mother, Lilith, so I'm sure you can figure out which side they landed on."

The side that had no problem selling enchantments to use on humans who'd ended up slaughtered. Anger simmered, prickling at my skin.

"We'd figured they'd be willing to help save Layla to score brownie points with Lilith," he explained. "Cayman went to see them and came back with a cure. I didn't know until later that they'd demanded Bambi in exchange."

"Would knowing that have changed anything?"

"No," he answered without hesitation. "They could've asked for my life and I would've handed it over to save her."

I had already guessed that, but I was still surprised. His actions were so…undemon-like.

"I could've refused," he added.

"Why didn't you?"

"If I had, then Cayman would've died. He's a demon broker, Angel Face. Their life is bound to their word."

I stared at his profile. Again, so very undemon-like.

"Anyway, I want Bambi back, and you're going to help me get her." He pulled into a parking space.

I blinked. "How am I supposed to help?"

Roth smiled at me, and a chill swept along my neck. "You're going to use your special Trueborn badassery and take that coven out."

14

My *grace* came alive like a spark giving way to flame.

Now that was definitely a very demon-like thing to request, but still, I was shocked. I stared at Roth, dumbfounded and sure I must have heard him wrong.

Did he seriously just ask me to kill not just one but an entire coven of people? Bad people. Bad people who'd betrayed us, but come on. He couldn't be serious.

He let out a laugh that would've been charming if it hadn't come after him demanding that I kill an entire coven of witches. "You should see your face."

"I don't need to see it to know it has *WTF* written all over it," I told him.

Roth leaned toward me. I tensed, and I thought he noticed based on the way his smile grew. "It's almost like you forgot who I am."

"I haven't." The muscles in my back became rigid.

"You sure about that?" One dark eyebrow rose. "A lot of people forget what I am—who I am, in the core of my very being."

"Is that so?" I murmured.

He nodded. "They mistake my love for Layla as a kernel of goodness that will take root inside me like a seed, eventually blossoming into a flower of purity and light."

"I didn't think *that* for one second."

"But a lot do, probably even Stony," Roth replied. "As do a lot of other demons. Faye and her coven think that. Do you know how I know that?"

"A super secret, extra special demon ability?"

He laughed, and the hair on my arms rose, because the sound settled over me like smoke and ash. "Because they *had* to believe I'm a demon changed into something soft and good to even briefly consider betraying me like they did."

"Oh," I murmured. Was his…skin getting thinner?

"But I'm going to let you in on a little secret, my half-angel friend, because you also don't truly understand who I am." His finger landed on the tip of my nose. I flinched, not having seen him move his hand. "Every cell and molecule of who I am desires, needs and covets Layla. Humans call that love. I call it obsession. Same thing, I suppose, but I am a demon, Trinity. I'm brutally selfish and there are very few things I truly care about. While I may randomly commit acts of perceived kindness, I do them only so that Layla is happy. Because when she's not happy, it makes me want to do really, *really* bad things to whatever or whoever has upset her."

All of that was kind of romantic. Also super disturbing.

I pulled away from his hand. "Okay. Thanks for the sharefest, but—"

"But at the end of the day, I'm the Crown Prince of Hell. You do not want to mess with me."

My jaw locked as I felt the *grace* flare within me. "And at the end of the day, I'm still a Trueborn who can reduce you to a pile of ash, so you don't want to mess with *me*."

"True, but something else I know?" He leaned back and draped an arm over the steering wheel. "You might have a whole lot of angelic blood kicking around in you, but you're as far from holy as I am."

"What does *that* mean?" I demanded, ignoring the spark of power deep in my stomach.

He stared at me. "Angels were forbidden to do the nasty with humans a long, long time ago, by you know who." He pointed at the roof of his car, referencing God. "You might have been created to help fight some big bad that's decided to have a playdate with Earth, but just in case you begin to go the route all Wardens have and think you're somehow above a demon, don't forget where you came from. You were created out of an act of pure sin."

"No offense, but Wardens *are* sort of above demons on the whole good-versus-evil scale."

Roth tilted his head as his gaze flickered over my face. Then he laughed, a deep belly laugh as he shook his head. "You, too, huh?"

"Me, too, what?" Annoyance flared.

"You have no idea how Wardens came into creation, do you? Do you think God created them to fight the demon plague upon Earth?"

"Well…yeah."

"Well, no," he retorted, thrusting a hand through his messy black hair. He snickered. "Even Layla had no clue."

"No clue about what?" I gripped my knees, beyond the point of impatience. "You know what, never mind. Story time is great and all, and I'm a hundred percent convinced that you're the most evil demon to ever walk this Earth and all should quake and scream when they see you, but none of this has anything to do with you asking me to kill a bunch of witches. I get I owe you a favor, but I didn't think that meant—"

"Not knowing what the favor was doesn't matter. You still made the deal, Angel Face."

"I don't even know why you need my help with this."

"Normally I wouldn't, but the deal for Bambi was brokered through Cayman. If I go back on the deal, Cayman dies. I like Cayman, but Layla *really* likes him. If he dies, she'll cry. We've already established what happens when Layla is upset. Luckily, the coven hasn't left the city yet, but word has it, they will soon. We need to act now."

"You expect me to wipe out everyone while you play *Candy Crush* on your phone?"

"Not *Candy Crush*. I'd probably be playing *Wordsy*."

"*Wordsy?*"

"I like putting words together, but yes. That's what I expect."

"I don't kill people, Roth."

"I didn't think you did. I thought you killed demons who attack you and beings who wish you and others harm. Sometimes that includes humans. Sometimes it includes Wardens and…ex-best friends."

My entire body recoiled. "You know, I was starting to like you, but you're an asshole."

He lifted a shoulder. "And sometimes you'll kill witches who betrayed you. Or have you forgotten that Faye told Aym we'd been to see her, setting into motion a series of events that nearly killed the Warden you love?"

I gaped at him. "I don't love Zayne."

He quirked a brow. "My bad."

"I don't," I repeated, heart thundering for some reason. "I care about him. That's all."

Roth shrugged. "Still. The question remains. Have you forgotten what this coven did?"

The breath I took went nowhere as I curled my hands into fists. "No, I haven't forgotten."

"Then I'm sure you also haven't forgotten that because of that, Layla was injured, and Zayne, the Warden you're not in love with but care about, nearly died."

"Of course not." My heart rate kicked up as the image of an injured Zayne formed in my mind. I would never forget the smell of his charred flesh.

"And how did Zayne not die?" he asked.

"He didn't tell you?" I didn't know how much Roth and Layla knew about Zayne's new super status.

"It was your father, wasn't it?"

I didn't answer.

A beat of silence passed as Roth stared out the windshield. "Zayne's your Protector now, isn't he? Bonded and true."

I had no idea if that was just a good or an obvious guess, or if Roth knew something I didn't, but my palms grew sweaty against my knees. "He is," I said. "It was…meant to be."

"Was it?"

I let go of my knees. I didn't want to tell him what my father had said and what Matthew had confirmed about Layla and I.

"It was," I repeated.

Roth's gaze flicked to mine. "If your father hadn't decided to bond Zayne to you, he would be dead right now. Layla would be devastated, and I'm damn sure you would feel just as torn up or even worse." A pause. "Even though you only *care* about him."

I ignored that, because I was lost in the moment of imagining losing both Zayne and Misha. I wasn't sure I could have recovered.

"They betrayed us, Trinity, and they betrayed us knowing what the consequences would be. Yes, I want my familiar back, but I also want them to pay," he continued. "And I know you do, too. I can smell the rage in you. It reminds me of cayenne pepper. You want to make them pay, too, and, Angel Face, sometimes an eye for an eye is the right thing to do."

Dragging my gaze from his, I looked out the window. I saw nothing but a blur of gray across the street, but even if my vision had been crystal clear, I doubted I'd have seen anything at that moment. I tried to push down the anger the demon could smell, but it was no use. The rage tangled with my *grace*, burning me from the inside out, demanding to be used…or fed.

It wanted out, that rage. It hadn't ended with putting Misha down. It had started there.

Roth was correct. I wanted revenge, because Faye and whoever else had taken part deserved to die.

Layla had been hurt.

Zayne had almost died. I had no idea whether, if they hadn't sold us out, that night would've gone any differently, but they'd played a major role in what had happened and they deserved to suffer lasting consequences from that night.

Faye deserved whatever was coming to her, but…seeking revenge wasn't right.

I'd learned that when I was six years old and I'd pushed a boy at the park who'd knocked me over to get to the swing set. Mom had taught me that. She'd sat me down and explained that two wrongs never made anything right. Thierry had reinforced it numerous times when Misha and I were younger and I'd retaliated whenever he bested me in training by hiding his shoes or taking his favorite chips or cookies and eating them or throwing them away.

Man, I had been a little terror.

But anyway, killing Faye and her coven wasn't the same thing as hiding Misha's shoes or throwing away his favorite chips. It was more like what I'd done to Ryker after he'd murdered my mother.

I'd killed him.

Immediately and without regret.

No one had punished me for that. I'd never thought twice about the fact that I'd killed him. What I'd done didn't seem to matter in comparison to what he had done.

This wasn't the same, though.

Or was it?

Killing Ryker had been an act of immediate retribution.

The crimes were different. Just like killing…killing Misha. It was the same. I'd *had* to do it.

Low in my stomach, my *grace* burned and pulsed. It was the source of my strength and power. A weapon welded from Heaven's own fire coursed through my veins, and it wanted to be used. For what Roth was requesting. Confusion swirled. Shouldn't it be shrinking away from such a request? Or was I wrong? Maybe I was supposed to do this, not because I owed Roth a favor but because the coven was indirectly tied to this Harbinger. When they'd helped Senator Fisher obtain the enchantment for the humans who'd attacked the community I'd grown up in, they had helped Misha and Bael, who were both connected to the Harbinger.

I thought about the Warden who'd died last night. And I thought about all those innocent humans who'd been infected and left to rot in the abandoned building. The witches hadn't done any of that directly, but they were still a part of it.

I took a breath. It went nowhere.

"What if I refuse?" I asked as I stared out the window, seeing nothing.

Roth didn't answer immediately. An eternity seemed to stretch out between us. "I don't think you will, so why ask the question?"

I'd been wrong about that breath I took. It did go somewhere. Air swelled in my chest. Pressure clamped down as my *grace* pulsed like a hot flash. My thoughts raced as I tried to come to terms with the crystal clear fact that…I wanted to take out the coven.

I wanted to make them pay.

I wasn't even all that furious with Roth for making the request. Sure, I was ticked off. The bastard was using my need for revenge to do his dirty work, but I also understood his deadly desire and that understanding dampened my outrage.

I started to reach for my phone, tucked away in the pocket of my jeans, then stopped, wondering who I was going to call. Zayne? Yes. That was who I was reaching for, and wasn't that bizarre? It had to be the bond, because I rarely thought to ask anyone for advice. I kind of just did whatever without talking to anyone. Not Jada. Not even Misha before…well, before everything had gone to crap with him. What would Zayne say? I doubted he'd sign off on this.

Knowing him, he'd come up with a less deadly alternative.

I opened my eyes and looked at Roth. He was watching me in a curious way, as if waiting to see what I'd say even though he'd already claimed I wouldn't refuse. "What if I can make Faye release Bambi without killing her?"

One side of his lips curled up in a secretive half grin. "Well, why don't we see how you might accomplish that?"

"How are things going with you and Stony?"

I cut Roth a sharp look as we walked down the rather ordinary hallway of the thirteenth floor of the hotel where Faye's coven regularly hung out. "I'm not talking about Zayne."

"Why not?"

Straightening the sunglasses perched on my head, I said, "The list of the reasons would be longer than the time it would take for us to walk the length of this hall."

"Give me the CliffsNotes version."

"The number one reason is that I'm not talking about Zayne with *you*," I stated.

"Because I'm the Crown Prince of Hell?" He slid me a knowing look.

"No." I stopped. "Because you're the boyfriend of the girl he loves, and talking about anything personal that deals with him seems wrong."

"Hmm." Roth halted. "Loves? Or is it loved?"

I met his amber gaze. "Aren't you the one who not too long ago told me that he was still in love with her? That he would step over me to save her?"

"But he didn't, did he?"

My head jerked back. "What?"

"The night at the senator's house. When Layla was injured, he did not leap over you to get to her," he pointed out. "He remained in the battle, fighting at your side—and that was before he was bonded to you." He paused. "At least, in the metaphysical sense."

I opened my mouth to tell him he didn't know what he was talking about, but he was right. Zayne hadn't left my side for Layla. What did that mean?

Nothing.

"You were wrong?" I challenged. "Is that what you're saying?"

Roth shrugged. "It would be the first time."

I snorted. "Really?"

He smiled.

"Look, it doesn't mean that," I told him. "And even if it did—and that's an *if* as big as the entire continent of North America—we can't be together. It's forbidden between Trueborns and their Protectors."

"What fun is it if it's not forbidden?" Shoving his hands

into his pockets, he wheeled around and started walking. "You coming?"

Making a face at his back, I hurried to catch up. He was humming a vaguely familiar song that was going to drive me crazy until I figured out what it was.

"You got a plan?" Roth asked.

I almost laughed. "Of course I do."

That was mostly a lie. I had no plan other than to hopefully scare the Jesus into Faye.

Wait. Did witches even believe in Jesus? I had no idea.

"This should be interesting to watch," he commented. "Nearly as interesting as watching you and Zayne train."

I shot him a dark look as we followed the hallway around a curve. The restaurant came into view. All I could see above the tinted glass windows and walls of the restaurant at the end of the hall were dim ceiling lights.

How many people were inside? Were all of them witches?

Roth stopped, lifting his right hand. He snapped his fingers, and I heard a sharp cracking sound. The smell of fried plastic filled the hallway. "Camera," he said, jerking his chin toward the corner of the hall. "Want to make sure there's no evidence, just in case."

Just in case...

I shuddered.

"Just remember, you can't kill her while Bambi is on her—it will kill Bambi, too. Don't do that." Roth reached for the door.

"Wait," I called, and he looked at me. "Was this something that just Faye would've decided to do—"

"Unless they went behind the Crone's back, the coven is a

democracy. No decision is made without the full support of the entire coven," he answered. "They are not just complicit."

Dammit.

I didn't know a lot about covens, but I knew how powerful a Crone, the leader of the coven, was, and how insane it would be to go behind their back.

Taking out one witch would be easier to deal with than an entire coven, if it came down to that. Come to think of it... "How many witches are in this coven?"

"I really don't know." He turned away from me. "A little over fifty, perhaps."

A little over fifty?

Fifty?

Sweet Jesus and baby llamas everywhere. Maybe all of them wouldn't be here. I doubted Roth expected me to hunt down every one. That would be too time-consuming, and there was no way I could get that done before Zayne returned.

Sort of horrified by myself, I shook my head. Here I was, thinking about how time-consuming it would be to kill fifty or more witches.

What bad life choices had I made that had led to this moment in my life?

My eyes narrowed on the back of Roth's black shirt. Oh, yeah. There. Right there. Agreeing to owe a favor to a damn demon prince. This was Zayne's fault. Sounded about right. I mean, he'd introduced me to Roth. I was going to throat punch Zayne when I saw him.

Come to think of it, how had Roth known Zayne wasn't home? Was it a lucky guess and that was what yesterday had been about? Roth hadn't been bored, but had come hoping to find Zayne absent? Before I could ask, Roth opened the door, and the sound of jazzy music drifted out, along with the hum of conversation. The same dark-haired woman who'd been there the last time we'd come stood behind the hostess table.

She opened her mouth as the door slid shut behind me. I heard the click of the lock and knew that had been Roth's doing.

"We're not expected, Rowena. I know." Roth stopped her with a raised hand before she could speak. "And we don't care."

The witch snapped her mouth shut, and something unholy burned bright in her eyes. A gleam that wasn't entirely human. Sort of like me. Her gaze shifted to me and then away, as if I wasn't a concern. "I'll let Faye know you're here."

"How about you just stand right there and do whatever it is you do. We know our way."

We did. Rowena didn't look happy about it, nor did she appear to listen. As we walked past her, she was reaching for what I guessed was a phone, her movements quick and jerky, as if her show of cool annoyance was a cracking facade.

Cutting through a maze of booths and tables, I noted that there were at least twenty or so witches here. Did they not have jobs?

As it had last time, conversation stopped as we stalked past their tables. Forks halted halfway to mouths. Spoons clattered off bowls. Plastic straws wavered in front of lips.

Well, this was one place that wasn't environmentally conscious. I added that to my list of reasons for not feeling bad if I had to take them all out.

As I followed Roth, a part of me acknowledged that I

wasn't terrified about what might happen. All I could feel was anger—anger over what the coven had taken part in, what Misha had done and what that meant for Zayne and I, and anger at Roth for this damn situation.

And my *grace*.

It buzzed through my veins, causing my fingers and lips to tingle. Which was weird, because not once while I'd battled the zombies had I felt it fighting to get out, to be used. Was that because I hadn't been in jeopardy then, but it somehow sensed that I was now?

I had no idea.

Ahead, I saw the shape of a woman rising from a booth, and even though her features were blurry, I knew it to be Faye.

"Sit," Roth commanded. "We need to have another little chat."

Faye's blunt-cut dark hair swung around her chin as her head whipped from the demon to me. Her hand flew to her arm, fingers curling tight around a dark shadow.

Roth's lip curled in a snarl, and I realized that somehow the witch had stopped Bambi from coming off her skin like the familiar had done the last time we'd been here.

And that made for a very unhappy demon prince. Roth's eyes flashed a bright, intense red before mellowing to a cool amber.

Faye's expression leveled as she slowly sat back down. "To what do I owe the honor of *this* unexpected visit?"

"Honor?" Roth's laugh was like silk wrapped in darkness as he sat across from her and scooted over to make room for me. "You seem surprised to see us."

I sat, keeping my hands in my lap as I looked at Faye, really looked at her, in a way I hadn't the last time.

She was young, maybe in her midtwenties, and she looked like a normal woman one could pass any day on the street. She *was* mostly human, with the exception of demonic blood courtesy of someone in her family having hooked up with a demon in generations past. That was what gave witches their abilities and enabled her to have Bambi as a familiar. These witches were nothing like the humans who called themselves Wiccans. Not that there was anything wrong with Wiccans. They just didn't have the same kind of power that born witches had.

"Of course I'm surprised," Faye said. "It's not like I knew you two were coming, and we're very busy right now. As I told you before, we are leaving very soon. The whole coven."

"You don't look busy," I pointed out as Roth stretched an arm over the back of the booth, acting as if he was settling in for an afternoon nap.

"Looks can be deceiving," she said, barely sparing me a glance. Which was funny considering she'd agreed to help the senator with the enchantment in exchange for parts of a Trueborn—*my* parts. For that alone I should kill her.

"Looks *can* be deceiving," I agreed, feeling the anger on my skin like a thousand pissed-off hornets.

Faye smiled tightly as she closed a small black journal in front of her. "How can I help you?" This was asked of Roth. Not me, because obviously I was not viewed as remotely important. "The last time you were here, I told you everything we knew."

"Is that so?" Roth murmured.

The witch nodded as she leaned back against the booth and placed her hands in her lap.

"Let's cut the crap," I said, not wanting to play the coy game. "We know you told Aym or possibly Bael that we'd been to see you. Or maybe you told Senator Fisher. Who knows who you told, but we know *you* did."

Her eyes widened slightly. "I don't—"

"Don't do the whole innocent thing." Roth's voice was deceptively soft. "Aym betrayed you, just like you betrayed us. You should pick better people to team up with."

Even in the low light and with my eyes, I could see Faye pale, and I took a perverse pleasure in it.

"And I can safely assume you realized the moment you saw us that things didn't end well for Aym," I added. "He's super dead now."

She said nothing, and that angered me further.

"I might not know a lot about witches, but I was under the impression that you're not supposed to be team good or bad," I said. "But boy, did you saddle up with Team Dead, Dumb and Evil."

"And what team are you on?" Her dark eyes flicked toward me. "As you sit beside the Crown Prince of Hell?"

"Mmm." Roth hummed low in his throat, like a large cat purring. "I love the way you say Crown Prince."

I met Faye's stare. "Like you said. Looks can be deceiving."

Her throat worked on a swallow. She opened her mouth, closed it and then tried it again. "We didn't have a choice."

"There's always a choice," Roth said. "Always."

"You don't understand. We didn't go to them. They came to us shortly after you arrived. The very same night—"

"I don't care," I said, not recognizing my own voice or what was invading my system. It was like a whole new personality was unlocked and taking over. "You didn't have to tell them, but you did. Because of that, we walked into a trap. A trap *you* helped set up. People were hurt, Faye."

Her lips thinned as she passed a nervous glance at Roth.

"Layla," he whispered. "She was hurt."

Now Faye looked like she was about to choke. "We would never do anything that would put Lilith's daughter in harm's way. Never. That wasn't our intention."

"Intentions mean nothing at the end of the day. I mean, you could set a bush on fire and never *intend* for it to spread to the apartment complex next door, but when it does, it's still your fault." I opened my hands in my lap. "What *were* your intentions? What did they offer you for this information?"

She gave a quick shake of her head and glanced around the dining area and then back to us. "If we didn't tell them, they would've slaughtered everyone here."

"What made you think we wouldn't do that once we found out?" Roth queried.

Faye's lips parted.

"I'm thinking she didn't believe we'd survive," I told him, nodding when she mashed her lips together. I thought about what Roth had told me in the car, about how much of a big, bad demon he was. Something occurred to me. "They risked ticking you off instead of Aym and Senator Fisher, and—" I turned to Faye "—there's no way in Hell you didn't think for one second that if Roth was involved, Layla wouldn't be. So, not only were you hedging your bets on the other side, you don't seem to have cared about the fact that Layla is the daughter of Lilith."

"That's true," Roth agreed. "And that does not make me happy."

"Now, Aym was really annoying and talkative, but he wasn't *that* scary." The last part wasn't exactly true. Aym wasn't some low level demon. He'd almost killed Zayne.

Following where I was going with this, Roth chimed in. "And while Bael's presence might impress the...impressionable—" he said, and two pink splotches appeared in the center of Faye's cheeks "—he ain't me."

"Who were you really working with?" I asked, becoming aware of the silence surrounding us. "Who could make you and your coven stupid enough to cross us?"

"We only spoke to the senator, like I said—"

"*And* you said you didn't know why he wanted the enchantment that turned innocent humans into cannon fodder," I interrupted, heart pounding. "But I don't believe you. Did you know Misha?"

Her upper lip curled. "I have no idea who that is, and you might want to think before speaking to me like that again, *human*. I could curse your entire bloodline with a few words."

I almost laughed. Almost. "Misha was a Warden who was working with Aym and Bael."

"Okay? So?" She lifted a shoulder and focused on Roth. "We don't deal with Wardens. Ever."

I wasn't sure I believed her, but Roth inclined his head and said, "Witches don't trust Wardens. The whole indiscriminately killing anything with demonic blood thing. But, I got to say, I'm going to be super offended if you really thought it was better to risk angering me over Aym or Bael."

Faye inhaled, and several seconds passed. "We spoke only with the senator at first. That isn't a lie."

"But?" Roth goaded.

Her shoulders tensed. "But it wasn't the senator who came after you all arrived. It was Bael. And you're right. We wouldn't risk offending you over him."

"But?" Roth said one more time.

She reached for a glass of water but stopped and placed her hand on the table. "I told you that the coven is leaving this city— Hell, we're leaving the entire coast. For the last couple of months, our Crone has sensed something *growing*. Something we want no part in. I told you that already." She toyed with the edge of a napkin. "We thought we had time. We were wrong, though. It's already here. The Harbinger."

15

The Harbinger.

Faye had confirmed what I'd suspected. The coven knew about the Harbinger and had possibly knowingly aided the creature, whether directly or indirectly.

"Have you met it? Seen it?" I asked, because if she could give me any description, it would help.

Faye shook her head. "No. We don't even know *what* it is, but when Bael arrived after you left, I knew someone had been watching us. They knew you'd been here."

Roth shrugged. "But they didn't know what you told us. You told them, and you could've lied. This is starting to bore me, Faye."

"Bael knew we were planning to leave. He…knew we had sensed this—this great *unrest*. An unbalance that none of us have seen before." She lowered her gaze as her fingers stilled on the napkin. "When Bael came, he told us that we hadn't made a deal with only the senator, but with *it*, this thing he called the Harbinger. We didn't know until then that the Harbinger was what we'd been sensing."

"You betrayed us because he told you the name of something you knew nothing about?" Roth coughed out a dry laugh. "Bad choice there, witch."

"We knew enough." Leaning forward, she kept her voice low. "He showed us what the Harbinger is capable of. One of our coven members who'd been at home had been killed. Bael had pictures." Her skin puckered around her lips, blanching white. "Paul. Paul was murdered."

I had no idea who Paul was.

Apparently Roth did and didn't care. "So?"

Faye drew back, her shoulders leveling. It took a moment for her to speak. "I'd never... I'd never seen anything like that. His eyes were open in the picture, burned out. Empty sockets. He had no tongue, and his ears... It looked like someone had shoved ice picks into him, but he was...he was *smiling*. The look on his face was peaceful, as if he was *happy*. How could that be possible? His death was brutal. How could he be smiling?"

Well, that sounded gruesome to be sure.

"Why do you think that's not something Bael is capable of? I imagine burning out eyeballs isn't exactly hard, and neither would be convincing someone the whole process felt good while it was being done." Roth drew his arm off the back of the couch. "Demons may not be able to persuade large groups of humans into doing or feeling things, but one? Easy peasy."

"We are protected against demon persuasion," she insisted. "No demon can break that spell."

Roth looked like he wanted to try, but the method of death didn't tell us anything about the Harbinger.

The witch focused on Roth once more. "I'm sorry that Layla was put in danger. I am, but we made a deal with the senator, and you all…stepped into this deal and—"

"Ah, yes. The whole Trueborn thing," Roth cut her off. "You were promised a Trueborn in exchange for your coven's aid."

"Parts," I reminded him. "Parts of a Trueborn."

"Yes. That is what we were promised. Are still promised," she added.

My brows lifted as the anger simmered to near boiling point. "You still think they're going to deliver?"

"Why would they not?" She picked up her glass. "We held up our end of the bargain, and I didn't hear either of you say you killed anyone other than Aym."

I could feel Roth start to move, but I was faster as I tipped toward the witch. "I can one hundred percent assure you that they will not be able to hold up their end of the bargain."

Her dismissive, almost distasteful gaze flickered over me, and I realized that, even though she was mostly human, she didn't like humans. She didn't consider herself one of them.

Considering I kept referring to humans as *them*, maybe I didn't, either.

"And how would *you* know that?" she asked, voice snide.

It was wrong. It was flat-out dangerous and probably more than a little stupid, but her being so totally unaware of how close she was to getting punt-kicked into her next life got the best of me.

And I knew what I did next would mean.

I might not have come here wanting to kill a witch, but I was going to do it. The moment I showed her what I was, she was a liability—an irritating one. She'd betrayed us before, and once she knew what I was, she would most definitely use that information to her advantage.

Maybe I'd feel bad about this later. Maybe guilt would fester and rot inside me, because surely there could be a nonviolent way of handling this.

But at the moment...I didn't care.

I let my *grace* flow to the surface of my skin. The corners of my vision turned a golden white. "Because I'm the True-born that was promised to you."

Faye choked on her water, her eyes bulging as she jerked back against the booth. The glass slipped from her fingers and cracked off the table and, I guessed with the help of Roth, toppled toward the witch. Water splashed and spilled into her lap, but she didn't seem to notice as she stared at me.

"Yeah." I let my admission sink in before I pulled the *grace* back. Tucking it away was harder than it should've been. "Not ever going to happen."

"Oh my God," she whispered.

"Pretty much." I rested my elbows on the table and plopped my chin into my hands. "You didn't just betray Roth, the Crown Prince of Hell. You also betrayed me, and because of that, someone very important to me was gravely injured. Because of that, I had to—" I cut myself off, knowing that what had happened with Misha would've happened with or without the coven's interference. "You screwed up. Big time."

"You're afraid of her." Roth's voice was soft.

"Terrified," the witch admitted.

Probably made me a bad Trueborn, but the corners of my lips curved up.

Faye's gaze darted to the side, and then her lips parted as if she was about to speak.

"Don't even think it," Roth warned.

I glanced at him, brows raised.

"She was about to cast a spell," Roth replied. "Weren't you? Probably something lame that she thinks will paralyze us or make us squawk like chickens. What she's forgetting is that her spells won't work on me, and they sure as Hell won't work on a being rocking angel blood."

Her lips thinned as her chest rose and fell. A long moment passed. "There are over twenty witches in here, each of them powerful in their own right. Spells aren't our only weapons."

"Is that a threat?" Roth queried.

"If it is, you're out of your damn mind," I said. "Maybe you are. So, here's what's going to happen. You're going to release Bambi and Roth from the deal he made with you."

"What?" Faye gasped, her wide-eyed gaze swinging toward him. "We made a deal to save Layla's life. If you go back on the deal, your barter demon will pay the price."

"He's not asking to be released from the deal," I said, and I didn't have to look at Roth to know he was smiling. "I'm telling you. You're going to offer Bambi back to him. It will be your choice, so thank you for that. The deal will be null."

"Those are technicalities," she sputtered, color flooding her cheeks once more. "He's asked you to do this."

"But I'm not the one asking you to be released from the deal." Smugness dripped from Roth's voice. "And you know that's the only thing that matters."

Faye began to tremble with anger or fear or possibly both. "And if I refuse? You'll kill me? You'll kill everyone in here? Because that's what will happen. If you attack me, they will defend me." She dipped her chin, and a blast of hot air flipped a napkin over and stirred the tendrils of hair around my face. "I will defend myself."

"Did you just do that? Cause a *breeze* to roll over the table?" I widened my eyes. "Scary. That was so very scary, I'm actually quaking in my shoes over here."

Roth snorted.

"And when did I say I'd allow you to live after you gave up Bambi?" I continued, my chin still resting in my hands. "That's pretty presumptuous of you."

Faye inhaled sharply.

"After all, you want me dead. You actually need me dead to make use of all my glorious parts, which I doubt will be used for the betterment of anyone but you or your coven," I told her. "How in the world could you ever think you would walk away from this alive?"

"That's a damn good question," Roth said. "And you should listen to her and make this easy. Release Bambi and null the deal. You know what to say. 'I end this deal bartered by the demon Cayman and release this familiar.' That's all. Say it."

"I…" Faye shook her head and then shuddered. Her hand floated to her arm, to where Bambi rested. She was going to release the familiar even though it was too—

She raised her hands.

The table between us slammed into Roth and me, pinning us into the booth. Pain lanced across my stomach as Roth cursed.

Okay. That was definitely not a breeze.

I worked my fingers between the table and my stomach as Faye rose from the booth, her black hair lifting from her face as her fingers splayed out. Her skin flushed and her dark eyes flashed a cinnamon brown. My gaze dropped. Yep. Her sensible black heels were several inches off the floor.

She was levitating.

I wished I could levitate.

"That's the best you got?" Roth laughed, and I really wished he'd shut up, because the table was now digging into my palms and it was starting to hurt. "You need to do better."

"I haven't even begun to show you what I can do." Faye's voice was thick like mud.

"And neither have you seen what I'm capable of." Roth placed his hands palms down on the table.

The scent of sulphur hit the air and the table shattered into dust within a nanosecond. Everything that had been on the table—the glass, the tea candle, the napkins—was gone. Even the journal Faye had had.

Okay. Now *that* was really cool.

As I shot to my feet, the witch's rage pulsed like a shock wave, rippling through the restaurant, and my *grace* answered, sparking to my skin.

"Deal with her." Roth spun toward the dining area. "I'll deal with them."

Them happened to be the other twenty or so witches who were also levitating.

Faye lifted a hand, and the air seemed to vibrate above her palm. Her lips moved in a low, quick chant I couldn't make out. A ball of fire appeared.

I darted to the side as the softball-size ball of flames hit the booth I'd been sitting in. The wood caught fire, swallowing the entire booth way too fast, reminding me of the fire the demon Aym had wielded.

"That was so not nice!" I spun back to the witch.

Instinct kicked in, and I could feel my *grace* powering down my arm, demanding to be used. I couldn't. Not yet. Not with Bambi still on the witch. If I killed her, it would kill the familiar.

Another ball of flames formed above her hand as a shriek of pain and a blast of heat came from the direction of Roth. Faye's gaze darted to our right.

I charged her, catching her in the stomach with my shoulder. She shouted as I brought her to the floor. The ball of flames flickered out as her body bounced off the hardwood. I went down with her, digging my knee into her stomach. She grunted as she swung her hand toward me.

"Oh, Hell no." I caught her arm at the wrist and then the other. "No more fire tricks. Release Bambi."

Faye tried to buck me off, but she wasn't trained to fight, at least not physically. I easily restrained her, pinning her arms at her head. "Get off me!" she screamed.

"Not going to happen." Another burst of hot air exploded, from Faye this time, and the air around her began to distort. Her skin heated under my hands, and holy crap, she was about to light up like the Human Torch.

Oh, Hell to the no.

I grabbed her by the throat, cutting off her air before she even realized she'd taken her last breath. "Don't even think it."

With her concentration broken, the heat evaporated from

her body. Her lips peeled back, but no air was getting in or out. Not with my fingers digging into her windpipe. I needed to let up, or she was going to asphyxiate, but my hand stayed there. Rage consumed me, causing the fine hairs on my body to rise. It was like the night with the Ravers. The need to split skin and tissue was replaced with the desire to crush the fragile bones of her throat. I could do it. Easily.

Faye's eyes bulged, her skin turning a violent shade of red as she opened her mouth, gulping for air that wasn't coming.

Stop, I told myself. *You need to stop or Bambi will die.*

I forced my fingers to loosen and watched her drag in lungfuls of air. A tremor rolled through me. Cursing under my breath, I glanced at Roth and saw him holding a man several feet off the floor. There was no one else left. Nothing but piles of ash and piles of...

Oh, man.

Stomach churning, I quickly looked back to Faye. My gaze met hers, and as close as we were, I saw the panic behind the brimstone. It made her eyes look like orbs of fragile glass.

My fingers twitched, loosening even more. Faye had betrayed us—betrayed me. She needed me dead to be able to use parts of me for spells or whatever. She'd just tried to turn me into a great ball of fire. I'd known she had to die the moment I showed her what I was. Maybe I'd known that when Roth came to collect on his favor. Hell, I could've already known that deep down when we'd realized she'd betrayed us.

But she was *afraid.*

I could see it in her eyes. Fear and panic. Had Ryker's eyes been like that? Everything had happened so fast then, but even if I had seen fear in his eyes, it wouldn't have stopped me. Not after he'd killed my mother.

The shock I'd seen in Misha's eyes hadn't stopped me, either.

It wouldn't stop me now.

Faye reared up, breaking my hold. She swung at me, her fist catching me in the jaw. It was a weak punch, but it got my attention.

Catching her flailing arms with one hand, I got her back where I'd had her before, arms pinned and hand around her throat.

"Release Bambi now," I ordered, digging my fingers into her throat, putting just the right amount of pressure on her windpipe. "Say the words. Do it."

Faye gagged as her eyes bulged. "If I do, you'll kill me. You won't with her on me."

Appearing at my side, Roth knelt. "Just so you know? If Bambi dies because of your actions, I will drag out your death until you beg me to end it. And when you beg? I will hunt down every living family member of yours and they will pay for your transgressions. Then, and only then, after you've watched everyone you know and love die because of you, I will end your life."

"Really?" I said to him.

He didn't respond to me, still focused on Faye. "Do you understand me?"

The witch shrieked as I eased up on her throat. "I'll be dead, so why would I care?"

"*Really?*" I repeated, staring down at her.

Faye took a deep breath and then stopped straining against

me. Her body went limp against the floor. "Do it. Kill me. But I will never release the familiar."

"Why?" I demanded.

"If I can't have her, no one will."

"Are you serious?" Furious, I jabbed my fingers into her side, cracking at least two ribs. She screamed. "Sorry. My fingers slipped."

"Did they, though?" an unfamiliar voice demanded.

Looking up, I about choked on my own breath. A little old lady stood between two broken tables, only a foot or so from us. And she wasn't just old. She appeared to be well over a hundred years old and then some. Tufts of snow-white hair framed a dark-skinned face. She was close enough for me to see how creased and wrinkled her cheeks and forehead were. Her pale pink shirt read WORLD'S BEST GRANDMA and matched a pair of pink linen cropped pants that draped her frail body. The white thick-soled sneakers completed the AARP and then some package. She was flanked by a man and a woman I recognized as Rowena, the hostess. I had no idea how she was standing on her own and not resting eight feet under, but those eyes were as sharp as a blade and her voice as strong as any of ours.

"The Crone," Roth explained in a murmur, his entire body gone taut beside mine. "This will either go very badly or somewhat less badly."

Great.

That sounded just great.

"Look at what they've done!" Faye shrieked, struggling against my hold, but I didn't let her go. "Look at what they've done to the coven."

"What *they've* done?" the Crone responded, and white caterpillar-like brows rose. "Was it not you who led them here? Was it not you who brokered a deal with a demon in the first place?"

"Wh-What?" Faye stammered, confusion flashing across her face, and I was right there with her.

The Crone stepped forward on thin legs. "When you offered the elixir in exchange for Lilith's daughter's life, you did so outside the bounds of this coven. I warned you then that every act, every word designed to benefit one comes back threefold."

I peeked at Roth. He was watching the Crone with amber-hued eyes. It was becoming clearer by the second that Faye and some of the coven had gone behind the Crone's back.

"But it was Lilith's daughter and—"

"And you wanted a familiar, a powerful one you did not work for nor earn on your own merit." The Crone cut her off. "We do not interfere with nature, and if nature demanded Lilith's child's life, then so be it."

Roth wisely and a bit surprisingly kept his mouth shut.

"But you were greedy, and that greed led to another deal with another demon, and now you've brought something far worse to our coven's door."

Underneath me, Faye stopped fighting again.

"You think I did not know about the human enchantment? The bargain you made?" The Crone's cackle raised the tiny hairs on my body. "It looks like you got what you wanted, but not in the way you expected."

She knew.

The Crone knew what I was.

"And it looks like those who followed you also received their blessing threefold." The crone turned her head just the slightest. "I knew I would see you again, young prince."

Roth bowed his head. "Honored once more."

She chuckled as if amused. "You always bring such…interesting creations with you. Never thought I'd see a Crown Prince or Lilith's daughter, but I did because of you and now the child of an angel is before me." She smiled, revealing dull yellowed teeth. "What odd company you keep."

"It makes life interesting," he replied, lifting his chin, and then he slowly rose.

I stayed where I was.

"I'm sure it does." The Crone's steely gaze found mine, and silence stretched out. A shiver danced along my skin. She stared at me like she could see inside me. "You are not like them. You do not see in black-and-white. You see gray and all that exists in between, and I know not if that is a strength or a weakness."

Having no idea how to respond to any of that, I decided to stay quiet.

"Release the familiar, Faye." The Crone's voice hardened to steel. "Now."

Faye closed her eyes, the fight gone. There was no begging. No bartering. "I end this deal bartered by the demon Cayman and release this familiar."

Air warped behind Faye's head, and for a moment I thought it was my funky vision, but then Cayman stood there.

His long dark hair was pulled back from his handsome face. No romper today. Instead, he was wearing a purple velour jumpsuit that looked vintage. In his right hand he held what appeared to be a…contract.

Cayman grinned down at the witch. "The bargain brokered is voided." Flames licked over the thick sheet of paper, leaving nothing but ash. "Blessed be, bitch."

The demon broker gave Roth and I two thumbs-up and then disappeared in a ripple of air.

And then it happened.

A shadow peeled off Faye's arm, rapidly expanding and thickening until I could see thousands of little beads. They swirled like a mini tornado and dropped to the floor, taking form and shape. Bambi appeared as a snake the size of the Loch Ness monster—a baby Loch Ness monster.

The familiar shot toward Roth, its rear waving like a puppy's tail did when it greeted its owner after a long absence.

"My girl." Everything about the demon prince's face softened as he placed his hand on her oval-shaped head. Bambi's forked tongue flickered in response. "Layla is going to be so happy to see you."

Bambi wiggled joyfully.

The two of them were oddly adorable—

Hands slammed into my hips, rocking me backward. I tumbled off Faye as she scrambled to her feet, breathing fast. Her eyes were wild as she whipped toward the Crone. The two silent witches had moved to block Faye. She took a step back as I rose. She spun again, clutching something in her hand.

My dagger—she'd swiped one of my daggers. I braced myself for her attack, but she didn't come for me, and the second I realized what she was about to do, fury exploded within me.

Faye threw herself at Bambi, her arm arced high, dagger poised to sink into the thick back of the familiar. It was iron, deadly to demons, and I didn't stop to think.

Letting the *grace* finally rush to the surface, I welcomed the burst of strength as I snapped forward and gripped a handful of Faye's hair. I tore her away from Bambi and Roth, throwing her to the floor as golden-white flames exploded along my right arm. My hand curled around the heated handle forming against my palm. The weight of the sword was welcoming as fire spit and hissed from the sharp edges of the sword.

"You know what you need to do, Trueborn." The Crone spoke, her voice carrying high. "It is what you were born for."

The words landed like a punch. *What I was born for.* A weapon from birth. I was not the child of my father. I was the Sword of Michael.

I lifted the sword and swung it down, catching Faye at the shoulder. It was like a knife slicing through air. The sword met no resistance, burning through bone and blood before it could even spill into the air. It took seconds.

And Faye was no more.

The *grace* recoiled, flowing back into me as the flames around the sword flickered and then extinguished. Wisps of smoke and golden, glittery dust danced in the air as the light seeped back into my skin.

I stumbled back, breathing heavily as I stared at my dagger, lying inches from a pile of ruddy brown ash. There was silence. Nothing outside or inside my head. Just vast emptiness in this moment of quiet, and all I felt was…

Anger.

The anger was still there, muted and a little more hollow, but present.

"Thank you," Roth spoke, shattering the silence. Slowly, I looked at him. "Thank you."

"It had...it had to be done," I said, my voice sounding thready.

Amber eyes met mine. "It did."

"It was unavoidable," the Crone stated. "We do not choose sides, and Faye's repeated actions could be perceived as such. While her aid favored you in the past, self-serving deeds cloaked as gifts always turn. There's always a price to be paid," she said to Roth. Then to me, she said, "Do you know what she could've done with just a quarter's worth of blood from a Trueborn?"

I shook my head.

"She would've been able to overthrow me and acquire another wanted item without earning it. Greed for power is one of the most dangerous things, as volatile as a loss of faith." The Crone lifted her sharp chin. "You have nothing to fear from the coven. Your identity is safe."

I nodded my thanks as my gaze flicked back to Faye's remains. I bent down, picked up my dagger and then sheathed it as I rose, thinking of the Crone's words about what Faye had led to her coven. Something worse than demons.

"May I ask you a question?" I asked.

The Crone's eyes were shrewd. "You may ask one."

Did she mean that literally? I didn't want to ask in case she did. "Do you know who or what the Harbinger is?"

Those ancient eyes fixed on me and then shifted to Roth. "What did I tell you the last time you were here, Prince? That what you seek is right in front of your own eyes."

Roth stiffened but did not respond, and I had no idea what that could mean since the Harbinger wasn't right in front of us. I didn't get a chance to question her further.

"You both need to leave." She shuffled around but stopped. She looked over her shoulder, her gaze meeting mine. "I have a feeling I'll be seeing you again, but not with the prince. You will bring me something I have not seen before. A real prize."

Uh.

I had no words. None whatsoever as I watched one of the witches lead her out of the restaurant. Only Rowena remained, and she was staring at the mess in a way that told me she had just figured out that she was going to have to clean this up. My gaze found its way back to the ash.

"A real prize?" Roth said. "I'm kind of insulted that she doesn't consider me a real prize."

"Well, she didn't consider me one, either, and I'm part angel, so…" I really needed to stop staring at Faye's ashes. "What did the Crone mean when she answered my question?"

Roth didn't answer immediately. "I'm not sure. The last time she said that, I thought she was talking about Layla, but then she would've been wrong."

"The Crone is never wrong," Rowena snapped, and when I looked up, she was carrying a Dyson.

She was going to vacuum up what was left of her coven.

That was…

I had no words.

"I don't know what she meant," Roth added. "But I'm sure one day, when it's too late, it will be glaringly obvious."

A tap on my shoulder snagged my attention. I turned and swallowed a shriek of surprise.

Bambi's diamond-shaped head was mere inches from mine. Her ruby-red forked tongue flicked as she opened her mouth.

And smiled at me.

16

I'd lost my damn sunglasses—and they were my favorite pair—somewhere between having a table slide into me and killing a witch. Luckily, the sun was behind thick clouds and, based on the color of the sky, it looked like it would stay that way. My eyes would still ache, but it wouldn't be as bad.

Dammit.

"I don't want to go home—I mean, back to Zayne's place," I announced, and that was the first thing either of us had said since we left the restaurant, Rowena muttering under her breath as she began to vacuum up what remained of her coven.

When he didn't answer, I looked at him. Roth's fingers tapped the steering wheel as he navigated the congested streets of the capital with more patience than I imagined most humans had. Bambi was much smaller now, ensconced on his arm, with half her body hidden by his shirt. Her head was tucked just under his collar, but every couple of minutes I had the strangest sensation that something was staring at me, and when I looked at Roth, Bambi's head would be visible on his neck.

"She likes you."

"What?"

"Bambi," he explained. "She's trying to keep an eye on you while she's resting."

Yet again, I wondered if Roth could read thoughts. He claimed he couldn't. "I'm…happy to hear that."

"You should be. Normally she likes to eat people."

My brows lifted. "Did you hear what I said?"

"You don't want to go home. Where do you want to go?"

I had no idea. "Surprise me."

"Do you think that's wise?"

I frowned. "What's that supposed to mean?"

"You out in the city without Zayne." At a stoplight, he tipped his head back against the seat. "He thinks you're back at his place, waiting on his arrival."

"I don't need his permission to go anywhere, nor do I need anyone to babysit me." I couldn't believe I was saying this. "I can take care of myself. I'm confident you already know that."

"I do." He lifted his head off the seat and the car revved as he went through the intersection. "I'm fairly observant. Did you know that? I notice things."

"That's what *observant* means." I felt my forehead crease. "Hopefully you're observing my expression right now."

He chuckled at that. "You don't see very well, do you?"

My lips parted on a sharp inhale.

Roth slid a brief, knowing glance in my direction. "That's why you were doing the blindfolded training. That's why you jerk or flinch when something gets too close to your face." A pregnant pause. "Why you didn't see the witch go for your daggers."

All I could do was stare at him while wondering why, if he'd noticed that, he hadn't intervened.

"You were also wearing glasses the other day, and I have a feeling it's something more than just bad eyesight. And there's also the fact I know damn well a Trueborn's vision would be better than a normal human's. It would be better than a Warden's or a demon's."

I shifted my gaze away. Christ, was it that obvious? I shook my head again, irritated and embarrassed even though the rational side of me knew I had no reason to be either, but Roth was asking if it was wise if I went out there alone.

My earlier fears resurfaced. There was a big, bad world out there I couldn't see.

"I don't see well," I muttered. "Actually, I don't see very well at all."

Roth was quiet for what felt like an eternity. "God is ironic, isn't He?"

I curled my lip. "Why do you assume God is a he?"

He laughed. "God's actually a being beyond a biological sex, but calling God 'it' just seems offensive."

"And why would you worry about offending God?"

"Just because I don't answer to God doesn't mean I don't respect Him."

Roth was such a strange demon.

A grin appeared. "The Boss hates the fact that God is beyond the whole biological sex thing, which is why the Boss always changes appearance. It's not like humans who identify with a different gender. The Boss does it to be more God-like."

"When you talk about the Boss, you're talking about… Satan?" I asked, shivering when I said the name out loud. No one who knew beyond a doubt that Satan was real spoke the name.

His lips quirked. "The one and only, but if Lucifer ever heard you use the name he was given after being kicked out of Heaven, he'd turned your insides out."

"But…he's an angel." Confusion swamped me. "Or was. Whatever. How can he change what he appears as?"

"What damned Lucifer in Heaven is what powers him in Hell," he answered. "Pride."

"Pride?"

"Yep. He's basically *The Little Engine That Could*."

Now the image that statement provided was something I could never unthink.

"The Boss operates purely on the mantra of 'if I think I can, I will.'" His lips pursed. "He's like the first motivational speaker, if you really think about it. Well, the first scammy one, but aren't they all?"

"Uh…"

"Anyway, I digress. The texts got a few things wrong. For starters, Lucifer is still an angel, which leads to another thing that's usually incorrect. Questionable timelines. He was the first to be cast from Heaven, and since God had no experience when it came to booting angels off their lofty clouds of self-righteousness, he didn't strip Lucifer's wings. He still has his *grace*, and it's just as dark and twisted as you can imagine."

I really didn't want to.

"Of course, God learned after that. The rest who fell lost their wings and their *grace*."

Those fallen angels might have lost their *grace*, but based on what I'd learned about them, they made demons, even ones like Roth, look like fluffy puppies.

He slid me an amused glance. "Good thing the Wardens wiped out the Fallen eons ago, eh?"

"Yeah." I had no idea how we'd gotten on this topic. Something about God being ironic?

Roth chuckled as if he knew something I didn't. "Will you do me a favor, Angel Face?"

"Does it involve breaking your nose when you call me that?" I asked sweetly.

"No. Even better."

"Considering what I just did, not sure I want to do you any more favors."

"This is nothing like that. I want you to ask Zayne what happened to the Fallen." Roth lifted a shoulder. "Or ask one of the Wardens that raised you. I can't wait to hear what they say."

I knew what had happened to the angels that had fallen. The Wardens killed them. Hell, it was why Wardens were created in the first place, because no mortal could fight a Fallen. Duh.

"Anyway, you ending up with shit eyesight sounds like some kind of messed-up thing Lucifer and God agreed to."

I blinked at the swift switch back to the topic. "They... they still, um, talk?"

"You have no idea."

My mouth opened. Then closed. My brain was starting to hurt.

"Why don't you just use your *grace*? Whether you see well or not, anything that gets near you won't survive that." I was having a Hell of a time following this conversation. "Why stress yourself out or put yourself in danger by trying to compensate for your eyes in a different way?"

That was a good question, but answering it might reveal too much. Roth was the damn Crown Prince of Hell, but I...

God.

I actually *trusted* him, which probably meant there was something drastically wrong with my abilities to make reasonable life choices.

But Zayne trusted him as well.

Well, that might change if Zayne found out about today. Which was never, ever going to happen.

"Using my *grace* can tire me out." It then struck me that I wasn't tired. I touched my nose, finding it dry. It hadn't bled. Shock flickered through me. Was it because I'd used the *grace* only briefly? Or because I was bonded to the one I was meant to be bonded to?

That was a possibly interesting development—an amazing one, if that was the case.

"But you can still wield it when necessary, when your eyes are failing you, without any real harm coming to you. Right?" he asked. "It's not like you pass out in the middle of a battle."

"It makes me weak, but I can power through it if need be." But now I wasn't sure if that was the case, since I felt no effects from using it earlier.

"Then perhaps there's a different reason you don't use it."

My gaze sharpened on him. "What do you mean?"

"You were raised by Wardens?"

"And my mom," I said. "Before she died."

"But you were raised with their beliefs and opinions, their thoughts and persuasions," he explained. "If I've learned anything from Layla, it's that Wardens are strong proponents of guiding those not like them to fight their natural instincts. They're good at convincing others that *not* using their natural abilities is what's best for them."

I had no idea what to say to that because Thierry, Matthew and even my mom had urged me to call upon the *grace* only when all else failed, so much so that resisting its call had become inherent. But they'd had a good reason. Besides the fact that it left me weak, it revealed what I was. Using my *grace* was always a risk, but...

"We're here," Roth announced.

Startled, I pulled my gaze from him and looked out the window. I saw a brown sign I couldn't read and a whole lot of trees surrounding a wide path.

"Where are we?"

"Rock Creek Park. It's sort of connected to the zoo. Lots of trails. It's where I go when I...need a place to go."

I had a hard time picturing Roth strolling through a park, but it was the perfect choice. The trees provided shade, and while there were people out jogging and walking dogs, it was nowhere near as overwhelming as the sidewalks and streets.

I wondered if Roth had chosen it for that reason. "Thanks," I said, reaching for the car door. "I guess I'll see you around."

"You will."

Nodding, I opened the door and stepped out into the sticky air.

"Angel Face?"

Sighing, I turned and bent down so that I could see into the car. "What, Demon Spawn from Hell?"

His lips quirked into a grin. "Just so you know, what I felt for Layla and what she felt for me was forbidden. That didn't stop us."

The unwanted spark in my chest felt a lot like hope. That burst of wanting was overshadowed by annoyance, because we were now back on the topic of Zayne. "Good to know. Happy for you both, but nothing like that is going on between Zayne and I."

"I almost believe that," he replied. "Both parts of your statement."

I threw up my hands. "Why are you all up in my nonexistent love life, Roth?"

"Because I saw the way he looked at you, and I know the way he used to look at Layla. It was different."

My brows snapped together. "Well, I'm not sure how that's a good thing."

"Different is not bad, Trinity. Different can be good."

"Or it can mean nothing, like it does in this case." I started to rise.

"Hey," he called out again.

"What?" I snapped.

The demon prince smiled at me, seeming unperturbed by my annoyance. "What you did today needed to be done. Don't waste air on guilt. It would not have been wasted on you."

The door slid from my grasp, closing in my face before I could even respond. I straightened and stepped back as Roth peeled away from the curb.

Roth's words cycled over and over as I stood along the side of the busy road for several minutes. He was right about the last part. Faye wouldn't have spent a second feeling guilty if I'd been given to her in pieces.

Slowly, I turned and walked into the park. It was cooler here under the thick canopy of trees. Still humid and damp, but bearable as I mindlessly followed the path. After all the walking I'd done in the evenings patrolling for the Harbinger, making use of my leg muscles wasn't exactly on my to-do list, but this was…

It was nice, and it was calming.

Accompanied by the distant hum of conversation and the trill of cicadas, I sank into my thoughts. Not about Zayne. I didn't have the brain capacity to deal with anything Roth had just shared about him. Not when I'd just straight up killed someone.

Someone who was only mostly human and who had wanted—actually, needed—me dead. Who wouldn't have mourned me. Who would've used my death for nefarious ends.

Still…someone I had killed.

I didn't want to go back to the apartment. I didn't want to be…trapped there with these thoughts. I needed to file them away before I faced Zayne.

I walked and walked, passing stunning waterways, ancient rock scrambles and even a rustic log cabin that looked one windstorm away from crumbling. I crossed a boulder bridge, awestruck by the fact that the thing was still standing, and as I walked, I replayed what I'd done.

Part of me couldn't believe that I hadn't found a different way. Another part of me knew I should've kept my cool and not given in to the anger that had led me to showing the witch what I was. The moment I'd done that, there was no going back. And I acknowledged that that wasn't the first time I'd killed something other than a demon.

There'd been Ryker, then Clay.

And there'd been Misha.

All of them had been acts of self-defense, but although Faye had attacked me, I'd been able to restrain her. She'd been no real threat to my safety. Plus, I'd goaded her and then some, and…if I was being honest with myself, serving retribution had felt *good*.

Coming to a bench, I sat down heavily and lifted my gaze to the trees. This place reminded me of the Community, where I'd grown up. The air smelled fresher here. I sat back, realizing I didn't feel any demons nearby.

Guess they didn't like parks.

I stared at a sign across from me, having no idea what landmark it announced, and all I could think was that, when Faye had screamed, I hadn't flinched, and when I'd ended her life, I hadn't felt anything other than righteous retribution.

That was why I needed to walk. Those were the feelings I needed to sort out. Roth's parting words had been powerful but pointless, because I didn't feel an ounce of guilt. I wasn't sure if I was supposed to or not, and if I was, I didn't know what that said about me.

Or what I was capable of.

17

I had no idea how much time had passed when my phone started ringing. But I had a sinking suspicion about who it was as I pulled out my phone.

Zayne.

I really should've found my way back to the apartment before he returned, but I would've had to hail a cab or figure out how to use the Uber app, which I would barely have been able to see. Two things I'd never done before.

Probably should've thought of that before I let Roth drop me off.

I answered, wincing when I squeaked out a criminal-sounding "Hello?"

"Where are you?" Zayne asked, concern so apparent I could picture him pacing. "Are you okay?"

"I'm fine." I felt bad for making him worry. "Completely okay. I'm at Rock Creek Park."

"You're where?" Surprise flooded his voice.

"It's a park near the zoo—"

"I know where it is. How did you get there?"

"Oh, I just sort of walked...and ended up here."

"That's one Hell of a distance to walk, Trin."

Watching a couple jog by in matching spandex, I wondered how far I was from his apartment. "Yeah, I know. That's why I'm sort of just sitting here on a bench." I crossed my ankles. "So, did you take care of everything you needed to?"

"Yeah." Zayne fell silent, and for a second I thought the call had disconnected. "Do you want me to come get you?"

A tiny part of me was on the verge of saying no, but I was going to have to deal with Zayne's questions face-to-face sooner or later. "Can you? Because that would be great."

"I'll be there in about thirty minutes."

"Perfect," I said with so much chirpiness, the one word could've turned into a cheer. "Do you want me to meet you at the entrance?"

"I'll find you in the park." There was a beat of silence. "Trin, I..."

A child toddled past me, chasing the leash of a dog that was three times its size. "Yes?"

He didn't answer immediately. "Nothing. I'll be there in thirty."

Zayne disconnected, and I was left staring at my phone, wondering what he'd wanted to say. There was no way he could know what I'd done today. Distance definitely seemed to mute the bond, so even if he'd felt my anger, it couldn't have been enough to worry him, because he hadn't checked in on me.

I opened my missed calls. All of them were Jada's except

one from Matthew. He'd called this morning, before I'd woken up on the couch with Zayne...

I saw the way he looked at you yesterday.

"Stop it," I whispered. My thumb hovered over Jada's name. I missed her. I needed to talk to her. I owed her a return call and then some. I started to tap her name, but my stomach dropped so far I thought I might dry heave. I was being ridiculous. I needed to talk to her, but I wasn't ready.

Tapping the text app, I typed a quick message and hit Send before I could chicken out. I wasn't even sure what I'd said, other than I was sorry that I'd been out of contact and I'd call her soon. I turned the phone to silent like the coward I was before slipping it back into my pocket.

I looked up and noticed an elderly couple ambling along, leaning on one another for support. The sun had broken through the clouds, and bright rays of light filtered through tree branches, seeming to follow the couple. They made their way to a bench across from mine, their gray hair nearly white in the sunlight. The old man sat first, hand still clutching a cane as he gazed to his left while the woman remained standing. I thought she might be speaking to him, but he was still staring away. Maybe he was hard of hearing? Or maybe—

The woman's form flickered and then stabilized. I squinted, realizing the glow around her wasn't due to the sunlight.

She was a spirit.

Possibly the man's deceased wife, and she was right next to him—she had helped him to the bench—and he had no idea she was there. A suspicious wetness gathered in my eyes. I'd never seen anything so sad and so beautiful. I started to rise just as the spirit turned toward me. Although I couldn't make out her face, I knew she was aware of me. Spirits always were. I could help her—help them both—if that was what she wanted. She must have a mes—

A chill tiptoed over the nape of my neck and settled between my shoulders. Twisting, I scanned the area behind me, but there was nothing but grass and trees. No one stood there like a creeper, but the feeling remained and it reminded me of what I'd felt in the zombie building.

I looked back at the couple. The spirit was gone, and the old man was still staring into the distance, seeming unaware of just about everything. I shifted on the bench, unable to shake the strange shivery sensation. Muscles along my spine stiffened.

I didn't just feel watched. I felt watched like a field mouse being eyed by a hawk. Becoming hyperaware, I inched one hand closer to one of my daggers. Something was near me.

My fingers drifted over the handle…and then the iciness vanished and the feeling of being watched with it.

What in the Hell?

I looked around again. Nothing had changed. In front of me, the old man stood and began shuffling down the path, relying on his cane instead of his wife.

By the time I felt the warm ball in my chest pulse brightly, I had no explanation of what I had felt. Zayne must've driven like a bat out of Hell, because I didn't think thirty minutes had passed. I sat straighter, looking toward the bridge. I squinted, but things were just a fuzzy blur. Zayne had to be close. I could feel his presence—

My head jerked the other way, and under one of the dazzling streams of light, Zayne strode forward, his golden hair taking on a halo effect in the sunlight.

In human form, he looked more like an angel than I did. Nearly a carbon copy of the battle angels in the paintings on the ceiling of the Great Hall back in the Community. It had been a long time since I'd been able to see them in any detail, but my memories were clear. Mom and I used to sit under them, and she'd make up silly stories, giving them names like Steve and Bill.

While I couldn't see his eyes since they were shielded behind silver sunglasses, I could feel his gaze on me.

I know the way he looked at Layla.

A vastly different kind of shiver curled down my spine. *Stop it.* My heart rate kicked up as his steps slowed. Two women jogging past nearly tripped over their own feet when they got an eyeful of Zayne. A smile tugged at my lips. I couldn't blame them for that.

"Hey." Zayne spoke first, stopping in front of me. I took a deep breath, catching his wintermint scent.

I waved at him. "Hi."

His lips twitched. "You must be exhausted."

It took me a moment to realize what he meant. "I'm not that tired. It was a good walk."

"Bet you burned a whole lot of calories." His hands were shoved into the pockets of his jeans. "With all that walking."

"I'm starving." That was the first truth I'd spoken. "And I'm sure that's a surprise."

He chuckled. "Not at all— Wait." His head cocked. "Where are your sunglasses? The sun has to be killing your eyes."

Oh, man, he'd noticed. Half of me was all warm and fuzzy that he'd noticed and was worried. The other part wished he hadn't, because how I was going to explain this? "I, um, they fell off when I was crossing a street. I had to run, and they slipped off…" That sounded sort of believable. "By the time I realized they'd fallen, they were crushed and dead."

"Damn. You got another pair at home?"

I nodded.

"Wish you'd said something. I would've grabbed them." He reached up and pulled off his own sunglasses. "Here. Take these."

Surprise flickered through me. "Thank you, but what about you?"

"My eyes will be fine. Yours won't." He held them out. "Take the sunglasses. Please."

Feeling like a goober, I slid them on. I blinked, immediately seeing and feeling the difference even though they were nowhere near as dark as mine. "Thank you."

"Can I sit?"

I nodded, wondering why he felt the need to ask.

Pulling his hands from his pockets, he sat beside me, close enough that his thigh touched mine.

It was different.

I hated myself, and I hated Roth for putting these thoughts in my head. "Thank you for coming to get me."

"No problem." He shifted, stretching out his legs as he tipped his chin back. The sun seemed to lovingly caress his face. "I was surprised to hear you made it all the way here. Been forever since I've been to this park or the zoo."

"The zoo." I tapped my feet. "I like animals. Thought

about finding the entrance but I had no idea if it cost money or anything. I probably could've looked that up, but…" I shrugged. "I like this place, too. You know what's weird?" I rambled on.

"What?" Lowering his chin, he looked at me.

Having his full attention made me feel guilty and dizzy and hopeful…and bitter. I cast my gaze to the ground. "I haven't felt a demon since I've been here."

"It's because of the zoo."

"What?" My attention jerked back to him. I hadn't expected an actual answer.

"The animals can sense them, especially the large cats. They go crazy when demons get near them," he answered. "It's rare you'll find a demon around here."

"Huh." Then what I'd felt definitely might not have been a demon. Then again, Roth claimed to like the park. "I guess the zoo is a safe place."

"Safer than most at least, even a church."

Which was all kinds of messed up, as a lot of demons could cross hallowed ground. "So, I…felt something while I was here," I said, deciding that if I wasn't going to tell him about Faye, I should tell him about this. "Something weird. Like a coldness where I'd normally feel the presence of a demon. Just like that, actually, but cold instead of hot. I felt it once before."

His gaze searched my face. "When we were at the abandoned building? You asked me if I felt something when we were there."

"Yeah, that's when I felt it before. Both times, nothing seemed to be there. I don't know what it is." I lifted my shoulders. "It feels like when I accidentally walk through a ghost or a spirit, except this is localized to one area."

Zayne's brows lifted. "You mean…a cold spot? Those things are real?"

I laughed softly. "They are."

He looked away with a quick shift of his head.

"You're now worried you've been walking through ghosts? Maybe even Peanut." I bumped my shoulder into his. "Don't worry. People walk through ghosts, like, all the time. It's as weird for the ghost as it is for you."

"Not sure knowing that makes me feel better."

I grinned. "Anyway, I don't know if it's just a new ghosty feeling or something else."

"You think it's a bad thing?"

The fact that he was deferring to me made me like him even more, and I didn't need to like him any more than I already did. "Nothing bad has happened when I've felt it— well, I felt it before the whole zombie-horde thing, but I don't know if the two are related or not. Nothing happened now, other than me being creeped out a little."

"It could be related, though. Definitely something to keep an eye on." He looked at me. "So…"

I waited. "So what?"

"Are you really okay?"

Whatever relaxation I'd been feeling belly flopped out a window. "Yeah, of course. Why wouldn't I be?"

"Well…" He sat forward, dropping his clasped hands between his knees, and I tensed to the point I thought my bones would break. "You're out here, by yourself, sitting in a park."

"Is there something wrong with that?" I crossed one leg over the other as I leaned back.

"No. But I know you've… A lot has happened, and you haven't done it before."

"And you haven't left me alone in the middle of the day for an extended period of time before," I pointed out. "You had stuff to do, and I had laundry combined with a singing, dancing Peanut."

He coughed out a dry laugh. "That actually sounds like something to see."

"It's not. Trust me," I assured him. "A lot has happened, but I'm okay." That was the truth. For the most part. "And it was you who lost someone last night. Not me."

"Just because I lost someone doesn't zero out what you went through, Trin." His voice was quiet, too quiet.

The whole time I'd worried about what I was going to tell Zayne to hide what I'd done, I hadn't considered that he'd think my walk in the park had something to do with… Misha and everything. "I just wanted to get out. You know? I wanted to see the city during the daytime," I lied. Well, it was a partial lie. I did want to see the city during the day. "And I thought today was a good day, since you were busy."

"Hell." Zayne dragged a hand through his hair. "I didn't even think about that."

"Think about what?"

"That you'd want to do that." He looked over his shoulder at me. "Do something normal during the day instead of just eat and train."

"Hey, those are two of my favorite pastimes," I joked. "And training is important. More so than seeing the city."

Zayne didn't smile as he sat back, twisting toward me. "There's nothing more important than seeing the city."

I tilted my head as I raised my brows above the sunglasses.

"The city is always going to be here, Zayne. It's not that important."

His gaze met mine. "But your vision won't be."

The next breath I took got stuck.

"I know you're not going to lose your eyesight tomorrow and maybe not even next year, but why wait and take that chance?"

I was struck silent.

He glanced at the sky. "Since we'll run out of daylight in a couple of hours, let's grab something to eat and do an early patrol, so we don't get back too late. Tomorrow I'll show you all that I know. Make a whole day of it."

A wild mess of emotions buffeted me from every side. "But...but we need to be out there as long as we can tonight. The Harbinger—"

"—isn't as important as you."

I gaped at him. "It's extremely more important than me, and you, and my eyeballs and everything. It's killing Wardens and demons. We need to find it and stop it before it moves on to killing humans." I kept my voice low. "That's the only thing that's important."

"Nah." He shook his head. "It's not. You, and you getting to see the city, is a Hell of a lot more important."

My heart stuttered as the mess of emotion swirled even more. I stared at him, realizing that no one had ever put *me* before my duty. Yes, my life was valued and constantly placed above others, but no one ever put me before what I was designed to do, and that always made me feel like I wasn't a person but a thing. A weapon. I knew that no one meant to do that, especially not Thierry, Matthew or my mom, but training had always come first. Knowing that I'd one day be called upon by my father had always been the future—the only future. But not to Zayne.

It was so strange to hear a Warden say what he was saying. Wardens were born to fight evil and to mate so that they could procreate. Sure, they had more of a life than me, but they were also strictly duty-bond.

I wanted to hug him. I wanted to kiss him. I also wanted to punch him, because he wasn't being remotely helpful in keeping the ZAYNE file cabinet door closed. It was almost like he was yanking on it! And he knew better than to do that.

"You make this so hard," I muttered.

"Make what so hard?"

Irritated and charmed, and annoyed because I was charmed, I glared at him. "Not liking you," I admitted.

Zayne's lips tipped up and a wide, beautiful smile appeared, stealing my breath again.

My eyes narrowed as I crossed my arms. "I don't know why you're smiling."

"Maybe because…" He rose, extending his hand toward me. "Maybe because I'm not trying to make it easy, Trin."

18

Grabbing a bite to eat turned into a legitimate sit-down dinner at a steak house we'd walked by many times on patrol, much to my surprise.

Based on the amount of men in dark suits and women in skirts and slacks who were enjoying their dinners, it was the kind of place that had a dress code as fine as the cuts of steaks. Which Zayne in his jeans and me in my loose-fitted T-shirt were totally violating, but that was overlooked the moment the hostess laid eyes on Zayne. I didn't even think the young woman even knew I was there.

I also didn't think the waitress, who was old enough to be *my mother*, realized that Zayne wasn't dining alone.

But who cared? Not me, with my belly full of juicy red meat, grilled asparagus and truffle fries. Not when seconds ticked into minutes that turned into hours while we talked about *human* things. No Harbinger. No demons. No duty. That all faded into the background.

I learned that we had the same tastes in music. He was an oldies fan, like me, and we agreed that half of what was played on the radio now was nowhere near as good as the music that had come out between the '80s and the early 2000s.

While I'd chowed down on the thickest rib eye I'd ever seen and Zayne had meticulously eaten a lean filet, I discovered he'd never watched a single episode of *Game of Thrones*, something I was determined to rectify as soon as possible. I explained how I'd recently became obsessed with older '90s sitcoms like *Fresh Prince* and *Step by Step*. His favorite movie turned out to be *Jurassic Park*, randomly enough. I admitted that I didn't have a favorite movie and couldn't understand how anyone could pick just one, which led to a heated discussion.

We did not have the same tastes in movies or TV.

"I bet you could quote all five hundred of the *Fast and Furious* movies," I said, toying with the hem of my shirt. "By heart."

Zayne chuckled as the flame of the votive candle danced. "'Look, I'm one of those boys that appreciates a fine body, regardless of the make.'"

I blinked. "Come again?"

He grinned as he leaned forward, resting his forearms on the table. "It's a quote from *The Fast and the Furious*. The first one, and just so you know, I stopped on *Furious 7*."

"There's seven of them?"

His eyes widened. "There are more than seven, you deprived young lady."

I snorted as I leaned back. "Action movies aren't my thing."

"What is?"

I didn't have to think about that. "I'm a sucker for funny horror movies."

"*Funny* horror movies? Sounds like an oxymoron."

"Not really. There're a lot of them that are scary and gross and actually pretty hilarious. Like the old *Scream* movies— they were clever and funny. So was *Cabin in the Woods*."

Zayne rolled his eyes. "*Clever* and *horror* also sounds like an oxymoron."

My mouth dropped open. "I don't think we can be friends any longer."

He laughed as he picked up his glass of water and then took a drink. "Just saying."

"And you think action movies are clever?" I challenged.

"Nope. Most are pretty mind-numbing." He placed his glass down. "Unlike you, I acknowledge the inherent flaws in things I like."

Now I was rolling my eyes. "And unlike you, I have good taste."

Zayne smiled at me, and my stupid breath caught as his gaze snared mine. My chest felt as full as my stomach as we stared at each other over the flickering candle. He bit down on his lower lip, dragging his teeth over the flesh, and my toes curled inside my boots.

I'm not trying to make it easy.

Those were his words—words that couldn't mean what I thought they did—but the longer he held my stare, the more uncertain I became. The air was chilly in here, but my skin felt too warm. My pulse was staccato, and while there was a small part of me that felt silly, like we were playing pretend at being normal for a few hours, I was having the best night I could remember in a long time—and we still had tomorrow. A day of sightseeing and just...hanging out. I was so excited for it that I wanted to fast-forward time as well as press Pause to actually savor the anticipation. Sort of like how I always enjoyed Christmas Eve over Christmas. It was the buildup, the excitement and wonder of what was to come.

A feminine throat cleared, and I jerked my gaze from Zayne's to the source. It was the waitress. What was her name? Daisy? Dolly? Her loose blond hair looked super glossy and bouncy—and quite different from the ponytail she'd been rocking when we first walked in.

Zayne looked up with a smile. "Have we worn out our welcome yet?"

The normal answer should've been yes. We'd been here too long and hadn't ordered dessert. We hadn't even looked at the dessert menu.

That was, of course, not the answer.

"Of course not, honey." The woman clasped her hands together, creating a rather deep display of impressive cleavage. "You're more than welcome to stay as long as you like. I just wanted to make sure there wasn't anything else you needed."

"I'm fine." Zayne looked over at me. "Trin?"

I glanced at my half-filled Coke and shook my head.

"We're good." Zayne glanced to where his phone sat on the table. It had been lighting up every so often, and I'd wondered who was texting him. He'd responded once. "Actually, we should get the check." His gaze found its way back to me. "Unless you want dessert?"

"God." I laughed. "If I did, the next stop will be Nap Town, population me."

He gave me a lopsided grin. "Just the check, please."

As the waitress hurried off, I cocked an eyebrow, and Zayne stared at me like he had no idea why I was looking at him. Could he be that oblivious? "What time is it?"

"Almost nine," he answered.

"*What?*" I exclaimed. We hadn't come straight here from the park; we'd gone back to the apartment, because Zayne had needed to run down to the office manager or something, but we'd been here for almost three hours.

Zayne sat back, lifting his shoulder. "Time doesn't exist when you're enjoying yourself."

That was true.

He gave a curt shake of his head. "You know, I lied to you."

My brows lifted. "About what?"

"Remember when you asked me if I'd ever wanted to be something other than a Warden?" he asked, and I nodded. "I don't know why I started thinking about that, but I didn't tell you the truth. I think I lied because I was caught so off guard by the question."

I remembered that he'd said no one had asked him that before, and I was guessing that even meant Layla. "What was it?"

Zayne nodded. "When I was a kid, I… I wanted to be a doctor." He turned his head, and I would've sworn on my life that his cheeks were pink. "A trauma doctor."

"A trauma doctor? Wow." I couldn't help myself. "That's a great profession for egotistical personalities."

He laughed that laugh of his, making me grin like a fool. "Are you calling me an egomaniac?"

"Never," I teased. "What made you want to be a doctor?"

"I don't know. Actually, I do." He shoved a hand through

his hair. "Every Saturday morning, my father used to take me to this ice cream shop in the city. It's one of those old-style parlors that looks like something out of a different era, and it was a tradition that I ended up carrying on with Layla."

Expecting to feel a familiar surge of jealousy, I was surprised when all I felt was a twinge of sadness. Not because of Layla. Not because that could've—should've—been me, but because Misha and I had had our little rituals, too.

"Anyway, one time when I was there with my father, a woman ran in carrying a boy who'd been hit by a car. Blood was everywhere, and nobody moved as the kid's mother screamed for help. Even Dad had frozen. Can you imagine that? A Warden like him, rendered incapable by an unexpected human accident?"

"No," I whispered, though I couldn't imagine what I would have done, either.

"And then this woman stepped out of somewhere in the parlor and just took over. No fear of the blood or that she was going to do something wrong. She knew to keep the boy's head and neck immobile and was able to keep that kid's heart beating until paramedics showed up. I was about six or maybe seven, and I was fascinated. I overheard her tell the paramedics she was a doctor before she started talking in medical jargon that sounded like a different language."

He leaned toward me, pale eyes intense. "I have no idea if that kid survived, but all I could think was how amazing the woman was. I wanted to be that random person in the crowd who could step up and save a life. So, I wanted to be a doctor."

"Did you ever tell your father that?"

"No." He laughed under his breath as he reached for his

glass but didn't lift it to his mouth. "There'd be no point. You know that. I was raised and groomed to take... Yeah, well, you know that story. It's not like he'd have laughed or gotten mad. Knowing him, he would've picked up medical textbooks for me to read. But I knew that wasn't why I was here."

I nodded slowly, understanding that what he meant by *here* was not a place so much as a purpose. "You know, you might not have become a doctor, but you are that person."

His brows knitted in confusion.

"That random person in the crowd who can step in and save someone's life," I explained, finding myself leaning toward him. "You've done that before. Probably more times than you can count. You're not a doctor, but you *are* that person."

Zayne stared at me for so long that I started to worry I'd said the wrong thing.

"Are you okay?" I asked.

"Always," he murmured, and then he caught that lower lip of his again. "I just never looked at it that way."

"Look at me." I smiled. "Being all useful and stuff, showing you a whole new way of thinking."

"You're always helpful." Thick lashes lifted, and I felt pierced to the core by his stare. "And you've already been showing me a new way of thinking."

I opened my mouth, to say what, I had no idea, but Zayne shifted topics. "Been thinking about our living arrangements these last couple of days," he said. "We can't stay there, at least not in that apartment. We need something with two bedrooms, two baths. That's one of the things I was taking care of today. Met with the property manager to see if they have anything open."

Looking for a bigger place made sense. Zayne couldn't keep sleeping on the couch, and while the morning schedule was working, it still was a bit of a pain. But I was weirdly caught off guard, because he hadn't broached the idea with me.

He ran a finger along the base of the candle. "The rental contracts at the building are month to month, so if we move, we're not stuck."

I was nodding, because that also made sense. He and I, as long as I lived and so did he, were a permanent thing. A forever thing. And it was smart and safer for us to live together. That was why Misha and I had lived in the same house back in the Community.

I had no idea why I was acting as if he was speaking a language I didn't understand.

Giving my head a good shake, I was relieved to find common sense had returned to me. "Is there a place open?"

"There are two, but one needs extensive remodeling, and that concerns me considering the building is new. Who knows what the previous tenant did to the place."

Immediately my mind went to a murder scene that required biohazard cleanup…which was a sure indication there was something wrong with me. "What about the other place?"

"It's currently under contingency, but the people haven't signed the lease yet, so maybe they'll back out. If they do, it's ours."

"Ours?" I let out a nervous laugh. "Then that means I want to help with rent. I have money now." I paused, still seeing the zeros and not quite believing it. "I need to pay my way."

"If that's what you want, that's what we'll do."

I smiled and nodded again, no longer feeling like a total freeloader. But then something else occurred to me, and my smile faded. I thought about what he'd said the night before, about how his apartment was just a place to rest his head. "You're really not planning to move back in with your clan, ever?"

Zayne shook his head. "No."

"Is it because of me and the bond?"

"The moment I moved out, I knew I wasn't coming back. Who I was when I lived there, within those walls, under that roof and with my clan?" he said. "I'm not him anymore, and that has nothing to do with being your Protector."

I mulled that over. "Because of your father and…and what happened with Layla?"

"Yeah, because of that, but there are also too many things I don't agree with to be a part of them like I was before. And they know that. Many of them don't trust me anymore, and obviously, I don't trust a lot of them, either. Me leaving was the best answer."

He was talking about his stance on demons. I could see how that would drive a major wedge between him and the other Wardens, even though Nicolai seemed more open-minded.

Well, Nicolai didn't spit and do the sign of the Holy Cross when Roth's name was brought up. Not sure if that meant he had a different stance on demons.

I also knew, beyond a doubt, that even though Zayne had basically ostracized himself from the clan and had done so the moment he'd stood with Roth and Layla, he'd still have any of those Wardens' backs.

Dolly Daisy the waitress returned with the check. Her body angled toward Zayne, her back to me as she propped a hip against the table.

I made a face at Zayne that he either didn't see or ignored.

"Take as long as you want." She placed the bill folder on the table, which Zayne grabbed immediately, opening it. "And if you need anything, you just let me know. I'll be happy to help you."

Zayne saw it the moment I did. Even I couldn't mistake what rested on the bill. A card with a number written on it in large bubbly handwriting, next to a name I couldn't read. The only thing missing was the imprint of her never-fading bright red lips.

Holy flying gargoyles everywhere, I couldn't believe what I'd witnessed.

The waitress just gave him her number in front of me! For a moment I was simply stunned, and I wanted to laugh, except I was—well, I was offended. Granted, this woman might be old enough to have legit birthed me, but she looked damn good for her age, and from what I could tell of her makeup, it was on point. The grown-ass woman was a stunner, but even if she thought I was yesterday's trash, that was a bold move.

I reacted without thinking—without waiting to see what Zayne's response would be. Impulsivity, as per usual, got the best of me.

"Hi," I said loudly. "Daisy? Dolly?"

The woman turned to me, eyebrow raised quizzically. "My name is Debbie, sweetie. Did you need anything?"

"Well, my name is not sweetie." I smiled at her. "Did you just give him your phone number?"

Her mouth opened.

"With me sitting right here, on a date with him?" I continued. The woman's tanned cheeks deepened to a rosy color while Zayne emanated a strange choking sound. She opened her mouth. "I'm all about ra-ra women empowerment, embracing our sexual needs and all that good stuff, but try respecting your fellow sisters first and that was not at all respectful."

Debbie stood there, arms lowering to her sides. I looked at Zayne. One hand was curved over his mouth as he stared at the table.

"You want to add something to the conversation?" I paused, eyes narrowing. *"Honey?"*

"Oh, no. I think you've just about covered it." He lowered his hand and looked up, eyes dancing. "You can keep the number. I'm not going to need it."

Debbie didn't pick up her card. She muttered, "Excuse me," under her breath and hurried off as fast as her heels would carry her.

"Well," Zayne said, drawing my attention. "I doubt she'll do that again."

"Probably not." Reaching across the table, I picked up the card. "You want it?"

"No." He laughed quietly.

"You sure?" I tossed the card to his side of the table. "I can't believe she did that. She didn't know who I was. If I was your girlfriend or not."

"Maybe she thought you were my friend," he said, sending me a long sideways look. "Or maybe my sister?"

I gaped at him. "Seriously?"

He laughed. "I'm kidding."

My eyes narrowed once more. "Ha. Ha."

"Seriously, though, it was rude, and I was about to point that out before you did in such a cheeky manner." Zayne leaned over and pulled out a slim wallet.

"I have money." I reached for the wad of cash I'd grabbed before we left the apartment. "I can pay—"

"I got this." He dropped several bills, one of them fairly large.

"I'm already living in your place, eating your food and I stole your—"

"I got it, Trin." He closed the bill folder. "That's what I do on a date."

I about choked on my own spit. Thank God I hadn't taken a drink. "A date?"

Zayne nodded, pushing the folder to the end of the table with a long finger. "Isn't that what we're on?"

Oh my God.

My face burned brighter than a thousand suns. "Look, I didn't say that to Dolly—"

"Debbie," he corrected.

"—because I thought we were on a date. I was just proving a point."

"I know."

"And it's not like I think that's what this is about." I was going to die. Right here. Wither up in embarrassment. "I didn't say that to get you to pay."

"I know," he repeated, standing. "But if it walks like a duck and quacks like a duck, it must be a duck."

"What?" I scrambled to my feet.

"This feels like a date and looks like one." He waited for me to make it around the table. "So, maybe it is a date."

"It's not a date," I hissed. My gaze bounced from him to the dimly lit narrow, convoluted spaces between the tables.

"Why not?" He walked a bit in front of me.

"Because we can't date," I told him, my hip bumping into the edge of the table. Cheeks flaming even more, I hastily apologized to the people whose table I'd jarred. "I'm so sorry."

Zayne turned and quickly assessed the situation. Without saying a word, he placed his hands on my shoulders, guiding me so that I was front of him. We took a couple of steps before he spoke again. "You know I'm teasing you, right?"

I opened my mouth and then closed it. Of course he was joking. And of course I was an idiot. "I hate you."

Chuckling, he squeezed my shoulders. "You wish."

He had no idea how true that was.

I kept my mouth shut as he steered me out of the packed restaurant and into the balmy night air. I took a second to scan our surroundings. There was an old church across the street and several more restaurants and shops.

Staying close to the buildings as we walked, I glanced at Zayne. That stupid, sexy grin was plastered to his face. Nervous energy buzzed through me. "I can't believe we were in there as long as we were. We should've been out here by now."

"Possibly, but we're allowed to have lives," he replied, but my father would probably disagree with that. "Speaking of having a life, what are some places you want to see tomorrow?"

"Um… I don't know." I stepped around a guy on his phone and realized I hadn't checked my own since I'd texted Jada. "I'd like to see the dinosaurs."

"That's in the natural history museum. Has a lot of cool stuff in it. Lots of fossils and artifacts. Even has a butterfly pavilion."

That sounded pretty. "And I would like to check out the Holocaust museum. Is that near the other one?"

"Yeah, about a fifteen-minute walk. Any place else?"

I nodded. "The African American museum—oh, and the one with the rockets and stuff."

"The Air and Space Museum."

"Yeah, that. And I'd like to see some of the memorials," I went on. "Probably the Washington Monument, too."

"Sounds like we'll make a day at the National Mall then."

"Is that okay?" I glanced at him. "I mean, you've probably seen this stuff a million times."

"It's perfect, and actually, I've only been to some of them a couple of times and it's been a while," he explained as he scanned the streets. "It's weird when you live here your whole life. You want to check the stuff out, but since you can go anytime, you put it off."

I guessed that made sense. "How is the, um, the lighting in the museums?"

"Some of them are pretty bright, so they might be a little harsh on your eyes, and others are dark. If you have any problems in any of them, let me know."

Relieved, I nodded. I hated wearing sunglasses inside because I worried, stupidly, what other people thought when they saw me. Like I was too cool or something. And while I knew I shouldn't care what random strangers thought, it still made me uncomfortable. I also worried whether I'd be able to see some of the exhibits if I couldn't get close, but I hoped

I could. Even if I could see only half of them, it would still be amazing and—

Zayne cursed. That was the only warning. One second I was walking, and the next I was off my feet.

19

The street became a blur as Zayne moved alarmingly fast. I heard a shout as he turned and spun us away from an eruption of angry voices where the sound of screeching metal was followed by the smack of flesh into something solid. The streetlights dimmed as he stepped into an alley, and then my back was pressed against a wall as Zayne caged me in, blocking my body with his. Whoops of laughter and the tinny sound of metal wheels on cement drowned out the chaos of my pounding heart.

"What in the world?" I lifted my head and saw the outline of Zayne's profile behind his hair. I felt the low buzz of a nearby demon, but that was normal for DC.

"Kids on skateboards and Rollerblades coming out of this alley like idiots with a death wish. One of them slammed into a guy getting out of a cab."

Well, that explained the ongoing shouting.

Zayne's tone was hard. "They're going to either hurt themselves or really hurt someone else, hopefully the former. Assholes."

"I didn't even…" My gaze dropped from his profile to where my hands rested on his chest. "I didn't see them."

"I know. They were coming from the side, too fast for you to see." He looked down at me. "It was like a gang of skateboarders."

"Scary."

His face was shadowed, but I saw a faint grin appear. "They're probably going to cause more headaches and damage than a horde of Fiends."

"Probably." My heart had slowed, but it was still pounding, and that had nothing to do with the skateboard gang. There was only an inch or so separating us. I drew in a shallow breath. "Then again, humans probably do more damage than most demons."

"True." His chin dipped.

I took another breath, a bigger one, and my chest brushed his. An elicit shiver danced over my skin. Had he moved closer? It was probably time to put some distance between us. I didn't say that, though. I also didn't move away. My hands remained where they'd landed, and I could feel each breath he took, long and slow, and not all that steady.

"Thank you." My voice sounded strange to my own ears. Thicker. Richer.

"For what?"

I let my head fall back against the wall as I searched his expression in the shadows. "For dinner. I didn't thank you. So, thank you."

"You having a good time was thanks enough."

My heart gave a happy little skip. "You always say the right things."

"I say what I'm thinking. I don't know if it's right or wrong." Zayne had moved closer as he spoke. His thighs touched mine. His hips met my stomach, and I knew he was picking up on what I was feeling. Warmth blasted my cheeks, but a different type of heat infused my skin as a low rumble radiated from deep within Zayne's chest. There wasn't even a centimeter between our bodies, and I felt that sound in every part of my being. My fingers dug into his shirt as whatever air I managed to get into my lungs slowly leaked out.

"Trin," he said, my name a raspy low growl of warning.

Of *wanting*.

I slid my fingers down his chest, stopping on his taut stomach. *Why not?* That was the question cycling through my thoughts. Why couldn't I stretch up and take what I wanted, what I suspected he wanted, too? In a physical sense, I knew he did. There was no denying that we were attracted to one another. That didn't mean Roth was right. That he looked at me differently or that…that I loved him. It just meant that I wanted him.

No one had explained why a relationship was forbidden between a Trueborn and their Protector. Maybe the rule had made sense when there were more Trueborns, but now there was only me, and I couldn't fathom why it would be a big deal.

I'd finally found someone that I liked—a lot—someone I was interested in beyond the whole physical attraction, and I couldn't have him.

Life was unfair and the heart was cruel, wasn't it?

Zayne's breath danced along my cheek, and all I would need to do was turn my head just the slightest bit to the left and our mouths would be lined up. He wasn't letting me go or putting distance between us, and he knew the rules. Maybe he was thinking the same thing I was?

What harm could a kiss bring?

Just one?

I turned my head. Zayne's lips grazed the line of my cheek, coming within an inch of the corner of my mouth. Every nerve in my body seemed to fire at once, and something heavier, spicier, invaded my senses, slipping from that warm ball of light in my chest.

Zayne.

He was the thick heaviness in my chest, next to my heart, and it was mixing with the same feeling that had settled low in my stomach.

God, it really was coming from him. He *was* feeling what I was feeling. There was something between us, more than just a bond between Protector and Trueborn, and whatever it was made me feel hot and dizzy, like I'd been sitting in the sun all day.

I didn't see him move, but I didn't flinch when his fingers brushed my cheek, his thumb on my jaw. He tilted my head back even farther. Anticipation danced along my skin. In that moment, I wanted a kiss as badly as I needed the air I breathed. Every part of me was in agreement. I wanted to feel his lips against mine once again. I wanted to taste his breath on the tip of my tongue. I wanted *so very much.*

There was a wicked little voice in the back of my head that

dared me to provoke the frustration and need I felt swirling inside him, to push the line between us as far as I could.

"Whatever you're thinking, stop." Zayne's voice sounded like it was full of gravel.

"Back off, then."

He didn't back off.

And I didn't stop thinking about how kissing him felt like lightning or how it felt to be in his embrace, skin against skin. My muscles turned to liquid in a way that was as pleasant as it was painful.

Zayne's forehead dropped to mine and I felt his chest expand with his next ragged breath. "Behave."

The corners of my lips tugged up. "I'm trying to."

"You're not trying hard enough."

My eyes drifted shut as my hips arched off the wall and then my breath hitched when his other hand curved around one hip. "You're not trying, either."

"You're right," he said. "I'm not trying, and I should be. We should be smarter than this."

"Being smart is overrated," I muttered.

He chuckled. "We're supposed to be patrolling. Hunting the Harbinger. Not this."

This.

Whatever *this* was.

"Agreed," I admitted. "But you started this. Not me."

"I don't know about that."

"You cannot put this on me," I argued. "Not when you're the one holding me. This is your fault."

"I can feel you." His voice was just a whisper but it stretched my nerves tight. "The heat. The want. I can feel you. I find it hard to resist."

My mouth dried. "And I can feel you. Did you think about that? Because *I* find it hard to resist."

"Okay." His warm breath made another pass over my lips. "How about we're mutually at fault."

"More like sixty percent your fault and forty percent mine but whatever."

His chuckle was a rasping, seductive sound. "We need to get our heads in the game."

We did.

And what Zayne had said a few seconds ago was right. Not the *mutually at fault* thing, but about us not being smart. We had no idea what the consequences would be if we were to be together, but I knew it couldn't be anything warm and fuzzy. The rule had been created by the archangels, the highest order and most powerful of all angelic beings. They even oversaw the Alphas, who were responsible for communicating with the Wardens.

Not only were archangels notoriously strict and old school, they were often of the Old Testament variety, meaning they operated by an eye for an eye, literally. God only knew what kind of penalty they would whip up, having eons of experience behind them when it came to doling out punishment like it was candy and every night was Halloween.

Fear spiked, leaving my skin chilled, and it wasn't for my own well-being. Considering how archangels often overdid things when it came to the punishment-fits-the-crime deal, they could hurt Zayne.

They could even kill him.

As fear turned my blood to slush, I thought of my father, of how unaffected he'd been by how Misha had turned out and by his demise. My heart tripped over itself. I doubted he'd step in if punishment were to be handed down, even with Zayne destined to be my Protector.

I was possibly overreacting about the whole killing-Zayne part. They needed me to find the Harbinger, and they needed me at peak performance to do so, and that meant they needed Zayne alive and whole, so maybe that meant we had the upper hand. Maybe—

A scream pierced through the distant hum of cars and people. We jerked apart, and I staggered away from the wall, turning toward the mouth of the alley. Another scream tore through the air, followed by shouts.

"What the Hell?" Zayne grabbed my hand. "Come on."

Zayne took off, and with him guiding the way, I was able to easily keep up as we made it onto the sidewalk and dodged clusters of people.

Another shout ratcheted up my adrenaline. Up ahead, a small crowd of people on the sidewalks spilled into the street and blocked traffic. Zayne's steps slowed as I struggled to see what was going on. The buzz at the nape of my neck told me there were demons around, but not close. So…human-on-human violence?

A flash of light caught my attention, followed by another. It took me a second to realize people were… They had their phones out and were taking pictures of something…

"Good God." Zayne's hand tightened and then released mine.

"What…?" I followed his gaze to the building everyone

was standing in front of as the distant whir of sirens drew closer.

The building was a church, one of the old stone ones, the same church I'd seen when we left the restaurant. Something hung from one of the steeples—something large with wings, but wait...not hanging. More like pinned.

Unease formed a lead ball in my stomach. I took an unsettled step forward and squinted. "What is it?"

Zayne growled low in his throat, causing the tiny hairs along the nape of my neck to rise. "It's a Warden."

20

Zayne shifted so fast I doubted anyone near us would realize the massive winged Warden had appeared human a second before.

"Stay here," he ordered, and for once, I didn't get my hackles up over the demand. Not when there was a dead Warden strung up on a church.

Not when we should have been patrolling instead of eating dinner in a nice restaurant and doing whatever it was we'd been doing in that alley. It took no leap of logic to conclude that, if we'd been doing what we were supposed to, we might've seen who had done this. We could've caught the Harbinger or whoever was responsible.

This was the second time a Warden had turned up dead where we'd just been.

With a rush of wind, Zayne's powerful wings lifted him into the air. Gasps followed as those in front of us wheeled around and craned their necks to watch Zayne fly toward the church. More lights burst from phones as he became nothing more than a blurry winged shape to me.

I knew that in the time it would take me to figure out how to spell *falafel*, pictures of the dead Warden would be plastered all over social media. What did they call it? Tragedy porn.

People were sick.

"Christ, he's huge," a nearby man exclaimed, awe filling his voice. "Man, I did not know they were that big."

"You never seen one?" another guy asked, and I turned and spotted two middle-aged men, both dressed in dark slacks and white dress shirts. Both had leather messenger-type bags slung over their shoulders and some sort of badge dangling from their necks. Office guys. Maybe they worked at the Capitol.

The guy with lighter hair shook his head. "Not up close like this."

"They're all big," the other guy answered, thumbing the phone he held. "Like wrestlers on steroids."

"Yeah, and someone tacked that big SOB up there like it's nothing. Freaking crucified the thing." The dark-haired man shook his head. "Let that sink in."

"Don't really want to, man."

I glanced to where Zayne was removing the Warden from the church and then back to the men. "Excuse me?" I said, and both faced me. "Did you guys see what happened to that Warden?"

"The one strung up there?" the fair-haired guy asked as flashing blue-and-red lights filled the sidewalks. The police were here. "No. We were just on our way to the Metro and someone screamed. People were pointing up at the church."

The other man shook his head. "Yeah, it was weird. It just *happened*. The thing appeared up there in the blink of an eye. Didn't see anything— Holy shit, there's another one. Look!"

My gaze followed to where he pointed. Against the cloudy night sky, the darker shape of another Warden headed toward Zayne and the church. Relief loosened some of the tension in the muscles of my neck. I had no idea who the deceased Warden was, but it had to be someone Zayne knew and possibly had grown up with or spent years with, like Greene. I was grateful he had backup, because I wasn't much help all wingless and standing on the sidewalk.

"Damn," the fair-haired man said again. "I can't get over how big those things are."

"They're not things," I snapped, earning dubious looks from the two men. "They're Wardens."

"Whatever," one of them muttered, and they both turned away from me and lifted their phones to take a picture.

It took a *lot* of restraint I didn't know I had to resist the urge to snatch the phones out of their hands and stomp on them. I figured I'd made enough poor life choices today to last me at least the next week. Drawing in a shallow breath, I scanned the crowd. Someone must have seen how that Warden got up there. Unless whoever had done it could move so fast that the human eye couldn't track them. Very few Upper Level demons were that powerful. Roth was, but was he even that fast? Able to crucify a Warden to a church on a busy street without being seen at all?

Once more, whatever had done this had been out here while we were patrolling—well, where we were supposed to be patrolling. It could be here right now, and we had no idea.

"Dammit," I muttered, frustration rising. Where was this—

The brush of icy fingers over the nape of my neck sent a shiver down my spine. Tiny hairs all over my body stood up as my breath hitched deep in my chest. It was *that* feeling again. I spun, scanning the people who stood near me, all of them looking up at the church. They all seemed human to me. No one suspicious.

Reaching back, I rubbed my fingers along the base of my neck. The skin was warm, but that chilled feeling was still there.

Wait.

One of them didn't look normal at all.

Near a parked white delivery truck, a woman's body was blinking in and out like poor reception on an old television. She was wearing a dark blue service uniform, and while I could see no visible injuries, her face held the pale gauntness of death. She was a ghost…and she was staring at something or someone.

The ghost faded out and then reappeared on the sidewalk, her body angled away from me. Surprise rippled through me. The ghost didn't know I was there, which was odd.

As I watched her drift through the onlookers as if she had a target, something occurred to me. I couldn't be sure the little old lady in the park had seen me earlier. She'd looked my way, but then I'd felt that coldness.

I stepped around people until I reached the edge of the onlookers. The ghost was only a few feet in front of me when her form began to flicker rapidly. I opened my mouth, fully prepared to look like I was talking to myself.

The ghost woman jerked, her wispy arms flailing, back

bowing as if an invisible string attached to her waist had been yanked hard. A second later, she blinked out of existence.

I drew up short. Ghosts and spirits both had an annoying habit of randomly disappearing. That wasn't breaking news, but the way her body had jerked, as if she'd been caught—

Something dark and large moved along the corners of my vision, snagging my attention. I turned but saw nothing but a brick wall. I stared, seconds passing without anything happening.

I had no idea if I'd seen something. It could have been a person, or a weird trick of light from a passing car, or the outcome of my mind trying to compensate for the gaps in my side vision. It could've even been a ghost or a spirit. Maybe that guy who'd followed me to Zayne's apartment. Or absolutely nothing. With my eyes, who knew?

But the icy awareness pressing on the nape of my neck had vanished, which made for a very strange…coincidence.

"Trin."

I whirled around. Zayne had shifted back into human form, which I knew he'd done beyond the prying eyes of humans. My gaze flickered over him. There were dark smudges splattered along the tattered remains of his shirt.

Blood. Warden's blood.

"Who was it?" I asked, shoving what had just happened aside.

His jaw was hard as he said, "Morgan. He transferred to our clan a year ago." His hand clenched something he was holding as he let out a low rumble of a growl that I really hoped no one around us heard. "New to the area, but well trained and more than capable of handling himself. Dez is taking him back to the compound."

A huge, terrible part of me was relieved to learn that it hadn't been Dez up there, but the relief was short-lived. I knew nothing of Morgan. He could have a family—a significant other and children. Even if he didn't, I knew there were others who would miss him, mourn him.

"I'm sorry." I swallowed hard as I lifted my gaze to Zayne's. "I'm so sorry."

He nodded and then stepped closer, lifting his hand. "This was what was used to impale him to the church."

Zayne opened his hand. Resting against his palm were two long, narrow spikes, definitely not of the normal garden variety. These glowed a faint luminous gold. I wasn't aware of any type of metal or stone that glowed like that.

"What are they?" I started to reach for them, but Zayne closed his hand around them.

"I have no idea," he answered, chest rising with a deep breath. "I've never seen anything like them before in my life."

I stood in one corner of Nicolai's office, trying to stay out of the way of the Wardens filing in and out. Several sent curious or suspicious glances in my direction once they realized I was there, tucked away like someone who didn't belong. Seeing a virtual stranger in the heart of the DC compound while they dealt with the loss of yet another Warden had to be disconcerting.

I'd learned from Jasmine, Dez's wife, that the Warden Morgan had been mated but had lost his wife in childbirth shortly before his transfer to the DC compound.

My gaze trailed to the spikes, resting in the center of Nicolai's desk, glowing softly. Now that was not something you saw every day.

"Whatever this metal is, it was able to kill Morgan with one puncture to the back of the head," Zayne was saying. "When we pulled it out, we could tell that it severed the brain stem internally."

I cringed. That had to have been…messy, and it was definitely shocking. Other than the claws and teeth of demons and Hellfire, I wasn't aware of any weapons that could easily puncture a Warden's skull.

"It has some kind of writing on it. I have no idea what language it is," Gideon said as he knelt eye level with the desk.

I'd seen Gideon briefly the night we'd returned here from the senator's house, but we'd never been officially introduced. I did know that he was the Wardens' resident tech and security specialist. Apparently he was also a scholar of sorts, because Zayne and Nicolai were staring at Gideon as if he'd admitted to collecting creepy porcelain dolls.

"What?" Gideon demanded, lifting the thicker end of the spike with a set of kitchen tongs. "I don't know every language in the world."

"That's a shocker," Zayne replied dryly. "I thought you knew everything."

"Well, this will be one for the record books." Gideon shook his head as he stared at the spike. "It seems similar to ancient Aramaic, but it's not the same."

My brows lifted. Ancient Aramaic? That was from one of the earliest known periods of written language and wasn't something one heard referenced often.

Nicolai, who was the youngest clan leader I'd ever heard about, dragged his thumb over the growth of russet-colored hair at his chin. For the first time since we'd showed up, he looked at me. Unlike the other Wardens, there was no suspicion in his gaze, but there was a wariness.

"I'm assuming you haven't seen a weapon like this?" Nicolai asked.

I shook my head. "Never."

He refocused on Gideon, finger still at his chin. "You think you can figure out what it says and where it possibly came from?"

Gideon nodded his dark head as he placed the spike back on the white cloth. "Might take a couple of days, but I should be able to."

"Good." Nicolai dropped his hand and crossed his arms. "Because I would sure like to know what kind of metal glows."

"Same," Zayne murmured. He cleared his throat. "I'm thinking Morgan was killed elsewhere and then transported to the church to be displayed. Just like Greene."

"None of the people on the streets saw what happened." I chimed in with useful information instead of being about as helpful as a houseplant. "I asked a few who were standing around, and they said he appeared on the church in the blink of an eye."

Gideon was staring at me curiously, probably wondering why I'd been out there on the streets alongside Zayne. Since he had no idea what I was, I wasn't surprised by his interest.

"No demon is that fast," Nicolai said. "Not even the most powerful Upper Level demons. Not even Roth."

At the mention of the Crown Prince of Hell, I stiffened.

God, for the last hour or so, I had actually forgotten about what Roth and I had done. Man, that now felt like a week ago, but how terrible did that make me? Weight settled on my shoulders.

"We've pretty much come to the conclusion that whatever this Harbinger is, it isn't a demon." Zayne glanced toward me. "We have no idea what could be behind this."

"Meaning we have no idea what we're hunting for," I added, inching out of my corner. "Greene was...left in an area where we'd just been, and the same tonight. I think the locations were chosen on purpose."

"What do you think?" Nicolai asked of Zayne while Gideon frowned.

"I think the same as Trinity." Zayne crossed his arms. "It's like it's taunting us."

"And neither of you saw anything?" Nicolai asked.

"We were having dinner at the restaurant across from the church, and then we were patrolling. We'd made it one block when we heard the screams."

Nicolai frowned. "Dinner?"

"That's what I said," replied Zayne.

Nicolai's jaw worked. "Was there *anything* either of you noticed that was abnormal?"

Zayne shook his head, but I thought about the sensation I'd felt and the ghost I'd seen. I had no idea if it was related to the Harbinger, but it was something.

I glanced at Gideon, unsure what I could say in front of him, and decided to go with the least amount of information as possible. "Well, I did see a ghost."

Gideon's head whipped toward me. "A ghost?"

Nodding, I found myself staring at Zayne. "It probably has nothing to do with the Harbinger, but the ghost was behaving weirdly."

"You see ghosts?" Gideon asked, speaking slowly.

"And spirits," Zayne answered, his arms unfolding as he angled his body toward me. "You didn't say anything about this earlier."

The tone of his voice pricked at my skin. "Well, we were kind of busy with getting back to the compound because there was a dead Warden to deal with."

"Hold up." Gideon stared at me. "You can see ghosts and spirits?"

"Yeah, it's not a big deal—"

"Not a big *deal*?" Gideon huffed out a dry laugh. "You do realize that means you have an angel perched on a limb of your family tree somewhere."

Yeah, there was one perched right on top of my family tree. He was an archangel, and his name was Michael, as in *the* Michael.

Somehow I managed to keep my face blank. It took an impressive effort, because usually my face didn't know how to not show what I was thinking. "So I've heard."

"Wow." Gideon looked at Nicolai, who appeared to be smiling...or grimacing. "I've never actually met someone who could see the dead. Man, you would've come in handy a few months back when we had a wraith running around in here. Would've saved all of us a world of trouble and..." He trailed off with a little shake of his head. "Definitely would've been helpful."

"How was the ghost acting?" Zayne cut in before I could question any of that.

"It didn't know I was there, which is weird. It was focused on something, but before I could figure out what, the ghost sort of jerked and then disappeared."

"Perhaps this ghost could sense the Harbinger," Nicolai surmised as he leaned against the side of his desk.

"It's possible," I said, mainly because anything was possible at this point. "Ghosts and spirits both have a habit of randomly disappearing, so it could be nothing, but…" But I wasn't sure if I could say what I'd also felt without having to explain it to Gideon.

Luckily Gideon was moving on. "By the way, still haven't found anything on where this school the senator plans to build is located, and I delved deep—deep-state-level deep. I'm still combing, but I'm wondering if land was purchased under a different name or company."

"And the senator hasn't been in the city since before the fire, when he was spotted with Bael," Nicolai reminded us. "His aides have been handling everything while he's dealing with an unexpected family emergency in his home state."

I snorted. "More like an unexpected demonic emergency."

Nicolai smiled. "Got some of us wondering if the senator is even still alive."

"Based on previous experience with demons like Bael, if the senator is no longer useful, then you can bet we'll hear about an untimely accident resulting in death," Zayne commented.

"I hope not." The three of them looked at me. "Well, he'd be a dead end then. Literally."

"Good point." Gideon carefully wrapped up the spikes. "I'll

tap into the street cameras and ones from nearby stores to see if they caught anything tonight. Hopefully they'll show us something. What might not have been visible to the human eye could've been captured on film."

"Like with ghosts?" I suggested.

Gideon nodded.

I grinned, thinking of how often people dismissed ghostly images on film as being a weird trick of the camera. I was willing to bet a case of root beer that people caught evidence of ghosts more often than they'd want to know.

"Let me know what you find," Zayne said. "Even if it's nothing."

Looking down at the bundle he held, Gideon nodded. "The one thing I can tell you is that these spikes weren't created by humans, and they're not something I've ever seen a demon use." He looked up. "Makes you wonder where they came from, doesn't it?"

21

The moment the door closed behind Gideon, I faced Nicolai and Zayne. "If humans didn't create those spikes and neither did demons, that doesn't leave a lot of options."

"Exactly," Zayne agreed, watching me.

Chest feeling strangely tight, I crossed my arms. There was one potential source I could think of—one that made no sense. "I've never seen angelic weapons before."

"I have. Both of us have," Zayne answered, glancing at Nicolai. "The Alphas carry swords. Not like yours. Yours is special."

Mine *was* super special.

"Alphas' swords appear to be some strange mixture of iron and gold," Nicolai explained. "At least, from what we've been able to see. None of us have actually held one."

"You know what's messed up?" I shifted my weight from foot to foot. "I'm part angel, and the only angel I've ever seen is my father, but you see the Alphas all the time."

"Yeah, well, none of us have seen an archangel," Nicolai replied.

"Except for me," Zayne reminded him.

"And doesn't that make you unique." Nicolai brushed a strand of shoulder-length brown hair back from his face as Zayne smirked. "I've never seen an angel carry anything like that, and besides, why would this Harbinger have something that was forged in Heaven?"

That was a good question. "Maybe it was stolen from an angel," I offered with a shrug. "I mean, if it's not of human or demon creation, then what does that leave? Aliens?"

Zayne's brows lifted. "Aliens *are* the next reasonable conclusion."

"Do you know of a race or species I'm not aware of but everyone else is?" I asked.

"Yes, everyone knows there's a whole other species out there and only you don't know." Amusement trickled through the bond, annoying me. Zayne's grin kicked up a notch. "It's more likely that it's an angelic weapon we've never seen before. And yes, I always have value to add."

Ugh.

What he said was more likely.

But...

My stomach dropped a little. "But that would mean that this Harbinger took it, and *that* would mean—"

"Aliens?" Zayne asked.

"I'm going to punch you. Hard," I said. "As I was saying, that would mean it was able to take out an angel. And what can do that?"

"Well, Roth's familiar ate an Alpha once, so killing angels

isn't unheard of," Zayne mused. "And yes, witnessing that was as disturbing as you might think."

The image of the snake that made anacondas look wimpy formed in my thoughts. Bambi was terrifying, but I remembered how happy she had been to see Roth. Like a very eager puppy, and she had...smiled at me.

For killing Faye.

"And it burned the other Alpha to death," Zayne went on. "Thumper turned that angel to nothing but ash in, like, a nanosecond."

I stared at Zayne. "You're not talking about Bambi, right?"

A ghost of a smile appeared. "Roth has several familiars. One of them is a dragon," he explained, and I remembered seeing the vibrant blue-and-gold tattoo on Roth. "Long story, but yeah, Thumper got a good meal that day."

"Wow," I whispered, wondering how Roth was still alive after that. "And you don't seem concerned about the fact that Roth's familiar killed two angels?"

Looking up, Zayne met my stare. "The Alphas were there to kill Layla."

"Oh." I averted my gaze. His lack of concern made sense, because that would probably be the only circumstance in which Zayne wouldn't care if angels were killed.

"I see where you're going with this," Nicolai said. "But we don't know all the facts yet to start panicking and operating on the idea that this Harbinger can defeat angels."

"I'm not panicking. I'm just pointing out the possibility that we might be up against something we've never seen before. *Not* an alien." I shot Zayne a look. "But definitely something that can take down the most powerful beings ever created."

"She has a point." Zayne picked up a small circular object from Nicolai's desk. "But we also don't know yet. These spikes could be something ancient that we've just never seen before. And even if the Harbinger managed to take a weapon of angelic origins, that doesn't mean the angel was defeated. These spikes could've been found. We need a lead."

"Perhaps you'll find one the next time you're having dinner," Nicolai suggested.

I blinked.

"What's that supposed to mean, Nic?" Zayne asked. "Because it better not mean what I think it does. We need to eat. That's what we were doing. And we can eat wherever and whenever we damn well want to."

Nicolai stared at Zayne for a long moment and then pushed off the desk. "We do have another pressing issue we need to discuss. Some of the others have started to ask questions about Trinity."

Tension radiated from Zayne to me through the bond, and I felt it shimmy over my skin. "And you told them it's none of their business," Zayne stated, the warning in his tone making every word sound like a verbal punch. "Right?"

I turned slowly to Zayne, brows rising. The clan leader position alone demanded respect, even if the actual leader hadn't earned it. Zayne knew that, and not because all Wardens knew that, but because his father had been the leader, and because Zayne should have been the clan leader now. The title was passed down to a male heir of age, and Zayne was of age.

He'd simply turned it down.

Nicolai's jaw hardened once more, and I fully expected him to remind Zayne who he was speaking to, but his expression smoothed out after several tense heartbeats. "I can tell them that all I want, but it doesn't change the fact they have questions." He sat behind the desk and shifted his gaze to me. "Keeping what you are a secret isn't easy. You're staying with Zayne and patrolling with him. Both of those things garner attention."

"I know." I rested my hands on the back of the chair. "But we need to keep it a secret."

"Have either of you thought about the fact that, at some point, one of the other Wardens will see you in action?" Nicolai questioned. "The moment they see you fight, they're going to know you're not human. And if they see you use your *grace*…"

"Do you really think that hasn't occurred to me?" Zayne shot back, placing the circular object back onto the desk. I realized it was a shiny black paperweight. "You damn well know Wardens don't patrol in groups or in the same area unless something is going down. If we're careful, we're not going to cross paths with another Warden."

"You can only be so careful for so long. I know you used Dez to get her out of that warehouse before the others arrived. It won't always be that simple."

"It may get complicated, but it is what it is," Zayne said. "I don't care if it's easy or not. You're the clan leader. Make sure they don't find out for as long as possible. That knowledge is too much of a risk."

I figured it wasn't a good time to remind Zayne that there

were currently two demons and a half demon who knew exactly what I was.

And didn't that speak volumes?

Zayne trusted those demons over his own clan. Granted, he hadn't known that Roth would be able to figure out what I was, but he hadn't reacted this way when Roth had figured it out and exposed what I was to Layla and Cayman. If Nicolai discovered that, I couldn't even begin to imagine what he'd do—what the entire clan would think.

It would also be a very bad time to tell them that the Crone, Rowena and another random witch knew what I was.

"I'm surprised you remembered I'm the leader of this clan." Nicolai's voice was soft. "I was beginning to think you'd forgotten."

"I haven't." Zayne met Nicolai's stare. "Not for one second."

Nicolai's lip curled in a scary mockery of a grin similar to one I'd seen on Thierry more times than I cared to remember. It was a sign he was close to going nuclear. "Is there a reason to worry that any of our clansmen would put Trinity in danger?"

I held up my hand. "I want to make it clear that if I'm in danger, I can handle myself."

Both ignored me, as was becoming the theme of my life when people talked about me like I wasn't in the room.

"You don't want me to answer that question," Zayne retorted.

"I know you have your issues with the clan, Zayne, and I get it. I do." Nicolai leaned back. "But do you really think I would allow anyone in my clan to use what Trinity is against her?"

"No one thought my father would allow his clan to do what they did to Layla." Zayne planted his hands on the desk. "Did they?"

I sucked in a sharp breath. Oh, man, they were about to travel down a painful road, one that led right back to Layla. Time to intervene.

"There was a Warden back home who discovered what I was." My stomach soured, because this was one of my own painful roads. "No one knew that Ryker believed a True-born would harm a Warden. It sounds insane, right? Even my mother, who he eventually killed when he went after me, never suspected. Misha might've orchestrated it all, but Ryker had those beliefs long before Misha was able to exploit them."

Zayne silently moved closer to me while I spoke, and I didn't want to think about what he was feeling through the bond. It was a messy bag of hurt and guilt, sorrow and fury. His pale blue gaze was fastened on me as he spoke to Nicolai. "I would love to believe that every clan member here is sane and logical and wouldn't for one second believe that Trinity would be a threat to them, but we just don't know that. The last thing any of us needs is to be looking over our shoulders for Wardens while trying to find the Harbinger."

Silence stretched out. The office clock ticked like a bomb. The bright blue gaze of the leader drifted to mine. "Was that why you were attacked at the Potomac Community when we were there?"

He was talking about Clay. I shook my head. "No. He

just…" Aware that Zayne was watching me, I recalled what Misha had told me. "That had nothing to do with what I was. But Ryker wasn't the only one who believed I was dangerous. There were others who felt I needed to be put down. They were…dealt with." I ran my fingers over the back of the chair. "I honestly don't know why any Warden would feel that way, but some did. There could be more who do."

"You don't know why?" Genuine disbelief filled Nicolai's tone.

Taken aback, I frowned. "Yeah, no. I don't."

Zayne's focus returned to his clan leader. "Why would any Warden fear a Trueborn?"

"A Trueborn pulls strength from a Warden—"

"That goes both ways," Zayne cut in. "The Protector gains strength from the Trueborn. It's not like she's a parasite."

A parasite.

Wow.

Never quite looked at it that way, but now that was stuck in my head to obsess over later.

"I wasn't suggesting that." Nicolai's fingers tapped the arm of his chair, a slow, steady beat. "It's just not entirely surprising that some would be concerned about what she is."

"Surprising or not, it's imperative that we keep what she is on the down low." Zayne got us back on track. "I need you to agree to this, Nic."

"I'll do what I can, but both of you need to prepare for when the clan discovers the truth."

"I never said I wasn't prepared. I am." Zayne moved so that his body blocked mine. He faced his clan leader, the man seated in the position that was supposed to have been Zayne's. "I was a Warden, but now I'm a Protector. Her Protector. If any of them so much as asks a question about Trinity in a way that is of the slightest concern to me, it will be the last thing they do."

22

"**D**o you think that was necessary?" I asked the moment we stepped out of Nicolai's office into the empty hallway.

"What?" Zayne headed down the narrow hall brightly lit by sconces. It was late, and the large compound was quiet in a way that reminded me of the home I'd grown up in.

I ignored a sting in my chest as I hurried to catch up with his long-legged pace. "What you said to Nicolai in there. You know, to your clan leader."

"I know who Nicolai is, Trin. Just like I told him, I haven't forgotten for one second who I was speaking to."

"Sure didn't seem like it."

One large shoulder lifted in a shrug as we entered a silent, roomy and yet somehow still cozy kitchen that managed to have a table that could seat an entire football team. "He needed to know I won't think twice about eliminating threats to you, no matter who they come from."

Zayne pushed open swinging white double doors that led into a smaller kitchen that had wall-to-wall stainless steel appliances. I guessed the food was prepped here. Normally I'd wonder why anyone needed two kitchens, but there were a lot of Wardens in the compound.

"While I appreciate that, you can't go after someone just because they ask questions about what or who I am—" I swallowed a squeak as Zayne spun to face me. "Hi?"

Zayne dipped his chin and a curtain of blond hair slid forward, brushing his jaw. "I'm your Protector. No one, demon or Warden or human, is going to put you in a position of danger."

I met his stare. "You're my Protector, not my rabid guard dog that bites anyone who gets too close."

"Oh, I'll do way more than bite," he replied, and I rolled my eyes. "My job is to keep you safe, and I'm not about waiting around for questions to become problems."

"But they're already asking," I pointed out. "And Nicolai is right. Eventually they are going to find out. Maybe…maybe we're wrong? Maybe we need to tell the clan. Take that risk."

"That's not the risk we should take right now. Like I said to Nic, we don't need to be looking over our shoulders. My clan won't find out. Not if I have anything to do with it."

I planted my hands on my hips. "And what are you going to do, Zayne?"

"Whatever I have to. I will not allow you to be harmed." He thumped his fist off his chest and then held it there, above his heart. "That is the vow I made."

Two halves of me went to all-out war. Part of me boiled over with annoyance. Not only because his warning was unnecessary and could further damage his relationship with his clan, but also because I could damn well take care of myself, thank you very much. I didn't need him going all He-Man on other Wardens without due cause.

The stupider half of me was all fluttery in my lady bits, because he was willing to put himself between me and a bullet, so to speak, even go up against his clan to do so.

That part was dumb as Hell, because of the reason behind his vow. The bond made him feel that way—willing to step in front of a speeding train for me—when it came to him and his clan. It was *not* the same thing that had driven him to kiss Layla even though he knew the danger, or that had allowed him to stand back and watch familiars munch down on Alphas because they'd threatened her, or to pursue a relationship with the half demon even when he knew his clan would never support it.

He *needed* to protect me. He'd *wanted* to protect Layla. And there was a world of difference between need and want. My chest twisted, even though I wasn't comparing myself to Layla out of jealousy or bitterness. There was no competition between us. It was just the…the simple difference that, even if Zayne and I shared amazing dinners, and he said kind, sweet things to me, there was a difference between needing to do something and wanting to do it.

Zayne's head tilted. "What?" His gaze flickered over my face. "What's wrong?"

I looked at the steel-paneled door we'd stopped in front of. "Nothing's wrong."

"You seem to keep forgetting I can feel what you're feeling."

"Trust me, I have not forgotten that." It was time to change the subject. "How are we getting back to your place?" We'd caught a ride to the compound with another Warden who'd showed up shortly after Dez had left with Morgan's body. "Are we flying again?"

Zayne didn't respond for a long moment. The silence stretched my nerves, forcing me to look at him again. The moment our eyes connected, I couldn't look away. Couldn't get enough air into my lungs with the shallow breath I took. "You're sad," he said, his voice low. "It feels like...a heaviness in my chest. I can feel it, Trin."

I closed my eyes, thinking I *really* needed to get better control of my emotions.

"Talk to me," he whispered in the quiet.

"I was... I was thinking about Misha." That was a lie, yet another I'd told today, and also not something I wanted to talk about, either. But it was better than the truth. "It was just a random memory. Not important."

His hand touched my shoulder, surprising me. The weight was light, but I could feel the warmth of his hand through the material of my shirt, branding my skin. "But it is important."

Exhaling roughly, I said nothing.

"I know you miss him." His fingers curled around my shoulder. "Even with everything he did, you still miss him. I understand."

Did he really? Things might have been tense between him and his father before his passing, but it wasn't like his father had wanted him dead or had sought to betray him. Or orchestrated the death of his mother. Then again, his father *had* gone after Layla.

"I know I'll never replace him. I'll never be what he was to you."

My eyes flew open as my hands curled into fists. "That's a good thing. I wouldn't want you to be anything like him. Everything about him was a lie, Zayne. I didn't really know him."

His lashes lowered, shielding those extraordinary eyes. "But there are good memories, Trin. What he became doesn't change that, and they're not going away because of what he ended up doing."

"But they *did*." I stepped away from his touch. I needed space before everything to do with Misha cracked wide open. "Because what if he'd always been like that, and it was all fake?"

"You don't know that."

"That doesn't matter. He tainted those memories, Zayne. He made them not real."

His hand fell to his side. "They're real as long they belong to you."

I sucked in a breath, his words hitting me hard in the chest. When I looked at him again, I found him watching me, his expression stark.

He took a step toward me, arms rising as if he was about to pull me into his embrace, but he stopped short of doing so. Relief and disappointment flooded me. His stance stiffened and then he turned toward the steel door. "Come on. Let's head home."

Home.

Sighing, I waited until he opened the door. The faint scent of exhaust wafted into the kitchen as Zayne turned on a light, revealing a large bay housing several vehicles. He smacked a button on the wall, and the garage door rattled open. A warm, sticky breeze blew into the space.

I closed the door behind me and heard the lock automatically click into place.

Zayne snatched a set of keys off the wall and skirted the grills of two SUVs as he walked toward something covered with a tarp. "You're not afraid of motorcycles, are you?"

"Uh. I've never been on one, but I don't think so? I mean, I shouldn't be," I reasoned as I watched him grab a fistful of the beige cloth and yank it aside, revealing a black motorcycle that looked like it went fast—really fast. "Is that yours?"

Zayne nodded as he reached for the handlebars. "Yeah, haven't taken it out in a while."

I was trying to wrap my head around the fact that Zayne owned a motorcycle and that I found that so…hot. It was just a method of transportation, no big deal, but I was feeling a little flushed.

"I keep meaning to ride it back whenever I'm over here," he said, turning something on the center part of the bike as he lifted a foot and placed it on one of the shifters.

Nudging the kickstand up, he straightened the bar. The security floodlight kicked on, illuminating Zayne and the bike as he wheeled it into the driveway. "Can you grab two helmets? They're on the shelf to your right. Sorry. No pink ones."

"I was really hoping for a pink helmet with kitten ears." I did as he said, grabbing two black full-face helmets. They were heavier than I expected, but I guessed that was a good thing when you wanted something between the pavement and your skull when going sixty miles an hour or faster.

The garage door closed behind me as I joined Zayne in the driveway. Stopping, I looked back at all the dark windows. Most Wardens would be on the streets right now, but they'd be returning home soon. "Do you not miss being here at all?"

Zayne shook his head as he swung a heavy thigh over the bike and sat in a way that said he'd done this hundreds of times. Holding on to one of the handles, he steadied the bike as he reached over and took one of the helmets from me. "These have microphones in them, so if you need to talk to me, I can hear you."

"Cool." I stared at the helmet I held and then peeked up at Zayne, thinking of those Wardens out patrolling—of Morgan and Greene and all the others I didn't know. "I'm really sorry about Morgan. I can't remember if I said that yet, but just in case I haven't, I'm sorry."

"Thanks." He looked back at the mansion. "What I said before hasn't changed. Another name on the list to grieve. Just wasn't thinking another would replace the last one so quickly."

"Me, either," I admitted, stomach twisting as my thoughts shifted to the park and the dinner and us in that alley while—

"I think I know what you're thinking," He tipped his gaze to the sky, exposing his throat. It was cloudy, so I couldn't see any stars. "If you are, it's what I'm thinking."

My grip on the helmet tightened. I didn't want to say what I was thinking.

Head still thrown back, he closed his eyes as he palmed the helmet between his large hands, and I thought he didn't want to give those words life, either. He opened his eyes. "Get the helmet on and hop on, so we can get out of here."

I slipped on the helmet and then, after a couple of seconds of trying to figure out how to get on the back of the bike without looking like an idiot, I scrambled onto the seat behind Zayne. When I looked up, Zayne had his helmet on.

He tapped something on the side of his helmet, waited a few seconds, and then reached over to my helmet and pressed something on the side. His voice was suddenly inside the helmet. "You're going to need to hold on to me."

Biting my lip, I placed my hands on his sides and tried to ignore how hard that area was. I had no idea why it had been so easy to cling to him like a sexed-up octopus in the alley earlier, but now it felt as awkward as trying to navigate a maze in the dark.

There was a pause. "You're going to have to hold on harder than that." Amusement lanced his tone, and I rolled my eyes. "And scoot up, or the moment this Ducati moves, you're going to fly right off the back of it."

"Sounds like if that happens, it's your fault," I retorted, but flattened my hands against his sides. "And if I get any closer, I'm going to be riding your back like a book bag."

"That's a sentence I never thought I'd hear." His voice crackled through the microphone.

"You're welcome."

His chuckle came through the speaker, and the next thing I knew, his hands were on mine. He tugged until my thighs were snug against his hips and my arms circled his waist. "You want to go fast?" he asked, and I thought his voice sounded deeper, rougher. The warmth in the center of my chest was burning brighter.

I looked around the driveway, unable to see much through the tinted face shield. "Sure."

"Good." His hand coasted over mine, where they were joined across his abdomen. "Hold on."

The engine rumbled to life underneath us, a purr that traveled up my legs. I started to pull back, and then the bike was off, tearing down the driveway. I swallowed a shout of surprise.

Heart rate kicking up, I held on to Zayne as if my life depended on it. I kind of thought it did as the wind whipped around us, all sound drowned out by the roar of the engine. I hoped Zayne could see where he was going, because all I saw was a blur of darkness and speed.

Fear trickled through me, heightened when he hit a bend in the road, and I swore we tilted sideways as he sped through it, but as the bike straightened out and my heart slowed down, it reminded me of that night Zayne had helped me fly.

This was a lot like that.

The whipping wind. The feeling of weightlessness. The emptiness the speed and darkness brought along with them. Being on the back of his bike was freeing, and I wanted to enjoy it without the festering burn of guilt. Guilt I hadn't felt over Faye, but that was threatening to swallow me now. Even though I hadn't said it out loud and neither had Zayne, what was unspoken between us didn't go away. No matter how freeing the wind tugging at me felt, it didn't change the truth.

We'd lost sight of our purpose tonight. We'd lingered too long in that restaurant and even longer in that alley. The Harbinger had known it, and Morgan was a message that it knew what neither Zayne nor I wanted to acknowledge.

We'd messed up…and someone had died.

23

After pulling on a long tank top that doubled as a sleep shirt because it was too big to wear normally, I walked out of the bathroom and climbed under the covers. I knew I wouldn't fall asleep, even though it was late and I was exhausted mentally and physically. I was too antsy, my mind occupied with a hundred different things,

Today had been at times wonderful and then terrible, and I'd experienced everything from apathy to horror. While that was a lot to deal with—what I'd done to Faye, how I'd felt at dinner with Zayne, and the grief and guilt surrounding the death of Morgan—I knew that Zayne was feeling a lot of these things, too.

I wanted to go to him, but I wasn't sure if that was smart. My head lolled to the side, and I found myself staring at my mom's old romance novel. I still couldn't believe my father had been here without me knowing. I started nibbling on my thumbnail. Not that I didn't appreciate the money, but it would've…it would've been good to have seen him. I had questions. Lots of them. We needed to know more about the Harbinger and why he'd spoken about it as if it would cause human destruction on an apocalyptic level. As far as we knew, it hadn't attacked humans. I wanted him to confirm what I suspected about the spikes—that they were of angelic origin.

I turned off the bedside lamp and then scooted down, tugging the covers under my chin. When I closed my eyes, the first thought that entered my mind was, what if Zayne and I hadn't gone to dinner? What if we hadn't been distracted with one another in that alley?

Would Morgan still be alive? Or would he have been killed and then displayed somewhere else? There wasn't a single part of me that doubted he'd been crucified as a message to us.

I'm right under your noses.

That's what it said.

What I didn't understand was, why hadn't the Harbinger revealed itself? What was it trying to accomplish? It was like it was waiting, but for what, I had no idea.

A soft knock jarred me from my thoughts. My breath caught as I rose onto my elbow.

The door cracked open and a thin sliver of light appeared. "You awake?" Zayne asked.

"Yeah," I answered. "You?"

The moment the word *you* came out of my mouth, I wondered if there were periods of time where my brain just did not function correctly.

Zayne didn't point out the ridiculousness of my question.

The door slid open, and I saw the outline of his body. A shiver of awareness rolled through me. "Want company?"

All common sense flatlined right there, in the dark. "Yeah," I whispered.

Zayne stepped inside, closing the door partway. My heart was hammering as he crossed the dark room. He hesitated at the side of the bed, and then he was settling in beside me. I took a breath and tasted winter on the tip of my tongue.

Neither of us spoke for a long time.

Zayne broke the silence. "We messed up tonight."

I closed my eyes. I shouldn't have been surprised that Zayne had the courage to give voice to those words first. "I know."

"But I don't regret it. The dinner," he added. "Any of what came after, in the alley."

My head jerked in his direction and my eyes opened. "Nothing happened in the alley."

"But it was going to."

I couldn't get enough air into my lungs as I stared at his shadowy profile.

"If we hadn't heard the scream, something would've happened. Even after I said we shouldn't be doing anything other than looking for the Harbinger, it was going to happen," he continued. "You know that. I know that."

Throat dry, I turned away. A huge part of me couldn't believe he was speaking so openly. I didn't know if I should be thrilled that he was acknowledging this or concerned because of where it could lead.

Heartache.

Because even if his words led somewhere, *we* couldn't go anywhere, and even with my lack of experience, I knew that being physically attracted to someone didn't mean everything or really anything.

But I owed him honesty. I owed it to myself, and in the dark, it was easier to go there. "I know."

Then I heard the next breath Zayne took. It was heavy and full. "You're under my skin and in my blood. I can't get you out."

Every single muscle in my body tensed. I didn't say a word. I couldn't.

"Maybe it wouldn't be like this if we hadn't started it that night—if I hadn't kissed you. Or maybe it would've eventually gotten to this point." His voice was deeper, rougher, like it had been when we were on the motorcycle. "Because it isn't just your taste that has me spinning in circles. It's *you*. All of you. Not just the memory of how your mouth felt against mine, or what it was like to hold you like I did. It's the way you talk and laugh, when you really laugh. It's the way you fight and how you don't back down." He let out a low laugh. "Even when you fight me. When I'm sure you're arguing with me just to argue. It's all you."

The latter part was totally not a surprise. I often did disagree with him just to be antagonistic, and I did secretly believe he enjoyed it. But the rest of what he said? My skin felt numb and yet hypersensitive.

"So, yeah," he said. "I'm in a constant state of distraction, and we messed up tonight. It's not your fault. I'm not saying that. I *should* know better. I should be able to do this... professionally."

I found my voice. "It's not just your fault, Zayne. I... I feel the same way. I just can't say it as eloquently as you." I gave a little shake of my head. "I'm distracted, too, and I know what my duty is. I know what I'm supposed to be doing. *We* messed up. Not you. We."

"Then what do we do?"

"Maybe if we weren't resisting it so much, it wouldn't be a distraction," I said, snorting.

"I was actually thinking that."

"What?" My head snapped in his direction. "I was joking."

"I wasn't."

In the darkness, I could feel his gaze on me. "You…you're serious?"

"I am," he answered, and those two little words blew me away. "I know we're not supposed to, but that doesn't change this."

Oh God, it didn't. No matter what I told myself over and over, it didn't change. "You think…what? If we stop fighting our attraction, things will be easier?"

He shifted to face me. "Sounds crazy, doesn't it? But pretending this isn't between us isn't working. Tonight is evidence of that."

I'd thought that caving in would make it so much worse, but my body and my heart were already way on board with his line of thinking. The numbness had vanished from my skin, which now tingled, and my limbs felt heavier.

"We can't be together," I whispered. "There are rules."

"We don't even know why they exist."

"But they *do*."

"Some rules exist only to control someone," he said, his voice as quiet as mine. "I, more than anyone, know that."

I guessed he was thinking about the rule that would've

prevented him from pursuing Layla before Roth came into the picture. The rule that would prevent him from settling down with anyone other than another Warden.

"Some rules need to be broken."

"Not these rules," I told him, even as I rolled onto my side, leaving nothing but a few inches between us.

"Rules are broken every day." His fingertips brushed my cheek, and when I jerked, it had nothing to do with me not seeing him move and everything to do with him touching me. "I've already broken more rules than I can count. This one surely cannot be any less favorable than working with demons."

"You might have a point there." My senses zeroed in on his fingers tracing the line of my jaw. Logic was still fighting to the surface. "But if we can't risk your clan finding out about me, then how do we risk whatever consequence might come from this?"

"You *are* considering it?"

I bit back a gasp when his finger glanced over my lower lip. "I didn't say that."

"What are you saying then?"

"I'm saying…" I lost track of my thought as his fingers slipped down my chin, over my throat and to my shoulder. A wake of shivers followed his touch.

"You were saying?" His voice threaded with amusement and something thicker, richer.

"I was saying that I have a problem with impulsivity and jumping into things without thinking them through."

"Never."

My lips twitched. "And I spend the other half of the time overthinking everything."

"Never would've guessed that, either."

"You have to be the reasonable one in this."

"I can't do that, Trin." He toyed with the flimsily loose strap of my tank top. "I'm so damn tired of being reasonable, logical and especially responsible."

I moved into his touch without intending to, lifting my shoulder as his finger slipped under the strap. "You're no help at all."

"No, I'm not."

Stomach dipping, I willed him to do *something*. Anything. Either to keep touching me, or to back away. When his hand stilled but didn't pull away, I wiggled closer, stopping only when I felt his steady breath against my lips.

His fingers became his palm, and his grip tightened. "I want you, Trinity."

A swift swelling motion invaded my chest, and all I could say was his name, and it was both a prayer and a curse.

Zayne rolled me onto my back as he moved over me, the bulk of his weight on his arm as his hand slid from my arm to cup my face. I moved with him, kicking the covers down and reaching for him. My hand fisted his hair as I touched his face with my other, loving the feel of the stubble along his jaw.

His forehead dropped to mine, and the breath we took was shared. "Whatever happens, this will be worth it," he said, and it sounded like a promise. "This is right, no matter what."

I hesitated, fingers on his cheeks as I tried to search his face in the darkness. If we did this, could we go back? Would it be worse? Or would it be better once we sated this need?

Would it be a one-time thing or would every night be like tonight? My toes curled at the thought, and the throb from deep inside, the purely physical response, was nearly painful.

Boundaries. Rules. Lines. If we kept this physical, then we weren't really together. *Semantics*, whispered the surprisingly sane-sounding voice. But was it really? People did this all the time without letting feelings grow. I could do this. We could do this.

And I wanted this. I was *ready*. Ready for more than just kissing and touching. I was ready for Zayne, for all of him and everything that entailed. My heart raced at the thought of it. Being ready was a huge decision, a monumental one. There were things we needed, like condoms. Maybe not plural. Probably only one, but we needed that, because I had no idea if baby making was possible between us. But I was ready, and wasn't that the strangest thing, to suddenly be so sure? To have woken up today not even considering the whole losing-my-virginity thing, and still be so damn sure, I wanted to shout it?

"Do you want this?" he asked.

God, did I ever want this—want him. So much so it was a little embarrassing. "Yes."

A tremor rocked his body and his head tilted. His warm breath touched my lips—

"No kissing." My hand tugged at his hair when he stilled over me. "Kissing…kissing makes this *more*." My logic had so many holes in it, but it made sense to me. And not just because I'd seen *Pretty Woman*, but because kissing was… It was beautiful when it was right, and it would be too beautiful with him. "No kissing."

Zayne's chest rose against mine and then he shifted onto his side.

Pressing my lips together to stop the sudden urge to cry, I looked at him. I wanted to take those words back, but I couldn't. It had to be this way—

He settled beside me and his fingers curled around my chin. For a heart-stopping moment, I thought he was going to ignore my newly established rule.

"We can work on that," he said.

I relaxed and then tensed as his thumb dragged over my lower lip.

"I'm...greedy enough for anything." His thumb moved along my chin and then the line of my jaw. "Or maybe it's that I'm desperate for anything that you will allow."

A terrible, insidious part of me broke through the surface, forcing words out of me that I hadn't thought I'd dare speak. "It could be easier."

"What could be?" His fingers made their way back to my chin.

"This," I said, exhaling roughly. "You could do this with literally anyone else, and it would be easier."

Zayne's fingers halted. "You're right. It could be. No rules. No complications." He started moving again, tracing the line of my throat. "It would be so much easier."

I thought about the waitress. "Not like there's any shortage of willing participants."

"There's not."

My eyes flew open. "Then why me?"

"Good question."

I wasn't sure I liked that response, but his fingers reached the collar of my top. My lips parted as the tips trailed down my neck and lower, between my breasts, and then even lower, down and over the slope of my stomach. His fingers glided back up and over my lower ribcage. That terrible, insidious voice slinked back into whatever hole it had climbed out of, thank God.

He flattened his hand, and his thumb tugged at my shirt as he followed the swell of my body until my back arched and a breathy moan left me. His soft hair grazed my chin as his lips followed the path his fingers had made.

"I hope this doesn't count as kissing," he whispered against the thin material of my shirt.

Did it? "I... I don't think so."

"Relieved to hear that." He was on the move again, his mouth skating above my shirt to where his thumb was moving in slow, lazy circles.

My hand fisted the back of his shirt. I had no idea when I'd grabbed him again, but obviously I had. My legs moved restlessly, squeezing together as the thin material of my shirt became damp under his mouth.

Zayne's hand moved to where the hem of my top had ridden halfway up my stomach, exposing a whole lot of skin to a Warden's perfect night vision. The calluses on his palm created a unique friction as he inched my shirt up. "Yes? No?"

"Yes," I breathed.

Cool air followed in the wake of my top, and I'm not quite sure what kind of magic got it over my head and off me, but with his breath against my skin, I didn't care.

"What about this?" he asked. "Is this considered kissing? I feel like it might be."

"No," I said, feeling the lines blur, but I couldn't bring myself to care.

"Hmm."

His lips pressed against my skin, and I thought surely this was the most exquisite torture in the whole world. I lost all sense of time, and his shirt might have begun to tear under my grip.

Slowly, I became aware of his hand opening and closing along my waist, my hip and then the bare skin of my thigh. One of his fingers slipped under the band of narrow cotton along my hip and his thumb moved along the elastic, dipping low enough to cause my head to kick back.

Zayne's head lifted. "I want… I want to touch you. Do you want that?"

"Yes." There wasn't even a half second of hesitation.

And neither was there any on his end. I could make out just the outline of Zayne, but I knew he was watching himself. I could feel the intensity of his gaze as he slid his hand under undies that I now remembered had tiny sharks all over them. In the distant part of my still-functioning brain, I wondered if he could see them.

Then he obliterated that small working part of my brain with the first featherlight touch. My entire body reared as I gasped. We'd done a lot the night of the Imps. I'd been completely undressed, and we'd both found release, but we hadn't done this. *He* hadn't done this. No one but me had gone there, and that had felt nothing like it did now. Each pass became bolder and shorter until…

Every breath left me. Every thought scattered as Zayne made a sound that only added to the sensation of fullness. I'd been wrong earlier, because I lost all sense of everything. My hips moved with his hand, and a maddening, tightening rush swept through me. I was speaking. I thought I was saying his name as I drew one of my legs up.

"Zayne, I…" Tension curled impossibly tight as my eyes widened.

He made that sound again, a throaty groan. "I can see you. Each breath you take. The way your lips are parted. How wide your eyes are and how flushed your skin is. That light inside you. The spark. I can see it and it's beautiful. You're beautiful."

Maybe it was his words or what he was doing, or maybe it was just because it was him and it was us, but whatever it was, I tipped over an edge and fell into pulsing waves that seemed to come from everywhere.

At some point I became aware of Zayne's forehead resting against mine and that his hand was now at my hip, his grip tight but not painful in the least.

My eyes fluttered open, and again, I wished I could see him. I finally eased my grip off the poor shirt and touched his cheek. His head lifted the scantest of inches. Everything about him seemed incredibly rigid, and then his head tilted in a way that I knew what was coming next.

"No kissing," I reminded him. "Kissing makes this mean more than it does."

Zayne lifted his head, and I reached for him, my fingers brushing the band on his pants. He caught my wrist.

I stilled, lifting my gaze and wishing I could see his face. "I want to—"

"I know. I want you to do whatever you want to me, but no."

"No?" I repeated dumbly. My senses were too all over the place to even begin to decipher what was coming or going through the bond.

"No," he said. "Because that would make this mean more than it can to me."

Hearing my own words from him was jarring. What he was saying didn't sound fair. He could do that to me, but I couldn't give him the same? And there was more left. I was *ready*, even after all I'd just experienced. I knew there was more, and I wanted him to feel what I felt.

"Zayne," I started, but he shifted onto his back. A moment passed, and then he rose from the bed. I sat up. "Where are you going?"

"Nowhere." He stepped away from the bed and then stopped. "Good night, Trinity."

My mouth dropped open in confusion as he walked out of the bedroom. With the brief flash of light from the living room, he was gone, closing the door behind him, and I was left sitting there, wondering what in the world had just happened.

Had I done something wrong? I must have, considering he'd gone from full throttle to not just pumping the brakes, but getting out of the car and walking away. But I *hadn't* done anything wrong.

I hadn't even initiated this.

Pulling my legs from where they were tangled in the blanket, I scrambled off the bed. I started toward the door, realized I was shirtless and then went back to the nightstand and smacked around until I found the switch. Golden light flooded the bedroom. I found my top at the end of the bed, tugged it on and then hurried to the door and yanked it open. Zayne was standing at the island, downing a bottle of water like he'd been dying of thirst.

"What's wrong?" I demanded.

Zayne glanced at me as he lowered the bottle. "You forgot your pants."

"I almost forgot my shirt," I replied. "That *you* took off me. What just happened in there? Everything was fine. Great, actually. Perfect, and then you just walked out—"

"Figured that's what you'd prefer."

"What?" I stared at him. "Why would you think that? Makes no sense."

"Makes no sense?" Zayne laughed, but it sounded wrong. He took another drink. "You got what you needed, right? I don't know what you're complaining about."

Now my jaw was on the floor. "Excuse me?"

"You're right. It was great and perfect. Then it wasn't." He started toward the couch. "And if you don't mind, I'd like to get some sleep."

"Oh, Hell no. I don't even know why you'd say something like that. Got what I needed? Buddy, I'm not the one who started this. That was you." My heart thumped heavily as something dark and oily seeped through my chest. "I don't understand. You're the one who wanted to get me out of your system!"

Zayne huffed, shaking his head. "I didn't say that."

"And I didn't say—"

Peanut appeared suddenly, drifting out of the interior wall. He took one look at me, standing there in my tank and undies, and then at Zayne glowering.

"Nope." The ghost wheeled right around and disappeared back into the wall.

Zayne followed my gaze to the wall. "Is that ghost here?"

"That ghost has a name," I snapped. "And no. Not anymore." Crossing my arms, I met his stare and tried to rein back my anger. "This sounds like a terrible miscommunication of sorts. I don't know why you'd get the impression that—"

"That this means more to me than just getting off?" He jumped in, and my eyes widened. "Yeah, I'm seeing that hasn't crossed your mind."

"I have no idea where this is coming from!" I shouted and winced, hoping his neighbors couldn't hear me. I forced my voice lower. "I told you I wanted you. I *showed* you and—"

"And there *was* a miscommunication." He swung toward me, pale eyes flashing. "When you said no kissing, I wasn't picking up on what you meant by *more*. If I had known, none of that would've happened."

I tipped forward, the oily feeling spreading. "All of this because I wouldn't let you kiss me? Are you kidding me?"

His head cocked to the side, brows raised. "Wow, Trinity. Your selective memory is not one of your endearing traits."

"Selective memory? I told you no kissing because—"

"It would make it mean more than what it does. Your words. Not mine."

I sucked in a sharp breath. Oh my God, I had said that. I unfurled my arms, heart now thundering. "I didn't mean—"

"Look, I've already been someone's pastime when they were bored or wanted attention. Been there, done that, and should have had the damn common sense not to go there again."

My entire body jerked. Not just because of his words—I realized the thick gunk slithering through my veins was coming from him. Anger. Disappointment. Worse of all, *shame*. I felt his shame as he took another step toward me.

"Maybe what we were doing in there doesn't mean anything to most people, but it does to me. It means a whole Hell of a lot to me, so I'm not going down that road again," he said, his gaze sweeping over me. "No matter how tempting that road is."

Blinking back sudden wetness, I lifted my hands as horror tore through me. God, no wonder he was feeling the way he was. He'd opened up to me, speaking honestly and telling me that I got under his skin and in his blood, and I… I hadn't told him why I'd said no kissing. I hadn't told him my fears about the Alphas and what they'd do. I hadn't told him…

I hadn't told him the truth. That even though I knew I shouldn't and was doing everything in my power not to allow it, I was falling in love with him. That I might even already be there. I didn't say anything other than that I wanted him. I'd even told myself that, if we kept it purely physical, it would be okay, but I had to draw those lines. I just hadn't told him why.

I took a shaky breath, needing to explain even if it couldn't fix this. "I didn't mean to make you feel that way. I wasn't thinking about you—"

"Of course you weren't." He looked away as the water bottle crinkled under his grip. "That's your thing, right? Always thinking about yourself."

Ice drenched my skin. I'd said that to him by the tree house, after everything had gone down with Misha. I'd told him I was selfish, and Misha had been right. Zayne had told me that wasn't true.

Taking a step back, I tried to breathe through what poured out of me, but it was deep-rooted and it overwhelmed what I felt from him.

"Dammit," he growled, tossing the water bottle onto the couch. It bounced off the cushion and thumped onto the floor. He thrust a hand through his hair, dragging it back from his face. "We need to end this conversation."

I stood there, arms at my sides.

"I don't know what I was thinking tonight. Why I said any of those things to you," he said, sounding very weary. "Tonight was a mistake, and we need to forget all of this."

"Yeah," I heard myself whisper.

His gaze shot to mine, and his jaw hardened. He smiled, but it was nothing like the smiles I knew. "Good news is, I don't think we have to be worried about being distracted any longer, because this…this isn't going to happen again."

24

The next couple of days *sucked* for a multitude of reasons.

Obviously the whole museum-tour thing had been nixed, not just because of what had happened between Zayne and I, but because it hadn't felt right after the last Warden death. Still, that didn't stop the rush of disappointment whenever I thought about those plans.

Hunting for the Harbinger each night had been a snooze-fest—an awkward, strained snoozefest. We found nothing each night, not even a Raver. I guessed that wasn't exactly bad news, since no Warden had been killed, but it meant we were no closer to finding the Harbinger.

It also meant there was a lot of downtime with no teasing between Zayne and I, no playful bickering or long talks about his clan or if I missed the Community. Zayne wasn't rude toward me; he was remote and utterly unreachable while we trained and looked for the Harbinger. Everything was just...

professional between us, and while that helped during training with the blindfold, it made me so, so sad. Heartsick, really.

I picked up nothing from him through the bond. And there was a tiny, *selfish* part of me that was grateful, because I wanted to forget that slimy feeling of shame that was the result of my own actions, intentionally or not.

Zayne was there every day, but he wasn't and I wondered if this was how it was going to be from now on. We were bonded till death, which, hopefully, was a long time off.

That was also a long time to miss the easiness between us, the camaraderie and the *fun* we'd had just being in each other's company. It was a long time to mourn the loss of everything that had made Zayne become what he meant to me, which was more than my Protector, more than just my friend.

It seemed a little too late to realize that pretending hadn't stopped my feelings for him from growing. Neither had my stupid, faulty mental file cabinet. All I'd managed to do was camouflage my emotions. That drawer named ZAYNE had been ripped open and everything I'd felt for him dumped out, scattered all over me. It was a mess I sifted through each night after returning to the apartment.

I never explained to Zayne what I'd meant about the whole no-kissing rule and why I'd sought to establish it. I never told him that he was the furthest thing from a pastime. That he and I weren't him and Layla. That what I felt for him had nothing to do with boredom or seeking a physical release and had everything to do with wanting too much of what we could not have.

Zayne didn't bring it up. It became something we didn't acknowledge but that remained a wall erected between us.

By the next week after what I was now referring to as Trin Is an Idiot night—TIAI for short—I woke still aching but resigned. Maybe this was for the best. We couldn't be together.

And we wouldn't be.

I twisted my damp hair up and shoved a clip into the mass, grabbed my phone and then slipped on my glasses. When I padded barefoot into the living room, Zayne was on the couch. He didn't look up as I made my way to the kitchen.

"Morning," I mumbled as I opened the fridge and grabbed a soda.

Zayne murmured roughly the same as I sat down at the island, figuring he would announce when he wanted to start training.

"Gideon is on his way over," Zayne said after a long moment of silence. "Says he has an update for us."

I looked over my shoulder at the back of his head. "Did he figure out what the spikes are?"

"Don't know. Guess we'll find out in a few." Zayne rose and disappeared into the bedroom without another word.

My chest squeezed. This was pretty much how every morning was now. Turning back around, I started biting my thumbnail as I stared at my phone. Jada hadn't texted me back after I'd reached out to her from the park. I wasn't sure what to think of that. I felt guilty, like a bad friend, because I *was* a bad friend. I'd been selfish, just like Misha had accused me of being, just like Zayne had reminded me I was.

Shoving my glasses on top of my head, I unlocked my phone and typed out a quick text that read I'm sorry I haven't been around. I miss you.

I hit Send and didn't expect a quick response, so when I

saw the little bubble appear then disappear before reappear-
ing, my stomach dropped. Within a few seconds, Jada's response came through.

I'm sorry too.

My chest hollowed. The bubble came back. She was still
typing.

I know it's been a lot for u to deal with. I'm trying to be understanding but it's also been a lot for all of us. I needed to talk to
u. Not just abt Misha. I needed to make sure u were ok. That's
what friends do. U didn't let me be there for u. I'm trying to
not let that get to me but it has.

I squeezed my eyes shut and pressed my lips together. A
burn crept up my throat. Man, I'd messed up. I'd been thinking only about what I didn't want to do and not what Jada
might need, both as someone who had grown up with Misha
and someone who was my friend.

Opening my eyes, I swallowed that knot as I told myself
I needed to tell her that. I couldn't just sit here and think it.
I wasn't telepathic and she wasn't psychic. Hands trembling,
I got to typing.

You're right. I cut you out when I shouldn't have & I was only
thinking about myself. I'm sorry. I don't know what to say except I'm sorry & I know that doesn't undo that I've been a shitty
friend. But I am sorry.

Several minutes that felt like a lifetime passed before Jada responded.

I know. Call me when you're ready and I know you're not ready bc u texted instead of calling. We'll talk then.

The fact that Jada knew me well enough to call me out on that last text made me want to cry. Not because it hurt my feelings, but because it was evidence of just how well she knew me. She knew that, even though I'd become aware of how crappy of a friend I'd been, I still wasn't ready to cross that bridge.

I put down the phone and rested my face in my hands. What was wrong with me? It wasn't like I was incapable of speaking my mind every other five seconds, so why couldn't I do it when it mattered most? Why was I taking the coward's way out? Because that's what I was doing. It was so opposite of everything about me. I could chase after Upper Level demons and jump off buildings and argue over everything from the consumption of water to what the best Marvel movie was, but I went graveyard silent when it was time to confront real personal issues.

When I needed to confront myself.

I scrubbed my fingers down my face as if rubbing my cheeks and eyes would somehow bring some sort of clarity to the situation.

It didn't.

Slowly, I became aware that I was no longer alone. I lifted my head, dropping my hands to the cool granite as I looked over to where Zayne was standing just inside the living room.

He looked like he was about to say something, but then he just walked straight past me and grabbed a water from the fridge. Awkward silence ensued. Luckily, it was short-lived, since the buzz of Gideon's arrival came soon after.

Gideon didn't arrive empty-handed or alone. Surprisingly, Jasmine's younger sister was with him. Danika's glossy black hair was hanging loose around her shoulders. Seeing a female Warden outside a Community or a compound was unheard of.

"Hope you don't mind me tagging along," Danika said as she strolled past Zayne, punching him lightly on the shoulder. He grinned at her, and I felt a pang in my chest, having missed that grin. "I was bored and the twins are going through the terrible twos, so I needed out stat."

"Aren't the twins older than that?" Zayne asked.

"The terrible twos do not just start and end in one year, I'm learning." She looked over at me. "You should see the look on your face right now."

I blinked and then slid my glasses down. Her face came into more detail. "I'm sorry. I'm just not…"

"…used to seeing a potential child-bearing female out in the big, bad world?" She grinned as she came around the other side of the island. "I know. Wardens all over the world are rolling in their graves. I don't care, and Nicolai knows better than to try to stop me."

I really wanted to confirm whether she and Nicolai were together, but it was none of my business.

"Nice place," Gideon commented, joining us. He carried a laptop, which he placed on the island as he looked around. "Very…industrial."

I hid my smile behind my fingers.

He looked across the open space, the vibrant blue eyes missing nothing. "One bedroom?"

"About to get a two-bedroom a floor down," Zayne answered, and my hand slipped away from my mouth. "You'll be happy to hear it's just as industrial as this one."

"The apartment is available?" I asked.

Zayne glanced at me. "Yeah. Just heard from the manager yesterday evening. Should be able to move in by the end of next week."

"Oh." I shifted my gaze to Gideon's laptop, trying to not be hurt that he hadn't mentioned it to me. Not like he hadn't had time while we'd sat in silence before Gideon and Danika showed up. "That's good news."

"You've had to share a bathroom with this guy?" Danika jerked her chin toward Zayne. "Oh my God, that's unfair."

I cracked a grin at that, liking the girl. "It's been okay. So far."

"I think you're being kind." Her sky blue eyes were dancing. "These guys shed worse than we do."

A surprised laugh parted my lips. "You know, I've noticed that. So much blond hair everywhere."

"Yeah, you think that because you haven't seen all the dark brown hair that's literally on everything," Zayne commented, and before I could figure out if he was teasing or being a jerk, he turned to Gideon. "What you got for me?"

"For us," I muttered under my breath.

Danika's grin kicked up a notch.

"Two things," he said, sitting on the stool. "The spikes are still glowing, in case you all wanted to know."

"I've seen them." Danika hopped up on the island and spun

halfway on her butt so she was facing us. "Glowing spikes are freaky."

"That they are," I agreed.

"Haven't found anything that tells me what kind of language is written on them," Gideon continued. "Leads me to believe that it either predates any known record of language or it's a language we've never seen before."

"Or it's not language at all," Danika suggested, and when we looked at her, she shrugged. "It just looked like scratches and circles to me. Could just be some kind of drawing."

"You have a point." Zayne leaned against the island. "It could be what Gideon suggests, or some kind of drawing."

"Or it could be of angelic origin." I still believed that was the answer. Danika looked at me, expression thoughtful. "I mean, has anyone ever seen angelic writing?"

"Does angelic writing exist?" Zayne asked.

"I haven't seen it." Gideon opened the laptop.

I arched a brow, thinking the same could be said about me. "Just because we haven't seen something doesn't mean it doesn't exist."

"That is also a good point." Danika tipped her head as she looked at me. I thought I caught a hint of speculation.

I looked to the screen Gideon was pulling up, realizing that I should keep quiet at this point. The fact that I was even here while they were discussing this was suspicious.

"I was able to tap into the security cameras around the cathedral, and while I wasn't able to catch a single glimpse of this thing, I did find something interesting."

Disappointment surfaced as Zayne came around to stand

on the other side of Gideon. Catching the Harbinger on camera, even if it was just a glimpse, would've been something.

"See this?" Gideon pointed at the screen. It was surprisingly clear black-and-white film of the street and the church. Half of its steeple was visible. "Look at the top here, on the right."

I stared, unable to see what he was pointing at.

"9:10 p.m.," Zayne murmured. "See it."

Gideon hit Play. "This camera is outside Morton's. Keep a close eye once it clicks over to 9:11."

Biting down on the nail of my forefinger, I squirmed as the burst of guilt whipped through me. That was the restaurant we'd been at.

Suddenly the video feed flashed a brilliant, intense white, as if a bomb had gone off and kept exploding.

"Hold up." Zayne leaned forward at the waist. "What is that?"

"Don't know. Lasts for about thirty seconds and then—" The video feed returned to normal. "And then there's…yeah, there's Morgan."

I drew a sharp breath, able to make out just enough of the large body, arms outstretched, to know what I was seeing.

"Show them the others," Danika urged.

"I got feeds from the District, Chase Bank and a retail store." Clicking on his computer, he brought up another feed, this one a sideways view of the church. "The same happens."

And it did.

On each video feed, the same thing happened. The screen turned white for thirty seconds, and when the visual returned, the Warden was staked to the church.

"It's some kind of interference." Gideon leaned back. "It

hit all the cameras that had the church within view. None of the cameras facing the other directions are affected. I checked them all."

Zayne let out a low breath, straightening. "I don't know what to think."

"Neither did I, so I got curious." Gideon glanced up at Zayne. "I checked out the camera feeds from the Eastern Market, which face the platform where Greene was found. Two cameras had the platform in view, and the same thing. Intense light that blinked out the whole screen for about fifteen seconds."

"Is it possible someone did this to the feed?" Zayne asked. "Sabotaged it?"

"Possible on the feed from Eastern Market, but these feeds from the church aren't monitored, and you know that since this was a Warden, police wouldn't have pulled the feed."

Zayne nodded. "Police wouldn't get involved unless we went to them."

"Exactly," he replied. "And I checked for video manipulation or cutting of the film. I see no evidence of that. The interference came from outside the feed."

"What could do that?" I asked.

"An alien?" Danika offered.

A slow grin pulled at my lips as I looked up at her. "I like the way you think."

Zayne's tone was bland when he said, "Let's not start the alien conversation again. Please."

Danika's eyes narrowed.

"Look, I'm a believer. Not for one second do I think God created Earth and mankind and called it a day," Gideon said.

"So, I'm not saying it's impossible, but I scoured all the demonology books, including the *Lesser Key*, and I haven't found a single demon that can do that to film without destroying it."

Like Roth had done. He hadn't caused a disruption at the hotel. He'd outright destroyed the camera. This was different.

Then I realized what he'd said. "The *Lesser Key*? Like *the Lesser Key*? The real one?"

Gideon eyed me with open interest. "If you're thinking about the *Lesser Key of Solomon*, then yes."

"Holy moly," I murmured. The *Lesser Key* was a demonic bible of sorts, containing a whole lot of incantations that could summon just about any demon out there. Thank God it was in the Wardens' hands.

"Whatever this thing is, it has weapons we've never seen before and abilities that we can't even comprehend." Gideon closed the laptop. "And that's not much help, but all of us are on high alert. Even more so now."

The conversation moved on to other Warden business, and then they prepared to leave, heading to some store to buy a new TV for Jasmine. Something about one of the twins having knocked hers over. I was still surprised that Danika was out like she was. It was dangerous for her, and I admired the Hell out of her for not staying in her gilded cage.

Gideon motioned Zayne to the side, and they stepped away. I watched them, wondering what he was saying to Zayne.

"Hey," Danika whispered, and I looked at her. She slid off the island, landing nimbly on her flip-flops. She bent down so that she was close to me. "I've got to ask you something."

Figuring it was going to be about Zayne and me sharing a one-bedroom apartment, I braced myself. "What's up?"

Her gaze flicked from me to behind me and then she said in a low voice, "What are you?"

Okay. I hadn't expected that.

"I know you can't just be some girl that grew up with Wardens," she continued. "No one in the clan believes that."

Muscles stiffened as I met her gaze. That was not a good sign, but also not unexpected. I didn't know how Zayne expected to keep his clan from finding out.

I didn't sense anything other than curiosity from her, but that didn't mean it was caring and sharing time. "I'm just a girl who grew up with Wardens."

"Really?" Her voice dropped as she drew the word out.

"I was trained to fight," I said. "That's about the only unique thing about me."

"Interesting." She wrinkled her nose. "Never heard of humans being trained to fight, because you could be a trained assassin, but you'd still be a field mouse compared to even a lower level demon. You're not a field mouse."

"Danika?" Zayne called. "What are you whispering about?"

She straightened, raising her brows. "What were you two whispering about?"

"Nothing." Gideon tucked the laptop under his arm.

"Oh." She winked at me. "We were talking about periods and cramps and bleeding—"

"Okay." Zayne raised his hands as I choked on a laugh. "Sorry I asked."

She pulled away from the island. "I hope I get to see you again soon. Get Zayne to bring you by. Or leave him here. That would be even better."

"Thanks," Zayne muttered.

Danika ignored him. "I'm sure Izzy can't wait to wing herself at you again."

I smiled at that, wishing I could visit her. Somehow I didn't see that happening anytime soon. I waved goodbye as they stepped into the elevator bay.

"Hold up," Zayne called to them as he snatched his keys off the counter by the stove top. "I'll walk you guys out."

Gideon caught the elevator door. "Sure thing."

It was then when I realized Zayne wasn't dressed for training like I was. He was wearing jeans and a pale blue shirt that was almost the same shade of his eyes.

I swiveled on the stool, lowering one foot to the floor. "You're going out?"

Zayne nodded as he went to the couch and grabbed his cell. "Got stuff to do. Won't be back for a while."

Questions formed on the tip of my tongue. I wanted to know what stuff, and I wanted to know why he hadn't told me about the apartment before anyone else. I wanted to talk about what Gideon had discovered. I wanted to *talk*, so we— so I—could feel like we were a team and not whatever it was that we were now.

Except by the time I opened my mouth, he was already stepping into the elevator and the doors were sliding shut behind him and the other Wardens.

My lips peeled back as red-hot anger flooded my system. I reached for my phone, half-tempted to chuck it at the wall, but I managed to resist.

I spent the next several minutes pacing around the couch and then giving up and scavenging for something to eat. All we had was eggs and avocado and mayo.

"God," I groaned, slamming the fridge door shut. If Zayne was out there eating anything that wasn't advertised on a low-carb diet, I was going to seriously hurt him.

Stalking from the kitchen, I decided it was time to find one of those local grocery delivery services. I was going to order every fattening, high-carb food with literally no nutritional value whatsoever and stock the entire kitchen with the crap. His cupboards would be overflowing with potato chips and cheese puffs, frozen pizzas and bags of french fries would line his freezer, every type of soda would stock his fridge, and I was going to replace all his coconut oil with good old *lard*. Smiling to myself, I opened my laptop and did just that, and when the bags and bags of pure junk food arrived two hours later, I gleefully did what I'd planned.

I couldn't wait to see Zayne's face.

After plopping the sack of white bread on the counter near the stove, I headed to the couch, popping another salty slice of fried—

I drew up short as a familiar prickle of awareness darted down my spine. I turned toward the kitchen area, thinking it was Peanut.

What I saw was not my ghost roommate, who had been MIA since last night. I lowered the chips, the bag crinkling in my grip.

It was the spirit from the night Greene had been killed, standing in the same place I'd last seen him, behind the island and in front of the stove.

The spirit was back.

25

"You," I said, curiosity replacing the wariness at seeing the spirit again in Zayne's place.

"You can see me," the spirit replied. "I have so many questions about how you can see me."

Most did, so that wasn't surprising. "I can see dead people. That's all you need to know."

The spirit cocked his head. "Like the kid in *Sixth Sense*?"

It had been ages since Jada made me watch the movie because she thought it would be funny. "Yeah, just like him. So, what's your name?"

"What's yours?" he queried.

I arched a brow as I tossed another chip into my mouth. "You followed me here and you haven't picked up on my name?"

"I wasn't following you," he answered. And before I could question that, he went on, "I didn't even mean to come here at first, but then I came back…" His words warbled as he faded out and came back in. "…and saw that really rude ghost. I need your help."

They *always* needed help.

He faded out again, disappearing completely. I opened my mouth but gasped as he appeared directly in front of me.

"God." I stumbled back against the couch as I threw my arm out. The bag slipped from my fingers, and little pieces of salty Heaven spilled across the floor. "My chips!"

"Sorry!" He reached out to grab my arm. That was no help, because his hand went right through it, leaving behind a wake of cold air.

I caught myself before I high-fived the floor with my face.

"Oh, damn. So sorry. Seriously." He pulled his hand back and glanced at it with a frown. "I didn't mean to scare you."

"You shouldn't just poof in and out like that." I knelt and scooped up what would probably also be my dinner. Five-second rule. "It's freaky."

"Why? You know I'm dead. It shouldn't scare you."

"You don't scare me, but that also doesn't mean the poofing thing isn't startling." All chips saved and back in the bag, I rolled the top down and placed it on the counter. "Anyway, I'm guessing you have a message you need me to help you with since you've crossed over."

"How can you—" He faded out without warning, and I found myself staring at the empty space again.

A few seconds later, he started to take form, his messy brown hair showing first and his boyish face next. His slim shoulders appeared, as did his waist, but beyond that? I could see the kitchen island where he legs should've been.

"Man, I *hate* it when that happens." He shuddered. "Makes me feel like I'm made of wind."

"I can imagine," I murmured, trying not to stare at his missing lower half. I knew spirits could be…sensitive about these sorts of things. "Look, I can help you, but you need to tell me what you need before—"

"Before I disappear again? I know. That's why I bounced before. The longer I'm here, the harder it is for me to stay. I can't really control it."

I nodded. "It's because you're not supposed to be here, at least not for extended periods of time."

"I know. That's what They tell me whenever They catch me leaving. 'You moved on,' They say. And it's okay to check on people I care about, but not too much, because I could get…stuck."

I had a feeling They were whoever monitored the comings and goings of souls. Probably an angel of the Second Sphere. They were kind of like the Human Resources of Heaven. "What do you mean that you can get stuck?"

"I might not be allowed back in or something. They weren't very specific," he explained, and I didn't find that surprising at all.

"Okay. Then let's get this show on the road," I said. "Tell me your name and what you need from me, and maybe I can help."

"There can't be any *maybes*—" He glanced down at himself and grinned. "Hey, my legs are back. Awesome. By the way, did you know that dead jellyfish can still sting you if you step on them?"

I was seriously beginning to think that when people died, they developed a mad case of ADD. I would know, since there was a good chance I had that myself.

"No, I didn't know that."

"Sorry." He lifted his shoulders. "Spewing random facts is a nervous habit of mine."

"Yeah, that was pretty random."

"Anyway, I need your help," he repeated. "Please don't say no. You're my only hope."

I tilted my head. "I'm not your Obi-Wan."

A goofy grin broke out across his face. "Did you just break out a *Star Wars* reference? I like you. Look, I've been trying to get the message across for weeks, but she's, well, she's been hard to reach." There was a fondness to his tone that was kind of adorable. "I love her with all my heart, but man, she's not the most observant person in the world."

I put two and two together. "It's a girlfriend you need to get a message to?"

His smile slipped as his stare grew distant. "Girlfriend? She was almost...she was almost that."

The gruffness in his tone tugged at my heart. It might've been only a handful of words, but they were full of un-achieved potential and heartbreak that made the back of my eyes burn.

Man, I could relate to that.

He looked away. "I need you to get a message to her. That's all."

I glanced at the door. "I want to help you, I really do, and

I'm not saying I won't, but you have to realize something. If I tell her whatever you want me to, she's probably not going to believe me. Based on previous experience, she'll think there's something wrong with me."

"No, she won't. She… Well, she's experienced some weird stuff in her life. Maybe not seeing-dead-people level of weird, but definitely some extreme weirdness." He came closer, flickering again. "Please. It's important. I know it's a lot to ask, but I can't—"

"Leave me alone until I play medium for you, or find real peace until this is achieved?" Nibbling on my thumbnail, I looked at the door again. "Where is she? And how am I supposed to find her? I'm not familiar with this city at all."

"I can show you. It's not far from here."

I hesitated, because this wasn't like Roth dropping me off in a park. What if the spirit got sucked back to Heaven, and I was out there, unable to see much? A flutter of nervous energy filled my chest.

What was I thinking? I could do this. I was independent, and if this spirit disappeared on me, then I would manage. Just like I'd managed when Zayne had left me on the sidewalk and I'd followed the Upper Level demon. I hadn't hesitated then. I wasn't going to hesitate now.

I was a Trueborn, and I was a badass, and this spirit needed my help.

"Okay," I said, lifting my chin. "Let's do this."

Relief poured into his features and he shot toward me, arms out as if he were about to hug me, but he stopped and let his arms flop to his sides. "Thank you. You have no idea what this means to me."

I had some idea of how important it was, which was why I was helping. "My name is Trinity, by the way. Are you going to tell me yours?"

He looked like he was about to offer me his hand in a greeting, but remembered that wasn't going to work. "I'm Sam—Sam Wickers. It's good to meet you, Trinity."

Walking down the street beside a spirit was super weird, but it wasn't the first time I'd conversed with one in public. Back in the Community, I'd usually had Misha or Jada with me, so it hadn't looked like I was talking to myself.

I didn't have that luxury today, but I had creativity.

Sam looked at me strangely as I slipped on my dark oversize sunglasses. It was overcast and looked like it would start raining at some point today.

He spoke up finally when I tugged a pair of earbuds out of the front pocket of my bag, which I'd grabbed from the bedroom before we left. I plugged them into my phone and popped them in my ears.

"What's up with the earbuds?" he asked as we walked down the crowded sidewalk toward Fourteenth Street. Well, I walked. He glided a few inches above the stained sidewalk. "Are you going to ignore me and listen to music? I hope not, because I'm chatty. Annoyingly so."

I kept my gaze focused on making sure I didn't knock into anyone. Talking also kept me from freaking out over the possibility that I was going to get super lost. "Listening to music would be kind of rude."

"Yes, it would."

"The earbuds make it seem like I'm talking on the phone."

I lifted the string, wiggling the mouthpiece. "I can talk to you without people thinking I'm talking to myself."

"Oh. Damn. That's clever." He kept pace beside me. "You must have a lot of experience with this sort of thing."

"Some." A sticky breeze whipped down the sidewalk, tossing my hair across my face and bringing with it the heavy scent of exhaust.

"Like what kind of experience?"

I glanced in his direction, hearing the genuine interest in his tone. Words bubbled up to the tip of my tongue, but this guy—this poor dead guy—didn't know me. Probably had no idea that he'd roamed into the apartment of a Warden. So, how could I explain what it had been like when I'd done things like this before?

"I have a question for you," I said instead.

"I'll have an answer."

I shoved the hair out of my face. "You…passed on, didn't you? Saw the light and went through it?"

That question earned me some weird looks from people passing by, but oh well.

"That's right! You said that before and I wanted to ask, but I faded. How can you tell?" he asked. "That I saw the light and went to it?"

"There's a difference between ghosts and spirits," I explained, keeping my voice low. "Ghosts are stuck. They don't know they're dead, or they refuse to accept it, and they usually look like they did when they died. You don't look or act like that, plus you have a…glow about you. A heavenly light, I guess."

"I do?" He glanced down at his arm. "I can't see it."

"You do." I thought about how Sam had looked different at first. "When spirits have passed on and they come back to check on their loved ones or do whatever spirits do with their time, they look normal except for the glow. They might look younger than they were when they died, or the age when they died. But when I first saw you, you looked like…like you had no features."

"Maybe I showed up looking different because…when I died, I didn't cross over immediately. I couldn't."

We came to an intersection packed with people waiting to cross. "Straight or turn?"

"Straight. It's just another two blocks."

I nodded and started chewing on my thumb again. "Why couldn't you cross over immediately? You didn't want to, or…"

Sam stayed quiet as we crossed the street. I looked down but couldn't see the curb through the legs of people. I figured I had—

The toes on my right foot slammed into the curb, sending sharp pain shooting across my foot. I tripped, catching myself. *"Crap."*

"You okay?" someone who wasn't Sam asked.

"Yep." I looked to my right and saw an older man in a suit talking to me.

"You should pay attention to where you're going and not who you're talking to on the phone," he advised and then walked on, shaking his head.

"Thanks, douche-canoe, for the unsolicited advice!" Sam shouted to no avail. "Maybe I should go push him into that hot dog vendor."

"Can you do that?"

"Sadly no." He sighed forlornly. "I haven't figured out how to become a poltergeist and move stuff."

Not many spirits or ghosts could interact with their surroundings, but I kept that to myself as I breathed through the obnoxiously horrid pain of a stubbed toe. "I think I just killed my foot."

Sam drifted closer to me, trying to avoid going through an older lady in a trench coat. "You know why stubbed toes are so painful? It's because they have a whole bundle of nerve endings that provide sensory feedback to your central nervous system. So, when you stub your toe, that pain gets sent to the brain quicker. Plus, there's little tissue there to cushion the blow."

"I cannot believe you know that."

"Like I said, I know a lot of stuff. Not sure how useful that is now," he said, shoving his hands into the pockets of his jeans. "Being dead and all."

"I have a piece of random knowledge for you."

"Hit me up."

A grin tugged at my lips. "I don't think poltergeists are actually ghosts or spirits. There's some evidence pointing to poltergeist activity being a buildup of energy from a live person."

"Really?"

I nodded. "They're manipulating things around them without knowing. It's usually someone going through something pretty intense."

"Wow. I didn't know that." Sam was quiet for a moment. "I actually did go to the light first, but I got...trapped and went someplace else."

"Someplace else?"

Sam didn't answer.

I looked at him and unease blossomed. "Hold on a second."

He frowned. "What?"

I stopped alongside a pub, keeping my back close to the brick wall.

Sam stopped, too, his expression marked with confusion. "What are you doing?"

"Look, I want to make sure that whatever message you want to give this girl isn't something mean or creepy. If you want to mess with her, I'm not doing this."

"Why would you think—" His eyes widened as a man jogging cut right through him. He faded out like wisps of smoke before coming back together. "Let me try that again. Why would you think I'd seek someone out to say something horrible?"

"Because people are assholes, and some of them even more so when they're dead," I told him. "Some ghosts, even spirits, are just bored and like to scare people or mess with their heads."

"For real?" The surprise in his tone was genuine, or at least I thought it was.

"And you said you went somewhere else first," I tacked on. "There's only one other place I can think of, and you don't go there accidentally."

"You're talking about Hell? I didn't go there accidentally. I was trapped there, and it wasn't my fault. Obviously, I wouldn't have a heavenly glow if I was supposed to be there," he argued. He had a point, but I was beginning to have serious doubts about this. "It's a long story, but I wasn't that kind of person when I was alive and I'm not now. I'm not here to hurt anyone, especially not her. I'm trying to save her life and the lives of others."

26

Chills swept across my skin. I hadn't expected him to say something that freaking intense. "What does that mean?"

"It means that I need to get a message to them before it's too late."

"Too late for what?"

"Come on," he said instead of answering, his jaw clenched with impatience. "We're almost there."

Inhaling the greasy scent of nearby fried food, I pushed away from the wall and followed Sam. I realized he'd said *them* instead of *her*, but he was gliding at a fast clip, and it was a struggle to keep up with him with all the people crowding the sidewalk.

Another block, and then Sam stopped outside an ice cream parlor, a super cute one from what I could tell from peering in through the large window. Black-and-white-checkered floors. Red booths and stools, and a line that nearly reached the door.

I wasn't much of an ice cream fan, but when the door swung open and I smelled hot fudge and yummy waffle cones, I was suddenly craving a big old bowl of chocolate drowned in syrup.

"She's here." Sam walked right through the wall, leaving me outside.

Trying to shake the feeling of unease, I used the door like a normal *living* person and stepped into the store, surrounded by the scent of hot fudge and vanilla. I pushed my sunglasses up and looked around. There were booths lining the walls and framed pictures hanging everywhere. I couldn't make out the details, but they seemed like pop art versions of some of the monuments in the city.

I stayed close to the door since the place was so busy. My heart started thumping heavily. There were so many people, some waiting in line, others hanging around the booths, digging into their ice cream, and as I scanned the faces, there were a few I wasn't quite sure were alive. The lights of the shop made it hard to focus for any length of time.

For a few seconds, I lost track of Sam as I fiddled with the cord connected to my earbuds, but then he reappeared beside me, standing in front of the door.

"Is she here?" I asked.

"She's right there." Sam pointed to the area left of the ice cream bar. "In that booth."

Following where he pointed, I saw a...girl with chin-length brown hair seated facing the entrance. Something about her was familiar. I inched closer, blinking rapidly like that would somehow soften the glare of the bright fluorescent lights. I took another step, and her blurred features came into some level of clarity. I recognized her pretty face and heavy bangs.

"Holy crap," I whispered. "That's Stacey. I know her—well, I've met her." Understanding flooded me. "That's what you meant when you said you didn't follow me. You were following her."

Sam was what I'd seen when Stacey came to the apartment with Roth and Layla. He was that strange shadow I'd seen behind her, and that meant—

"You know Zayne?" I asked.

"Yes, but that doesn't matter. You need to talk to her."

"Doesn't *matter*? It totally matters." A father and his daughter passed us, getting in line as I continued to pretend I was on my phone. "Why didn't you tell me that?"

"Because I didn't know who you were." He was still staring at Stacey. "Or why you were in his apartment. When I realized you could see me, I didn't know if I could trust you—not until I knew you'd help me."

I stared at him, thunderstruck. His sudden appearance was no coincidence. He knew Zayne, and he was a friend of Stacey's. He was—

Suddenly I remembered what Zayne had said about Stacey. That she had lost someone, just like he had. They'd bonded over it, and I now knew without a doubt that this spirit—Sam—was who she'd lost. I had no idea what had happened to him, but based on the minimal information he'd shared, I had a feeling it wasn't a natural death.

Oh, man, all of this had *bad life choice* written all over it. If he'd told me who he was—who he was to Stacey and that he'd known Zayne, I would've demanded to know exactly what the message was before agreeing to help. I would've sure as Hell contacted Zayne first, not just to tell him that Sam's spirit was hanging around but also to find out what had happened to Sam.

Come to think of it, why hadn't Sam asked why I was living with Zayne? He hadn't asked a single question about who I was or how I was involved.

"Dude…" I said.

"It's okay." Sam's gaze swung back to mine. "Really. Let's go up to her."

"You need to tell me what's going on."

Sam turned to me. "This can't wait. You don't understand. I'm running out of time."

I stared him down. "You're not at all curious about who I am?" I whispered. "*What* I am?"

"I figured since you're with Zayne, you're good people." His gaze bounced to where Stacey sat. "I know what he is."

"But you said the reason you didn't tell me who she was was because you didn't know me. You didn't trust me—"

"I lied. Okay?" He threw up his arms, one of them going through the chest of a man who walked past us. The man stopped, frowning, and then walked out, shaking his head. "I know what you are. The moment I realized you could see me, I knew what you are, and I knew if you were with Zayne, it had to mean something, but I didn't know if you were…if you were one of the good ones."

"What?" I gaped at him. "Okay. You need to tell me everything, and you need to make time—"

"Trinity?"

My head jerked up at the sound of Stacey's voice. She was staring in my direction, starting to rise. Crap.

"Look." Sam grabbed for my arm, but his hand went through it. "She's seen you."

Every instinct was telling me this was going to end badly, but it was too late to duck and run. Mentally cursing myself and Sam up and down the street, I shuffled over to the booth. As I drew closer, I saw Stacey's fingers flying over the screen of her phone. I drew in a shallow breath as I glanced over the table—

Was that a...pack of Twizzlers next to the ice cream in front of Stacey?

It *was*.

Oh my God, who ate Twizzlers with ice cream? That was the grossest thing ever.

"I didn't expect to see you here." A thick fringe of bangs fell over her forehead as she placed her phone down and looked around the parlor.

"Same," I murmured, and Stacey's brows disappeared under her bangs.

Exhaling loudly, I glanced at Sam, who was sitting next to Stacey. "This is going to sound really random, but—"

"I'm used to random. Are...are you okay? You look a little pale..." She trailed off, frowning as she looked at where Sam sat.

Their faces were inches apart, his thigh pressing against hers, but she couldn't see him and that...that killed Sam. As ticked off as I was at the spirit, I could see raw pain as he stared at her.

"She felt me, didn't she?" The pinch eased from Sam's features. "Wow. She *felt* me."

I couldn't answer him. "Are *you* okay?"

"Yeah." Stacey's frown smoothed out as she rubbed her hands over her arms. "Just... I don't know. I'm sorry? You were saying something about this being random?"

"It's okay." I forced an easy smile I hoped didn't come off as weird as it felt. I started to speak...and felt warmth flare in my chest.

Zayne.

He was nearby. Dammit. If I felt him, then he was feeling me and probably wondering what in the world I was doing out in the city. Despite the way things were between us right now, I *so* planned on telling him about this development. I just hoped he didn't freak out.

"Trinity?" Stacey's brows lifted when I focused on her.

I took a deep breath. "I have something to tell you. It's going to sound really out there, and you're probably not going to believe me."

A half smile appeared. "Okay."

"I..." This was always the most awkward part. "I see... spirits."

Stacey's mouth opened, but she said nothing, which caused Sam to grin. "That's her she-doesn't-know-how-to-respond face. I know that face pretty well."

"Yeah, I figured that," I muttered, and Stacey's nose wrinkled. "I know this sounds completely bizarre, but there's someone here who wants to talk to you. He's apparently been hanging around, trying to get your attention."

She looked at me and then around like she was waiting for

someone to intervene, which was a common reaction and also meant it was time to bite the bullet.

"It's…it's Sam," I told her. "And he wants to talk to you."

Blood drained so rapidly from her face I was afraid she might faint. All she did was stare at me.

"You…you know a Sam, right?" I asked, startled when I felt the pulse in my chest intensify.

"Yeah. I *knew* a Sam. Did Zayne tell you about him?"

"No, he didn't." I glanced at the spirit. "He's actually sitting right next to you."

Her head swung to her left so quickly I wondered if she pulled a muscle.

"I'm right here," Sam said, and I repeated what he said.

Stacey didn't respond. She stared at where Sam sat for so long I started to really worry she'd passed out sitting up with her eyes open.

Was that even possible?

Adding it to my list of things to google later.

Stacey's cheeks flushed a mottled red, and my stomach sank. Her gaze lifted to me. "Is this some kind of joke?"

"Tell her it's not a joke," Sam said needlessly.

"It's not a joke. I know it may seem like that, but Sam *is* here. He's actually been around for a while," I repeated. "And he wants me to tell you something. It seems to be really important—"

"Good God." Her lower jaw moved as she leaned against the table, toward me. "What is wrong with you that you would do something like this? Is it because of Zayne?"

"What?" I jerked. 'This has nothing to do with him—"

"Because we had a thing once? And you're mad about it?"

"Oh my God, no. Seriously. Nothing is wrong with me. I swear. You can ask Zayne. Or even Layla. They know I can do this. I'm not making this up." Feeling the heat in my face increase, I turned to Sam. "I think it's time for you to tell me your message."

"I know there's a lot of weird stuff out there in the world that I don't know a lot about, but I'm not stupid. You need to leave right now," Stacey said, her voice low. "Like *right* now."

Sam cursed. "Tell her that she can't go back to that school."

Confusion thundered through me. "What kind of message is that?"

"Are you pretending to talk to him?" Her voice rose as she placed her hands on the table. I didn't need to look around to know people were probably starting to stare. "Are you freaking serious right now?"

"Yes." My attention shifted to her. "Sam is here, and I have no idea why he says you can't go back to school, but that's what he's saying."

Stacey laughed, made it sound coarse and twisted. "Do you really think I'm going to believe you? If it was, why has no one mentioned your little talent?"

"Because it's not really any of your business," I snapped.

"Excuse me?" Her eyes widened.

"Look, I'm not making this up. He—" I sucked in a sharp breath as the warmth in my chest flared intensely.

Oh, no.

Oh, no, no.

No way.

"Zayne!" Stacey called out, shooting to her feet. "You need to come get your girl."

My stomach dropped to my toes. I took a breath, but it got stuck in the rising disbelief and confusion.

Sam was saying something, but I couldn't hear him over the pounding of my heart. Stacey was staring behind me, her brown eyes wide, and she was saying something, too, but none of her words were making sense.

My gaze shifted to the table—the table that wasn't meant for only one person—and I thought about what Sam had said, referring to *them* instead of *her*. My breath felt funny in my chest as things began to click into place. Zayne hadn't told me what he was doing today. Just that he had stuff to do.

Just like he'd had stuff to do the last time he'd made plans and, other than meeting with the apartment manager, he hadn't told me what they were.

Slowly, I turned around.

In the mess of blurred faces and bodies, I saw him in the light blue shirt he'd left the apartment in, parting the crowd like some kind of hot Moses.

I took a step back, looking around this cute little ice cream shop, and I realized I knew this place. *This* was the ice cream parlor his father used to take him to, a tradition Zayne had kept with Layla as he grew older. This place was important to Zayne.

And he'd never brought me here.

This place was important to him, and yet he'd never shared it with me. But he'd gotten mad because I'd said a kiss meant more? A kiss could be anything or nothing, but sharing a piece of your past with someone meant a whole lot.

Even though a rational part of my mind recognized he didn't have to take me anywhere nor did he have to tell me

squat, the slicing pain in my chest felt all too real. I felt...
betrayed. A burn built in the back of my throat and crawled
up, stinging my eyes.

The urge to cut and run hit me hard and my muscles tensed
to do just that. I wanted space—I needed distance to get control of what I was feeling as I watched Zayne's steps slow. The
look of surprise was hard to miss, and it was as if he'd felt me
and couldn't believe I was here.

I was intruding.

Heat swept across my cheeks as my stomach churned. Oh,
man, what exactly was I intruding on? Zayne had claimed he
and Stacey were just friends, and friends met up for ice cream
all the time, but friends didn't hide that.

My head was shorting out like there was a loose wire somewhere between my synapses. Under a coarse coating of embarrassment was...disappointment.

Not jealousy.

Not envy.

Disappointment.

Zayne inhaled, and something flickered over his face.
"What are you doing here?"

My emotions were too all over the place to pick up anything from the bond, but the way he'd spoken the words
told me everything I needed to know. He wasn't happy to
see me here.

"She just showed up, and I thought she was with you, but
she said—" Her voice, thick and coarse, drew my gaze. "She
said *Sam* is here."

Her words jolted me out of the spiral of emotion.

"Sam?" Zayne shifted so he was in my line of vision. "What's going on, Trinity?"

"I am here," the spirit in question spoke up from where he still sat beside Stacey. "Tell them I'm here."

My heart was thrumming and my muscles were still tensed to run, but I held myself still. I hadn't done anything wrong. Well, I probably should've demanded more answers from Sam before I'd agreed to help, but I was just doing what I was meant to do. It wasn't my fault that it had led me to Zayne's little rendezvous.

"Trinity," Sam pleaded, and I looked at him. The golden shimmer around him was fading. "I don't have much more time. I can feel it. I'm being pulled back."

Get it together.

This is your duty.

I shoved everything I was feeling aside. My face was still burning, as were my throat and eyes, but I ignored all of that. I had a job. I had a duty. I got it together.

"Sam is here." I hated how hoarse my voice sounded. "I saw him at the apartment once before," I continued, not looking at Zayne or Stacey. "But he disappeared before he could tell me who he was. He followed Stacey when she came with Roth and Layla, but I didn't realize he was with her then."

"I did." Sam nodded.

"He just confirmed that," I said.

Stacey looked like she was close to fainting or having a complete breakdown as she stared up at us. "Zayne…?"

"Is it true?" Zayne asked, touching my arm. "Is Sam really here?"

Stunned he'd question me, I jerked my arm away as a new

wave of hurt pulsed through me. "Why would I lie about that, Zayne?"

He blinked. "You wouldn't."

"No shit," I spat, hurt giving way to anger. I wanted to pick up Stacey's ice cream and toss it in his face. Instead, I gestured at the booth. "Sit down."

Zayne hesitated like he wasn't going to listen, and I turned to him, widening my eyes. His lips thinned, but he dropped into the seat and slid across the booth, leaving space open. Sitting next to him was the last thing I wanted, but we were already drawing enough attention to last a lifetime and Sam *was* running out of time.

Tugging the earbuds out of my ears, I shoved them into my pocket and then I sat, back stiff. "I had no idea until we got here that Sam was bringing me to Stacey. He conveniently left that out."

Sam had the decency to look sheepish.

"And as Zayne can confirm," I said to Stacey, "I didn't know who Sam was. No one told me about him. If anyone had, I might've realized right off who he was."

She stared at me. "This is real?" Her wide eyes darted to Zayne. "She can see him?"

"She can see ghosts and spirits." Zayne dropped his arm on the table, next to the pack of the Twizzlers. "If she says Sam is here, he's here."

"I can't…" She looked at where Sam was sitting, shaking her head. "Tell me what he looks like."

I did just that, and Stacey pressed her palm to her mouth. "But you could've seen a picture of him online," she reasoned. "That doesn't mean anything."

"She's telling the truth," Zayne insisted quietly, saving me from having to ask why in the Hell I would even be looking up a picture of Sam.

Stacey said something, but it was too muffled for me to understand. She lowered her hand, fingers curling into a tight ball over her heart. "Sam?"

"I'm here," the spirit said, reaching for her but stopping short. "I've been here. Always."

I repeated what he said, and Stacey's face crumpled. "I'm sorry. I don't know what's wrong with me. I just—I'm sorry. Tell him I'm—"

"He can hear you," I said.

"He can hear me? Okay. I guess that makes sense." Tears tracked down her cheeks as she looked at me and then Sam. "I miss you," she whispered, lifting her hand from her chest to her chin.

"I miss you, too," Sam said, and I repeated it.

"Oh God." Her slim shoulders shook. "I'm just so sorry. I…"

Zayne made a sound of distress, reaching across the table. He placed his much larger hand over hers. "It's okay," he told her. "It's okay."

But it really wasn't.

Normally I'd be more considerate of the emotions these types of situations caused, but I had zero craps to give at the moment and we didn't have a lot of time.

"He has something he needs to tell you—"

"Tell both of them," Sam corrected, and my eyes narrowed on the spirit. "I knew they were meeting today."

A spirit had known and I hadn't.

"They used to come here once a week after…well, after everything," he added.

Nice.

That was just freaking great.

Hands opening and closing, I kept my eyes on Sam. "He has a message for both of you. Something to do with a school?"

Sam nodded and then twisted toward Stacey. "She can't go back to that school. Something is happening there. It's not safe."

"You're going to need to give me more detail, Sam. I need to know why it's not safe."

"He's saying the school isn't safe?" Zayne questioned.

"There's a lot of…souls there. Too many. It's like they're gathering for something," Sam explained, his form flickering more rapidly now. "I've been checking on her since…well, since I could, and it hasn't always been like that."

"What do you mean souls are gathering there?" I asked, and Zayne shifted forward.

"Souls. Dead people who haven't crossed over—"

"Ghosts?" I suggested, and when he nodded, I glanced at Stacey, who was staring at Sam but not seeing him. "There are a lot of ghosts there? How many?"

Stacey's eyes widened even further. "At school?"

The spirit nodded. "Over a hundred. I tried counting one day, but they disappear and they're confused. Sort of running around all hectic-like. It's like they're stuck."

"The ghosts are stuck at the school," I repeated. "Over a hundred."

"How can that happen?" Zayne asked.

"Spirits and ghosts can be summoned to a place," I explained.

"Like through a Ouija board?" Stacey let out a nervous, wet-sounding laugh.

"Yeah, actually those things can work under the right circumstances," I said. "But you almost never get who you think you're communicating with. Not unless you know how to... channel a certain spirit, and even I can't do that."

Stacey stared at me. "They sell them in toy stores."

Beside her, Sam laughed. "God, I missed that look on her face." A smile appeared. "Did you know the Ouija board marketer fell to his death while supervising the build of a Ouija board factory?"

I frowned at him.

He shrugged. "Kind of freaky if you think about it."

"How can ghosts be stuck?" Zayne asked.

"I don't know. I'm sure there are spells that could do it, but I don't know why you'd want to. A trapped ghost or even a spirt could become a wraith. Could take months or years, but being stuck would corrupt them," I said, horrified by the possibility of something like that occurring. "How could this happen at a school?"

"It's a Hellmouth," Stacey murmured. "Layla and I weren't joking when we said that."

I ignored her. "Are the ghosts putting people in danger?"

"Someone fell down the steps a week ago. They were pushed by one of the ghosts," Sam said.

When I repeated that, Stacey sat back against the booth. "A guy did fall down the steps. Last Tuesday. I don't know the details, but I heard that it happened."

"I've heard whispers," Sam continued, and then he blinked out and returned in a more transparent form. "And yes, I'm being literal. I hear whispers when I'm here—about it not being much longer and that something is coming. I've tried to find the source but when I saw them, I knew I couldn't get any closer. I can't keep going back there. I want to, I want to keep her safe, but I'm… I'm afraid if I keep going back, they'll see me and they'll know I'm not like the others."

A chill swept down my spine.

"What is he saying?" Zayne asked, pulling his hand away from Stacey's. "Trin?"

"Who are they?" I swallowed. "Do you know who is whispering?"

Sam's hazy form twisted toward me. "Shadow People."

27

Shadow People.

Two words in the English language I'd never hoped to hear spoken out loud. Goose bumps spread across my arms.

"Oh, man," I whispered.

"What?" Zayne touched my arm, and this time I didn't pull away. "What's going on?"

Pulse pounding, I gave a short shake of my head and focused on Sam. I needed to get as much information as possible out of him before he poofed into oblivion. "Have you heard them say what's coming?"

"No."

Even though he couldn't confirm it, I had a feeling I knew. And there was something else I needed to know. I tipped forward. "How did you know what I was?"

"Because there's someone there, at the school, who can do what you can," Sam said, and another chill powered down my spine. "I've seen him talking to— Oh, man. It's happening."

I blinked, knowing what he meant. He was being pulled back. "Can you tell me what he looks like, Sam? I need—"

"I'll try to come back as soon as I can." He turned to Stacey, and for what I could see of his face, my heart cracked a little. "I wish I'd had the guts to tell you how I felt about you. I wish… I wish we had more time. Tell her that. Please? Tell her I did love her." He lifted an arm that was more see-through than solid and touched her cheek. Stacey sucked in a sharp breath. "She felt that. Tell her it was me. And tell her I want her to be happy. That she needs to be happy."

Without warning, the space beside Stacey was empty. He was gone, and I had a feeling he wasn't coming right back.

"Dammit," I muttered.

"What?" Stacey placed her fingers over the spot on her cheek "What just happened?"

"You felt him when he touched your cheek," I said, and then I told her what he'd said without looking at her as I spoke. I didn't want to see the emotions her face would expose. "He's gone now, but he said he'll try to come back. He doesn't know when."

Or if he could again.

I left that part unspoken, because the message he'd imparted made it sound like he wasn't entirely sure. He'd been coming back too much.

"Excuse me." Zayne tapped my arm. "Can you let me out?"

I slid out of the booth and stepped aside as Zayne moved to where Sam had been sitting. He folded an arm around Stacey's shoulders, tugging her against him as he spoke to her.

I cast my gaze to the pack of Twizzlers, pressing my lips

together. I was a third wheel on a painfully intimate moment of two.

"When?" Her voice sounded rough when she spoke again. "When can he come back?"

"I don't know. I have a feeling he'll try, but…" I stared at the candy I'd actually never tried before, because it always looked gross to me. "But spirits are not meant to repeatedly visit the living."

"Why not?" she demanded.

"Because moving on isn't just the process of crossing over. It's a continuous journey for the, um, the deceased, and if visits are continuous, it's hard for those left behind to move on," I explained, dropping my hands to my lap. "It's hard for those who have died to find peace when they're still wrapped up in the lives of the living. Spirits can come and go as they please, but there are rules. Their travels are monitored. Based on what he said, he's been here a lot already. He's been trying to get your attention for a while."

"Oh God." Her voice cracked. "If I'd known, I would've talked to him. I would've done something. Anything. I just didn't know."

"There wasn't any way for you to know. It's all right," Zayne assured her. "Sam had to know that. It's not like he'd blame you."

Some people were far more perceptive of things like spirits and ghosts, but Zayne was right, Stacey wouldn't have known Sam was there.

"God. I just—I didn't expect this today. It was just supposed to be catching up over ice cream and maybe a nice walk. You know? Like we used to do." The ice cream in front of

Stacey was more like soup as she picked up the Twizzlers. "I even picked up these for you. I remember how you like to put them in your ice cream."

My lip curled.

Zayne ate Twizzlers with his ice cream? I lifted my gaze. He still had his arm around Stacey, but his eyes were on me, the pale shade of blue anything but cool. I averted my gaze to the glossy vinyl records framed on the wall.

"It's okay." Those were turning out to be two of Zayne's favorite words. "We'll try again, as soon as possible."

I thought and felt nothing in response to that.

"Yeah," Stacey said, dragging her palm under her eyes. "Promise?"

"Promise."

"Good. Because I'm going to need some nonmelted comfort food after this." She cleared her throat. "So, what's going on at the local haunted and cursed school from Hell?"

"You sure you want to talk about it?" I asked. "After everything with Sam?"

"She's sure," Zayne answered, and I bit down on my thumbnail. "Stacey can handle this."

Stacey laughed again, the sound stronger as she picked up her water and took a drink. "If you knew the things I've seen and experienced, you wouldn't ask if I was sure. I'll deal with…with Sam later, most likely when I'm alone and have a bag of Skittles to consume. Obviously what Sam was trying to tell me is important. We need to deal with that."

Surprise flickered through me, quickly followed by respect for her ability to push aside a riot of emotions and prioritize.

God, Zayne had been right. Stacey and I probably would get along...if it wasn't for him.

"He told you something that had you freaked-out." Zayne shifted, pulling his arm away from Stacey. "What did he tell you?"

"Other than the over-a-hundred-trapped-ghosts creepy tidbit?" I said.

"Over a hundred?" Stacey let out a low breath. "Yeah, other than that creepy tidbit."

"He's said there are Shadow People there," I told them, keeping my voice low.

"Shadow People?" she repeated. "Do I even want to know what that is?"

"Probably not." I glanced at Zayne. A muscle was ticking along his jaw. "Do you know what they are?"

"I'm assuming some kind of ghost or something?" he said.

I coughed out a dry laugh. "Not quite. I've never seen one. All I know is what my mom told me about them. They're like wraiths, but they were never human in the first place. They're like the souls of deceased demons."

"Oh, man," Stacey whispered.

"I don't understand. Souls of demons?" Zayne rested his forearms on the table. "How is that possible? They don't have souls."

"We think they don't," I corrected, thinking of Roth. "But I said they're *like* souls. More like the essence of them." Based on the way Zayne was staring at me, I could tell this was something that had never crossed his mind. "What did you think happened when demons died? That they just ceased to exist?"

"I figured they went back to Hell."

"They do, but they're dead, and unless someone with a lot of power gives them back corporeal form, they don't just cease to exist without being destroyed, and I can only think of a few people who have that ability."

"Grim?" he suggested.

I nodded. "If you mean the angel Azreal? Yeah, he'd be able to do that."

"Wait. What?" Stacey glanced back and forth between us. "You mean the Grim Reaper? The guy Layla met?"

My brows lifted. Layla had met the Grim Reaper. How had that happened?

Zayne nodded.

"He's not the only one who can destroy Shadow People," I said, catching Zayne's glance, and I saw the moment he realized what I couldn't say. With the Sword of Michael, I could destroy Shadow People just like an angel could. "But these things are inherently evil. Like, worse than when they were living, breathing demons bent on destruction. Like, if you see a Shadow Person, you turn and run in the other direction. They're powerful and vindictive, malicious and deadly."

Zayne reached for the Twizzlers and dragged one ropey piece of candy out. "I'm guessing they look like shadows?"

I tilted my head. "Yes. They look like shadow outlines of people. Sort of in the name."

He bit down on the rope of cherry and sugar and stared back at me.

"And they're at my school?" Stacey said.

"That's what Sam says, and that's not all."

"It's not? Trapped ghosts and Shadow People aren't enough to get between me and my diploma? There has to be more?"

My lips twitched. "He says there's someone there who's able to communicate with the ghosts and the Shadow People." I looked at Zayne again. "Someone like me."

"And what are you exactly?" She stared at me and then shifted her gaze to Zayne. Her puffy eyes sort of ruined the hard-core look she was trying to deliver. "Anyone care to fill me in? Because she's not just some chick that grew up with Wardens."

I frowned. "I *am* the chick that grew up with Wardens."

"Who can also commune with the dead?" she challenged. "Like other normal humans?"

"I never said I was a normal human." I smiled. "Like you." Now her eyes narrowed.

"Was he able to tell you what this person looked like?" Zayne changed the subject. "Any information on who it is?"

"All he told me was that it was a guy before he ran out of time," I answered.

"So, we don't know if it's a student or a teacher or just some random person roaming the school." Zayne finished off the candy with one last frustrated snap of his jaw. "All we know is someone is rounding up ghosts and trapping them in the school, and Shadow People are involved."

Not knowing how much Stacey was aware of, I chose my next words carefully. "That's not all we know. I'm pretty sure it's related to what everyone is looking for."

Zayne's hand halted halfway to the bag. "You think so?"

I nodded.

He cursed under his breath as he grabbed another strip of candy. "I don't know if that's good or bad news at this point."

"Good," I decided. "It's a lead."

"I have no idea what you two are talking about." Stacey took a drink. "I don't like to be left out."

Zayne spared her a brief grin. "I'll fill you in later."

He would? When his gaze shifted to me, I arched a brow. "We need to go to that school."

"Agreed."

"Well, you're going to have a problem doing it during the day, because there are always people there, and right now they're doing renovations in the evening and overnight." Stacey placed her empty glass down. "Except on the weekends."

What was today? Monday. So, that wasn't too long of a wait, but I wanted to go now, see if I was right—that this was connected to the Harbinger.

Could it be that Sam had given us our first real lead? Damn, it was almost too convenient, so much so that it was also disturbing to think that, if Sam had not had followed Stacey when she'd come to Zayne's place, we wouldn't know about what was going on at the school.

Made one wonder about cosmic interference.

Looking across the table, I saw that Zayne was finished with the second Twizzler. I couldn't believe he actually ate them with ice cream. The same guy who removed buns from grilled chicken sandwiches.

There was something wrong with him.

And there was something wrong with me because not having known Zayne ate ice cream with Twizzlers made my chest ache.

How stupid was that?

My gaze flicked over Stacey and Zayne, taking them in sitting side by side, him so much larger and broader than her tiny frame. They looked good together, even if they were just friends who had been more at some point, and things would be easier for them if they wanted to be more again. Yeah, Wardens weren't supposed to date humans, but Zayne did a lot of things Wardens weren't supposed to do. It wasn't the same with us.

It was time for me to hit the road.

"I hope it…helps to know Sam obviously cares about you and wants to make sure you're safe," I announced awkwardly as I focused on Stacey. "I know it probably feels good and horrible all at once, knowing that he's been around, but when you've had time to sit with it, I think—or at least I hope—it's a good thing. He wants you to be happy, and if you can do that, you'll be doing the best thing for you and for him."

"You…" Stacey lowered her gaze as she toyed with the spoon jutting out of her soupy ice cream. "You really think he'll be back?"

"I do." I wasn't sure if that was going to be a good thing in the long-term. I bit back a sigh. "Anyway, sorry I busted up your ice cream social. I honestly didn't mean to." I glanced at Zayne as I slid out of the booth. "I'll see you later."

Zayne's jaw was working overtime as I gave them a quick wave. For the briefest moment, I felt what was coming through the bond, and it had me backing up and turning around as fast as I could. Soon I stepped out into the hot air and started walking, the scents of melted fudge and vanilla following me.

Anger.

Simmering anger was what I'd felt, and it had left a peppery taste in my throat.

Zayne was angry, but at what? His ruined ice cream social? Me showing up? Sam's unexpected appearance and how it had affected Stacey? Ghosts and Shadow People hanging out at the school? The whole situation, including what had happened between us? The options were limitless.

Whatever. At the end of the day, at least we had a lead.

I didn't know where I was going. Back to the apartment, I guessed, but I had no idea if I could get back there. I really didn't care right then. I'd just keep walking and walking, trying to put as much space between me and that damn little ball of warmth in my chest. My path was blissfully clear as I hit the intersection. I was never—

A horn blew, the sound deafening as my head whipped to the left. The car was *right* there, in my blind spot. Tires squealed as brakes pumped. It was too late. The car wouldn't be able to stop in time.

Someone screamed, but it wasn't me, because I was incapable of making sound. In those seconds that stretched into eternity, I knew this car was going to ram into me. It wouldn't kill me, but it was most definitely going to hurt. Bones might even be broken, and God, wouldn't time in a body cast just top today—

A band of steel circled my waist and pulled me back. I slammed into a hard, warm surface that smelled of winter. My feet left the ground as I was turned. Within a heartbeat I was staring at...

Staring at Zayne's pale blue shirt, as the man in the car

shouted and then peeled away, laying on his horn. I lifted my gaze, and furious pale eyes met mine.

"Are you out of your mind?"

I felt the words rumble out of him, because he had me all but plastered to his chest. I tried to lift my hands to push away, but my arms were clamped to my sides. I was stuck against him, and his body was throwing off heat like a furnace.

Crap.

"Trin—"

"Let me go." I knew we had to be gaining an audience, considering we were in the middle of a sidewalk.

He glared down at me. "What were you doing?"

"I said let me go." The next breath I took was like swallowing fire. "Now."

Zayne drew in a deep breath, but he let go, sliding his arm away from me in a slow drag that infuriated and frustrated me for half a dozen different reasons.

I stepped back.

But I didn't make it very far.

His hand shot out and wrapped around my wrist, his grip firm but far from painful. "Where do you think you're going?"

"Anywhere but where I am right now."

Zayne's laugh was harsh. "Oh, I don't think so."

Without another word, Zayne wheeled me back toward the ice cream shop as an older couple wearing matching windbreakers eyed us. Their heads were bent together as they sent nervous glances in our direction. They didn't intervene. No one did. I guessed it was because it was rush hour in the nation's capital and people just wanted to get home before dark.

Real concerned, helpful citizens right there.

I tugged on my hand. "Zayne—"

"Not yet," he said, threading his fingers through mine. "Not here."

The hand around mine was firm, and his long-legged pace was annoying to keep up with. I peeked over at him. "I do not understand why you're the one with the attitude right now."

"You don't?" he demanded. "You know better than to walk across a street without checking. You could've been injured, Trin. And then what?"

I tried to pull my hand free again. No such luck. "But I wasn't hurt, and look, I busted into your ice cream date. I didn't—"

"Not yet," he clipped out.

I started to frown. "But I—"

"Trinity, I'm serious. I don't want to hear a single word from you right now." He cut in front of me, nearly causing me to trip. I didn't, because he righted me before I could topple over.

"But you asked me a question!" I pointed out. "Did you not want me to answer it?"

"Not really."

Now I was *really* frowning as he pulled me into an alley I'd passed on the way to the ice cream shop. Zayne stopped by a fire escape, far from the packed sidewalk, and faced me. The light above us flickered, casting strange shadows over his face.

"You going to let me go now?" I demanded.

"I don't know. Are you going to go play in traffic again?"

"Oh, yeah. It's a favorite pastime of mine, so no promises."

The look he gave me told me he wasn't impressed. I drew in a shallow breath and started to try to tell him what happened, but he opened his mouth and beat me to it.

"You have so much explaining to do." He stared down at me.

That was the wrong thing to say. "*I* have explaining to do? Me?"

"Are you not the person who just randomly popped up here and then ran off into the street?"

"You make it sound like I did all that on purpose, which I did not, and I also did not run off." Even though I'd wanted to. "I *walked* off."

"As if that makes a difference." His eyes flared wide as he dipped his head. "You were out here for who knows how long, unprotected and alone."

"Oh, like you care," I blurted out. It was such a typical thing to say, but whatever.

"Really? You think that?"

"Based on the way you've been acting the last couple of days? Yeah."

"God, I shouldn't even be surprised that you'd think that."

I gaped at him. "You need to chill with the attitude."

"I need to chill?"

"Obviously. That's what I said." I yanked on my hand again. I was done with the hand-holding crap. I broke his hold just to remind him exactly who had the strength here. "In case you're confused, I don't have to tell you anything about what I'm doing, so you need to check yourself with the whole you-didn't-know-where-I-was spiel. That is not how this works. Ever. Second, I can protect myself—"

"Except when you're crossing streets, apparently," he fired back.

"You know what. You can go—" I cut myself off, taking a step back.

His lips twisted into a smirk. "Finish that sentence if it'll make you feel better."

Instead of doing just that, I lifted my hand and flipped him off.

One eyebrow rose. "Did *that* make you feel better?"

"Yes."

Lips thinning, he looked away and dragged in a deep breath. "You didn't tell me the truth the night you were in the kitchen."

My ears must have been deceiving me, or the Lord was testing me. Or both. "Come again?"

"That was why you had your dagger with you." He faced me again. "You weren't getting something to drink. Sam was there, and you didn't tell me—"

"You didn't tell me you were meeting up with Stacey!" I shouted loud enough that people on the street had have to heard me. "You failed to mention that when you talked about the 'stuff' you needed to do, so don't stand there and lecture me. And it's not the first time, either, right? That's where you were the day you met me in the park. The night we—" I cut myself off. "The night Morgan was killed."

His gaze flew to mine. "I had lunch with her that day. I didn't tell you—"

"I don't care." And that was the God's honest truth at that messy moment. "I don't care why you didn't."

Zayne stepped toward me. "Are you sure about that, Trinity?"

I tensed. "I'm positive. I'm just pointing out the hypocrisy."

"Then if that's the case, I can't wait to see your face the moment the hypocrisy turns right back on you."

"Oh, you think you're smart." I started to turn away, but I stopped. "I didn't tell you about Sam because I had no idea who he was that night. He disappeared before I could get a name, and I thought he was just some random spirit who'd seen me and followed me back. It's happened before, and I didn't bring it up because I figured hearing there was another dead person in your apartment would creep you out."

Zayne looked toward the street, arms crossing over his chest.

"I didn't know he was bringing me to Stacey until I saw her. If I had known who he was, I would've contacted you. I'm not stupid."

His head whipped back to mine. "I didn't say you were."

"I guess I misinterpreted the playing-in-the-street comment then." I held on to my anger like it was a favorite blanket. "And why are you even here right now?"

"What is that supposed to mean?"

"Really?" My tone was so dry, a desert would seem like a damp destination in comparison. "You have *stuff* to do, and the whole Sam thing seemed to hit Stacey really hard. So, you should be in there, where you're needed. Not out here, giving me crap."

Zayne's nostrils flared and his pupils changed, stretching.

"You're right. I had stuff to do today, and *that*, back there?" He jabbed a finger at the street. "It did hit Stacey hard, because when Sam died, she didn't even know. None of us did, because a damn Lilin had assumed his form and pretended to be him in every way possible."

My eyes widened. A Lilin was the offspring of Lilith but nothing like Layla. A Lilin was a demonic creature way forbidden to be topside, because they could strip souls by simply brushing up against a human, creating wraiths like a mogwai feeds after midnight. And now I understood what Sam had meant by saying he hadn't crossed over as soon as he'd died. His soul would've been stripped and he would've been...

Oh God.

"I didn't know," I whispered. "I don't know anything about these people—"

"These *people* are my friends," he said, and I sucked in a sharp breath. "And why would anyone tell you? You didn't ask who Stacey lost, even though I mentioned it."

I jerked back. "I didn't think you'd want me to ask."

"Yeah, and I wonder why you thought that."

My mouth dropped open. "That's bullshit. I tried to ask you the night we talked on the couch, and you told me there were a lot of things I didn't know."

"You were asking about Stacey being at my place before. You weren't asking about *her*. You were asking about *us*. Big difference there."

A prickly sensation swept across my skin as his pupils shrank back to their normal size. I didn't know how to respond to that. I felt like I'd belly flopped over a line.

"I didn't tell you about meeting with her because I didn't

think it would be something you'd want to hear. Maybe I was wrong. No. I *was* wrong. I should've said I was meeting her among the other stuff I needed to do today. Hindsight is twenty-twenty." He glared at me. "Stacey is my friend, and I haven't been a very good friend to her of late. That was what today was supposed to be. That's what the other day was about. Nothing else. Nothing more. No matter what she and I used to do or not do."

My face started to sting. "You don't owe me an explanation—"

"Apparently I do. So, here's what you need to know. Stacey thought she was telling the boy she knew for years that she loved him, but she wasn't. She never got to tell Sam," he said, causing me to flinch. "And that boy was in Hell until Layla freed him. Stacey knew that, once we realized what we were dealing with wasn't Sam. There wasn't a damn thing she could do, so, yes, hearing that he was there hit her hard.

"And after what happened between us, I cannot believe you're questioning me," he continued. "You don't want anything serious between us, so it shouldn't matter what the Hell I was doing with her or with anyone. You made your choice."

"Choice?" I barked out a harsh laugh. "You have *no* idea, so please, keep standing there, making me feel bad when you're the one who chose not to tell me about Stacey. And what nerve of you?" I stepped toward him. Anger and frustration was a tumultuous storm in me and the emotions got the best of me. "I had no *choice*. I had to draw a line, because if whatever was going on between us became more than something physical, I have no idea what would happen to you. It's forbidden, so I drew a line at kissing, because it does make things

mean more to me. You tore me down for that, making me feel like I was using you like Layla did. You projected *your* baggage all over me, but you brought Stacey to that ice cream parlor. I know what that place is. It's the one your father took you to. It's important to you, and never once have you even considered taking me there."

"It's a damn ice cream shop, Trinity."

"Oh, don't you dare try to play it off as if that place means nothing to you. If it was anyone else? Sure. I know better. You get to think I'm terrible for excluding you from something you find important, but you can do it to me?"

A muscle ticked in his jaw as he looked away.

"I guess you're resisting saying it's not the same?"

"Just like you not telling me about Sam is not the same?" he shot back. "Or when you refuse to tell me the truth when I know you're not okay? Or when I know you're not telling me the whole story about things?"

"Oh my God." I shook my head, and I don't know why I admitted what I did next. It was like the situation was spiraling out of control and I followed right along with it. "You know what, I have lied. That day in the park? I wasn't out roaming around. I'd gone to see the coven of witches with Roth."

His gaze sharpened on me.

"He wanted me to help get Bambi back, and I thought it would be a good chance to try to get more information out of them," I continued, hands clenching into fists. "I killed that witch, Faye. So, yeah, we're both great at lying about the important stuff, right? We're both hypocrites. Does that make you feel better, knowing that? It should. Now that you know what I'm capable of, you should be *thrilled* I drew that line."

He stared at me. "You're wrong. I'm better at keeping things a secret than you."

"Is that so?" I challenged.

"I knew about Roth and the coven," he said, effectively blowing my mind and the smugness right out of me. "I knew that he asked you to help. And I know that you didn't want to kill her or any of them. I also know that you didn't kill that witch until she went after Bambi and the Crone told you to."

"Well," I said, and that was all I could say.

"Roth called me after he dropped you off."

My jaw was on the ground. That demonic SOB had told me not to tell Zayne!

"He didn't think it wise for you to be out there by yourself," he continued, and I about fell flat on my back. "I was just waiting for you to tell me, and I guess you have."

I had nothing to say.

"There it is. The expression on your face I was waiting for when the hypocrisy turned right back around on you. Too bad it's not as enjoyable as I thought it would be," he said. "And you know what? I *should* be in there with Stacey, because that's what a friend does. Instead, I'm out here with you."

The sting returned, mixing with the burn. "I didn't tell you to come out here."

Zayne shook his head as he dragged his lower lip between his teeth. "Do you know your way back to the apartment?"

"I can figure—"

"Do you or do you not know your way back to the apartment, Trinity? Do you even have any apps downloaded on your phone to help you? Can you see those street signs? Did you pay attention when Sam led you here?" When I didn't answer—when I *couldn't* answer—he said, "It's not like I can just let you roam around, so whether or not you want me here or I want to be here, this is where I am."

The burn and sting became a knot I could barely swallow. All my anger pulsed, dissipated, returned as something entirely new. My chest ached, but my skin burned with embarrassment and my shoulders slumped under the sudden weight as I stared at the pebbled alley floor.

Burden.

That's what that weight was. A burden of duty, and a burden of having to be aided. Zayne was right. I didn't even have Google Maps on my phone. Hell, I wouldn't be able to read the stupid directions if I did. He knew that, and he was here because of that and because he was my bonded Protector.

Not because I was a friend in need.

Not because this was where he wanted or needed to be.

And *that* was a world of difference. Even if things hadn't gotten so complicated between us, this situation right here would've probably still happened.

"I want to go back to the apartment," I said, feeling so very heavy. "I would like that."

"Of course." His voice was flat. "It's your world, Trinity."

It's your world.

Hadn't Misha said something similar? I turned toward the street, squinting behind my sunglasses. "I can do an Uber if you—um, if you help me with seeing the app and…" Heat flowed over my cheeks. "And help me with the car when it gets here. I can't see license plates, and some makes—"

"Got it," he clipped out, and when I looked over my shoulder, he already had his phone out. No more than a few seconds later, he announced, "The car will be here in less than ten minutes."

And that was all he said.

28

About two years ago, Misha and I got into this huge fight. Jada and Ty and several other Wardens were leaving the Community to spend a day in one of the nearby towns and Outback cheese fries were involved, so of course, I wanted to go with them. Thierry refused my request due to some inane reason and, knowing my penchant for not listening to his orders, he went as far as stationing spare Wardens at all the possible exits of the house. Misha had told me he wasn't going and would be working on something with Thierry. He'd lied and gone with the group, and while coming to find out that lie wasn't his biggest crime, it had been world ending to me then. I knew that my anger and upset had everything to do with me feeling left out and like life was generally unfair, but Misha had still lied instead of just fessing up to the fact that he'd wanted to go with everyone. I would've still been jealous, but I wouldn't have said anything other than *have fun*. We were both at fault, even though I shouldered most of the blame; we yelled and shouted at each other before retreating to our respective rooms, slamming the doors shut. The following morning we had to train, and I wanted to apologize but was still too angry and hurt to cross that bridge, so the entire session was incredibly awkward and conversation stilted throughout the remaining day.

That was a lot like how tonight was going with Zayne.

He hadn't come back to the apartment until it was almost time to leave, and all he said as he passed me in the living room was that he thought it would be a good idea to check out the area that surrounded the high school.

We'd probably exchanged three complete sentences since then, which wasn't exactly different than the past several days.

So, fun times.

As we walked along the rain-drenched sidewalks toward Heights on the Hill, which was what the school was called, I felt a lot like I had with Misha following our argument, but unlike earlier, when I couldn't figure out why I was being such a coward, I thought I might have figured it out now. And I wanted to apologize. I was mouthy and confrontational on a good day and didn't back down from a fight, but I absolutely loathed conflict with someone I cared about. The problem was, like with Misha that day, I was still furious and hurt and about a million miles away from being ready to apologize.

But I wasn't completely to blame.

I could understand, now that I'd had time to dwell obsessively over what had happened, why he hadn't told me he was meeting Stacey. He'd felt my emotions when Stacey had come over, and he'd seen through my questions about her. He probably wanted to avoid hurting the feelings he sensed in me or avoid them in general. But that didn't mean he shouldn't have been honest, same as with Misha. Honesty would've sucked in the moment, but would have been far easier to deal with than uncovering a lie designed to cover a hurt. Contrary to what Zayne believed, his lie was nothing like me not telling him about what had appeared to be a random spirit in his apartment.

No one could convince me otherwise.

And the fact that he'd known about what had happened with the coven this entire time? I couldn't be mad at him for not saying anything, because I had kept that from him, but I didn't understand why he hadn't confronted me. Had he really just been waiting for me to tell him?

I doubted he was happy now that I had.

Lightning streaked across the night sky, a jagged arc of light that lit up Zayne's stoic profile. His hair was pulled back, all except those shorter strands. They were tucked behind his ears.

The one time I would've appreciated him being dishonest would've been when he'd told me that he'd rather be with a friend than dealing with me.

Than *helping* me.

That, he could've kept to himself.

"You want to say something." Zayne shattered the silence. "Just say it."

I jerked my gaze from him, flushing at being caught staring. "I have nothing to say."

"You sure about that, Trin?"

Trin.

At least we were back to nicknames and not formal names. "Yep."

He didn't respond.

"Do you have something *you* want to say, Zayne?" I didn't even try to keep the snideness out of my tone.

"Nope."

Thunder cracked like the blast of a cannon aimed at the Heavens. The pounding rain had stopped about an hour ago, but another storm was coming in. Getting soaked and possibly electrocuted would be a fine way to wrap up today.

Definitely not seeing any stars tonight.

"I wonder what happens when Wardens are hit by lightning?" I walked ahead of Zayne to an intersection.

"Probably the same thing that happens to a Trueborn."

I rolled my eyes, making sure there were no cars coming before I crossed. Not like I was about to repeat earlier. I started forward, my steps clunky as I reached the curb before I thought I would. I really hoped Zayne hadn't seen that, because God knows, I wouldn't want him—

"Trin?"

"What?" I snapped.

"Are you going to the high school with me or someplace else?" he asked, amusement dripping from his tone like thick honey. "I'm just curious, since you seem to have other plans in mind."

Stopping halfway across the street, I sucked in a breath and did everything in my power to keep myself from screaming. I pivoted and found that Zayne had hung a left at the intersection. Stalking my way back to the sidewalk, I all but power walked past him, noticing the sidewalk was no longer following a flat course but a rather steep incline. A deep, rumbling chuckle came from behind me.

"Glad you found that funny," I replied, squinting as the outlines of trees gave way to open lawn. "Because you're going to think it's really funny when I break your face."

"You're incredibly aggressive."

Up ahead, I saw a two-story building with its main floor lit up. "And you're incredibly annoying."

"And you're still going the wrong way," he said.

I stopped.

God had to be testing me.

Wheeling around, I saw that Zayne was crossing the lawn. I frowned, glancing in the direction I was going. I couldn't make out much about the large building ahead of me, but it looked like a school to me. "Is that not the school right there?"

"It is." He kept walking. "But I don't think you want to walk right up to the front doors, do you? We're here to scout the place, not announce our arrival to whoever is working right now."

My God, I was going to tackle him and pound him into the ground, and *not* in the fun way.

"Did it cross your mind to maybe say something?" I complained, breaking into a jog to catch up with his freakishly long strides. A flag whipped around its pole, making snapping noises.

"It did." He slowed down. "For about a second."

"Ass," I muttered, remaining a few feet behind him and to the side. The ground was mushy and soft in certain areas, as if the soil had been recently laid down.

"What was that?" Zayne looked over his shoulder, his face hidden in the darkness. "I didn't quite hear you."

Yeah, he had; he just wanted me to repeat myself. Not going to happen. "Where are we going?"

"To check out this side of the grounds. There's a small neighborhood directly behind the school, and I want to see if we pick up on anything."

All I felt was the constant low hum of nearby demon activity. "The only thing I'm picking up on is your combative attitude."

Zayne laughed—he laughed loud enough that I wondered if we'd be overheard.

"That wasn't meant to be funny."

"It sure made me laugh, though." Zayne stopped suddenly, throwing out an arm and nearly clotheslining me.

"Jesus," I gasped, stumbling back a step.

"Careful," he advised. "It's hard to see, but the lawn ends here and there are six narrow steps down."

Yeah, I definitely wouldn't have noticed that. Granted, tripping and falling down those steps would've hurt only my pride. The words *thank you* burned my tongue, but I didn't speak them as I tentatively went down the steps.

"I don't know if I can sense a Shadow Person," I said as lightning cut across the sky again. "Since they're not living demons, I don't know how that works."

"With our luck, probably not." He scanned what I realized was a small, narrow parking lot that likely was for faculty.

Beyond a temporary makeshift fence, several lighter colored vans and trucks were parked along the back of the building, blocking whatever entrances were there. The words *Bar Rhinge and Sons Construction* were scrawled in big, bold red letters across the vans, lit by the side entrance lights. As we drew closer, I could hear the steady thump of hammers and…

"By the way, I talked to Roth this afternoon," Zayne announced as we started across the parking lot. "He wants to check out the school with us on Saturday."

"Cool," I murmured. "He's like the opposite of a good-luck charm, so why not?"

A rumble of thunder silenced the trill of cicadas and my steps slowed, then stopped. I looked behind me. Wind continued to beat at the flag and the branches of the trees that dotted the lawn. Tiny bumps rose on my arms as I strained to hear…what, I had no idea. It was a low murmur. Maybe even the wind?

"Trin?" Zayne's voice was close. "You feel something?"

"No. Not really." I turned back to the school and lifted my gaze to the dark windows. The goose bumps spread as a fine shiver chased them along my skin. "It's just a weird feeling."

"Like what?"

I lifted a shoulder. I wasn't sure if it was anything, but there was the sensation of hundreds of unseen eyes on us. Could be the ghosts Sam had said were trapped. They could be at those windows, and I just couldn't see them. "I don't know. Just a weird vibe. Maybe this school *is* a Hellmouth."

Zayne was silent.

I looked over at him. "Now that was supposed to be funny."

"Was it?"

"How mad will you get if I just drop-kick you into one of those trucks?"

"Pretty mad, to be honest."

"Okay." I nodded. "Just going to weigh my odds over here to see if it's worth making you madder than you already are."

"I'm not mad."

"Oh, really?" That I laughed out. "I've seen you happy. This is not happy."

"Didn't say I was happy, either," he returned. I threw up my arms in frustration. "There're doors back here, along the side, if I remember correctly. I'm going to see if it's accessible or if any windows are boarded up. Map out the area for Saturday night."

"Have fun."

Zayne faced me. "You're not coming?"

"No. There's probably debris and crap all over," I pointed out. "I'm just going to stumble and trip all over everything."

"Then what are you going to do?" He stepped toward me.

"Play in traffic."

He made a noise that sounded like a cross between a laugh and a curse. "Sounds like a good time. Just try not to get hit and killed. Sort of like to survive the night."

"Getting hit by a car wouldn't kill me." I tossed the words back at him.

Zayne lifted his hand, and I thought maybe he'd give me a thumbs-up before he walked around the fence.

"Jerk," I muttered, turning my gaze to the dark windows.

Of course I wasn't going to play in traffic. While Zayne was scoping out a good entrance for Saturday, I wanted to figure out what I was feeling and possibly hearing. Plus, I would probably break a leg and alert everyone to our presence trying to navigate an active work site in the dark.

I lifted my gaze to the neat rows of the second floor. It

could just be insects, but the vibe...yeah, the vibe was way off, and I didn't think it had anything to do with the fact that I knew what could be inside.

The air was thicker here, like soup. The steady clang of hammers made me wonder if the workers had noticed anything. Missing tools. Disembodied voices. People seen in the corners of their eyes but gone when they focused on the area. Those things would be experienced if there was just one ghost in a place, but over a hundred? God.

Why would someone trap them here? And if this was related to the Harbinger, what could it want with ghosts? And Shadow People? The plot was thickening, but the problem was I had no idea what the damn story was.

Another flash of light streaked the sky, illuminating the windows for a second. Anyone else would've probably been able to see whether anything was in those windows, but they were blurs to me. Thunder immediately followed, and then a big, fat drop of rain smacked my nose. That was the only warning before the sky ripped open and rain poured from above.

Soaked to the bone within seconds, I sighed heavily. The rain was kind of warm, so at least there was that.

I was debating the merits of crawling under one of the vans when I felt cool, icy fingers slip over the back of my neck. I cranked my head around, expecting to see either someone with freezing hands and absolutely no concept of social propriety, a ghost or an abominable snowman.

No one was behind me. I struggled to see through the veil of rain, scanning the lawn. It was impossible for someone to have touched me and disappeared that quickly. The cold feeling was still there, settling between my shoulders, forming a pressure. It was that same brutally cold sensation I'd felt that night we found the zombies.

I turned and walked back to the steps. Instead of climbing them, I jumped and landed in the thick grass. The cold feeling was still there, and the sensation of being watched intensified.

Someone was out here.

I knew it in my bones and my blood. My *grace* sparked deep within me as I took a step forward. *There.* By one of the trees.

Out of the rain and the darkness, a thicker shape peeled away from the base of the tree. Was it a person? A ghost? A Shadow Person? I couldn't tell. Not with the distance and the rain.

Squinting, I could see it about four feet from the tree. I walked forward, and then instinct took over. My pace picked up until I was jogging and then running as I reached for one of my daggers, just in case—

The soft, mushy ground sank under my feet, and for a heart-stopping second, I froze. So stupid, so incredibly stupid, because that was a second too long. The ground gave way under me, sucking me down before I had a chance to scream.

Clumps of dirt and grass fell with me as I plummeted into nothing. Panic rose, but I squelched it as I folded my arms and tucked my legs, bracing myself as best as I—

—slammed into the hard ground, air punching out of my lungs as a flare of pain shot across my pelvis and down my left leg. My head cracked off something, and starbursts blinded me as another spike of pain erupted along the back of my skull and then shot down my spine. The sudden impact stunned me into immobility. I lay there on my side, legs still tucked as I breathed through my clenched jaw, eyes squeezed shut.

Holy crap.

I had to have fallen ten feet or more. The distance explained the deep, steady throb in my leg and my head. That kind of fall would've done serious damage to a human. Unclenching my mouth, I took a deep breath and about choked on the overwhelming scent of rich, wet soil. The icy pressure was still between my shoulders, and whatever I'd fallen into was unbelievably chilly, at least twenty or so degrees cooler.

Opening my eyes, I saw...*nothing*. Nothing but complete, utter darkness.

A seed of panic took root as I jerked upright and scurried backward until I rammed into something hard and solid. Nausea swept through me as a streak of pain lanced my temples.

Okay. Maybe I did some damage to myself.

"Shit," I moaned, lifting a hand to my temple, realizing I was against a wall. I twisted at the waist, wincing as I reached out, placing my hand against the damp, slimy surface. A stone wall—a moldy, slimy stone wall.

What the Hell had I fallen into?

I strained to see anything, but there was only inky darkness. Was the place devoid of all light? Or was it my eyes? Had they taken this moment to give out on me? The seedling of panic unfurled. No. *No.* That was not how RP worked, and my skull was thick enough to protect all the important brain cells and nerves responsible for vision. I knew that, so I just needed to calm my heart...and my breathing, because hyperventilating wasn't doing me any good. I needed to look for a way out—my phone. I could use the light from my phone to see, and Zayne must have felt my panic. For once, I was grateful for the bond I could feel in my chest. He would look for me.

Hopefully not on a nearby street.

I began to reach for my phone while praying that it hadn't been damaged in the fall, because that would suck. I needed light. I needed to be able to see—

A soft thump echoed not far from me. I stilled, trying not to breathe too heavily or too deeply as I stared into nothing. What was that—

Another barely audible sound caught my attention. A softer thud and then one more, a sound that reminded me of...

Realization kicked in, and my stomach dropped as my *grace* burned in my core.

I wasn't alone.

29

The sound of footfalls ceased as I held myself completely still. I knew beyond a doubt that there was someone with me.

What that someone was, I had no idea.

Because it wasn't Zayne, and no human could've made that jump as quietly or safely, but I also didn't sense a demon. Could it be another Warden? If that was the case, why not say something?

I scanned the darkness, hearing only the steady splatter of rain and the rumble of thunder. There was no other noise, not even the sound of breathing, but I could feel *it*. Every sense I had was hyperaware of the presence.

I needed to see.

Chills swept down my arms as I slowly, carefully reached for my back pocket. My fingers slipped over my phone. Heart pounding like the rain, I held my breath as I pulled it out. If the phone still worked, the moment I hit the button, it would light up, alerting whatever was down here with me. It was the risk I had to take.

In the darkness, I found the button on my phone. The small flare of light as my home screen came into focus brought relief and worry, along with a burst of pain in my eyes at the sudden brightness. There was no movement as I dragged my thumb along the bottom of the screen. Sparing a brief glance at my phone, I squinted until the little flashlight icon came into focus. I hit the button and exhaled roughly.

Intense white light streamed from the phone. I followed the funnel of light to…another glistening wall that was about five feet from me. Something was carved into the stone. I couldn't make out what it was, but I realized I was in a tunnel.

I shifted the phone toward my left as I reached for a dagger with my other hand. My fingers curled around the handle as I followed the light, seeing grayish-green stone, clumps of grass and dirt—

Weight came down on my arm, so fast that I lost my grip on my phone and shrieked. It fell to the floor and before I could even feel embarrassed over the tiny scream, the tunnel was once more thrown into complete darkness.

Instinct roared to the surface as my *grace* clamored inside me. I pitched forward, unsheathing the dagger and swinging out, slicing at nothing but air. I pulled back, panting as I pressed against the wall. I tensed, bracing myself for a blow I couldn't see to deflect. I thrust the dagger out again as I went for my other blade, hitting nothing.

"Where are you?" I shouted. "Where in the Hell are you?"

Silence greeted me.

Panic spread, invading my consciousness like a noxious

poison as I tried to remember my blindfolded training with Zayne. Wait for the change in the air—the temperature, the shift that would occur around me. There'd be a warning that something was close. My gaze darted wildly side to side. Everything around me was cold and the air was too thick, too stagnant. I felt nothing but the sweat dotting my clammy skin. A distant part of my brain knew that I was caving in to hysteria, but I couldn't rein in the panic. The complete and utter void of light struck a terrifying chord in me, tearing open a Pandora's box of fear and helplessness. I jabbed the dagger out, causing nothing but a whisper of air.

A soft clucking, a *tsk tsk* sound, replied, crawling over my skin.

Every part of my being focused on the direction of the disapproving noise. It had come from…directly in front of me. From my angle on the floor, I was at an extreme disadvantage. I pushed myself to my feet, putting weight on my left leg—

My right ankle was snagged by someone and jerked out and up. I went down hard on my back, the impact punching the air out of my lungs. I kicked out with my other leg, but the tight grip pulled, *dragged* me farther into the tunnel, away from the sound of the rain.

I sat up, swinging both daggers. The hold on my ankle was released suddenly, and a very male, very low chuckle echoed around me. My body sprang into action. I scrambled to my feet, ignoring the dull burst of pain. Panting, I gripped the daggers—

A cool, damp touch pressed against my face, the contact a solid slide down my cheek. Flesh. The touch was one of *flesh*. Gasping, I swung out as I brought my right knee up, kicking. The grunt told me my foot had connected with whoever was down here. I started forward, following the sound, when something hard and sharp—an elbow—caught me under the chin, knocking my head back. Pain threw me off balance. A hand caught my wrist, twisting sharply. My fingers opened on reflex and the dagger fell even as I swung the other dagger around. The same happened. Another hand caught my other wrist. That dagger fell and clanged on the stone floor.

Rearing back, I moved to use the hold against the attacker. Weight slammed into me before I could get my legs up. The weight was a body—a hard, incredibly cold chest and torso—pressing me into the wall. The full-bodied contact was a shock to the system. I tried to push off, but the weight kept me in place as the hands at my wrists drew my arms up, pinning them above my head.

Terror exploded in my stomach as my arms were stretched, causing my back to bow. Blood in my veins turned to slush as icy breath moved against my cheek, followed by the feel of drier, softer lips.

My struggles stilled. A thousand different horrific scenes rapidly played, each one more disturbing than the last, being forced into a helpless position where I couldn't fight back, couldn't do anything to stop whatever might be coming—

No.

I *wasn't* helpless. I *wasn't* captured. I *wasn't* without a weapon—a weapon I should've used by now. A weapon that I'd been repeatedly trained to use as the last resort. Clarity struck me with the force of a bullet to the brain.

Those years of training were *wrong*.

And listening to them had been my greatest weakness. Not

my vision. Not my feelings or my fear. I shouldn't ever allow things to escalate to the last resort. I should never be in a position like this when I could've prevented it.

Terror gave way to rage, turning that slush in my veins to fire. My *grace* roared to life, and I tapped into it. The corners of my eyes flared with golden-white light.

Whoever this bastard was, he was about to get the surprise of his life.

The grip on my wrists shifted until one hand bit into my bone. The other gripped me by the neck, pulling me forward while holding me back. Muscles stretched to the point of tearing.

"It's a little late to use your *grace*." The voice was distinctively Southern, a deep twang that would've been charming in any other situation. It wasn't at all lost on me that he knew what I was. "That should've been the *first* thing you used, darlin'."

"Did you seriously just call me darling?" I growled, feeling the intense heat power up my arm.

"What should I call you? Trueborn?"

"How about your worst nightmare?"

"How about no? Because that would be a lie, darlin'. In reality, I'm *your* worst nightmare."

I was suddenly released, and I staggered forward before catching myself. My *grace* flared from my palm, the handle forming as my fingers curled around the weight. Flames licked down the length of the blade, spilling a golden glow into the tunnel.

I saw enough of him.

Standing across from me, dressed in all black, hair so blond it appeared white and skin an alabaster shade that was near translucent. There was just a glimpse of his face, but I saw that his features were all perfect angles, although the sardonic twist to his lips turned the asymmetric beauty into something far too cruel and cold, like a young man carved from ice and snow.

The Sword of Michael spit fire as I lifted it high, more than prepared to end his life without hesitation.

"Cool toy," he quipped, extending his right arm. "I got one myself."

The shock of what I saw caused me to lose control of my *grace*. It pulsed brightly and then exploded into sparking ash.

"Impossible," I whispered.

Golden light tinged in blue had powered down his arm, taking the shape of a long, narrow spear of fire.

Grace. He had a *grace*.

"Does this look impossible to you?" he asked, his tone almost teasing. "You thought you were the only one, didn't you? Your shock is damn near palpable." He made that *tsk*ing sound again, and then his *grace* retracted, throwing the tunnel into darkness once more. "Darlin', there's a lot you don't know."

The rush of air was the only warning before his hands clapped down on either side of my head. "But you'll learn soon enough."

There was no time to brace or prepare. Shocking pain exploded along the back of my skull as my head slammed into the wall, and then there was nothing.

Nothing at all.

A soft, warm touch to my cheek led me out of the darkness. I came to, gasping for air in a brightly lit room that hurt my eyes. I started to sit up, blinking the burn from my eyes until buttery-yellow walls with dark molding came into view.

"Trin." Zayne was suddenly there, placing a gentle hand on my shoulder. "You need to lie still. Jasmine will be back soon."

I went to speak, but my tongue felt heavy and woolly as he eased me back down on a thick pad or pillow.

"Please just keep still," he said.

Zayne's features were a little blurry as my eyes worked to adjust to the brightness. Damp strands of hair clung to pale cheeks, and the shirt he'd worn was shredded and hanging from his shoulders. He'd shifted at some point into his true form and his pupils were still stretched vertically.

"Where...?" The back of my head throbbed, causing me to draw in a shallow breath. "Where am I?"

Zayne's pale eyes flickered over my face. "You're at the compound." He sat next to me on the bed. "When I found you, you wouldn't...you wouldn't wake up, and you were bleeding from the head. Bad." A muscle tensed along his jaw. "How are you feeling?"

"Okay." I started to reach for said head, but Zayne was fast, gently capturing my hand. "I think."

"You think?" He gave a small shake of his head and then added quietly, "Your wrists."

My gaze followed his to bluish and deeper violet marks along my inner wrists. Everything that had happened started to come together. Several emotions spiked—fear and anger churned together, quickly followed by disbelief.

Zayne's gaze flew to mine. "They look like finger marks."

Because they were. I stared at them, thoughts still fuzzy. "I fell through the ground into some kind of tunnel."

"I felt you—through the bond." He laid my hand on my lap, his fingers lingering on mine for a few seconds. "Panic and anger. I got out of the school as fast as I could, but I didn't see you. The bond," he said, placing his hand to his chest. "It led me to you, but it took me too long to find you."

"I fell into some sort of tunnel," I told him. "Was I alone when you found me?"

"You were when I reached you." He rose, voice hardening. "What happened, Trin? The injury to the head could've happened in the fall, but not the other bruises."

I looked down at myself. Holy crap. There were streaks of dried blood on my arms and chest. My shirt was dark and felt damp in areas, either from rain or more blood. How badly was my head injured?

That didn't matter right now.

I shifted my gaze up, tracking Zayne as he passed beside the bed. As the fuzz cleared from my head and my body, I could feel his anger through the bond, and it was as hot as the sun. "There's another Trueborn."

Zayne stopped and then slowly faced me. "What?"

"That's what was in the tunnel with me. He's a Trueborn, like me, and I think he's been what I've been feeling. That weird coldness and feeling of being watched? I think it's him." My focus shifted to my wrists. "A Trueborn is the Harbinger."

Shock splashed over his face and through the bond. "You're the only one."

I laughed and then winced as that made my head hurt. "Yeah, apparently I'm not."

Zayne was immediately at my side, concern pinching his

features. It was strange to see him so concerned after days of being standoffish or annoyed with me.

"It makes sense," I said once my head stopped feeling like a cracked egg. "It explains why the Harbinger hasn't been sensed by Wardens, and a Trueborn can take out a Warden or an Upper Level demon. It doesn't explain the video feed interference, but I saw his *grace*. He has a spear like my sword, and he was fast." I paused. "And he sounded like he was from the South."

"Did he say anything?"

"Nothing of real value." I closed my eyes. "You didn't see him?"

"I didn't hear or see anyone but you." A moment later I felt his fingers graze my cheek. He scooped up a strand of my hair, brushing it back from my face. "And you were gone maybe twenty minutes."

"I think he… I don't know. He could've killed me after he knocked me out, but he didn't. If you didn't run him off, then…"

"Then this was a message. He was finally showing himself."

I opened my eyes and saw that Zayne's expression was downright murderous. What I was about to say wasn't going to help. "He was at the school, watching us. I saw him on the lawn. I didn't know what he was when I started toward him, and then the ground just gave out."

"I'm sure that wasn't a coincidence." Zayne's gaze met mine. "He wanted you down there, alone."

That couldn't be argued. "We need to get back there. Like now. There were things written on those walls, and he could still be there—"

"We're not going anywhere right now."

"I'm fine. Look." I lifted my arms. "I'm okay."

"Trin, you have been unconscious for nearly an hour—"

My eyes widened. That did seem like a long time. "But I'm awake and perfectly functional."

He stared at me like I was trying to walk around on a broken leg. "I don't think you realize how badly injured you are."

"I think I can tell if I'm hurt or not."

His eyes flared an intense pale blue as he leaned over me, planting his hands on either side of my shoulders. "I think you, of all people, can't tell that. You were knocked unconscious. There are bruises all over you, and I know there are, because I was here when Jasmine checked you out. You bled enough to soak what is left of my shirt."

When he said that, I realized there were rusty-colored smudges all over his chest, peeking out of the torn clothing.

"You've also bled through the pillow and the towels we placed under your head." He stayed close, caging me in like he planned on keeping me in the bed. "Jasmine thinks that the back of your head is split open, and she's gathering up stuff right now to work on you, so no, we're not running off to check out a damn tunnel or even a movie. You're staying right here."

"But what if I want to see a movie, Zayne?" I snapped, even though my stomach dropped. My head could be split open? Were they going to have to shave off my hair?

Okay, that was, like, the last thing I needed to worry about.

His lips twitched and some of the heat went out of his eyes. "Well, you're out of luck. Even if I did let you out of this bed, all the theaters are closed. It's almost two."

I crossed my arms, knowing that my expression was about as sullen as it could get. Just because a blow had knocked me out didn't mean I was *that* injured. "We have to go back there."

"We will. Not now, though." Several moments of silence passed. "I was scared."

My gaze shot to his, and I was snared, unable to look away.

"When I saw you like that, bleeding all over the damn place, and I couldn't wake you up, I was scared, Trin."

My heart flopped over. "Because you thought you might die?"

"You know damn well that's not the reason." His voice was low.

A hundred different things I needed to say rose to the tip of my tongue. I didn't know where to start, but it didn't matter. The door opened, and as Zayne leaned back, I saw Jasmine hurry into the room carrying a tray of bandages, towels, bowls and shiny silver objects. Her long dark hair was pulled up and out of her face and she was wearing some kind of house robe. She drew up short. "You're awake."

"I am." I expected to see Danika follow her sister, but she didn't.

"She woke up about ten minutes ago," Zayne added. "And already thinks she can get out of bed."

"I'm sure you advised her that wasn't a wise idea." Jasmine sat the tray on the stand near the bed.

"More like demanded," I muttered.

Zayne shot me a dark look.

"I'm sorry it took so long to gather everything from the medical facility. It would've been quicker to treat her there." Jasmine hurried around the bed.

"No one else needs to see her right now. Just you," Zayne answered.

Jasmine didn't reply as she sat beside me on the other side. "I want to take a closer look at the back of your head as that's the most pressing concern. I wasn't able to see it well when he brought you in."

"Okay." I was wondering what she thought she was going to do with those tools. "You need me to sit up?"

"How about you just turn your head toward Zayne. That should work."

I did as she ordered.

"Okay, I'm going to need you to roll onto your side. Can you do that?"

"Yeah—"

Zayne intercepted when I started to roll, curving a hand over my shoulder and hip, turning me onto my side like I was a log. He held me there. I scowled, thinking he was being a bit dramatic.

"Zayne, can you hand me that pen light?" Arms moved over my head as I stared at what I realized was Zayne's exposed navel.

"How's the bleeding?" Zayne asked.

"Let me see…" Jasmine pushed my hair aside. Her soft inhale concerned me.

"What?" My gaze met Zayne's. "Is my brain visible or something?"

"Quite the opposite." Jasmine sounded too unsettled for that to be something good. "Your skin is…"

"What?" I asked, starting to twist toward her, but Zayne stopped me. "Is my skin missing?"

Zayne frowned as his gaze moved beyond me. "What is it, Jasmine?"

"Does this hurt?" she asked instead, and then I felt her fingers just below the crown of my head, probing gently.

I winced at the flare of pain. "Doesn't feel exactly that great, but it's manageable."

"That's good," she murmured. She poked and prodded a little more and then she sat back, letting my hair fall into place. "There's just a fine cut. I don't think it even needs stitches. Head wounds bleed a lot, but I was expecting more damage."

That probably explained the whole tray of scary medical instruments and was also proof that Zayne was overreacting. It took more than a knock on the head to warrant all this, even if a Trueborn had delivered the blow.

Jasmine asked for one of the sterile cloths and, once it was handed over, she cleaned the area. I kept staring at Zayne's belly button, thinking it was kind of cute.

"Remarkable," she murmured. "You were unconscious for a while, so I feared swelling was possible and swelling could've been an indication of serious issues, but the bleeding has stopped and the swelling is minimal."

I hoped Zayne could see my face right now.

"There's still a chance that there's more damage beyond what I can see," she continued, swabbing my head some more. "A CAT scan and MRI would need to be done to rule out anything more serious than a concussion."

I opened my mouth.

"But I have a feeling you're going to refuse that," she added. "You can let her onto her back now."

Zayne did, thank God, and I scowled up at him. He ignored me. "You're positive she doesn't need stitches?"

"Are you trying to inflict pain on me?" I glared at him. "Do you remember the last time I had to get stitches—"

"I haven't forgotten," he responded coolly.

"There's no need for stitches. There should be, but there's not." Jasmine tossed bloodied cloths into a bin.

"What do you recommend?" Zayne's hand was still on my hip, and I had no idea if he was aware of that or not.

"Can we be honest with each other for a moment? There's just the three of us, and if you want sound, educated medical advice, you need to be open about something."

I shifted my narrowed gaze to Zayne and said, "What do you want to know?"

"Are you human?" she asked.

"Well, that's kind of an offensive question." I sat up and when Zayne moved to stop me, the look I gave him should've burned out his retinas. There was pain as I went upright, but nothing serious. "I'm not going to pass out if I sit up."

"A part of me wishes you would, because then you'd at least—"

"If you say *be quiet*, I will show you exactly how okay I am," I warned.

The corner of his lips tipped up in a way that reminded me of when he was amused, but I had to be reading it wrong. "I was going to say, then at least you'd be still."

"Oh." Well then. "Fine." I glanced at Jasmine, and her lips were pressed together as if she was fighting a smile or a grimace. "To answer your question, I am human."

She tipped toward me. "No human bleeds as if they're seconds away from a massive brain hemorrhage and is able to sit up and argue like you an hour or so later. Now what I think is that you have incredibly tough skin and a thick skull—"

"Well…" Zayne drew the word out.

"The other option is that you were seriously injured, but you have some level of accelerated healing that allows you to heal within an hour," she continued, and I honestly didn't know. Previously, whenever I was injured, medical aid was always rendered immediately. "What I do know is, either of those things would mean you're not human, and it's not like Zayne overreacted by bringing you here. He doesn't."

"I beg to differ on the last point." I sighed. "But I am human. Partly."

"You're not part demon," she said.

"She's not," Zayne confirmed. "Dez knows. So does Nicolai, but I can't—"

"I'm a freaking Trueborn," I said, so tired of lying, and what was the point? Her husband knew, and there was another Trueborn out there. Hell, there could be a league of them for all I knew, with their own softball teams.

Zayne slid me a long look. "Really, Trinity?"

I shrugged and then grimaced, which caused Zayne to appear as if he was seconds from forcing me to lie back down.

"You're…you're half angel?" Jasmine whispered, placing her hand against her chest. "And that…" Her eyes shot to Zayne. "Are you her Protector?"

"Yes. We are bonded for forever and ever," I murmured.

"My God, I never thought… I mean, I thought there were no more Trueborns."

"Yeah, so did we," Zayne muttered. Confusion marked

Jasmine's features, but Zayne went on, "This is something we were trying to keep quiet."

I met the look he sent me with raised brows.

"I won't say anything. I mean, I'm totally going to talk to Dez, because you said he knows, but otherwise I won't." She let out a little laugh. "I have so many questions."

"I'm sure you do, but now that you know what she is, can you tell us what you think we should do from here?" Zayne said, getting us back on track, as always.

"Well, I'm not sure with her being angelic blood, but I don't think you have to worry about her blowing a blood vessel in her brain," she said, and I wrinkled my nose. "But with her being unconscious, that human side probably got a nasty concussion. She should probably take it easy for a couple of days."

Couple of *days*?

I didn't know how Zayne got Jasmine out of the room or how long it took, because I spent the time gearing up for the major battle I knew was coming.

As soon as we were alone and he turned to me, I said, "I'm not taking it easy for a couple of days. We finally found out what the Harbinger is, and those tunnels have to be important. There is no way I'm spending days in bed when I'll be fine in a few hours."

"You have no idea if you'll be fine in a few hours." He sat down on the bed. "Have you ever been knocked out for an hour?"

"Well, no, but I know I don't need to be bedridden."

"How about forty-eight hours—"

"Twelve."

"Twenty-four."

"No," I argued.

Zayne looked like he wanted to strangle me but was resisting. Thank God, because that would probably result in more *taking it easy* time. "Tomorrow. You take it easy all day *and* night. That's it. And you could use the time, because you've got to pack up your clothes, which are scattered all around the bedroom. We're moving in to the new apartment on Thursday."

Wow. I hadn't been keeping track of time. "How about we go to the tunnels tomorrow, during the day, to look around, and if we come across any potentially dangerous situations, I will sit it out or run as fast as I can in another direction."

He exhaled noisily through his nose.

"And I will stay in during the night, packing my clothes, which are *not* thrown all over the room."

"That's a lie." He scrunched his hand through his hair. "I can't believe you even said that with a straight face, but okay. That's the deal, but I'm going to call Roth. I want backup in case the Harbinger shows up again."

I nodded, thinking that if the Harbinger showed up, we didn't need backup. We needed me and my *grace*. "You know, what happened today was a blessing."

"I have no idea how you can even say that."

"Because this whole time I thought my vision was my weakness. That it would be what takes me out for the count. And yeah, I don't like to think of my eyeballs as a weakness and I hate how I feel like I can't even think of them as such, but I was wrong. That's not what I should've been focused on."

Zayne's head tilted to the side. "What are you saying?"

"My training. My belief that I shouldn't use my *grace* until I have to. *That's* my weakness. All that training is hard to break. When I fell into that tunnel, I should've used my *grace* immediately, but I didn't, and he got the upper hand. Not only that, he called me out on not using my *grace*." I stared at my hands. "I will never let that happen again."

30

Since there was a small chance I might have a tiny concussion, Zayne insisted on treating me like I was a human who was on their deathbed.

Upon arriving at the apartment, I showered while Zayne waited outside the bathroom with the door cracked. I didn't know if he expected me to faint and bash my head open again on the stall, but with every passing minute, I felt stronger and the throbbing along the back of my head lessened. Shampooing the blood out of my hair, however, was not a pleasant experience, as it caused the cut to sting like a wasp had tried to mate with my head.

Afterward, Zayne had coaxed me into the living room and forced a bottle of water on me. He didn't want to leave me alone in the bedroom, at least not for the next couple hours, and I was secretly glad to have his company and the soft, flickering glow of the television. After the complete darkness of the tunnel, I didn't think I'd be able to relax for one moment in that bedroom without every light turned on.

Things weren't as caustic between us as they'd been before I fell into a tunnel, but I wasn't foolish enough to think that meant things were okeydoke between us. But I still enjoyed being able to sit next to him and not want to bite his head off like a female praying mantis.

At some point, I did fall asleep, and Zayne didn't intercede. I woke up hours later with the sunlight streaming through the windows and the soft quilt tucked around my shoulders. The gesture was sweet and made my heart ache more than my head.

But I woke up alone and not like I had the last time I'd slept on this couch, all warm and toasty, snuggled against Zayne. Swallowing a sigh, I sat up, holding the quilt around me like a cape. I found that Zayne hadn't gone far. He stood in front of the fridge, one hand on the door, the other on his hip as he shook his head.

I'd totally forgotten what I'd done the day before.

"Uh…" I murmured, slowly rising from the couch.

Zayne's head jerked over his shoulder. I was too far from him to make out his expression when he said, "How are you feeling?"

"Fine. Almost perfect."

There was a pause. "Do I even want to know why it looks like the junk food aisle of a convenience store threw up inside the fridge and every cabinet?"

Lips twitching, I struggled to keep my face blank. "I…got hungry yesterday, and ordered groceries through one of those delivery services."

Closing the fridge door, he placed a carton of eggs on the island, next to what appeared to be his jar of coconut oil. "And thirsty?"

I lifted a shoulder.

"Because I didn't even know there were that many versions of Coca-Cola," he said.

"There are a lot of different kinds," I agreed. "Lime. Cherry. Vanilla. Regular. Sugar-free. Real cane sugar…"

He placed a skillet on the stove top. "It took me about ten minutes to find the coconut oil."

"Really?" I widened my eyes, giving him my best shocked face.

"Yeah, for some reason, it was tucked away behind mixing bowls and a tub of lard," he said, cracking an egg perfectly over the skillet. "Actual lard."

"How strange."

"Indeed." Another egg was cracked. "I'm making breakfast. Eggs and toast." Another pause. "Unless you want to finish off that bag of chips or the packet of chocolate chip cookies."

Unable to hide my grin any longer, I ducked my chin. "Eggs and toast will be perfect."

"Uh-huh," he replied, and I held the edges of the blanket over my mouth, smothering my giggle. He looked up, and even though I couldn't see it, I felt the drollness of his expression. "I talked to Roth. He's going to meet us in about two hours."

"Great."

Breakfast was almost normal. The silence between us as we ate eggs and toast—Zayne did not eat the toast, because like Hell was I buying whole wheat—was a lot less tense than it had been the past couple days. When I was finished, I rinsed my plate and excused myself.

There was a phone call I needed to make.

Closing the bedroom door behind me, I picked up my phone and called Thierry. He answered on the second ring.

"Trinity," he said, his deep voice a balm to my soul, which made what I needed to ask and say even harder.

I wasn't going to beat around the bush. "There's another Trueborn."

"What?" he gasped, and unless Thierry was a skilled actor, his shock was real.

I sat on the bed. "Yes. I met him yesterday."

"Tell me what happened," he said, and I heard a door close on his end.

Quickly, I broke down why we'd been at the school and the confrontation in the tunnel. I didn't skip over being injured. "I have no idea what his name is or who he's related to, but he knew me. He has to be the Harbinger." I took a shallow breath. "Did you know that this could be possible? That there was another?"

"Absolutely not." He was quick to respond. "Your father always spoke as if you were the only one, and there has been no reason for us to doubt that."

"I doubt he didn't know. Why wouldn't he have told us—told me?"

"I wish I knew, because I don't see how keeping that information from you or any of us would do any good. Not knowing made you vulnerable."

It could've also gotten me killed.

"How old did he appear?" Thierry asked.

"Roughly my age, maybe older. I'm not sure. What I don't understand is why he even exists. I was created by my father to be used as the ultimate weapon in a battle—this battle. How could there be another, and how could he be…evil? Because he definitely was not a friend."

Thierry was quiet for so long, unease formed a heavy ball in my stomach.

"What?" I gripped my phone.

His heavy sigh came through the phone. "There's a lot we never told you, because Matthew and I and your mother didn't think it was relevant."

"What do you mean by a lot, and what does it have to do with what's happening?"

"It's not that we knew of another Trueborn, but we knew why Trueborns were a thing of the past," he explained. "It's why some Wardens who know the history would be wary of any Trueborn. And why Ryker was so easily convinced to turn against a Trueborn."

My stomach flipped. I was not expecting his name to come up. "You're going to need to explain this to me, because Trueborns and Wardens are like best friends forever. Wardens are the Protectors of Trueborns, and Ryker was afraid of what I could do—"

"He was afraid of what you could *become*," Thierry corrected.

"What?"

"I wish your father had explained this to you. It should come from him."

"Yeah, well, as you know, my father is about as useful as you're being when it comes to information," I snapped, patience running thin. "We don't keep in touch and have dinners on Sundays. I can count on a few fingers the times I've seen him in person."

"I know. It's just…" There was a gap of silence. "I wish you were here so we could talk face-to-face. So you understand why we never believed this could be an issue for you. That you're good, to your very core."

The unease intensified as his last words settled on me.

"Trueborns are only half angel. Your other half is human, and because of that, you have free will. The choice to do great things with your abilities or to cause incredible harm with them," he said.

"I'm not Spider-Man," I mumbled.

"No, but you're more powerful than any Warden or demon. Because of a Trueborn's human side and the nature of their creation, they are more prone to being…corrupted, more prone to giving in to the allure of power."

At once, I thought of what Roth had said about how I was born of a great sin. "Because angels are not supposed to knock boots with humans?"

"That's one way of putting it. 'The sins of the father are visited unto the son.'"

"That's archaic, and how do we know it's really true?"

"Because, as with the corruption of mankind from the acts originated in Eden, the soul of a Trueborn is darker than a human's and not as pure as a Warden's."

I remembered what Layla had said when she'd seen my aura—my soul. She'd described it as both dark and light, and I hadn't paid much attention.

"There is a balance in a Trueborn just like there is a balance in the world, but those scales can be tipped."

I was floored. "So, you're basically saying I could turn evil?"

"Not at all, Trinity. Not even remotely. You are good. You've always been good, and we took steps to prevent you from being lured by your abilities."

But was that true?

I was selfish and prone to acts of pettiness and barely restrained violence. I wasn't a great friend, and the list of my character flaws was a mile long. Look at what I'd done to Faye. I hadn't felt remorse.

"There was an uprising of Trueborns against Wardens," Thierry was explaining, snagging me from my thoughts. "This happened centuries ago, and a lot of the history has been lost to time. All I know is that it had to do with a bonding, and as a result, a lot of Wardens died. Bonds between Wardens and Trueborns were severed, and after that, Trueborns died out."

"I… I don't know what to even say." Shock had scattered my thoughts. "Except you all should've told me this. Someone should've told me this."

"You're right," he said, voice heavy. "We should have, but we never thought it would be an issue—"

"Because I'm a paradigm of a decent human being?"

"Because you *are* good, and we also made sure you didn't rely on your *grace* and use it too much."

I sucked in a sharp breath.

"*Grace* is a beautiful thing. It's your angelic ancestry shining through. But it's also the deadliest weapon known to Earth,

Heaven and Hell, and that kind of power is dangerous," he went on. "It can be seductive. We didn't want you getting accustomed to it."

The room seemed to tilt even though I was still sitting. "But you all were wrong. I understand what you were trying to avoid, but you were wrong."

"Trinity—"

"Teaching me to use it only as a last resort ended with me being knocked out for over an hour last night. I should've used it immediately, and that turned out to be a major weakness this other Trueborn picked up on immediately," I told him. "Now I have to undo years of being taught to do everything else before I use my *grace*. *You were wrong*."

Thierry didn't respond for a long moment and when he did, the remorse in his voice was as thick as the frustration I felt. "You're right, and I'm sorry. We shouldn't have forced you to go against your nature, even if that nature could turn."

Leaning against a concrete wall, I adjusted my new pair of sunglasses. The arms were loose, so they kept slipping down my nose.

"I feel like we're loitering," I said. We were waiting for Roth, and I guessed Layla, to join us, near the corner of the street that led to the school.

"Probably because we're technically doing just that," Zayne responded.

I looked at him as I toyed with the tail of the thick braid I'd managed to weave before leaving the apartment. He was standing a foot or two from the wall, dressed as if he was going patrolling, as was I, even though I wasn't supposed to be engaging in anything. Luckily, Zayne had had the sense to find my blades and bring them back. They were attached to my hips, but if push came to shove, I wasn't going to use them.

Not anymore.

I sighed, shifting my weight from one foot to the next. I'd told Zayne about my call on the drive over here. He'd been just as dumbstruck as I had been.

Could I become evil?

That question kept popping into my mind. Every time it did, I thought about the other Trueborn, and I thought about what I'd done.

What I knew I was capable of.

Nervous energy buzzed through my veins as I tried to shove those thoughts aside.

Zayne looked at me, his features fuzzy in a ray of sunlight. "What are you thinking about?"

The bond between us was as convenient as it was obnoxious. "I was trying *not* to think about what Thierry told me."

He faced me. "You're not evil, Trin. You're never going to go evil."

I appreciated his faith in me, especially after everything that had gone down between us. "I don't know if I should be worried you knew exactly what I was thinking."

"You shouldn't be worried you'll end up like the other Trueborn."

A mail truck rumbled past us. "The thing is, we don't know anything about this Trueborn and why he's doing what he's doing, but I… I killed that witch."

"The witch who betrayed us and was responsible for the deaths of countless humans." He moved closer.

"I know, but she…"

"What?" he persisted softly.

I squeezed my eyes shut behind the sunglasses. "She was scared. She didn't want to die, even after she knew it was going to happen once the Crone arrived, and I… I don't know if I cared or not. I mean, I recognized she was scared, but there was this moment, before she released Bambi, that I *wanted* to kill her." Feeling like I'd bathed in dirt, I opened my eyes. "I had my hand on her neck, and I wanted to kill her."

"*I* wanted to kill her."

My head whipped in his direction.

"You're really that shocked? She handed over enchantments that not only killed humans but also put Wardens in danger. She did it to use parts of you," he reminded me. "I'm not losing any sleep over how it turned out for her. The only thing I wish is that you aren't bothered by it."

"Yeah," I whispered. "Me, too."

Zayne lifted his hand slowly, reaching out and guiding my sunglasses back up the bridge of my nose. "The fact you're questioning yourself and your reactions is proof you're not evil."

"You think?"

"I know."

I smiled at that, carefully leaning my head against the wall. His words did make me feel a little better. I just hoped I could hold on to them. That I could believe them.

"You getting tired or anything?" he asked after a couple of minutes.

"Of anything other than boredom? No."

"Just let me know if you tire of anything other than boredom," he said and then added, "or me."

My lips quirked. "I'm not sure I can make that promise about the last part."

"Do try to resist."

I pushed away from the wall, feeling like I should say something. To be honest. "I don't think I could ever get bored with you."

Surprise rippled through the bond like a rush of cool air. "Annoyed, a different story," I amended.

"Well, I know better than to expect that."

I inched closer to him. "Do you...do you get bored being stuck with me?"

His head tilted as warmth infused my cheeks. "I don't know how you could ever think a moment with you could be boring. You filled up my entire kitchen with junk food and hid my coconut oil."

"Unfair accusations," I said and then I laughed a little. "Okay. I did hide your oil."

His chuckle warmed my face even more. "I don't look at us as being stuck together, Trin," he said, and air lodged in my chest. "Things have been—"

I felt the shivery hot warning of a nearby demon, effectively stopping whatever Zayne was going to say. I swallowed a sigh of disappointment and stepped away. Seconds later, Roth and Layla rounded the other corner, walking toward us like the embodiment of light and dark. They crossed the street, hand in hand, and there was a little burst of envy in my chest as the happy couple joined us.

I wanted that.

I glanced at Zayne. I wanted that with him.

"Hey, sorry we're late," Layla said, a smile appearing as they came closer. The warm wind picked up pale strands from her ponytail, tossing them across her face.

"I'm not," Roth replied.

I rolled my eyes while Zayne snorted.

Layla ignored that comment as she looked at me. "Zayne filled us in on everything. The Harbinger is another Trueborn?"

"Yep." I nodded.

"Just when you think you're unique and special." Roth grinned. "You find out you're just another of the same thing."

I arched a brow at him. "At least we now know what we're dealing with."

"But there's still a lot of unanswered questions."

Like the glowing spikes and strange marks, the video interference or what it was doing with the trapped souls.

"Do you think we'll find something in this tunnel?" Layla asked.

"There was something written on the walls. I couldn't make it out, but the tunnels have to be important, right?" I glanced between them. "I mean, how many cities have tunnels underground?"

"A lot actually," Roth answered, his dark hair a spiky mess. "But in DC, half the tunnels were created by government administrations to get important people in and out of the city undetected. The other half, well, probably have more demonic origins."

"Huh." Learn something new every day.

"We've been in a few of them." Layla glanced at Roth.

"Not in a while, but they're super creepy. The fact I'm willing to check them out again is proof of my dedication to the human race."

"Or that you're prone to making bad life choices," Roth commented.

"That, too," Layla sighed.

Completely relating to that, I smiled. "Did you know about the tunnels?"

Zayne nodded. "I know they're there. All the Wardens do, but I don't know many of the entrance or exit points or what they connect to, and I didn't know there was one near the school."

"I don't think anyone has a map," Roth said. "And I imagine a whole lot of unlucky fools have entered them to never be seen again."

"Where did you fall in?" Layla looked toward the hill that led to the school.

"I can show you." I started toward the sidewalk. "It won't be too hard to find a Trinity-size hole in the ground."

We started up the hill, Zayne ahead of us with Roth following close behind. Layla fell in step beside me. "Stacey told me," she said when I glanced over at her. "That you saw… you saw Sam."

"I did." I wasn't sure what to say. "I'm sorry about what happened to him. I don't know everything, but I know enough to say I'm sorry."

Layla looked away, lips trembling before she pressed them together. She didn't speak until we started to cross the lawn. "Did he look…okay?"

I stopped, touching her arm. She faced me, sorrow etched

into her features. "He crossed over, into the light, and that means he's someplace good, with people he knows and loves. He's more than okay."

"But he's back—"

"Spirits can come back. They're not supposed to do it a lot, but he's worried about Stacey. I think once everything is resolved with the school, he'll be more at peace and won't come around as much," I explained. "But he'll always be here with you guys. As cliché as that sounds, I know it's true. He's more than okay."

As she closed her eyes, Layla's lips moved wordlessly and then she sprang forward, giving me a hug that left me standing there with my arms awkward at my sides. "Thank you," she whispered. "Thank you for telling me that."

My fingers wiggled. "It's only the truth."

She squeezed me. "And it means everything."

When she stepped back, she smiled at me and then turned. "What?" she yelled.

I followed her gaze to find Zayne and Roth standing several feet away, watching us.

"Nothing." Roth had his hands in his pockets. "Just that you two getting all handsy was kind of hot."

Zayne jerked his head toward Roth.

The demon prince shrugged. "Look, I'm just being honest. I'm a demon. I don't know why any of you would expect anything less from me."

"It's a good thing I love him," Layla muttered as she stalked forward, and I got moving. "And I do love him with every part of my being and then some, but he...he just doesn't people well."

I laughed at that, glancing at Zayne, who was watching us with an almost perplexed expression on his face. Having no idea what that was about, I headed toward the copse of trees, steps slowing.

"It was somewhere over here." I scanned the ground, not wanting to plummet through a hole again. "It happened pretty fast, but..."

Roth was to the right of me. "I don't see anything."

"Neither do I." Zayne had moved farther, head bowed. "And you're right, the hole was right around here."

"What the Hell?" I muttered, frowning.

"Hey," Layla called out. "Is it possible that the hole... recovered itself?"

I turned around. She was a couple of feet behind me, standing inches from where I'd just stepped. "That would be weird, but anything is possible at this point."

She was staring down as she slowly lifted one foot and then the other.

"You find something?" Roth was heading back to us.

"I don't know. The ground feels weird here."

"Like it's mushy?" When she nodded, I lifted my hands. "You should probably move. That's what the ground felt like where I fell."

Layla knelt and placed her hands on the lawn. Without any effort, she lifted clumps of grass. "Yeah, I think the hole totally closed back up."

"Then you should definitely move," Zayne advised, coming to stand by me.

"We need to get down there, right?" She lifted her chin. "Unless any of you know a close entrance to the tunnels."

We looked at Roth.

"I know of no entrances nearby."

"Then we've got to go down this way." Layla rose.

"What are you going to do?" Zayne asked. "Jump into the ground?"

"Sounds like a plan to me."

"Shortie," Roth began. "I do not think that would be wise."

"How far do you think the drop was?" Layla asked, and I told her. "That's not bad. I mean, I'll know it's coming, so I can brace."

"You're really just going to jump up and down?" Zayne looked at Roth like he expected the demon to intervene.

Layla did just that. She jumped. "Yeah."

"Uh…" I wondered what the four of us must look like to passersby as Layla jumped again.

"Oh. Wait. The ground is getting more mushy." She looked at Roth and jumped again. "I think I—" She disappeared before Roth could intervene, sucked into the Earth.

"Well," I said. "Not like anyone didn't say that was a bad idea."

Roth dropped to his knees by the hole. "Layla? You okay?"

Silence and then came her muffled response. "Totally worked!" A pause. "And that was maybe a couple feet more than you estimated, Trinity."

I raised my hands.

"It's cold down here and really dark," she said. "I can barely see anything, but it's definitely a tunnel."

"Move back," Roth called. "I'm coming down."

Zayne and I watched him slip into the hole and when we heard the thump of his landing, we looked at each other.

"They're your friends," I told him.

He chuckled as he walked forward and stopped at the hole, holding out his hand. "Let me get you down there."

I shot him a look. "I can make the jump now that I'm prepared for it."

"I know you normally can," he said. "But you promised to take it easy, and taking it easy isn't jumping down ten feet."

I opened my mouth.

"And you were limping."

"Was not!"

"You were," he argued. "A little. I saw you."

"You were totally limping," Layla shouted from the hole.

"No one asked you," I yelled back.

"Trin," Zayne all but growled. "Let me help you."

Part of me wanted to refuse, though I knew I was being ridiculous. But I did stomp on the way over to him, which didn't go unnoticed, because Zayne grinned in an infuriating way when I took his hand. He pulled me to his chest, and I tried not to think about how warm and wonderful and just *right* it felt being this close to him. I tried not to feel at all as he lifted me about a foot and folded his other arm around me. I tried not to inhale that wintermint scent of his, and I really, *really* tried to not think about how it had felt the last time we were this close.

"Hold on," he said, voice rougher than before, and before I could attribute that to what *he* might be feeling, Zayne jumped.

The moldy, musty smell seemed to reach up and grab us.

His landing was hard, but not jarring, and as he straightened, I realized the tunnel wasn't dark this time. There was a soft orangey glow.

Zayne settled me on my feet, his hands gliding over my back as he let go. Shivery, I turned toward the source of the light.

"Torches." Roth held just that, a thick stick about half the length of a baseball bat. "They're spaced every few feet out."

"I didn't see them last time," I admitted.

Layla grabbed one and tipped it toward Roth's. The top sparked and flames grew. She handed it to Zayne. "Is this where you came down?"

"I think so." I turned around, spying the greenish-gray stone walls. "But I ended up moving a bit, not sure in what direction."

Zayne took the torch toward the wall. "I don't see any writing."

"Maybe this isn't the section."

"There's a mound of dirt down here," Roth called several feet to our right. "This could've been where she landed, but there's no writing around here, either."

The corners of my lips turned down as I went from one wall to the next. There was nothing. "I don't understand."

"Let's keep walking. There's a chance you ended up farther than you think," Zayne suggested, keeping the torch close so that I could see.

We walked on, past a couple of halls that branched into other tunnels. "I really hope there are no LUDs down here," Layla said.

"LUDs?" I asked.

Roth sighed. "Have you never seen *The Princess Bride*? Little Ugly Demons? Like Rodents of Unusual Size?"

I looked at Zayne and he just shook his head. "I've never heard of LUDs."

"They look like little baby Ravers," Layla explained, stopping. "Just as ugly and somehow creepier when they're smaller. They live in tunnels."

"Oh, great," I murmured.

"There's a door here," she said. "It's sealed somehow."

She was right. There was no handle or lock, and when she pushed on it, it didn't budge.

"There's another one here." Roth tipped the torch to his right. "We're going to see a lot of doors and they're probably best left closed."

"It has to be fifty degrees cooler down here." Zayne looked up at the ceiling as we passed yet another opening into a dark corridor. "Do you feel anything?"

"No. I feel nothing."

"That doesn't mean we won't find anything," he reasoned.

"I don't understand, though." We passed more doors made of stone and easy to miss. "I know I saw something written on those walls."

"Could it have been dirt?" Roth asked.

"I don't think so, but Hell, I don't know. I really thought this would lead us to something."

Zayne touched my arm. "It did. You discovered who the Harbinger is."

"Yeah, but…" It was hard explaining the disappointment I was feeling. I didn't know what I'd been expecting to find, but an endless maze of tunnels wasn't it.

"One of these tunnels, I'm betting, leads directly into the school." Roth stopped and stepped back as he looked both east and west. "Probably opens up in the old lower gymnasium and locker area."

"Where the Nightcrawlers were?" Zayne asked, and I shuddered.

"Would explain a lot of things, like how that zombie got into the boiler room that one time," Roth said. "We never figured out how it got into the school without being seen."

"God, don't remind me," Layla groaned. "I'm still not emotionally or mentally over that and the popping eyeballs."

My lip curled. "There's got to be a hundred different doors and tunnels branching off down here. How in the world do we find the one connected to the school?"

"We don't need to." Zayne lifted his torch toward the ceiling. "At least not right now. We don't need these tunnels to get into the school. When the workers aren't here Saturday, we can walk right through the front doors. Or one of the doors. Windows. Whatever."

"Oh, yeah. Good point. Duh," I said.

Zayne grinned at me and returned to scanning the ceiling for the damn marks.

"Finding which one of these connects and destroying it would be beneficial. Might not stop spirits or ghosts from getting in or out," Roth mused. "But will stop demons and the Harbinger. I'll have some of my people check it out, find the entrance and blow it up."

"You have people?" My brows raised. "Fancy."

"I'm the Crown Prince," he replied. "I have legions of demons who serve me."

"Oh," I murmured. "Super fancy then."

We continued on several more football field lengths of twisty, winding tunnel before I stopped, exasperated, cold and starting to feel a little claustrophobic. "We're not going to find anything," I said, and they stopped, turning toward me. "I don't understand why there's no writing. I don't know if my eyes were playing tricks me on me or what, but it's clear we could walk forever and die down here before we find the Harbinger."

Up ahead, Roth glanced at Layla. "I hate to say it, but you're probably right."

"But we can keep going," Layla insisted. "Who knows what we'll find down here."

"Probably a group of cave-dwelling giant bats," I said, placing my hand against a wall. "And—"

Something happened.

A vibrating hum radiated under my palm. My head jerked toward the wall. A dim golden glow flickered and then rolled over the walls and ceiling in a quick flash before vanishing. The marks were now there, but if I'd blinked, I would've missed the quick golden light. "What the what?"

"Whoa." Zayne stepped in with his torch. "Did it do this last time?"

"No. I mean, not that I noticed, but it was completely dark when I touched the wall and I was…" I looked at Zayne. "I was kind of panicking."

"Understandable," he murmured, stepping closer to the wall. "You guys seeing this?"

"Yes," answered Layla. "It looks like…a really old language or something. This is what you saw?"

"Exactly."

"We've all touched these walls, right?" Layla was nose to wall. "And it didn't do this?"

Everyone had touched them except for me, which begged the question of why it responded to me. Slowly, I removed my hand as Roth walked toward us. The marks didn't fade, at least not yet.

"It's the same as the marks on those spikes," Zayne said, lifting the torch.

I was going to have to take his word for it. I stared at the scrawling marks etched into the stone. They looked like words spaced into sentences.

Roth had become very still behind us. "You have spikes with these words on them?"

I looked at him. The glow from the torch Layla held cast flickering light over his face. "You know this language? That these etchings are actually words?"

"Yeah, and I'll ask again—you have spikes with words like this written on them?"

"I don't know if it's the exact same words, since we can't read it," I replied. "But we found them impaling a Warden to a church. They also glow."

"Well, of course they do." Roth swore, and I tensed. "I know what this is, and I know why your spikes glow."

"What?" I asked.

"That's angelic writing," Roth answered, staring at me. "And that means you have angel blades in your possession."

31

Angelic language.

I'd called it!

My smugness over having been right was short-lived when I realized the confirmation also meant that the Harbinger was in possession of angelic weapons.

"Wait a second." Layla crossed her arms. "The Harbinger just left those spikes behind?"

"Appears that way," Zayne answered as he scanned the writing on the wall.

"That doesn't make sense." Roth turned to us. "Angel blades are not just left lying around. Those suckers can kill just about anything. Actually, not just about. Totally can kill anything, including another angel. If this Trueborn left those blades behind, he's either extremely careless or had a reason."

"He doesn't seem like the careless type," I murmured, staring at the faint markings.

"If those blades weren't found, how in the world did a Trueborn take them from an angel?" Layla asked. "I know a Trueborn is badass and angels aren't exactly invincible, but to possibly disarm or even kill an angel?"

"Not just any angel, Shortie." Roth inclined his head. "Only archangels carry angel blades and I doubt one would hand them over to their half-angelic spawns."

"Nobody really knows what Trueborns are or aren't capable of," Zayne said. "It's been too many years since they were anything more than myth."

"I don't even know if I share the same abilities with this one, other than him being able to see spirits and ghosts. That's an angel thing, but this isn't something we can google or read about in a book." I thought about what Thierry had shared with me this morning. "I think our history has been purposely forgotten. Erased."

"It wouldn't be the first time." Roth looked at Zayne.

He met Roth's stare, expression hard. I had no idea what that was about, nor was it important at the moment. "Can you read it?" I asked.

"Not exactly an expert at angelic language. One would think that you'd be more apt in that area. It's similar to Aramaic."

At least Gideon had been on the right track.

"I recognize some words." Walking a few feet down, Roth stopped. "I think this is some kind of spell. Not the witchy kind—more of an angelic ward."

"What kind of ward?" Zayne held the torch close to the wall.

"A trap," he said, stepping back. "I think it's a ward to trap souls, preventing them from entering these tunnels. Now I'm wondering if a similar ward is written inside the school."

Tiny hairs rose all over my body. "If so, it would stop the souls from leaving the school."

"God," Layla murmured. "Nothing good can come from this."

"Not at all," Roth agreed.

Layla unfolded her arms. "Stacey has two weeks or so of summer school left."

"She went back?" I asked, surprised.

"She has to, or she won't get her diploma," Layla explained. "And I told her she could just get her GED, but she doesn't want to do that. She's in class right now. Did Sam say if Stacey was in direct danger? That the ghosts were targeting her or anything like that?"

I shook my head. "No. Just that they pushed a kid down the stairs and that they're getting more angry. The longer they're trapped, the worse they'll become."

"There are spells that can get them out of the school." Layla looked at Zayne. "We've done them before with wraiths. Basically an exorcism."

He nodded. "There are. When we go in the school Saturday night, we can force them out."

I raised a hand. "I have a slight problem with that. Do you know what happens when you exorcise a spirit? You don't just force them out of a residence or building. You send them into oblivion. They don't get to move on. With a wraith, that's understandable. They're a lost cause. But there might be spirits and ghosts in there that are good, and they don't deserve that."

"Do we take that risk? Aren't there also Shadow People in there?" Layla argued.

"Yeah, and exorcism would send them back to Hell, but you can't just pick and choose who gets exorcised. It will catch every spirit or ghost in there." I twisted toward Zayne. "We can't just do an exorcism. We have to come up with a different plan."

Zayne was quiet for a moment. "You're both right. It wouldn't be fair to those trapped, but it's also a risk."

I glared at him. "That statement didn't help."

"I didn't think that it would, but I'm not sure what you want me to say. We might not have a choice."

Anger flashed through me as I looked away from Zayne. I refused to believe that was our only choice. It was wrong.

"While I would love to stand here and listen to you all argue, I think all three of you are forgetting a very important piece," Roth said. "These tunnels are warded, and I'm betting the entire school is also warded. Exorcism won't work."

He was right.

Layla swore under her breath, turning away. "Then what do we do? Because I'm guessing that also means Trinity can't go in there and move them on."

"That leaves us with only one option," Zayne said. "We have to take down the wards."

At that point, we collectively decided we'd seen enough. I hitched a ride with Zayne to get out, welcoming the open air, even if it smelled faintly of exhaust.

Walking across the lawn toward the sidewalk, I was grateful to be in the bright, warm sunlight. My skin and bones were chilled like I'd spent hours in a meat locker.

Taking down the angelic wards sounded like a great plan, but none of us knew how to accomplish it. Not even Roth, who one would think knew something about getting around angel wards. The only people I could think of was my father.

Retrieving that information from him was about as likely as me swearing off fried food and soda.

"I'll check in with Gideon," Zayne was saying as we reached the trees lining the sidewalk. "See if he's aware of a way."

"I'll ask around, too." Roth dropped an arm over Layla's shoulders. "Carefully and quietly." He looked toward the street. "And just an FYI, I have people keeping an eye out for Bael. Still hasn't been spotted."

"Neither has Senator Fisher," Zayne responded.

A white truck drove by, heading toward the school. It was like one of the trucks I'd seen parked outside the night before. "Hey." I spun toward Zayne. "That truck. What's the name on it?"

Zayne looked, head tilted. "It says 'Bar Rhinge and Sons Construction.' That's the name of the construction company working on the school. I didn't catch that last night."

"I saw it and forgot," I said. "We need to see if we can find anything on them."

Zayne already had his cell phone out, calling Gideon. The Warden answered quickly, and as Zayne told him about the tunnel, the school and the construction company, I stepped onto the sidewalk and looked toward the school.

"A Hellmouth," I said. "Isn't that what you and Stacey called it?"

"Yes," Layla said. "And we were only half joking."

Even as my skin was thawing under the hot sun, a chill powered down my spine. "Maybe you guys are onto something. Not the *Buffy* variety of Hellmouths, but something like that."

"Gideon's on it right now. He's blown away by the whole angelic language thing. Think he geeked out the moment he realized he had real angel weapons in his possession." Zayne grinned. "He wants us to head to the compound to talk to him about the plans we found at the senator's house. He thinks he might be onto something."

"That's good news," I said. We could really use some good news.

"Keep us updated," Roth said as we started walking back toward the intersection. "Especially if those damn blades go missing. Once the others realize what they have in their possession, I want to know if there's a Warden who decides he could use them."

Zayne nodded.

"Can you do me a favor?" Layla asked Zayne when we came to a street corner.

"Sure," he answered.

I couldn't help but notice how far both of them had come since the first time I'd seen them together. That was good, I thought, smiling.

"When you see Stacey later, can you try to talk her into staying out of school?" she asked, and the smile froze on my face. "Maybe she'll listen to you."

Zayne glanced at me before answering. "Yeah, I'll talk to her."

I wished Zayne had driven his motorcycle, because at least then I could pretend I couldn't hear him. Alas, we were in his Impala and I had problems with my vision, not my hearing.

"I was going to tell you about Stacey," he said, halfway to the compound.

Staring out the window, I nibbled away on my thumbnail. "You don't have to tell me."

"I know I don't," he replied, and I made a face at the window, unsure why he thought confirming that helped. "I was going to tell you because I wanted to."

"Oh," I murmured, focusing on the blurred buildings and people. "Cool."

He obviously didn't believe I thought it was cool. "She and I really didn't get to talk yesterday."

"Understandable." I was sort of surprised the ice cream social was only yesterday. Felt like a week ago. "I kind of ruined all of that."

"That's not what I'm saying," he corrected. "It's just with everything that happened with Sam and—"

"You don't need to explain yourself. Pretty sure that's already been established," I said around my thumb. "Works out, anyway, because I need to pack."

"I'm not trying to explain myself. It just slipped my mind with everything that happened between then and Layla bringing it up." He paused, and then I felt his fingers on my wrist, sending a jolt of awareness through me. He pulled my hand from my mouth. "I wasn't trying to hide it from you."

I looked down as he lowered my hand to my leg. His fingers lingered just below the bruises that were already fading.

"I promise you," he added. "I wasn't trying to hide it."

My gaze made its way to him. He was focused on the road, and I didn't know if I believed him or not. Everything I thought and felt for Zayne skewed my instincts when it came to him. I wanted to believe him, but knowing he was seeing her again also made my chest feel hollow and my stomach heavy.

Jealousy sucked.

"I believe you." I shifted my hand away as I returned to staring out the window. The buildings had given way to trees, and I knew we weren't far from the compound. "I hope Gideon found something."

"Yeah," he replied after a handful of seconds. "Same."

We didn't speak after that and arrived at the compound about ten minutes later. Gideon met us at the door and ushered us into Nicolai's study.

The clan leader wasn't there, but Danika was standing behind the desk, palms resting on the glossy cherry-colored wood. In front of her were two large, nearly transparent sheets of paper, and propped along the desk were two more rolled-up papers.

Danika smiled at us, and I returned the gesture with a wave.

Because I was a dork.

"Guys, do I have something interesting for you." Gideon crossed the room as Zayne closed the door behind us. "Something I wish we'd known before. That school that Layla went to? Heights on the Hill? It's the missing piece."

"What did you find?" Zayne asked as we reached the desk. I looked down, not able to make out what I was staring at.

"What our senator has been up to." Gideon leaned over the desk. "But first, I'm looking into ways to break an angelic ward." He coughed out a laugh. "That's going to take some time, and I'm not sure it's possible." Gideon's gaze met mine and then he glanced at Danika. "Never seen angelic writing before, so that's cool. What's not cool is this Harbinger having been in possession of angel blades and able to cast an angelic ward. The only beings out there I'd naturally assume could do that are an angel or someone with a whole lot of angel blood in them."

Keeping my expression blank, I stared at the papers. I had no idea how to read angelic writing, but this other Trueborn—the Harbinger—could, and I could only assume that meant his angelic father had been way more hands-on than mine.

"What is all this?" Zayne gestured at the papers, shifting the topic smoothly.

"The top layer is Fisher's building plans, which you found, and underneath that is the high school, which is the old layout I found in public records. As you can see, his plans fit within the footprint of the school."

"I see it." Zayne moved his finger over the outlines. "Same lines."

"But that's not all." Danika reached for the rolled paper closest to her. "Gideon was able to get the remodeling plans for the school."

"It was the name of the construction company," he explained, lifting the top sheet and pulling the bottom one out. "I was able to hack into their servers in like ten seconds flat, and this is what I found." He grinned at Danika. "Want to do the honors?"

She unrolled the paper, spreading it out over the senator's plans for the mysterious school. I saw the company's name scrawled across the top. "Tell me the first thing you notice."

I squinted, trying to focus on the blurry squares and lines.

"It's the same damn plans," uttered Zayne. "Look here,

Trin." He drew his finger along a rectangular shape. "That's the cafeteria and these are the classrooms." He continued to point out the areas. "It's Layla's old school."

"That's not all," Danika said, lifting her brows at Gideon.

"So, when I first looked up the company Bar Rhinge and Sons, I couldn't find much on it except a cheap website with a rather questionable portfolio and contact info. Nothing online about the owners, but I did some quick digging and found the name the company is registered under."

"Natashya Fisher." Danika pushed off the desk. "As in Senator Fisher's late wife."

"Obviously finding that these renovation plans match the senator's tells us that the senator is connected to the school, but that's further confirmation."

I stared at the name of the company, and I don't know why it stood out then or what made me see it, but it was like the words scrambled in front of me and I saw *it*. "Holy crap. The name of the company. Bar Rhinge. Maybe I'm seeing things, but don't those letters also spell *Harbinger*?"

"What?" Danika looked down and then she jerked. "Hell..." Grabbing a piece of paper and pencil out of the desk, she wrote down the company's name and then *Harbinger* under it. She quickly connected the letters. "You're right."

"It's an anagram." Zayne huffed out a laugh. "Good catch, Trin."

Cheeks flushing, I shrugged. "I mean, we already know they're all connected, so not a big deal."

"It is a big deal. It's more proof that we're onto something," he said.

"He's right," Gideon agreed. "I should've seen that. It's kind of obvious once you do."

"Can't always be the nerdiest in the room," Danika remarked.

"I disagree." Gideon picked up the other roll of paper and unrolled it on top of the plans. "This whole thing got me thinking—what in the Hell is going on with that school? Before this, we had too much demon activity there. It's the same place the Lilin was created. Now the senator will be 'renovating' it, and it's full of trapped ghosts and spirits plus has tunnels running near it or under it with angelic wards. There's no way all of that can be a coincidence."

"It has to be the Hellmouth," I murmured, staring at the paper he'd laid down. All I saw was hundreds of lines, some bolder than the others.

"It's not a Hellmouth, but it's definitely something." Gideon walked around to stand by Danika. "What you're looking at is a map of ley lines—intangible lines of energy. They're in alignment all over the world with significant landmarks or religious sites. Humans think it's a pseudoscience, but it's real. These lines are straight navigational points that connect areas across the world."

"I've heard of them." Zayne's brows knitted. "On a show where people investigate fake hauntings."

"Hey." I shot him a look. "How do you know they're fake?" Zayne grinned.

"A lot of strange things occur along ley lines. Major historical events in the human world, places where people claim to experience more spirit activity," Danika chimed in. "Areas where Wardens would often find larger-than-normal demon populations.

"Often incantations or spells are more powerful and therefore successful along the ley lines. They indicate powerful, charged areas," Gideon continued. "And this one here?" He drew his finger over a thicker red line and then stopped over a red dot. "This is the same ley line that connects from Stonehenge, all the way to Easter Island…and this dot?" He tapped his finger. "This is a hub, and it's not only around Washington, DC, but nearly on top of the area where Heights on the Hill is."

Holy crap.

"That could be why the Harbinger is interested in this school," Zayne said, looking at me. "It's not a random location."

"Would make sense if whatever he's planning is going to require a whole lot of the heavenly, spiritual variety of energy. That kind of power, wielded by someone who knows how to control it, could turn a balled-up piece of paper into an atomic bomb, and that makes damn near anything possible."

32

"You really suck at folding clothes," Peanut pointed out from where he was floating near the ceiling.

"Thanks," I muttered, wondering how I'd fit all these clothes in the luggage in the first place. I glanced up at Peanut. "What are you doing up there?"

"Mediating."

"Sounds legit." I folded a tank top as my mind slowly but surely circled back to what I'd been trying to not think about since Zayne had left the apartment.

What was he doing with Stacey? Were they having another ice cream social? Catching a movie, or going to that steak house he'd taken me to?

I shook my head as I shoved the tank into the luggage. It didn't matter, and this was for the best. He deserved to have some sort of life outside of being my Protector, with whomever he chose. Eventually the ache in my chest would fade, and I would come to look at Zayne as nothing more than my Protector or my friend. Maybe then I'd even find someone to…to pass the time with.

If we lived long enough.

What we'd found out today was a big deal, but it had also created more questions than answers and I couldn't shake the feeling we were missing something.

Something huge.

We still didn't know what the Harbinger planned to do at the school, how the plan involved the trapped spirits and why he not only had angel blades but had been able to use an angelic ward to trap the spirits. Something didn't make sense, because even if his angelic father was daddy of the year, why would an archangel teach a Trueborn angel wards? I didn't have an answer to that.

Meanwhile, Zayne was probably eating ice cream and Twizzlers.

I snatched up a pair of jeans, material jerking as I folded it.

"What did those jeans ever do to you?" Peanut drifted down beside me.

"They exist."

"Someone is in a bad mood."

I lifted a shoulder.

"Where's Zayne?"

"Out."

"Why aren't you with him?"

"Because I need to pack," I told him, not wanting to get into the whole thing.

"It'll probably take him ten minutes to pack," he said, glancing at the closet. "He's that organized."

I said nothing.

"And you are the most unorganized thing I've ever witnessed."

I gave him a look that promised certain death. Probably would've worked if he wasn't already dead.

He grinned at me, and with his head more transparent than solid, he looked like a creepy jack-o'-lantern.

I missed Halloween.

"You know, I followed Zayne to the new apartment yesterday. He stopped there before he came up here."

I hadn't known that, but it explained where he'd been after I'd Ubered my way back to the apartment. "What does the place look like?"

"Nice. Two bedrooms. Two baths. Kitchen and living area is the same." He crossed his legs as he lowered to the floor. "It's actually the apartment sort of below this one."

"Cool." I was only half-jealous that Peanut had seen the new place and I hadn't. "I guess the movers are showing up tomorrow to get the couch and stuff. They'll take the bed last."

"Really?" he drew the word out. "Then where will Zayne sleep?"

Good question. My stomach took a tumble, even though I knew it wasn't going to be with me. "I don't know. Maybe he'll stay in the new place."

"That would be lonely."

I shrugged.

"The new place is kind of like Gena's, but she has three bedrooms and a den," he said. "But I don't think anyone goes in the den."

Gena.

Dang it, I'd forgotten about that girl again. "Tell me about her," I said as I folded another shirt.

"There's nothing to tell."

I glanced at him. "You could tell me how you met her."

"Well, I was floating in and out of apartments, checking out people, seeing how the cool live."

My nose wrinkled.

"And I was in her kitchen, staring at the magnets they have on the fridge—and by the way, you all could use some magnets—and she saw me and said hi."

"It didn't freak you out that she could see you?"

"Did it freak me out when I knew *you* could see me?"

I lowered the shirt I'd picked up. "Uh, yes. You screamed like a banshee."

"Oh. Yeah." Peanut giggled. "I did."

Shaking my head, I balled up the shirt and tossed it into the luggage. "So, which apartment is she in?"

"Why do you want to know that?"

"Because I'd like to meet her."

"I don't want you to meet her."

"What?" I was sort of offended.

"Because you'd probably freak her out, and she's got enough to deal with."

I leaned against the foot of the bed. "What does she have to deal with? Homework and parents?"

"You have no idea."

My gaze sharpened on him. "Then tell me."

"Things are…complicated with her and her family." He flopped onto his back and sank halfway through the floor. "And that's all I can say."

I frowned down at him. "Why can't you say more?"

"Because I promised the little dudette that I wouldn't talk

to anyone about that stuff," he said. "And I keep my promises."

"But I'm not just anyone," I reasoned. "I'm— Dammit!"

Peanut had sunk completely through the floor, and I knew he wasn't coming back for a while.

The fact he wouldn't tell me anything about the girl or her family was concerning. I re-added finding out more about her to the list for the third time, worried that either something bad was happening to her, or she was doing something she shouldn't be.

The moment I heard the front door open, I sprang off the bed. It was late. Like night had fallen kind of late. I hadn't expected Zayne to be gone this long.

Moving around the suitcase I'd finally managed to pack, with the exception of clothes for the next couple days, I told myself not to go out there, because it would look like I'd been waiting for him. Which I had been.

I curled my fingers around the cool door knob.

But I had questions.

Like, what had they done? Did they share a romantic candlelight dinner between friends? Did they catch a movie afterward, or go for a walk? Or back to Stacey's place? Because it was close to eleven, so there was no way they just ate dinner. Did they spend hours catching up or making out? I hadn't felt anything...weird through the bond, but that didn't mean anything, since distance weakened it. And even though Zayne insisted they were only friends, Stacey was really pretty, and they had hooked up in the past. There was some level of attraction there, physical and emotional, and Zayne hadn't...

He couldn't be with me.

He probably didn't even want to be with me now.

My stomach twisted in knots. I needed to play it cool. I told myself that as I whipped open the bedroom door so hard that I nearly pulled it off its hinges.

So much for playing it cool.

My narrow vision swept over the living room, stopping on the blurry form of Zayne. He was standing behind the couch as if he'd stopped there abruptly.

He stared at me.

I stared back, and the silence stretched between us until I couldn't take it any longer. "Hi."

Zayne was too far away for me to tell if he smiled, but it sounded like there was one when he spoke. "Hey."

Resisting the urge to wave at him like a doofus, I clasped my hands together. "You're back."

"I am." He took a step forward and then another. "I wasn't sure if you'd still be awake."

And waiting up for him? I cringed. Was it that obvious? "I was just getting ready to sleep and I was thirsty."

That was a total lie, but at least I was in my pajamas.

I stepped out of the bedroom, telling myself to just walk to the fridge, grab a bottle of water and then head back.

That's not what I did.

"Did you have a good time?"

"Yeah," he said, and then there was a pause. "I guess."

"You *guess*?" I crossed my arms. "You were out pretty late, so I would think you did have a good time."

He tilted his head. "It's not that late."

"So…" I shifted my weight from one foot to the other. "What did you guys do?"

Zayne leaned against the couch, clasping the back of it with his hands. "We went to dinner and then went down to the mall. We just walked around and talked."

Irritation flared to life, and I tried to stamp it down, but *I* wanted to walk the mall with Zayne and do nothing but talk and laugh like normal people, like we'd planned to before everything had gone to Hell.

I needed to get a drink and go to bed. That's what I really needed to do.

So, instead of doing that and keeping my mouth shut, I said, "Sounds like a lovely date."

Zayne's back straightened. "Date?"

I lifted my shoulders in a shrug. "I mean, I haven't been on many." Or any at all, but whatever. "But that's what it sounds like to me."

"It wasn't a date, Trin. I told you that. It's not like that between Stacey and I, not anymore."

"It's not?" Irritation was giving way to anger—and jealousy. And oh God, I needed to get control, because it wasn't like that between us, either. "It's not a big deal. I don't care, anyway."

"Seems like you care an awful a lot."

"You're wrong."

"Yeah, I don't think so. You're jealous."

I opened my mouth as heat flooded my cheeks. I could not believe he'd called me out. "I'm not—"

"Don't even say you're not. I can feel it." He shook his head as he pushed off the couch. "You know, I can't believe you actually think tonight was anything like a date."

My back straightened. "Why wouldn't I think that? You're single. So is she. You two have a history. Don't get why you think it's such a crazy conclusion to come to."

"You don't?" He took another step toward me, and his features became less of a blur. He was definitely frowning. "Do you really think, after everything that's happened between you and I, I'd go out on a date with someone else?"

Slowly, I unfolded my arms. "What happened between us doesn't matter."

His brows shot up. "It doesn't?"

I shook my head, even though that was yet another lie, because what happened between us did matter.

It would always matter.

"It can't," I said, finally speaking the truth.

Lips curling in a cruel grimace of a smile, he shook his head as he looked away. "I don't know who you think I am, and Hell if I want to know, but let me tell you something, Trin." His gaze came back to mine. "There is no way in Hell I'd be out there screwing around just because I can't have the person I want."

My breath caught.

Zayne was now just a foot from me. "Maybe some people work like that, but not me. You should know that."

I should.

Part of me totally did, deep down—the logical part of me I rarely listened to. The same part of me that had apparently left me hanging at the moment.

"And if you think I'm capable of doing anything with anyone, then you obviously haven't been paying attention."

Swallowing hard, I took a step back from him and then another.

"You drive me crazy," he said, eyes narrowing. "Looking at you right now, I can tell there's still a part of you that has *no* idea."

"I—"

That's all I got out. Zayne moved so fast I couldn't even track him, probably wouldn't have been able to even if I had good eyes. He was there, and suddenly his hands were at my waist. He lifted me up, and within a heartbeat my back was pressed to the cool cement wall.

Then his mouth crashed into mine and there was nothing slow or tentative about this kiss—about the way his lips moved against mine—and my lips parted for him. The sound he made heated my skin, and I just reacted in the way I'd been wanting to, needing to. I kissed him back. And the kiss was...oh God, it was everything, because I didn't want soft or questioning. I wanted *this*. Hard. Fast. Raw. He kissed me as if he were drowning and I was air, and I wasn't sure I'd ever been kissed like this. Not even by him. I didn't even know you could be kissed like this.

"Sorry," he said. "I forgot kissing was off-limits."

I had no words.

"Just because I'm not supposed to want you, doesn't mean I've stopped wanting you," he said. "Just because what I feel for you physically isn't supposed to mean something more, doesn't mean I've stopped wanting you. That hasn't changed."

His words were a startling mix of warmth and coldness as

his mouth found mine again. I'd wanted to hear him say that. Needed it, because it felt good and warm and *right*. But his words also brought a shock of cold reality with them.

He wasn't supposed to be doing this.

Neither was I.

All of this felt like *more*.

"You want this?" he said, voice thick. "That hasn't changed?"

"No," I admitted. "Never."

His mouth was on mine again, his kisses like long sips of water, and I wanted more. I wanted too much. Breaking the kiss, I tipped my head back against the wall as my heart pounded. "The rules..."

Zayne followed, reclaiming the scant distance. His lips brushed mine, sending a tight shiver down my spine. "Fuck the rules."

My eyes widened as the back of my throat tickled with a laugh. *"Zayne."*

"What?" His forehead touched mine as his hands tightened on my hips. "Following the rules has never benefited me in the past. All I've ever done is follow the rules."

His skin heated under my hands as I stared at him. "I'm pretty sure working with demons is the opposite of following the rules."

"Exactly. When I finally broke those rules, for the most part, only good things have come from that." I wondered what he meant by *most part*. "There were other rules I wished I'd never followed. Rules that served no purpose other than to control me."

"But my father—"

"I don't care," he said. "Nothing happened the last time we kissed, or when we did more. Nothing happened before the bond, and nothing happened after it. We're both still here."

"We are, but that doesn't mean anything."

"How many rules are there that make absolutely no sense?" Zayne reasoned, and I couldn't answer, because there were a lot of rules that were a joke. He chuckled, and the sound rumbled through me. "I can't believe *you're* arguing for following the rules. Usually it's the other way around."

My lips twitched. "Maybe it's opposite day?"

"Maybe…" His hands flexed on my hips, and then he shifted me farther up. Instinct drove me to grab his shoulders and curl my legs around his waist. Our bodies were lined up in the most interesting way…and then he pressed against me, causing my breath to catch. "And maybe sometimes following the rules *isn't* the right thing to do."

"Maybe," I repeated, my skin humming from the contact as I drew a hand up the side of his neck, to his jaw. The bristle of hair grazed my palm as my eyes searched his face. This close, every detail of his features was startlingly clear. "Maybe you're right."

One side of his lips kicked up. "I'm always right. Haven't you realized that yet?"

A grin tugged at my mouth and then faded as my heart thundered in my chest with a yearning that made me feel like my skin would split wide open with it. Zayne was right here, where I wanted him, where I'd spent countless moments wishing he was. Now that he was here, it seemed impossible and yet somehow inevitable.

His hand slid up my side, stopping just below my breast.

Every cell in my body seemed to short out as if I were a live wire.

I wanted Zayne.

It was a physical thing, yes. My body burned for him—for his touch, for his mere presence. Each day we were around each other, it became harder and harder to ignore the almost overwhelming *need*, but it was more than a physical desire. It was him, everything about Zayne. His humor and intelligence. His need to protect those whom others did not find worthy of protecting. The way he sometimes looked at me as if I were the most important being ever created. It was even in the way I knew he had loved Layla, been hurt by her loss but still wanted her to be happy with Roth. It was the *moments*. When a chuckle turned into in real laugh. When he let himself go, slipped out of the role of Warden and Protector to just be Zayne. It was that dinner and the nights he was there to beat back the nightmares. It was the moments when he helped me forget about Misha.

And all of that...terrified me, because I was... I was falling in love with him, and that was forbidden. Even if it weren't, it was risky, because he'd loved Layla so fully, and I didn't know if that meant he had the capacity to feel that kind of love again.

But Zayne wanted me.

I could feel how much he wanted me, through the bond and in the way his body trembled against mine, and I realized he wasn't fighting this anymore.

And I... I stopped fighting.

I stopped thinking and worrying.

Our lips met, and the kiss was hard and deep, and when

the tip of my tongue touched his, I was lost in the low sound that rumbled from the back of his throat.

Zayne pressed me against the wall, his hand cradling my face as he kissed me, rocking his hips against mine. Trapped as I was between him and the wall, there was no escaping the rush of sensations each roll of his hips brought forth. I moaned into his mouth, and whatever control Zayne might have had shattered.

With a powerful surge, he pulled me away from the wall and turned, his mouth never leaving mine as he walked backward. Somehow we made it to the bedroom. He laid me flat on my back, and only then did his mouth leave mine. His lips trailed a path down my neck as his hands slid under my shirt. His fingers curled around the material as he lifted his head. A question filled his luminous eyes, the stark need pouring from every inch of his face.

"Yes," I told him.

His pupils constricted and then thinned into vertical slits. "Thank God."

I would've laughed, but there wasn't enough air in my lungs. I lifted my arms and shoulders, and he peeled my shirt off me and tossed it aside. He reared back, staring down at me as his chest rose and fell so heavily, it stretched the fabric of his shirt.

Zayne placed his palm on my stomach, just above my navel. "I've said this before, but I feel this need to say it again and again. You're beautiful, Trinity."

I felt beautiful when he looked at me like that, when he said my name like that, but then his hand moved, and all I could think about was his touch. His palm coasted up over my rib cage and then higher. My fingers curled into the thick comforter as his thumb glided in maddening circles around a most sensitive area.

Then his mouth followed his hand, and I arched into him, panting as I curled my legs around his hips, moving restlessly against him.

Zayne took his time, leaving me breathless when he finally blazed a path with his lips and tongue down the center of my stomach, lingering around my navel and then going lower. He easily broke the hold of my legs, pulling away as he tugged on my shorts.

I lifted my hips and with one quick movement, I was divested of all clothing. Everything. A heady flush swept across my body, and he followed it with his gaze.

"God, Trin." His voice was guttural, almost unrecognizable.

Hands trembling, I raised up onto my elbows. "This isn't fair."

"It's not?" He was still staring down at me.

"You still have all your clothes on."

"I do." Lashes lifted. "Want to do something about that?"

"Yeah. Yes." I nodded just in case I hadn't been verbally clear.

Zayne waited.

Sitting up, I grabbed his shirt and pulled. Material stretched and tore, giving way before I realized what I'd done.

"Oh. Crap." I let go. The ruined material gaped, revealing taut golden skin. "Sorry?"

"Don't be." He chuckled. "That was really hot."

I grinned.

Zayne tossed the shirt to the floor. I reached for his pants, managing to work the button free and the zipper down before he caught my wrists. "Not yet."

"Why not?"

"Because there's something I've been thinking about nonstop and I've been dying to do," he said, holding my wrists. He came down and pinned my hands to the bed. His mouth covered mine, and then he started all over again. Kissing me breathless, senseless, until, when he let go of my hands, I couldn't even move, but then he was following that path again, stopping at my breasts and then my navel before drifting lower and lower.

My eyes flew open when I felt his lips against my inner thigh. The sight of him there almost tipped me over the edge, and the feel of his tongue against my skin, drawing closer and closer, robbed me of the ability to speak.

I'd never done this.

Obviously.

A thousand thoughts entered my head, threatening to shatter the heat, but when he stopped, piercing me with those eyes when he looked up at me, I was...

I was *found*.

"Can I?" he asked.

Heat burned me from the inside. All I could do was nod, and then he said something that sort of sounded like a prayer.

The first touch of his mouth turned my muscles to liquid fire.

A sound came from me that surely would embarrass me later, but at that moment, I didn't care. All there was in this world was him and what he was doing. I didn't even know what I was doing until I was clutching his shoulder with one hand and had a fistful of hair in the other. I was moving against him, as much as I could with his hand flat on my stomach, holding me in place as he…as he *feasted*.

I lost all sense of myself, of control, and it was glorious. No worry. No shame. No fear. Just everything he was drawing out of me with every sweep and dip and—

All at once it was too much—the tightening, the coiling deep inside me. The liquid rush of raw sensations pouring and pounding through me. My fingers dug into his shoulder as I jerked my head back, gasping for air as my release whipped through me. I was trembling and shaking by the time he eased away from me, lifting his head. He planted a hand next to my hip and it took a moment for my eyes to focus on him.

"Zayne," I gasped, trying to catch my breath.

A slow smile pulled at his lips. "I think you liked that." He dipped his head, kissing my stomach. "I know I did."

"I did." I swallowed, my heart thrumming. I eased up on my grip. "That's not all of it, though."

"No." Those lips brushed over a swell as his hair tickled the side of my ribs. "It isn't, but it can be."

I dragged my hands down his arms, nervous anticipation replacing the sated languidness. "And what if…what if I wanted it all?"

Zayne lifted his head, his features almost stark. He didn't speak.

"Do you want that?" I whispered.

"God. Yes." His voice was rough. "I do."

My heart jumped as I took a shallow breath. "I'm ready."

"So am I," he said, and I knew what that meant for him.

I knew what it meant for me. I felt it all when he kissed me again. "One second."

I didn't quite know what to do with myself as he rolled off and stood, his jeans hanging indecently low as he went to a dresser. I sort of just lay there, curling my legs up as he opened a drawer.

"A condom?" I flushed. Which was stupid. If I couldn't say *condom*, then I probably shouldn't be doing what one needed a condom for.

"Yeah." He turned, holding a small foil between his fingers. "I know that neither of us can pass diseases even if we'd been with anyone, but..."

"Pregnancy," I whispered, arching a brow. That I hadn't thought of it was alarming, mainly because I wasn't sure that could even happen. "Is that possible?"

"I don't know. You're not completely human," he said, coming back to the bed. He tossed it on the comforter, and for some reason I wanted to giggle. "So, probably wise to be safe."

"Yes." I nodded, because, hello, not only would a baby be a terrible idea at the moment, there was a good chance I'd be the absolute worse parent known to the history of the world.

Even I could recognize that.

Zayne grinned and reached for his pants. I thought maybe I should look away, but I couldn't. Not even if a chupacabra tap-danced across the room.

When his pants hit the floor, I had a feeling I would've also hit the floor if I'd been standing. The first time we'd kissed—that we'd done anything—the room had been dark, and neither of us had been standing. I hadn't seen him.

I saw him now, and my mouth sort of dried. I felt a little dizzy and hot—*really* hot.

"If you keep staring at me like that," he said, pressing a knee onto the bed and then a hand by my shoulder. "Then this is going to be very disappointing for you."

"I don't see how." I dragged my gaze to his face. "At all."

He laughed as he settled beside me, placing his hand on my stomach. "Because it would end fairly quickly."

"Have faith," I teased. "You got this."

And he did.

Starting over like it was the first time he'd touched me, he got reacquainted with all the dips and swells of my body with his hands and his lips. It wasn't until my breaths were coming in short, shallow pants that he reached for that foil and then, after a moment, shifted so that he was over me, his weight braced on one arm as his lower body lined up with mine.

I knew this was it. There was no more pumping the brakes or pulling away, even though I knew if I did, he'd stop. But that wasn't what I wanted.

Zayne stared down at me, eyes so pale and yet so bright. His lips parted, and I thought… I thought he might say something, but then he kissed me as he reached between us.

There was a pinch, a feeling of pressure and fullness. The feeling stole my breath and Zayne's. He stilled above me, arms and body trembling.

Waiting.

Waiting until I told him it was okay, and when I did, he moved again, and within a heartbeat, there was no space between our bodies. There was a sharp, burning bite that snapped my eyes open wide.

"I'm sorry," he whispered, kissing my left cheek, then my right. Another dropped on the tip of my nose and then glanced over my damp brow. "I'm sorry."

Hands shaking, I smoothed them down his back, feeling his muscles bunched and tensed. "It's okay. It…it happens."

"I wish it didn't." He pressed his forehead against mine. "I don't want you to feel pain."

Pain was a part of life. Sometimes it left scars, physical and mental. Sometimes it led to something worse, and sometimes, like this, I thought it might be a necessary step toward something amazing.

"It's not bad," I told him, and it really wasn't. It was mostly just uncomfortable as his heart pounded against mine.

And slowly, it did become better. For a few minutes, I didn't think that would be possible, but it did, and when I tentatively moved, the sharp breath that left him sounded like a different kind of pain.

"Trinity," he gasped as I tilted my hips up once more, and between the sound of my name and the interesting friction, it was becoming more than just better. "I'm trying to give you time."

"I've had enough time."

"Okay." His eyes opened. "I'm trying to give myself time so this isn't over before it even gets started."

A grin tugged at my lips and then a wild laugh bubbled out of me. I moved, lifting my arms and wrapping them around his shoulders. I kissed his cheek.

"Have I told you that you drive me crazy?" he asked.

"Maybe." Then, because there was a strange giddiness in me, I nipped his earlobe.

Zayne's restraint snapped, and I guess he'd given himself enough time. He was moving. I was moving. Hands. Arms. Mouths. Hips. Legs. Wrapped together, there seemed to be no end or beginning, and everything swirled around the way we were joined together and that inexplicable deep coiling sensation.

When he lost all sense of rhythm, his back bowing, it happened. That moment. The rush of raw pleasure roaring through the bond, coming from him, coming from me, washing over us in endless waves and waves. We weren't two. We were one.

As if it was always meant to be.

33

Sex changed nothing and everything.

It wasn't like I was suddenly different, even though I did feel like I'd changed. That a small, hidden part that was just for me would never be the same again. It was a good feeling. It was also a strange feeling, and I didn't know what to make of it.

It was even more strange, I thought, as I lay in bed and Zayne went to the kitchen, that when I'd gotten up this morning, I'd had no idea that this was going to happen.

Part of me still couldn't believe it had happened. That we'd done it, and neither of us had been smitten or set on fire. My father hadn't arrived—*thank God*—while Zayne and I had lain together afterward, arms and legs tangled, exploring each other in a different, less hurried but even more intense kind of way.

The grin on my face grew as I snuggled down under the comforter. There was a delicious heaviness to my limbs, and the moment I closed my eyes, I felt him, as if he was still with me. Cheeks burning, I rolled over and planted my face in the pillow and stayed that way, my giggle smothered.

After a few minutes, I heard Zayne ask, "What are you doing?"

"Meditating," I said, repeating what Peanut had claimed earlier.

He laughed. "Interesting technique."

Lifting my head, I rolled onto my side. Zayne had pulled on a pair of sweats, and that was it, so all I got at first was an eyeful of chest.

And that was nice.

More than nice.

Then I saw what he held in his hands.

I sat up so fast, I almost hurt myself. "You have cookies," I said. "Cookies and soda."

"Yeah. I was hungry. Figured you would be, too."

"I'm always hungry." I lifted a hand, wiggling my fingers. "But *you're* eating cookies and drinking soda?"

"Thought tonight was the perfect night for gluttony." His eyes had a hooded quality to them as he stared at me. "I'm sorry, what are we talking about? I'm so distracted now."

Glancing down, I realized the comforter had pooled around my waist. "Oh." I folded my arm over my chest. "Sorry." I wiggled my fingers again. "Cookie?"

"I'm not." Instead of handing over one of those amazing double-chocolate-chunk cookies I'd ordered, he placed them on the nightstand next to the two cans of soda. "Scoot up."

Doing as he asked, I tugged the blanket up as I wiggled forward. The bed dipped behind me as Zayne settled in, propped against the headboard. I started to turn, but he snagged an arm around my waist and tugged me back between his legs. My bare back pressed to his chest, and as he reached for the cookies, I was struck by how infinitely more intimate *this* was than anything else we'd shared.

"Here." He offered the cookie. "Let me know when you want your drink, and I'll get it for you."

"Thanks," I whispered, taking one bite and then another. I heard the bag crinkle as Zayne fished out a cookie for himself. After a few minutes, I relaxed into him.

"Something I thought about when I was getting this stuff," Zayne said, and I liked being this close when he talked. I could *feel* his words. "I hope to God Peanut wasn't hanging around."

I laughed, almost choking on my cookie. "If he was, I wasn't aware."

"That's not the confirmation I was looking for."

Grinning as I felt his lips coast over my shoulder, I said, "I don't think he was. I can't imagine him not saying anything by now."

"Thirsty?" When I nodded, he reached for the soda, popped the tab and offered it to me. Another cookie ended up in my other hand. He shifted behind me, resting back against the headboard. "I could sleep like this."

"Really?" I alternated between my cookie and my Coke.

"Yeah." His arm tightened around my waist.

I grinned. "I think I could, too."

"Minus the cookie and Coke."

"I'd cuddle them."

He chuckled, and that felt even better, but then he dropped

his head to my neck, nuzzling there, sending a wicked little shiver down my spine. With no rules, Zayne was *cuddly*, touchy and sweet. Part of me wasn't surprised to discover that. It was *Zayne* after all, but I was still a little surprised—pleasantly surprised. I never thought I'd be the type who enjoyed the causal touches or kisses, the way he was holding me so close, but I did. And I didn't just enjoy it, I lo—

A cold, sharp slice swept through my stomach as I swallowed the last bit of chocolate. I didn't just *like* any of this. There was a far stronger emotion that seemed even more dangerous to acknowledge now.

Nothing had happened yet, but that didn't mean there wasn't a consequence waiting patiently for us around the next corner. No matter how right or beautiful what we'd just shared felt, it was forbidden, and as much as I hoped Zayne was right, that this rule was just a method of control, I feared he might be wrong.

Beyond that, our lives were… Well, either of us could bite the bullet tomorrow. This Trueborn—the Harbinger—was deadly. Zayne could die, and I…

"Hey," he said softly, hand brushing my arm.

I closed my eyes, trying to stop the bombardment of fears, but it was like a floodgate being breached.

The Coke left my hand, ending up on the nightstand. Cool, damp fingers curled around my chin, turning my head toward his. "What is it?"

"Nothing." I smiled, not wanting to ruin this.

His gaze flickered over my face. "Talk to me, Trin."

Talk to me.

How many times had he said that to me? How many times

had I blown it off, because talking meant giving breath and life to fears? It had always been easier to keep all of that neatly hidden away, but easier wasn't always better.

It wasn't always the right thing to do.

"I'm just… I'm scared that something is going to happen," I admitted. "That there will be a consequence for this."

"There might be, Trin."

I sucked in a sharp breath. "You're supposed to say something that reassures me. Not freaks me out more."

"What I'm supposed to say is the truth." He brushed his thumb along my lower lip. "Look at me."

Opening my eyes, I was immediately snared in his pale gaze. "I'm looking."

"No matter what happens, we'll face it together. I didn't kiss you without considering there could be a risk. I didn't share with you what we just shared believing nothing could come from it." His eyes searched mine. "I knew there was a risk for us—and there *is* an us. I also know that you're worth the risk. That *we're* worth the risk."

A ripple of pleasure danced its way around my heart. "You always say the right thing."

Zayne grinned at me. "You know that's not true."

"You say the right stuff a good ninety-five percent of the time." I reached up and touched his jaw. "Together," I whispered. "I like that. A lot."

His hand slid up to cup my cheek. "Happy to hear that. If you didn't, things would get a whole lot more awkward and annoying for you."

"How so?"

"Because I have no plans of letting you go anytime soon,"

he said, moving wickedly fast. Before I knew it, I was on my back and he was above me, his lips brushing mine as he said, "So, I'm glad to hear we're on the same page."

Then he kissed me, and yeah, we were *definitely* on the same page.

Zayne was perched on the parapet of one of the hotels not too far from Federal Triangle. In his Warden form, wings tucked back, he was a fearsome sight.

All day I'd kept waiting either for things to become weird between us or for an Alpha to randomly show up and mete out punishment.

Neither happened.

Well, things had been a little…goofy when I'd woken up this morning, all tangled up with him, and on and off throughout the day. I didn't know what I was supposed to do. Wake him up, or somehow maneuver my way out of the bed without waking him? I'd suddenly been extremely concerned about morning breath. Zayne woke before I could make up my mind, kissing my cheek before rising. He'd beaten me to the shower. Later, when he walked past me, dropping his lips to the side of my neck instead of tugging gently on my hair or messing with my glasses had been a pleasant behavioral shift, but he had left me blushing and stammering. Training had started off normal, but the moment one of us got the other on the mat, we ended up staying there, kissing, touching, until Peanut drifted into the room and then back out, screaming something about his eyes.

When we'd started patrolling, I'd wondered if it would be

weird to hold his hand as we walked. I hadn't quite worked up the nerve to do that.

But we hadn't spent the whole day training or making out. We'd planned for the Harbinger. I had come to accept that Zayne had been right all those days ago, when he'd said we wouldn't find the Harbinger until he wanted to be found. Once he came around again, we needed to get him to talk, because if we took him out, we wouldn't know what was going on with Bael and the senator and those spirits trapped in the school. And if the Harbinger had been the one to set those wards, he could possibly be the only one able to break them. So, we needed to make ourselves available.

We needed to be alert.

And we needed to be patient.

The latter was not a part of my skill set.

Under Zayne's watchful eyes, I was treating the narrow ledge of the building as if it were a balance beam. I thought that perhaps he had about four separate heart attacks each time I misstepped.

"Do you really need to do that?" he asked.

"Yes."

"The correct answer would be no."

Grinning, I pivoted like a ballerina, eliciting a harsh curse from Zayne. "It's practice. That's what I'm doing."

"Practice for what? Earning a new world record for how many times you can make my heart stop?"

"Besides that, it helps me work on my balance when I can't see."

"And that can't be done when you're not several hundred feet in the air?"

"Nope. Because I can't mess up when I'm up here. Down there, nothing bad would happen if I fell."

"That would be the point," he replied dryly.

"Don't be such a worrywart. I know exactly how wide this is. Nine inches." I carefully made my way back to him and stopped a couple feet away. I looked down, unable to see the width of the ledge or the shape of my boots. "The ledge is like my field of vision. Well, except the edges here are straight and not like a wonky circle where things are sometimes clear and sometimes blurry. Everything else is…" I lifted my arms. "Shadows. It's weird, because sometimes it's not even black. It's like gray. I don't know. That might be the cataracts."

"Do you think it's possible to get them removed?"

"My eyes?"

"The cataracts." He sighed.

I grinned again. "The last doctor I saw said they were actually protecting my retinas in a way, and until they're causing a real problem, they wanted to hold off on talking about surgery. There are a lot more risks involved with operating on people who have RP, and more possible side effects."

"I hate to think what might classify as a *real problem*."

I snorted, thinking that while I'd adapted the best I could to the restricted vision, the cataracts often annoyed the Hell out of me. "If they cause a lot of pain or fully obstruct my central vision, I guess."

"But you said your eyes hurt before."

"Yeah, but it's manageable. More of an achy feeling and that probably has nothing to do with the cataracts. I mean, not directly. I do think I need to have my eyes checked, though." Tipping my head back, I looked up at the sky. It took me a moment to see the distant, faint glow of one star and then another. "I had edemas once before. They could come back."

"Macular edemas? The swelling behind the retinas?" he asked, surprising me once more with his own independent research. "That could be what's causing your eyes to ache. We need to make an appointment. Call Thierry and see if the doctor they took you to could hook you up with someone closer, like the Wilmer Eye Institute over in Baltimore. They're a part of Johns Hopkins."

He really had done his research.

"We'll just have to be careful," he continued. "As long as there's no genetic testing—"

"They'll have no idea I'm not completely human." I lowered my arms, inching closer to Zayne. "Though, can you imagine if they did test? The look on the geneticists' faces when they got an eyeful of my DNA?"

He laughed. "They'd probably think you're an alien."

"I thought you didn't believe in aliens."

"I never said that. I just said it wasn't *likely* those spikes belonged to aliens."

"And I said that those spikes could belong to angels," I pointed out. "Just to remind you, I was right."

He snorted. "I've been thinking about the spikes. They'd be deadly against any being with angel blood. Between your *grace* and them, we'd be better prepared."

"Good idea."

"Of course it was a good idea. It was mine," he replied, and I rolled my eyes as a warm breeze curled around the bare nape of my neck. "By the way, I forgot to tell you I was not remotely successful in convincing Stacey to not go back to the school."

I waited for a surge of jealousy, but there was barely a smidgen of the ugly emotion. Since that was a massive improvement, I decided not to read myself the riot act. "She might be safe. Sam didn't make it sound like she was in immediate danger."

"Yeah."

Hopping off the ledge, nearly laughing at the ripple of relief that came through the bond, I walked to Zayne's other side.

I almost lost an eye almost walking into his wing.

Luckily, he sensed how close I was and lifted it before I made contact. "You're worried about her."

"I am," he admitted, and as close as I was now, I could make out his profile in the moonlight. "She's been through enough."

"She has," I agreed. "Hopefully once we get into the school, we'll be able to assess the situation. There's got to be a way to get the spirits and ghosts out of there."

Zayne stared at the street below, and I thought that if anyone could see him, they'd think a stone gargoyle had been installed. "I know you want to help them."

I stiffened. "I will."

"But you can't help them cross over with those wards in place, Trin."

Anger ticked away at my otherwise pleasant mood. "Well, you can't exorcise them with the wards there, either, so we can compromise. Get the wards down, and I can move on the ghosts who need to go and the spirits who were trapped. I can take care of the Shadow People on Saturday night, and

I'm betting, once I get rid of them, the ghosts and spirits might calm down."

He nodded. "I was thinking about some of the books my father used to keep in the library. There's a huge old book about angels. Probably be good to head over there tonight and grab it. Gideon might have already checked it, but..."

"But it wouldn't hurt," I agreed.

"Right. And I also think there's another avenue we can take."

"Like—" I jerked as an icy shiver slipped over the nape of my neck and settled between my shoulder blades as if a hand was pressed into my skin. "He's here."

Zayne came down from the ledge in one fluid motion. "Where?"

"Nearby. We need to draw him out." I kept my voice low as I turned to Zayne. In the shadows, his gray skin blended in, but his pale gaze stood out in stark relief. A plan quickly formed. "We need to split up."

"Yeah, already don't like this idea," Zayne growled.

"Neither do I." I placed a hand on his chest. The heat of his skin was warm against my palm. "But he didn't show himself last time until we were separated, and we need to get him to talk. I'll go to the next roof. You go elsewhere, hide until he shows."

"Trin—"

"I can take care of myself, and this time I won't let him get the upper hand," I promised. "You know I got this."

His wings twitched with irritation but he said, "I know."

I found his gaze and then stretched up, placing my other hand on the hard surface of his jaw. Three simple words rolled to my tongue but couldn't break free. I did what I knew I could. Guiding his head toward mine, I kissed him softly, quickly, and then settled back onto my feet. I took a step and turned.

Zayne caught my arm, hauling me back to his chest. A gasp of surprise left me, quickly swallowed by the press of his mouth on mine. The touch of his tongue and the almost forbidden sensation of the tips of his fangs against my lips nearly turned my muscles to liquid. I was lifted up until only the toes of my boots touched the roof as he kissed me like a man coming out of a deep slumber, and there wasn't a part of me that didn't feel it.

This kind of kiss was definitely *more*.

When he lifted his mouth from mine, I had to remember that there was stuff to do. Important stuff. "The fact that you can kiss me when I look like this?" His voice was like sandpaper. "It...it undoes me, Trin. It really does."

My heart swelled and then squeezed, torn between the understated beauty of his words and disbelief. "I can kiss you like this because you're beautiful like this."

A tremor rocked him as he pressed his forehead to mine, holding me tight for another all-too-brief second, and then he lowered me to my feet, letting go with a slow slide of his hand. "I'll be watching."

Stepping back, I smoothed my hands down my sides. "Creeper."

"Be careful," he growled, ignoring my comment.

"Always." Spinning around, I took off as fast as I could, admitting that, if I didn't get going, predestined duty or not, I would do something incredibly irresponsible and completely impulsive. I'd stay and find a way to prove that he was as beautiful to me in his true form as he was in his human skin.

Knowing exactly where the ledge was and the distance between the buildings, I jumped just as my foot touched the short wall. Brief, weightless seconds were as stunning as Zayne's kiss. I landed in a crouch, scanning the lit rooftop. Between the floodlights and the full moon, I had a decent view.

I rose and walked toward the ledge that faced the street below, still feeling the cool pressure on the nape of my neck. Hopping up on the parapet, I knelt and waited as cars traveled the narrow street and the laughter and shouts from the people below faded into the background.

"Where are you?" I spoke to the night, knowing in my bones he would come.

I didn't wait long.

A few minutes later, I felt the intensity of coldness increase. My *grace* simmered and then sparked. I kept myself still, holding my breath until I heard the *thump* of him landing on the roof.

He spoke first. "The last time I saw you, you were unconscious."

"In case you don't realize this," I said, staring straight ahead, "it's inappropriate to knock a girl out and leave without saying goodbye."

"I could've killed you, darlin', but you've made me curious."

My jaw ached at the endearment. "Could've. Would've. Should've." I rose then, pivoting on my heel, and dropped down to the roof. He was standing in the center, his hair nearly the color of the moonlight. Dressed all in black like he was the last time, he appeared otherworldly. "Why are you curious?"

"Why wouldn't I be?" he queried. "You're like me."

"I'm nothing like you. I don't give off Abominable Snow-man vibes."

"No, you're like a volcano, always seconds from erupting."

"Thank you," I replied. "Why do you throw off so much coldness?"

"Because my soul is cold."

"Well, that was disappointingly cliché." Stopping, I braced myself in case he charged me. "Not only are you rude, you're not really creative."

"I'm a lot of things." His head tilted. "None of which you know."

"You'd be surprised by what I know."

"Doubtful." He chuckled. "Because if you *knew*, you wouldn't be standing there, charming me with small talk."

"I'd be killing you?" I suggested. "Because I'm more than happy to get to that if you'd like?"

"No. You'd be running." He took a measured step forward, then stopped, turning his head to the left. "I was wondering when you were going to show up."

The graceful arcs of wings appeared on the other side of him as Zayne rose, having dropped out of nowhere. "I wouldn't miss this party for anything."

There was a hint of a smile when he spoke. "Protectors. The loyal hounds of Trueborns."

I sneered. "He's not a dog."

"Loyal they're not," he added as if I hadn't spoken. "I had a

Protector once. He was my age, and we were raised together. He was my best friend. A brother."

"I really don't care," I said. "Just being honest."

He turned his head toward me as Zayne kept a distance between them. "I killed him. Pulled his heart straight from his chest. I didn't want to. I had to."

"Cool story, bro." Zayne's wings swept down. "Sorry if I sound repetitive, but I don't care, either."

"But don't you want to get to know me? Know how it's possible that there's another Trueborn? My name? Or how long I've been watching? Waiting?" He paused. "You two have been very naughty."

"I'm not sure what part of *I don't care* is confusing to you, but let me repeat myself. I don't care what your name is or who your daddy is." I felt the *grace* roar through me. "All I want to know is how to break the wards trapping the spirits in that school—"

"You don't want to know about Misha?" he interrupted.

My heart faltered.

"What he told me about you—I wouldn't do that if I was you," he said, picking up on Zayne's quiet advance from behind. "I'm in a charitable mood, Protector. Do not test it."

"I'm in a murderous mood," Zayne snarled. "Please do test it."

"If you force me to kill you, I have a feeling everything will go south quickly."

"The fact you think you can kill me just proves how far south things have already gone," Zayne shot back. "You may be a Trueborn, but you touched Trinity, and that alone gives me more than enough strength to shatter every pathetic bone in your body, one by one. I won't kill you, though."

"No. You won't."

"I'll just force you onto your shattered kneecaps, so she can deliver the death blow."

God.

I wanted to kiss Zayne, right here and now.

"Speaking of delivering death blows," he countered, focusing on me. "Interesting you and I can tick killing our Protectors off on our shared-experiences list."

"I don't care what you have to say about Misha," I said, and I almost believed myself. "I want to know how to break the wards."

"Jealousy is a terrible thing," he said instead. "That was Misha's sin. Envy. He was told he was special, and he was dying to believe that. Literally."

I stiffened.

"It's such a human emotion." He shrugged. "I want you to know my name."

"I want you to just answer my damn question," I snapped.

"My name is Sulien—"

"For real?" Zayne cracked. "*Sullen?* That's your name?"

He sighed. "Not the way you're thinking it's spelled."

"That's a fitting name," I said. "You seem like the kind of guy who strums the guitar, but only knows a few chords and waxes poetic about the girl you loved but who didn't know you existed. Sullen and moody and cold. A real life of the party. Is that why you want to bring on the end times? Because you're stuck with the name Sulien?"

"Actually, I've never loved anyone. Not even my Protector," Sulien replied. "And I'm not bringing on the end times. I'm just here for the ride."

"Uh-huh," Zayne muttered. "So, *Sulien*, where's Bael been hiding?"

"Someplace safe."

"Safe from what?" he asked.

"Those who wish to do him harm. Like you."

I raised an eyebrow. "You're protecting a demon?"

Sulien chuckled. "Funny you of all people would ask that, but I'm protecting the plan."

"What plan?" I demanded.

"The one Misha died for."

My chest seized.

"Speaking of Misha, he was exactly how you just described me, but you never saw that side of him. That would mean you'd actually thought about him instead of yourself."

That barb was a direct hit.

"I have a feeling you didn't know him at all," Sulien continued. "That he did actually love you at some point."

"You need to shut up," Zayne warned.

"But then it all turned to hate," he went on. "That's why you were able to kill him. I won't be that easy, because I don't hate you, Trinity. I feel nothing regarding you, but you hate me."

The corners of my vision turned white as golden light powered down my arm, the sword taking shape rapidly. Angry, hissing sparks bit into the air. "You're right. I do hate you."

"All that rage..." Sulien sighed as if it pleasured him. "It will be your ruin."

Zayne lunged toward him, but Sulien dipped and spun

away. I charged forward, but he was fast, moving like a streak of lightning. One moment he was between Zayne and I, and then he was on the ledge.

"I can't break the wards," he said. "Because I didn't place them there."

"Bullshit." I stalked forward, holding the sword to the side as Zayne rose up, wings stretching out. "I know what you are. You're the Harbinger."

Sulien laughed, the sound like ice falling. "I'm the tool of retribution and you're the weapon of destruction. Those are our labels and the roles we must play."

"Do you always speak like you've lost all touch with reality?" Zayne asked. "Jesus. And I thought demons liked to hear themselves talk."

He snorted. "I was feeling charitable. You should've asked why I've collected all those souls. You should've asked why I haven't killed you. You should've asked what the final role *you* play is. But I know I'll see you again, Trinity, and when I do, it would be wise for you to come alone."

Before I could do anything—speak, go for him or take another breath—he tipped backward, falling from the ledge into the night.

34

I shouted as Zayne flew forward and landed on the ledge, wings lifted high. I darted to the edge as my *grace* retracted.

A laugh rose from the darkness below as I leaped up next to Zayne. Unable to see Sulien, I was able to figure out he'd landed on a balcony a dozen or so feet below. He jumped again, hopscotching from balcony to balcony until he reached the ground. My gaze swept the darkness, spotting lights on the balconies. I prepared to jump.

Zayne's arm snagged me around the waist. "Don't."

"But—"

"We can't give chase," Zayne argued. "Not right now. That's what he wants, and we're not giving him what he wants."

"Chasing him is what *I* want," I reasoned, grasping his arm.

Zayne turned me from the ledge and then let go. I spun toward him, instinct demanding I knock him aside and go.

He must have sensed that, because his wings spread out, an effective obstacle. "Chasing him is what you did before," he said. "And he led you to that tunnel. We do *not* let him lead us anywhere again."

Frustrated because he was right and because knowing that didn't damper the instinct to give chase, I balled my hands and swallowed a scream. "He's playing with us."

"You're right," he snarled. "And that's why we don't play along. That's not how we'll beat him."

"And how will we beat him, All-Knowing One? We don't know where he's staying or have any way of tracking him if we can't chase him." I spun away and stalked across the roof. "This whole time we've just been waiting for him—"

"That was the plan we agreed to."

"But we're not behind the steering wheel here." I stopped, taking deep breaths of the warm night air. The other Trueborn's presence was completely gone. "If this is a story, we're not driving the plot, buddy."

"This isn't a story, and even if it was, sometimes forcing things to happen is not only unrealistic but incredibly stupid. So, you know what, we'll rewrite the story."

Huh.

I turned around, seeing that he'd followed. "I'm completely lost now in this conversation."

His wings swept back. "Remember when I said I had an idea? Before Sulien the Douchebag showed up?"

My lips twitched. "You said *douchebag*. Peanut would be so proud."

"Glad to know," he replied. "There is another way, if we

can't take down those wards. Something that will definitely free those trapped there and get rid of the wards."

"What? Angel Spells Begone?"

"Didn't know such a thing existed. Wonder if we can order it from Amazon?"

"Ha. Ha. That was my enthusiastic, you-said-something-clever laugh, in case you didn't know."

Zayne's expression was indecipherable, but I sensed his rich amusement. "We can find a way to take down those wards, then find a way to take out the tunnels and that school, if need be."

I blinked once and then twice. "Are you, a Warden, suggesting we blow up the tunnels *and* the school?"

"That is exactly what I'm suggesting."

Blowing things up was probably—okay, definitely—a felony, so it should be a last resort, but it was a damn good idea. One that now seemed incredibly obvious.

The rest of the evening was spent discussing the logistics of doing so, which was a conversation I was glad we weren't having over the phone—I was pretty sure it would result in Homeland Security and the FBI showing up on the doorstep.

We didn't see Sulien again, nor any demons, and by the time we returned to the couchless apartment, we'd decided we would probably have to involve Roth. Hellfire wouldn't take down angel wards, so we were going to have to go the good ole human method of mass destruction.

Explosive materials.

Surprisingly, the Wardens didn't have any stashed away, so we figured Roth would be our best off-market bet.

I mean, I'd be disappointed if he didn't have access to any.

That night wasn't like the night before, but it also wasn't like any other night, either. Zayne and I, well, we were together. We were a thing, and even though it felt like we'd known each other for years instead of months, everything was still fresh. I didn't want to assume he'd sleep with me, both in the literal and figurative sense.

So, as I'd brushed my teeth and gotten ready for bed, I'd gone over all the possible nonawkward ways I could broach the topic. I ended up working myself into knots by the time Zayne had done the same.

All for nothing.

Because when he came out of the bathroom, pajama bottoms hanging low on his lean hips and hair damp around his face, he asked, "You want me with you?"

Plopping onto the bed, I nodded as I scooted over. He slid onto the bed with far more grace, leaving the bedside lamp on.

I lay down, unsure what to do. Should I initiate fun times? Was I expected to? Was he? I didn't think being together meant having sex every time you ended up in a bed with your significant other. Not that I didn't want to, but I was, well, I was a little sore. Like not cringe-worthy sore, but…different.

I wished I could call Jada and ask.

"Mind if I turn out the light?" Zayne asked.

"Nope," I said, hoping it didn't sound so much like a squeak as it did to my own ears.

The bed shifted and the light turned off. Then there was a shift again as Zayne rolled toward me. Like he'd done on the rooftop, he snagged me by the waist, arm under my back, and tucked me against his warm chest.

"You comfortable like this?" was his next question.

"Yeah." He was warm and smelled like fresh mint, and I liked how one of his hands found mine in the dark. Our fingers threaded together. "Are you...going to sleep?"

"Eventually." There was a pause. "We didn't get a lot of sleep last night."

In the darkness, I flushed. "Not my fault."

"I would say neither of us were at fault. Or both of us were."

"But you brought out the cookies, and that energized me."

He laughed, and a few seconds later, I felt his mouth against my temple, pressing a quick kiss there. He started telling me about the first time he'd met Roth, and how he had struggled to maintain his human form in public. I listened, laughing at how obvious Roth had been about goading him into shifting. He told me how Nicolai and Dez had both reluctantly come to like the demon prince, if not completely trust him, and about his own history with Danika. How his father had wanted him and Danika to mate, but he'd always viewed her as more of a sister.

Finally, he confirmed that Danika and Nicolai were, indeed, doing the couple thing. We both determined that Nicolai was probably having a harder time dealing with her than he was running the clan, because she was unlike any other female Warden I knew. He told me about Nicolai's first wife, who'd died during childbirth, and Zayne admitted that after being in the room with Jasmine's twins for an hour, he wasn't sure he'd ever want kids. He'd make the exception on adopting once they were old enough to shift, and I'd laughed, thinking how I'd overhead Matthew once say he'd adopt if the child was *housebroken*. I'd about died, because yeah, potty training had to be one of the circles of Hell.

We talked until our eyes got heavy and the breaks between responses grew longer. Never once did the topic of the Harbinger come up, or anything related to our duty, and while we lay together in the dark, there was no tomorrow to worry about, no pressures or fears.

And this was better than anything I could've hoped for. Anything I could've wanted or needed. Just us and words and our fingers, threaded together.

Those minutes that stretched out were simply…*more*.

An update we'd be waiting for came unexpectedly, right before we left the apartment to patrol—the eerily empty apartment. Movers had come that morning, a small army that quickly packed up the kitchen, the mats and punching bag, and everything in the bedroom. We'd been planning to swing by the new place before we left for the evening, but that wasn't going to happen now. The first time I'd see it would be tonight, and luckily, Peanut already knew where to find us. I'd reminded him this morning, and he'd responded that walls meant nothing to him and he was a "free range" ghost.

Sigh.

Zayne's phone rang as I stood where the couch used to be, twisting three sections of my hair into the lamest looking braid ever.

"What's up, Dez?" he answered as he walked past me, dipping to press a quick kiss on my forehead. "What? For real?"

Zayne stiffened, and all my attention focused on him as he

turned back to me. "Okay. Thank you." A pause. "Yeah, I'll keep you guys updated. Thanks again."

"What?" I asked the moment he disconnected the call.

Zayne smiled. "Senator Fisher is back in town."

"Really?" That was not what I'd been expecting. "I was really beginning to believe the guy was dead."

"Well, he's alive and checked in to the Condor, in one of the federal suites." Zayne told me the floor and room number. "Dez said he's got security with him, most likely stationed outside the suite, in the private hall and inside with him."

"So, we can take care of them," I said. "We're going now."

"Yeah, but if they're just government workers doing their job, we don't want to do…too much harm to them. We'll need backup." Zayne thumbed through the contacts on his phone. "Since there are definitely going to be humans there."

"Roth?" I knew Roth could mess with human minds, erasing short-term memories or replacing them with something different.

Zayne nodded as he lifted the phone to his ear. As he spoke to Roth, I quickly finished the braid I was trying to tame my hair into. It was uneven as Hell, but it would keep my hair out of my face. I tried to not get too excited about the news, because who knew what we'd find when we got there, but the senator could tell us where the Harbinger was. He could tell us what the Hell the Harbinger was planning and could tell me what Misha had said—

No.

It didn't matter what Misha had said, or why he'd done what he did. I had to let that go, because finding out was not the priority here.

I exhaled roughly, dropping my hands as Zayne hung up. "Roth isn't available, but he's sending Cayman over. He's going to meet us there."

"Awesome." I wondered what Cayman would be wearing today. "The plan?"

Zayne headed to the island, where a small pouch of keys resided. "We get in and we make him talk, one way or another. Find out where the Harbinger is staying and what's going on with the school."

"And if he doesn't talk?"

Zayne dumped out the keys as he peered through his lashes. "Humans are…fragile, Trin, and from what I've learned, humans who conspire to do evil are always the weakest, because it's the inherent weakness that led them to do evil. Find the weakness and exploit that. They'll spill the tea faster than an anonymous Twitter account."

I cocked my head. "You've had experience, haven't you? Making humans talk?"

"I have. I didn't enjoy it, but I've done it and will do it again without hesitation."

Surprise flickered through me as I tried to imagine Zayne threatening a human with violence and maybe even carrying through with the threat. I couldn't see it.

"I can tell you're surprised." A wry grin appeared. "There's a lot you don't know, Trin. I've told you that before."

He had. "I didn't think you meant that you were secretly a master interrogator."

"All of us are trained to get necessary information," he explained, and I knew that, but this was *Zayne*. "Why do you think I wouldn't be?"

"I know you're trained, but I'm just surprised that you… that you would, because you're… I don't know. You're inherently good."

Zayne's pale gaze was piercing. "No one is inherently good, especially not Wardens."

My stomach hollowed. "Thierry basically said I was, and that was why he believed I wouldn't turn like…like Sulien."

"We don't know enough about Sulien to know why he's the way he is, and while I agree that you have nothing to worry about, neither you nor I are *inherently* good."

"You're right," I said after a moment.

He studied me. "Does it bother you, knowing this about me?"

Did it? No. That was the truth, whether it was right or wrong. I shook my head. "Just surprised."

That odd half grin appeared. "It's something that has to be done, but it's always good to learn the reasons of why a human was led to where they were. Knowing might not change the outcome, but empathy will make it an easier one."

I thought about Faye and the coven members. They'd done what they did out of greed. "Is that why you didn't care that I took out Faye?"

"I wouldn't go as far as to say I didn't care, but it had to be done," he replied. "And it would've happened eventually, but at least this way, more harm was prevented."

I nodded slowly. "Killing is… I don't know. It's…"

"Never easy," he answered. "It's not meant to be easy, no matter the circumstances."

"Yeah." I walked to where he stood by the island. "And the senator? Once he's talked, what are we going to do?"

Zayne didn't answer immediately. "We'll decide when we cross that bridge."

I had a feeling I knew what was going to be on the other side of that bridge.

I inhaled then let the breath out slowly. This was a part of who I was. It would always be. I knew that. "I guess it's good that I feel weird about this aspect of who we are."

Zayne touched my cheek, drawing my gaze to his. He didn't say a word as he lowered his head, halting a mere inch or so from my mouth for an indelible moment. Then he kissed me, a soft, lingering press of his lips against mine. "I'd be worried if it wasn't."

I smiled at that as he straightened. "Ready?"

"Walk? Impala? Motorcycle?" he asked, hands hovering over the keys.

"You should know by now that I'm always going to take the option that doesn't involve walking," I said, wrapping a hair tie around the end of the thick braid. He grinned at me, and I felt a happy wiggle in my stomach, which felt strange after our conversation. "Motorcycle."

His grin spread as he curled his fingers around the lone key. "I knew there was a reason I liked you."

35

Traveling by motorcycle was much less difficult than by car, though a little frightening as Zayne cut in and out of traffic like he was in a race to beat his own personal record for how many times a car could lay on its horn.

I loved it—the air on my skin and the wind that tugged at my braid, how my thighs fit to his, and the way it felt to hold him this tight—but, most important, I loved how, whenever we stopped, he reached down and rubbed my knee or squeezed it.

Also, the fact that we weren't walking.

I really loved that, too.

Zayne was able to snatch a spot down the road from the massive hotel, which took up nearly an entire block and looked like it had been transported from France.

"The hotel is beautiful," I said as we walked down the sidewalk.

"And it's old. I think it was originally built in the 1800s." He kept a hand on my lower back as he guided me around a cluster of tourists snapping pictures of the tiny gargoyles and water spouts that were carved under many of the windows.

I sighed. "This place is going to be so haunted."

He chuckled. "Just ignore them until we're done."

"Easy for you to say," I muttered.

"He's here," Zayne said when we neared the entrance.

Under a blue awning stood Cayman, and I wouldn't have recognized him if it hadn't been for Zayne. He was dressed in a black suit—an expensive-looking black suit—and loafers. Actual leather loathers. His dark hair was pulled back in a neat ponytail, and when he saw us, he raised black brows.

"You look nice," I told him.

"I thought I'd dress the part." He glanced over us. "Obviously you two did not."

I looked down at my black leggings and gray T-shirt. Zayne was in leathers, and I guessed we probably should've thought about how we'd fit in. Or not.

"We're not here to walk a runway," Zayne commented.

"But if you did, I'd pay for front-row tickets," Cayman quipped, and I grinned. "You two ready?"

When Zayne nodded, Cayman stepped aside and opened one of the heavy doors. Cool air rushed out, beating back the heat. Inside, I knew at once I was going to need to keep my sunglasses on. I was overwhelmed by the dazzling bright lights from the crystal chandeliers, and the grandeur of the palatial lobby. I'd seen some expensive artwork and designs before—Lord only knew how much the Great Hall back in the community had cost—but this was insane. Everything seemed to be made of marble or gold, and I had the sudden urge to run back outside and wipe off my feet.

"Wait here," Cayman said. "I need to get us a key to the floor."

Cayman sauntered up to the registration desk and leaned in, catching a young man's attention. I had no idea what he said, but within a minute, he came back to us with a hotel key card jutting from between two fingers.

"That was fast," I commented.

"I got the magic voice." He winked at me. "Follow me."

We passed a koi pond and through a massive number of columns flanked by numerous potted palmy plants. Between some of the leafy green flora, I noticed a pacing woman, her hands clutching at voluminous violet skirts, who was surely a ghost.

We arrived at a set of elevators. Cayman led us to the last one, swiped the card and then stepped in.

"Come on, children," he called out. "No time to spare."

I lifted a brow as I glanced at Zayne, but he only shook his head as we stepped into the surprisingly cramped elevator. Light jazzy music floated from hidden speakers.

Cayman hit the button to the thirtieth floor. "I expect that, as soon as these doors open, we'll be greeted in a not-so-fun manner. I can take care of them—"

"In other words, kill them?" I cut in.

He looked at me. "Uh. Yeah."

"How about Zayne and I knock them out or otherwise incapacitate them, and you do something with their memories," I suggested. "That's what we need."

The demon broker pouted. "That's not nearly as fun."

"You're not here to have fun," Zayne pointed out.

"Says who?"

"God," Zayne sighed, stretching his neck from one side to the next.

"Well, God ain't my boss." Cayman rolled golden-hued eyes. "But whatever. I'll do as you ask, but I make no promises about the memories I'll leave behind. I think I'll give them a new obsession with BTS, who have officially replaced 1D on my best-things-ever list."

I opened my mouth, but the elevator came to a smooth stop. Zayne eased in front of me as the doors opened. "Three on the right, two on the left. Room 3010. I'll take the right."

"Excuse me," a deep male voice called out as soon as Zayne stepped into the hall. "I need to see some—" His words ended in a thump as Zayne shoved him hard into a wall.

I darted out, my narrow gaze focusing to the left as a man dressed in a black suit peeled away from the wall, reaching for his waist.

"Nope." I caught him by the shoulder and spun him, then grabbed the back of his head. I introduced his forehead to the wall and let his body fall as I shot forward. I heard another body crumple behind me, quickly followed by a yelp from what I assumed was Zayne reaching his third man.

The guy in front of me had grabbed his gun, but I was faster. Spinning, I kicked out and caught him along the fleshy inside of the elbow. The gun flew into the air as the man grunted. Zayne caught the gun as I gripped the man by the shoulder and used his weight against him to drive him to the floor. The crack of the back of his head told me he was going to have one Hell of a headache when he woke up.

"Nice," Zayne said, tossing the gun to Cayman, who was kneeling by the second man.

"You weren't too shabby your—"

Another man stepped out, his mouth open as if he'd prepared to shout out a warning. I sprang up and jammed my elbow under his chin, snapping his jaw shut and his head back. Zayne caught him as he went down, placing a hand over the man's mouth as he jerked his chin to my right.

I looked up, finding that we were outside door 3010. I turned, waving my hand at Cayman.

The demon hurried over, replacing Zayne's hand with his as he peered into the man's wide eyes. "Hi. Have you found Jesus, our Lord and Savior and all-around psychedelic bro?"

Slowly, I looked at the demon. He grinned widely, and I lifted my gaze, mouthing, *What the Hell?* Zayne just raised a brow and motioned me to remain quiet as he gathered up one of the unconscious men, hoisting him over a shoulder.

Damn.

Zayne was strong.

The features of the man on the floor had gone lax, as if he were on some kind of trip. He didn't make a sound as Cayman dragged him out of view of the door, into what appeared to be a laundry or storage room. Within moments, they had the hall cleared, and Zayne returned to stand on the side of the door that opened while Cayman lingered back. Zayne's gaze met mine, and I nodded.

He knocked on the door, and a second later, it opened a crack. "Wilson?" a male voice asked.

Zayne shouldered the door open, knocking the man back. "Senator's on the couch," he said, folding an arm around the man's neck and exerting just the right amount of pressure to make him go sleepy bye-bye.

I stalked into the room, taking everything in as Cayman slipped in behind me and quietly closed the door. The room was large, nearly the size of Zayne's entire apartment, and there was a whole lot of blue and gold on the walls and the carpet, causing me to blink. My gaze swept over framed pictures and past a door, over a dining set and to a royal blue couch and the older man who was rising from it.

Senator Fisher looked like the cliché of an ordinary old congressman who was way past the expiration date on being useful to the people he represented. Hair snow-white and trimmed, pale skin crinkled at the corners of his mouth and eyes and creased along the forehead. His clothing sported the colors of America, the suit navy blue, tie a bright red and dress shirt white. He was a walking advertisement for patriotism and privilege, rolled into one messed-up little ball of well-hidden evil.

"What is the meaning of this?" he demanded, reaching for his pocket and pulling out a phone. "I don't know who you are, but you're making a very terrible—"

"Mistake? Not as big as the one you've made." I snatched the phone out of his hand. "Sit."

His rheumy blue eyes narrowed on me before his gaze bounced nervously to where Cayman was whispering to the man Zayne had taken down. "Now, you listen to me, young lady. I don't know what you all think you're doing, but I'm a senator of the United States and—"

"And I'm Frosty the Snowman. Sit. Down."

The senator stared back at me, his cheeks mottling and then paling as I felt Zayne come closer.

"Check the penthouse," Zayne said to Cayman. The demon bowed and all but scampered off.

Impatient, I smacked my hands down on the senator's shoulders and forced him onto the couch. The surprise that widened his eyes gave me a measure of satisfaction. "Thank you for sitting." I smiled brightly. "We have questions, and you have important answers. So, we're going to have a little chitchat, and if you're smart, you're not going to make this hard for us. See the big blond guy behind me?"

Senator Fisher's lips thinned as he nodded.

"He's as strong as he is hot, and his hotness is off the charts." I sat on the edge of the coffee table directly in front of the senator. "And I just learned today that he is extremely skilled when it comes to breaking bones."

"Expert level," Zayne murmured.

"But we don't want it to come to that. Keep in mind, not wanting it to come to that does not mean it will not come to that. Understand?"

He looked between us. "You won't get away with this."

"Famous last words." Cayman strolled back into the living room and threw himself into the chair beside the couch. "The penthouse is boringly clear. No more security teams or hookers, dead or alive."

I frowned at him.

Cayman shrugged. "You should see the things I've found in some politicians' hotel rooms. Could write a bestselling memoir."

All righty then.

"Who are you people?" Fisher demanded, straightening the lapels of his jacket.

"Just your friendly neighborhood Warden," Zayne answered. "Oh, and demon and Trueborn."

How rapidly the man's face drained of blood was proof enough that he knew exactly who he was facing. His gaze focused on me.

I smiled again, lifting my sunglasses so that they were perched on my head as I tapped into my *grace*, just a little, letting it shine through. Fisher sucked in air as his chest rose and fell rapidly.

From the chair, Cayman said, "The whole glowing thing is super creepy."

Only a demon would think it was creepy.

I reined my *grace* back in.

"Do you know who we are?" Zayne asked. "Now?"

"I'm not really Frosty the Snowman," I hinted.

Fisher looked like he might bust an artery. "I know." He swallowed and cleared his throat. "Then you also know who I know."

"If you think we're even remotely afraid of the Harbinger, you're very misguided," I advised, leaning back. "You're going to help us."

"I can't," he said, hands landing on his knees. "You might as well go ahead and kill me, because I cannot help you."

I sighed, rising from the coffee table. "I guess it's going to be the hard way."

Zayne didn't take my place. Instead, he grabbed a chair from the dining table set and then kicked the coffee table back, the stubby legs scratching deep grooves into the wood floors.

"That was hot," Cayman said.

It really was.

Zayne placed the chair in front of the senator and sat. "Where is the Harbinger?"

Fisher shook his head as I moved to stand where Zayne had been.

"Where is the Harbinger staying?" Zayne tipped forward, eye level with the senator.

Silence.

Zayne picked up the senator's hand. The man tried to fight him, but it was like a rabbit fighting a wolf. "Do you know how many bones are in your hand? Twenty-seven. In your wrist? Eight. Three in each of your fingers. Two in your thumb. Each hand has three nerves in it, and, as I'm sure you know, a human's hand is incredibly sensitive. Now, I can break each one of those bones individually," he continued, voice soft as he turned the man's hand over. "Or I can do it all at once. I think I know what needs to be done, and I'm sorry you don't seem to know any better."

There was a crack that caused me to cringe inwardly as the senator shouted, his body curling inward.

"I wish I had popcorn," Cayman commented.

Zayne tilted his head. "That was just one finger. Three bones. A lot more to go. Where is the Harbinger?"

Dear God, Zayne was like the Chuck Norris of Wardens.

Chest heaving, Fisher groaned as he squeezed his eyes. "Jesus."

"I really do not think he's going to be any help," I said dryly.

Another crack caused my head to jerk to Zayne. "That was your thumb," he said. "So that was two more."

"I don't know where the Harbinger is staying. God," he gasped. "Do you really think he'd tell me? *Him?* He's no fool."

"Then how do you get in touch with him?" I asked.

"I don't." The man trembled, rocking slightly as Zayne slowly, methodically turned his hand over. He took his middle finger in hand. "I swear. I don't. He came to me only once before."

"Really? You've seen the Harbinger only once?" Zayne shook his head. "I don't think I've been serious enough—"

"It's Bael," Fisher groaned. "It's usually Bael I speak to."

"Hmm…" I crossed my arms. "You were right earlier."

"Told you," Zayne murmured, smiling with near friendliness at the senator.

"What's good old bally-ball Bael been up to?" Cayman shifted, dropping his legs over the arm of one of the chairs. "Haven't seen that punk in centuries. Has he been rocking his Harry Potter–esque cloak of invisibility? Spreading his web of lies? I imagine he has, considering he is the King of Deceit. You work for one of the oldest demons known to this Earth, birthed from the pits of Hell. Interesting company you keep. One would think that would make you stop and wonder if you're on the right side of whatever it is that they're planning."

"You're a demon," gasped the senator. "You're going to preach to me about being on the right side?"

Cayman gave him a half grin. "Sometimes the right side of history is made up of those you'd least expect."

"Where is Bael?" I asked.

"Nowhere near here," the senator responded. "He's far

away, hidden. I can give you a number I've called in the past, but that will do you no good. Not now."

Just as Sulien had said. Frustrated, I stepped forward. "Why is he staying away?"

"I don't know."

"Fisher," Zayne sighed. "You seem to know very little. That's disappointing."

"Wait—" A shout interrupted his words when Zayne shattered another finger.

And then Senator Josh Fisher shattered.

Only eight bones. Tiny ones. Painful ones, but tiny compared to equally breakable larger ones.

"I love my wife," he moaned, face crumpling and body curling onto his side, stretched as far as he could get with Zayne still holding his hand. "I love my wife. That's all. I love her. I can't do this without her. She's all I ever wanted." Body-racking sobs erupted from the man. "Loved her since the day she walked into my econ class in Knoxville. She's my everything, and I would do anything to see her again. Hold her. Have her back. That's all I ever wanted."

I unfolded my arms, exchanging a glance with Zayne. He let go of the hand, and all the Senator did was curl farther into himself. I shifted, uncomfortable with the visible raw pain. This man had conspired with a demon and witches, getting innocent humans and Wardens killed. He was connected to the Harbinger, who wanted to bring on the end times, so he sucked—big time—but unless he was an accomplished actor, he was collapsing under a kind of pain far greater than broken fingers.

"What does she have to do with Bael, Josh?" Zayne asked,

using his first name and in a voice so gentle it was easy to forget that he'd just broken the man's fingers.

Fisher didn't answer for several minutes, only sobbed, until, finally, he rasped, "The Harbinger heard my prayers and came to me."

I jolted as Cayman swung his legs off the chair and tipped forward.

"He looked like an angel." The man's eyes opened then, wide and unseeing. "He sounded like an angel."

I totally understood how he could mistake Sulien for an angel, but to think he and his twang sounded like one? Then again, Fisher was from Tennessee. Maybe he thought all of Heaven sounded like Matthew McConaughey in a car commercial.

"What did he say?" Zayne's voice was so soft.

The man trembled. "That he… That I could earn the one thing I wanted most. Natashya."

Oh God.

I had a sinking suspicion where this was heading.

"He told me a man would come to me and I was to help him with what he needed, and this man was a sheep in wolf's clothing," he whispered now. "I thought it was a dream, but then that man showed up. The sheep in wolf's clothing."

Did he mean a demon pretending to be bad?

"Bael?" Zayne prodded. "A man who wasn't a man at all?" When Fisher nodded, Zayne folded his hands under his chin. "Did you know what he is?"

"Not at first, but eventually…yes."

I wanted to ask if he'd thought that was, I don't know, a bright freaking red flag, but I remained silent.

"What did he want of you?" Zayne asked.

"Access to the school. I don't know why. He never told me, and I didn't ask. I... I didn't want to know." The man still trembled. "I just wanted my Natashya."

Anger crowded out whatever sympathy I'd felt. "And it didn't occur to you that it could be bad that a *demon* wanted access to a *school*?"

Zayne shot me a look of warning before refocusing on the senator, who didn't answer, only cried harder. "Did you ever go into the school?"

"No. Never. I just set up the company, made a few calls and was able to purchase it. A new school was already being built to replace it. That's all."

Plans for a school catering to children with disabilities, I wanted to shout, but clamped my mouth shut.

"And when he told me I needed to meet with them—the witches—he told me what to say, and I... I did it."

I had to put my hand over my own mouth to keep from speaking.

"Bael promised me he would bring Natashya back. That as soon as they had what they wanted, I would have her," he rambled, body heaving. "And I did it. I went against everything I believed, and I did it. I knew it was wrong, that the enchantment would kill, but you have to understand—she is my everything."

"Wait," Cayman spoke up. "Bael said he could bring your wife back to life?"

"The Harbinger and Bael promised me."

"No one has that power," I said, shaking my head. The senator's wild gaze swung toward me. He stopped shaking.

"Your wife is dead. She's probably crossed over. She can't be brought back."

"That's not true." Fisher's lips pulled back, baring his teeth. "It's not true."

"Bael cannot grant you that favor. I don't care who the Harbinger is, but neither can he," Cayman said, rising. "Other than the one in charge up there, there is only one other being in this world who can do such a thing and he's only ever done it once. It ended badly, so I doubt he'll do it again. Especially for a human. No offense."

Understanding clicked into play. "You're talking about Grim? But he can't bring someone back from the dead, especially not..." I looked down at the senator. "When did your wife die?"

The man's gaze shifted to his swelling fingers. "Three years, ten months and nineteen days ago."

That was...exact.

"She's super dead," I pointed out. "Like super decayed and dead."

"That doesn't matter," Cayman replied, stunning me. And apparently even Zayne, because he turned toward the demon. "Grim can do anything with a soul and that's all you need to reanimate a body."

My eyes widened. "Do you have...her body?"

The senator didn't answer, and my stomach churned. I wasn't sure if I wanted to know where her not-so-fresh body was being kept if it wasn't in her grave.

"You don't need the body," Cayman explained. "You just need the soul."

I gaped at him. "That's...that's not possible." I couldn't

believe it. After all the dead people I'd seen, it just couldn't be possible.

Cayman smiled. "Anything is possible, especially when you're Azreal, the Angel of Death.

"But like I said, he's only done that once before, and if you ask him if it can be done, he'll lie at first, but he can release a soul, he can destroy it and…" He paused for pure dramatics. "He can bring back the dead."

I didn't know what to say.

Cayman stepped toward the couch and then knelt so the senator was eye level with him. "I can also tell you that Azreal would *never* make such an agreement. There is literally nothing anyone can offer him. You were lied to."

The man did not move.

Zayne lowered his hands. "She was your weakness. They found it," he said, repeating what he'd said to me earlier. "They exploited it."

My gaze flickered over the man. "The sad thing is, you would've seen her again. If she had been good and you were good, you would've seen her when you died. You would've joined her, stayed with her for all of eternity. But now?" I shook my head. "You will not."

His eyes squeezed shut. "They promised me," he whispered. "They *promised* me."

I sighed, chest heavy, torn between hating this guy and feeling sorry for him. How could I feel both? He wasn't a good person. Maybe at some point he had been, but he'd turned a blind eye to everything wrong to get what he wanted, and I…

A coldness filled the pit of my stomach as I glanced at Zayne, thinking that I never wanted to know what it felt like to get to the point the senator had, where I'd do anything to bring back the love of my life.

I, who rarely prayed, prayed then to *never* know what that felt like.

Ever.

36

We left the senator a broken man with more mental and emotional hurts than physical. There was nothing else to coax from him other than heartbreak.

It hadn't been a waste of time, despite what Cayman said, because we now knew how a man like Senator Fisher had gotten wrapped up in this. But knowing left me with a heavy heart and distracted thoughts as we patrolled, hoping to lure the Harbinger out of whatever hidey hole he'd crawled back into.

It was tragic, what love could drive a person to do.

Zayne called an end to the evening earlier than usual, and for once I didn't complain or feel guilty about not scouring every nook and cranny of the city. Finding the Harbinger was paramount, but I suspected that the moment we entered the school on Saturday—in two days—Sulien would show up. And once we got into that school, we'd know exactly what we were dealing with.

I had a feeling we'd be blowing up some stuff shortly after.

As we walked to where the bike was parked, I said, "Something I've been thinking about. Why do you think Bael is being hidden? He's being protected. Isn't that weird?"

"If it were demons protecting him? No. But the Harbinger, who is a Trueborn? Yes." As we reached his bike, he slid his hand onto my lower back, and feeling the weight of it there was even better than holding hands. "I've been trying to come up with different scenarios, but all we know is that Bael is needed alive for whatever this plan is."

I sighed, staring up at the sky. With all the lights of the nearby buildings, I couldn't see if there were any stars. "I wonder what made Sulien become like this. We don't know what he's planning, other than to help bring about the end of the world, but obviously it's something insanely evil. He said he's never loved anyone, so we know it's not like with the senator."

Zayne tossed a leg over the bike, seating himself. "We're working with demons," he said, looking back at me. The glow from a nearby streetlight glanced off his face, creating shadows under his cheeks. "Not just because we see a different side of some demons, but also because we think what we're doing is for the greater good."

I followed where he was heading with that. "And you think he's working with demons because he thinks whatever he's planning is for the greater good?"

"It's possible. Throughout history, people have done messed-up things because they believed in something—because they believed they were right. Wardens are no different. I don't think there's any being that hasn't done bad things while believing it was for the right reason."

I nodded, thinking that whenever anyone believed what they were doing was right, it was nearly impossible to convince them otherwise.

I climbed onto the bike and wrapped my arms around his waist. He reached down, squeezing my knee in return, and we were off.

The ride back to the apartment was fast, but I used the time to sort of...detach myself from what happened with the senator and everything to do with the Harbinger. I thought perhaps Zayne was doing the same thing. We needed that, to carve out a tiny bit of time that belonged to us, to our lives, and by the time Zayne eased to a stop in the garage, next to his Impala, I was ready to be...normal. For a little while.

"Ready to check out the new place?" he asked as we walked to the elevator doors.

"I actually forgot about that," I admitted, laughing as we stepped inside.

"Wow."

"I know."

He grinned as the elevator rose. "It's a lot like the other place. Same layout and all. Just two bedrooms."

I leaned against the opposite wall as I tipped my head back. "Is two bedrooms really necessary now?" I teased.

"I hope not." He stalked toward me, placing his hands on either side of my head. "But two bathrooms will be amazing."

"True."

"Because I'm tired of you using my body wash."

"It's accidental."

"Uh-huh." He lowered his head. "I think you just like to smell like me."

I continued to grin. "The second bedroom is probably a good idea, because I'm sure I'm going to get annoyed and kick you out of the bed at some point."

"Sooner rather than later," he agreed. "Just don't kick me out entirely."

"You don't have to worry about that." The elevator came to a stop, and I stretched up to kiss him. Then I dipped under his arm and stepped into our new apartment. "You joining me?"

As Zayne pushed off the wall and followed, I turned back around. The apartment was virtually the same, except it was flipped. The kitchen was to the left and the living room to the right. The windows faced a different street, but the couch and furniture were set up just as before. Except...when I narrowed my eyes, I realized there was a short hallway where the door to the bedroom had been in the other apartment.

Zayne strode forward, turning so that he was walking backward. "Can I give you a tour?"

"Of course."

He grinned, taking my hand. "I think you can figure out the kitchen and living room."

"Yeah, I got that covered."

Chuckling as he turned, he tugged me into the hall. "The interesting parts are over here. To the right is a half bath, and the double doors next to that is laundry."

"Real exciting stuff," I teased.

"Just wait." He led me farther down, opening the door on the left. Reaching in, he flipped on the light. "This is bedroom number two. Through there is a bathroom."

I looked around. "The room is...completely empty."

"Observant."

I shot him a look.

"I only have one bed," he explained. "Had to order another, plus furniture."

"Wait." I tugged on his hand. "I should be ordering the furniture—paying for it."

"This isn't your room, though. It's mine, for whenever you're annoyed with me."

"But—"

"*This* is your room," he said, opening the other door.

Zayne didn't turn on the lights, but there was a soft white glow coming from something. Not the bathroom, which I assumed was somewhere in the shadows, or a bedside lamp. It was too faint for that. Confused, I looked up—

"Oh my God," I whispered, not believing what I was seeing.

Slipping my hand free, I walked into the bedroom, my head cranked back as far as it could go as I stared at the ceiling.

The ceiling that glowed a soft white from the glow-in-the-dark stars scattered all over it.

There were stars on the ceiling.

Stars.

"How?" I whispered, lifting my hands and then curling them against my chest. "When did you do this, Zayne?" I couldn't figure out when he'd have had time.

"The day you told Stacey about Sam," he answered. "I came back here and put these up. I tried to put them into a constellation, but that was harder than anticipated. Decided to make one up myself. So, it's Constellation Zayne."

My mouth opened and I couldn't find words as I stared at them. They started to blur, and I realized that was because my eyes were damp. "You did this when you were mad at me? Before we...before we made up?"

"Yeah. I guess so." He sounded confused. "Is that bad?"

Slowly, I turned to him. I could make out his outline in the doorway. My heart was pounding, and my hands were trembling. "You did this when we weren't talking? When I thought you might've hated me?"

"I never hated you, Trin. Mad? Sure. But I never—"

Running full speed, I launched myself at him. He caught me with a grunt that turned into a laugh as I threw my arms around his neck and my legs around his waist. I squeezed him as tight as my chest was squeezing and planted my face against his neck.

"I guess you like it." His arms came around me.

"Like it?" My voice was muffled against his neck. "*Like it?* It's perfect and amazing. It's beautiful. I love it. It's *more.*"

Zayne replied, but I don't know what he said, because something happened. Something cracked inside me, splintered wide open, and a rush of emotion poured through so fast and so unexpectedly that I couldn't stop it all from swelling up inside me.

It broke free in a sob that was part laugh. There were no walls. No stupid file cabinets. Nothing between me and everything I felt. Nothing between me and all that Zayne was.

Which was *more.*

So much *more.*

"Hey. Hey. Trin." His hand curved around the nape of my neck, tangling in the loose braid. "It's okay."

It was.

It wasn't.

Zayne carried me over to the bed and sat down with me in his lap, still clinging to him like a deranged spider monkey. My fingers curled along the edges of his hair, crushing the soft strands in my hands.

"Damn, Trin, I didn't mean to make you cry," he murmured against the side of my head. "You just said that you missed the stars from your bedroom back home, and I wanted… I wanted to give you stars that you could see every night."

Oh God. Oh God.

That made me cry harder, so much so that Zayne started rocking us as he rubbed a hand up and down my back, murmuring nonsensical words until I pulled it together, shifting so that my forehead rested on his shoulder.

"I know. I know you didn't mean to make me cry. This isn't your fault. I love the stars. I love that you did this. It's just…" It was just that what he'd done was kind, sweet, thoughtful, beautiful and as meaningful as he was.

And it was just that I'd known he cared for me—that he liked me as more than just a friend—and I'd known he'd begun to feel all of that before the bond. And I'd known I cared for him, and that I had already been falling for him long before the previous night…but this was so much *more*.

"Trin?" He guided my head back, sliding his thumb along my bottom lip. "What's going on in that head of yours?"

"I'm… I'm scared," I admitted in a whisper.

His pale blue eyes sharpened. "Scared of what? Of me?"

"No. Never." I drew in a shallow breath. "I'm scared of…

I'm scared of *us*. I'm scared of what this means. I'm scared we're not supposed to be *this*. I'm scared that I'll lose you. I'm scared of how much I…how much I feel for you. I'm scared."

Zayne's chest rose with a deep breath against mine and then those thick lashes swept down, shielding his eyes. His fingers splayed against my cheek. "So am I."

My body jerked. "You are?"

His hand curled around the back of my head, fingers tangling in my hair. "You want to know the truth?"

Yes? No?

He took my silence as a yes. "It terrifies me. Every aspect of it, Trin. Feeling what I do for you, wanting what I want from you?" His voice was deep and rough, and it made me shiver. "There have been moments when I wished I felt this way about anyone other than you."

Wait.

What?

I blinked. "Okay. I wasn't expecting that."

"Hear me out." His fingers tightened around my braid. "What I feel terrifies me, because I'm not supposed to feel this way and God knows I've already been down that road. Wasn't exactly looking to repeat history."

I clamped my mouth shut.

"But it's more than that, Trin. It goes way beyond my past," he went on, his gaze holding mine. "It's because of who you are. You go out there every night and put your life on the line. You're hunting the kind of demons that skilled Wardens dread. You're looking for something that can kill demons and Wardens in seconds. I'm terrified of something happening to you, and that has nothing to do with what that means for me."

Okay. I totally understood that. "You're doing the same thing, Zayne. I can't even think if something happened—" I cut myself off, not wanting to go down that road. "I wish you were a human who went to college and was studying to be a veterinarian."

His brows lifted.

"Okay, maybe I don't want you to be a human. Humans are too easy to kill, but you get my point."

A slow curl tipped up his lips. "I do." His head tilted to the side. "So, I'm scared, but what I feel—what I want is still there. It's always there, and when I'm not with you, all I want to do is get back to you. At first I thought it was the bond, but it's not. It's something entirely different." His mouth grazed my cheekbone, drawing closer to my lips. "And knowing that—knowing you feel...feel *right*—I'll be damned if I'll walk away from that, even though it terrifies me.

"I need you to understand something." His gaze caught mine, held it. "I know that what I feel for you is nothing like what I felt for Layla. *Nothing*. And I realized something the night Stacey and I talked."

That was the night he and I had gone to the next level. It had been only, what, two days ago, but it felt like weeks. "What?" I whispered.

"I...don't know if I was ever in love with her," he said. "I loved her. I know that, but I think I was in love with the idea of her and us. And I think...no, I *know* that the hardest part, what I've been dealing with since then, is realizing it would've never worked out between us, and how I couldn't see that." The hand around my braid slipped to my lower back. "I will always love that girl. There won't be a time that I don't, but I'm not *in* love with her."

My heart pounded, and when I took a breath it felt like it went nowhere. "And *Stacey* helped you realize all this?"

That crazy-cute half grin appeared. "Yeah, she sort of called me out on it. Said some things I needed to hear—things I'd already been thinking."

All right.

There was a swelling motion in my chest, one that threatened to lift me straight to the starry ceiling.

Maybe I shouldn't be so mad about him staying out late with her.

But…

There was always a *but*.

I took another deep breath. I needed to say this. I needed to get it out there, because I could feel it building between us. The rules weren't going to stop us. The dangers each of us faced weren't going to be a hurdle. "I'm scared of getting my heart broken."

His eyes met mine once more. "So am I."

I sucked in a sharp breath. "I couldn't… If something happened to you, because we're together, I…"

The hand on my jaw kept my gaze glued to his. "I know that my life is tied to yours, that if something happens to you, it happens to me, but that doesn't keep me from being terrified that I'll somehow lose you. I will do anything to get to you if something happens. There is nothing that will stop me," he admitted. "A part of me understands why the senator did what he did. Hell, not a part of me. Everything in me understands, and the knowledge of what I'd do if I lost you? Yeah, that scares me, too."

A tremor rolled down my spine.

"If my life wasn't bonded to yours and something happened to you? If you were taken from me, there'd be nothing that would stop me from getting you back. I'd go to the ends of the Earth. I'd barter with everything I have," he said. "I know that's wrong. I know how bad that could go, but I would do it. And that's not because of the fact that if you were to die, so would I. In death, nothing would keep me from you. That I swear."

It was wrong. It would most likely go bad, but I whispered, "I'd do the same." And that was the truth. "If you were killed?" Even thinking that hurt. "I'd do anything to bring you back."

"So, knowing that? I sure as Hell am not going to let some rule keep us apart. Nor the fear of seeing you get hurt, and definitely not the fear of me getting hurt. I'm a lot of things, Trin, but a coward isn't one of them." His eyes searched mine. "And you're not a coward, either."

"No," I whispered. "No, I'm not."

That half grin grew into a smile, the kind that broke and mended my heart in a matter of beats. It was the kind of smile full of promises and possibility, and damn straight, I wasn't a coward. My fingers tangled in his hair as I exhaled.

"Why is this coming up now and not two nights ago?" he asked.

Because then there'd still been walls. I hadn't realized it until now, not until those walls were gone. "Because you gave me stars, and that means this is…this is *more*."

His thumb swept over my cheek. "I don't know what *more* means to you, but it means that I love you, Trinity Lynn. That I'm in love with you."

I didn't know who moved first, who kissed who. We were separated and then we weren't. It was gentle and soft, like it could've been our first kiss, and there was something more powerful about this kiss, and maybe this was our first real one. I slid my hands to his cheeks and opened my mouth to his.

And then it became infinitely *more*.

It was love that I felt for him, love that had me worked up into so many tiny, twisted knots. It was love that coursed through me, even if the words never left my lips.

It was love that fueled the need to give him something as beautiful as the stars he'd given me, and I knew of only one thing, something Jada had once told me about.

Sliding out of his lap, I gripped his shirt and pulled. He needed little instruction, lifting his arms and letting me pull the shirt off, and when I reached for his pants, he rose, toe-ing off his boots. He undressed. I helped. Sort of. I mostly distracted him during the process, causing his strong legs to tremble. Actually, I distracted myself, learning and exploring as I went, pressing kisses against his hip.

Then, only when he pulled me up, did I shimmy out of my bottoms and kick them aside as I met his gaze. "I want you."

"That much is obvious." His eyes glimmered as he reached for me.

"I want you to be who you really are," I added, holding on to the hem of my shirt. Zayne opened his mouth, closed it. Not exactly the response I was looking for. "You're my Protector. You're a Warden. I want *you*."

He sat down heavily on the edge of the bed. "Do you know what that means?"

I knew what it meant.

It was what Wardens did when they mated, according to Jada, and it was pretty much just like humans, but it was only shared with their mates. For a Warden, it was a true expression of love, and while I couldn't do it, I knew what it meant if *we* did it.

Then it occurred to me that perhaps that was making things a little too serious. He loved me. I could look at the ceiling every day and see his love, but this might be too much, too soon. Embarrassment crept over my skin.

"You don't have to," I said in a rush. "It was just— Never mind. It's dumb and too soon. Can we forget it?"

"No." His pupils stretched vertically. "It's not dumb or too soon. It's just…" A wondrous look filled his features as he shook his head. "You amaze me."

A different kind of blush swept over me, but then Zayne rose, and he showed me who he truly was.

I might've stopped breathing as he extended his hand. "Forever."

"Forever." I placed mine in his and as his fingers curled around mine, he returned to the bed, sitting. I felt like I wasn't getting air in my lungs as I placed a knee on either side of his legs.

His eyes were wide, pale and luminous as he stared up at me. His sharpened nails snagged the material of my shirt as he lifted it up and over. I reached out, fingers fumbling over the tiny hooks on my bra. Carefully, he lowered his head, his fingers chasing the straps as they slipped down my arms, off my wrists, to fall to the floor below. I touched his cheeks, my palms flattening as I guided his gaze back to mine. Tilting my head, I lowered my mouth and kissed him. The taste of him branded my skin, the feel of him as I slid a hand down his chest, over the tight muscles of his stomach and even lower, tattooed itself into me, and the sound of his groan echoed like a prayer.

There was a pause to grab protection, and then I lifted up slightly only to ease back down, my breath mixing with his. Zayne did not rush me or move a muscle. I knew he would not until I did, forever patient as I adjusted, and when I did move, it was like nothing I'd felt before.

"Trin," he moaned, his hands at my hips, his nails gentle against my skin. His arm circled my waist, careful of his strength as he pulled me to his chest. "Forever," he repeated.

I whispered the word back against his lips. It was no simple word, but a promise. A different kind of bond. Forever seemed like a long time, especially at our ages, and to humans it might even seem foolish, but our forevers weren't guaranteed, and what *was* was what we felt for one another. It didn't mean things would be easy. It didn't even mean that tomorrow we wouldn't annoy the crap out of each other. What it meant was that no matter what, we were forever.

His wings swept around us, forming a cocoon that blocked out all light. The fear of the sudden darkness was nowhere to be found. Not when whatever chains that had been holding him back seemed to have snapped and his body surged against mine. Not when there was all this tension in me, in him. I gripped his shoulders, my fingers digging into his hard skin. We were like wires stretched taut, pulled as far as we could go, and then released in a beautiful rush, pounding through both of us.

It was like waiting for a storm to pass. His forehead rested against mine, his breath just as short and quick. An eternity seemed to go by before I felt the stir of air as his wings lifted and his skin against mine softened.

"That was... I wasn't expecting that. I..." He drew in another shallow breath, seeming at a loss for words. "I don't think you know what...that meant to me. I've always... God, I used to worry about how I really looked. I guess a part of me still does."

"You have no reason." I leaned back so I could see his face. His cheeks were flushed a deeper hue. "Like I said before, you're beautiful in both forms. And just to sound extra cheesy for you, it's because of what's in here." I pressed a hand to his chest. "You say I have a light about me, but *you* are my light."

Zayne reclaimed the space between us, kissing me. "You're never getting rid of me now."

"I wouldn't want to."

"I'll remind you that you said that." His smile held a sleepy quality to it. "You know, you're perfect for me."

A giddiness swept through me as I rocked forward, placing my hands on his shoulders and—

I stopped. There was something off about his shoulders. Three short grooves in his skin. Bright and seeping tiny beads of red. Blood.

Confusion replaced the bubbly warmth. "I think... I think I scratched you."

"Huh." He looked down, following my gaze. "You did."

They were scratches—scratches that I'd caused. I jerked my hands back to my chest. "Oh my God."

"It's okay." He grinned. "More than okay."

Cold air poured into my chest as I stared at his skin—skin that I'd scratched with my fingernails, which didn't make sense. At all. My wide gaze bounced to his face.

The smile faded from his face. "Trin, it's okay—"

"No, it's not." I scrambled off him, standing and backing up until I knocked into the dresser. "I shouldn't have been able to do that. Fingernails can't pierce your skin, not even in your human form, but you weren't... That shouldn't have happened."

"It's..." Understanding dawned across his face. His gaze shot to mine. "Oh, Hell."

37

Zayne's skin was no longer Warden hard, even after he shifted back into Warden form and then again into human form. His skin was virtually *human*.

Meaning he was susceptible to weapons. Knives. Daggers. Bullets. Claws. Teeth. We knew this because he'd snatched one of my daggers and sliced open his palm before I could stop him.

He was still a Warden, with the strength and power of a Warden, but otherwise he was basically human. That was how important their stone-like skin was. It protected a whole lot of important things, like every single vein and organ in their bodies.

I knew why this had happened. Deep down, so did Zayne. *This* was the consequence I'd been dreading.

"Why would this happen now and not before?" Zayne asked, sitting on the couch. We'd moved to the living room sometime after he'd sliced and diced his palm. It hadn't healed, but the bleeding had slowed enough that he was able to remove the cloth he'd bound his palm with. The cut was thin and beaded with blood. Just like the welts on his still-bare shoulder—welts left behind by my virtually human fingernails.

Tearing my gaze from the wounds, I returned to wearing a path in the floor. I was pacing back and forth in front of him, wearing his shirt, which nearly doubled as a dress on me. "I think...I know why. It's me."

"Trin..." He lifted his head, closing his hand. "This is not just your fault."

"I'm not saying it is." I chewed on my thumbnail. "What I mean is, I think—no, I know I was holding back before. Even though I knew I was...was falling for you. That I already had, but I wasn't allowing myself to really feel that or acknowledge it."

"And you did tonight?"

Pacing, I nodded.

"We don't know if that's why."

I stopped and looked at him. "I think it's pretty safe to assume that's exactly why. Maybe we were right in the beginning. Or I was. That sex or something physical wasn't what was forbidden. It was emotion."

"Love," he suggested in place of the word *emotion*. "It's love, Trin."

My feet got moving again. "That," I whispered.

He was silent, and then said, "It's not a big deal."

"What?" I nearly shrieked, my pace picking up. "It's a huge deal, Zayne. You can be killed—"

"I could always be killed. That's nothing new."

"You can be killed a Hell of a lot easier now," I pointed out. "Don't play this off as if it's nothing. It's huge, Zayne. This is why we should've fought this. This is why, just because something *feels* right—"

Zayne caught me around the waist as I passed him, pulling me into his lap. "No," he said. "This does not mean that, Trin. This only means it is what it is, and we have to deal with it. That's all."

My gaze fell to where his uninjured hand circled my wrist. His skin felt the same, impossibly warm. "How can you make it sound like it's nothing?"

"Because it doesn't change anything." He pressed his forehead to mine. "It doesn't lessen what I feel for you, and I know damn well, after what you just gave me, it doesn't lessen what you feel for me."

He was right, and I hated myself a little for that.

"This could be temporary," he continued. "We don't know anything other than the fact we'll have to adapt to it. Together. That's all we can do."

I shook my head against his. "I don't understand how you can be so calm."

"It's not like I'm not worried. I am, but I told you. I knew the risks going into this."

We'd known *of* the risks, but not what they were and there was a big difference. I pulled my head away, thinking about all we had to do—that we'd planned to do. "I don't want you going to that school with me."

"Trin—"

"Not until I know what's in there. You said we need to adapt, and this is how we adapt. You take a step back."

"That's not what I meant."

"I don't care!" I twisted in his arms, my heart pounding as I clasped his cheeks. "I don't care what you think you can do, but if this is our...our punishment, then this is how we adapt. We have to be even more careful, and being careful means you take a step back until we know what we're facing."

"Do you think I'm just going to sit here, reading a book, while you're out there fighting the Harbinger?"

"Starting a reading habit isn't a bad thing. You could start a book club."

"Trin." His pale eyes flashed. "I'm a trained warrior. I know how to prevent getting clawed or bit or stabbed. I'm not weak."

"You're the strongest person I know, but you're not invincible."

"I never was. And neither are you. When I found out about your vision, do you think it didn't scare me half to death, imagining all the ways it could affect you?"

I fell silent.

"It did. It still does. You're half human, Trin. Your skin is vulnerable to all manner of injuries, but I remind myself that you're trained. You have your *grace*. You know how to fight and to get out of a situation if it turns ugly. I have to remind myself of that every day. I'm there to protect you, but I'm not there to stop you. Are you going to try to stop me?"

I smoothed my fingers over his cheeks and then exhaled roughly. "I don't expect you to sit here and do nothing. I just expect you to...make smart choices. Like I do."

His brows lifted.

"Like I *try* to do. You go to the school with me, but you stay out of it until we know what's going on," I compromised. "And you're right. I could probably still get hurt faster than you, even now, but I've had my whole life to accept my limitations. You haven't had even a minute fighting with yours."

He leaned in, closing the distance between us and kissing me softly. "We'll figure this out, limitations and all."

"Promise?" I whispered, needing the confirmation, needing to know that this wasn't the start of something terrible.

"Promise." He held me. "Remember, Trin. Forever."

"I remember." And I did. I would never forget.

Later, once Zayne had coaxed me back to bed and he'd fallen asleep, I did something I could count on one hand the number of times I'd done before. Closing my eyes, I cleared my mind of anything except my father. I called to him. I summoned him. I prayed to him, hoping he'd show up and undo what we'd done. Begged that he return Zayne to his former state. I even offered something that would break my heart into tiny jagged pieces that could never be repaired.

I'll give him up, I silently pleaded. *I'll make him give me up. I'll undo forever. Anything. I'll do anything.*

But like all the times before, there was no answer.

38

I was riding the nervous hot-mess express by the time Zayne and I met up with Roth and crew Saturday evening. My *grace* was on a hair trigger. If anyone so much as looked at Zayne the wrong way, I was prepared to do full bodily harm.

Human and nonhuman.

Except for animals. Zayne better be able to run fast if a dog tried to bite him or something.

His skin hadn't returned to its stone-like quality, and I had to fight everything in me to not lock him in the closet or something. He was behaving as if this new state of things wasn't utterly life changing. He seemed quite unaffected by it, and I couldn't understand it.

I figured the first time he got clawed by a demon would change that real quick.

Thinking about that terrified me, because depending on where he was clawed, it could be serious or even fa—

"Trin." Zayne pushed off the concrete wall. We were waiting in the same place as last time, on the corner of the street that led to the school. "You're getting yourself worked up."

I frowned in his general direction, since he was a blur in the absence of lights. "No, I'm not."

"I can feel it." He sighed. "Why does that seem like something you repeatedly forget?"

"Maybe because I'm trying to forget it."

He laughed, moving closer. I caught the scent of wintermint, and then his hand was on my lower back. "Don't worry. I'll be fine."

Yeah, he was going to be fine standing out here, at a safe, smart distance.

"Here they come," he announced. "Roth, Layla and… Cayman."

"I didn't know he was coming."

"I guess he missed us."

I cracked a grin as I made out the vague shapes of three people heading toward us. They were dressed like burglars, but as they got closer, Layla's hair stood out like a slice of moonlight until they stepped under the streetlamp.

"Guessing you guys haven't heard yet." Roth was to the first to speak.

"Heard what?" Zayne kept his hand on my lower back as he guided us away from the wall to the sidewalk.

"About thirty minutes ago, Senator Josh Fisher was found on the sidewalk outside the Condor," Cayman said. "And he didn't just lie down. He came down about thirty floors."

My eyes widened. "Holy crap."

"Yeah. The whole street is blocked off right now," Layla said. "News crews and police cars every twenty feet."

"Do you think he killed himself?" I asked. "Or..."

"...the Harbinger paid him a visit?" Zayne finished. "Either is possible."

"Especially considering he was one Hell of a broken man," Cayman said, and I had to agree.

It was possible the senator had come to accept that the Harbinger and Bael had lied to him and that he'd never see his wife again. Considering what he'd taken part in, it was truly possible he'd ended his own life, but... "The Harbinger could've found out we'd been there. Taken him out."

"Possible," Zayne said.

"Well, I mean, who cares, though?" Cayman asked, and I looked to where he stood behind Roth. "He was a bad dude, and things were never going to end well for him."

"Tact," Roth explained, "is not something Cayman has ever learned."

"Mainly because tact is often pretending you care when you don't," he replied. "Look, all I'm saying is I wouldn't throw a life jacket to that guy if our boat was sinking."

Zayne rubbed his brow as he shook his head.

"Well," I said. "You are a demon, so..."

"I'd also kill baby Hitler," Cayman announced. "Easily."

"Jesus," Zayne muttered under his breath.

"I'd kill baby Harbinger, too," Cayman added.

"Really?" Layla pursed her lips. "A baby? But what if there was a chance you could change him?"

Exhaling heavily, Zayne dropped his hand but still looked like he was about to have an aneurysm.

"Some people can't change," Roth interjected. "Evil is their destiny."

"But a baby?" Layla shuddered. "That would be hard."

"Not really," Cayman said, shrugging when her eyes widened.

"Is this a necessary conversation to have right now?" Zayne asked.

"No, I agree," I jumped in, and Zayne sighed once more. "Knowing what the Harbinger has been doing, I'd go back in time and terminate his ass."

Layla was quiet and then she nodded. "Yeah, I'd kill baby Harbinger."

Roth crossed his arms. "You know I'd do it."

"Now, that's a shocker," muttered Zayne.

"I'd do it, but then again, I don't have a problem killing some babies, because I'm a demon." Cayman paused as we all turned toward him again. "Oh, was that an overshare?"

I lifted my pointer finger and thumb. "Just a little."

"What about you, Zayne?" Roth asked. "Would you kill baby Harbinger?"

"Yes," he said, and I imagined a vein was beginning to throb in his temple. "I would. Now that we've all agreed that we'd kill baby Harbinger, can we get a move on?"

"Sure." Cayman grinned. "I don't know about you guys, but this sharing-and-caring moment makes me feel like we're a real team that can get stuff done. Like the Avengers, but more evil."

"So, pretty much like Tony Stark?" Layla said.

"Tony Stark is not evil!" Cayman shouted, causing me to jump. "Why do you keep saying that? He's the only one who ever tried to set boundaries. He just has moral gray areas, thank you very much."

"You know he's not real?" I asked. "Right?"

Cayman spun on me. "How dare you?"

"Okay. Really." Zayne gestured to the sidewalk. "Seriously."

The plan was to enter around the side of the building, where the work trucks had been parked.

"I think we should check out the basement locker area, since we're certain that's where the tunnels lead," Roth suggested. "It's where the Lilin and Nightcrawlers were last time. We can access it through the gymnasium."

"Sounds like a plan," Zayne said and started walking up the sidewalk.

"What?" I caught his arm, stopping him. "What do you mean it *sounds like a plan*?"

His face was shadowed in the glow of the streetlamp. "Just what it sounds like."

"Zayne, we talked about this," I said, keeping my voice low.

"Yeah, we did. I'm going to be careful and—"

"That's *not* what we agreed on!"

"What did we agree on exactly?" He pulled his arm free.

"We agreed that you'd stay outside until we knew what we were facing."

"That's not what *I* agreed to."

"You have to got to be kidding me." I stepped back, hands opening and closing at my sides. "I thought we agreed—"

"We agreed to figure this out together. That doesn't mean I agreed to stay out here."

"So, you're going to go in there, where there might be

demons and pissed-off ghosts and Shadow People, who are far more dangerous than most ghosts?" I was aware that we were gaining an audience of three. "What if the Harbinger is in there?"

"Do you feel him?"

"No, but that doesn't mean he isn't there or won't show up—"

"While I'm outside?"

"Or he could be in that school and I just don't feel him yet. Neither of us can tell if there are more demons around, because, hello, there are several of them right here with us, eavesdropping on our conversation!"

"I'm only part demon," Layla murmured. "Why are you guys arguing over this? I'm confused."

"I'm enthralled," Cayman countered.

I turned from Zayne, not wanting to say what was going on, but they needed to know. "His skin is no longer like a Warden's. It's like a human's."

"Like yours," Zayne called from behind me.

I ignored that. "And he hasn't had any time to figure out what that means and how to work with it."

Layla stepped toward us. "How is that possible?"

"It's a long story," I said, not really wanting to get into our super personal business. "But I want him to stand back until we know what's inside."

"I can still fight," Zayne said.

"Yes, you can. We've already discussed this, but the moment they realize that your skin is as soft as a baby's butt, they're going to exploit that," I reasoned.

"She has a point, man." Roth's gaze shifted to Zayne.

"Would you sit out while Layla went in there?" Zayne demanded.

"Well, my skin would never be as soft as a baby's butt, so no."

I threw up my hands, exasperated, as I glared at Zayne. "You cannot go in there."

"Hold up." Layla jumped in, turning to Roth. "If something happened that made you more vulnerable, would you really put yourself in danger out of some backward caveman need to protect me? Even when I clearly don't need you to protect me?"

Roth opened his mouth.

"Think *really* hard about how you answer that question," she warned, holding up a hand. "Because you and I are going to have a very uncomfortable evening if you say yes."

Roth closed his mouth.

"I totally understand why you don't want him in there," Layla said to me. "I wouldn't want Roth to be in there, either, if something had made him more vulnerable. You're not in the wrong here, but *you*?" She pointed at Zayne. "You are in the wrong."

"Excuse me?" Zayne responded while I smiled.

"Would you be okay with Trinity going in there if the shoe was on the other foot?"

"Actually, the shoe—"

"Not the same thing," I interrupted, pinning him with a glare. "I know what my limitations are. I know how to work around them. You don't know your limitations yet."

A muscle ticked along his jaw.

"You wouldn't, Zayne. You would not be okay with her

doing it. Not only that, you'd be so distracted with worry about her that you'd also be vulnerable," Layla went on. "Is that what you want her to be? Distracted while dealing with Shadow People and who knows what else?"

His lips thinned as he shook his head, his narrowed gaze finding me. "No. I don't want her distracted."

"Then you can't go in there," she said, her voice softening. "I know it'll kill you to stay out here, but that's better than getting hurt or being the reason she gets hurt."

"Fine," he bit out, sounding not even remotely fine.

Relief swept through me so powerfully I almost started crying, and he must've felt that through the bond, because his eyes widened slightly. I went over to him, folding my arms around his waist as I stared up at him. "Thank you."

A sighed shuddered through him as he lifted his hands to my cheeks. "I hate this," he said, voice low. "I hate the idea of not being in there with you. I'm your Protector. This feels…wrong."

"I know." My gaze searched his in the darkness. "But I'll be okay. And you'll be okay. We just need time to adapt to this. Patrol. Hunt. We haven't had that time yet."

"Don't be logical," he said, lowering his head. "That's not your job. It's mine."

Before I could point out that I was entitled to be logical every once in a while, Zayne kissed me, and it was no quick, chaste kiss. He coaxed my lips open with his, and the moment the kiss deepened, the world around us faded away. I leaned farther into him, and when the sound he made rumbled through me, my toes curled.

"Well, now we know why Zayne's suddenly all soft and

virtually useless," Cayman commented dryly. "Look at the happy couple."

"I can still kill you." Zayne's lips brushed mine once more before he lifted his head, pinning the demon broker with a dark look. "Easily."

Cayman gasped. "I'm *affronted*."

I peeked over my shoulder, my gaze finding Layla. I didn't know what I expected to see when I looked at her, but what I saw was happiness. The sad kind I recognized and had felt myself, way back when I'd realized Misha had been interested in someone. It wasn't that I'd wanted him, or that I hadn't wanted him with someone else, but he'd been mine in a way, and then he was no longer. I imagined it was the same for Layla.

Emotions were weird.

"That was the consequence?" Roth asked, cursing under his breath. "You fall in love and it *weakens* you?"

"Apparently." Zayne's hands rested on my shoulders. "Messed up, right?"

"More than messed up," Roth replied. "That's downright—"

"Smart?" Cayman said, and I was beginning to wonder if he had a death wish today. "What? It makes sense. Love can be a weakness or it can be a strength, but no matter what, love is always the priority. You both would put each other first, before your duty, and the ones in charge would see that as a weakness. Something they'd want to prevent."

"Well, thanks for your input," Zayne said, sighing. "That makes us both feel better about everything."

Somehow, and I couldn't follow how, Roth decided that

Layla should remain outside as well, which caused Zayne to announce he didn't need a babysitter. Then Layla and Roth started arguing, but in the end, she agreed to wait with Zayne until the three of us—Roth, Cayman and I—knew what we were dealing with.

Finally, we headed to the school, and as we got close, I could see a few windows were lit from within. As we rounded one side, making our way to where the trucks had been parked last time, my gaze flicked to the second level. The vibe was still there, as if hundreds of unseen eyes were tracking our moves.

Skirting the temporary fencing, we neared the door, and I turned toward Zayne, admitting to myself that it did feel wrong to leave him out here.

Sometimes what feels wrong is right. That's what I told myself as I suddenly wanted to take back what I'd said. He was safer out here. This was smart and logical.

Zayne caught my hand as Cayman fiddled with the padlock, breaking it. "Be careful."

"I will." I squeezed his hand in return, those three words I hadn't said yet dancing to the tip of my tongue, but feeling too dangerous to speak. Which was dumb, since the damage was already done. Speaking them aloud didn't give them any more power than the emotion attached to them already had.

"You be careful, too," I said instead.

"Always," he replied.

39

The wide first-floor hallway was suprisingly lit with obnoxiously bright track lighting, something that we hadn't been able to see from outside since most of the classroom doors were closed. The light did very little to cast back the shadows clinging to the lockers and closed doors. I let Cayman and Roth lead the way, since this was the first time I'd been in a public school.

It smelled weird, like must and leftover cologne and perfume, along with the faint smell of sawdust and construction.

A flicker of movement caught my attention. A gray form darted into one of the closed classrooms.

"You think what's going on with Zayne is permanent?" Roth asked, voice low.

"I don't know," I admitted. A shadow appeared at the end of the row of lockers and quickly seeped back into its surroundings. "I hope it's temporary, but..."

"But you'd have to stop loving him," he finished. "Or he'd have to stopping loving you."

"Yeah," I whispered, looking around. Every couple of feet, there was a glimpse of something that didn't seem right, but it was gone before I could focus and decipher what I was seeing. However, I could feel them. There were so many ghosts in this building, it was almost suffocating.

"Do you think that's possible?"

I thought about how I'd prayed to my father, desperate, promising to do just that. "I... I don't know how you even fall in love, so I don't know how to fall out of it."

"You don't," he said. "At least, you can't make yourself fall out of love."

"You sound like you've tried."

"I did."

"You could get yourself a spell. There are some out there, but I'm sure they come with nasty side effects," Cayman replied, looking over his shoulder at me. "Or you could barter, if you knew where to find a demon with a certain skill set..."

I lifted my brows. "Are you offering to barter?"

"I'm a businessman to the heart, little Trueborn. Well, a business demon, but whatever." He faced straight ahead. "You know where to find me if it comes to that."

Roth frowned at Cayman's back. Barter my soul? Or parts of it? That wasn't something I'd considered.

"You see any ghosts yet?" Roth asked as we passed an empty glass case.

"I'm catching a lot of quick glimpses of movement. It could be nothing, or it could be shy ghosts."

"Or Shadow People?"

I nodded.

Cayman stopped, and I realized we were at the entrance to the gym. The doors were open, and a void of darkness waited for us.

Oh dear.

I could see literally nothing. Not even Cayman as he walked in and was swallowed up by the nothingness. Tiny hairs lifted all over my body. The vibe I'd had earlier increased as I stared into the darkness.

My feet were rooted where I stood. I, who was not afraid of ghosts, was a wee bit scared of the prospect of entering that gym.

"What is it?" Roth asked.

"Ghosts. There are a lot of ghosts in there. I can feel them," I said, looking at him. "I can't see them, though. I can't..."

Roth understood, nodding. "Give me your hand. I'll get you where we need to go."

I stared at his hand. "You told Zayne what I did to Faye after you told me not to say anything."

"I was wondering when you were going to bring that up," he replied. "I changed my mind after I dropped you off. My bad."

I frowned at him.

"You guys coming?" Cayman called out. "Because it's kind of weird in here. Like, I don't think I'm alone kind of weird."

"Maybe talk about this later?" Roth suggested.

"Definitely later." I put my hand in his. There was a strange burst of energy from where his skin made contact with mine, but I couldn't really focus on it.

Roth led me into the void, and it was like walking through

soup. The air was thick, and it moved, as if it was curling around us. The legs of my pants tugged as if tiny hands were grabbing them. I kept walking. A few more steps, and I felt *them*, pressing in, crowding us. What felt like a hand glanced off my hip and then my rear.

I was starting to get a really bad feeling about the kind of ghosts that were in here.

"You really can see?" I asked, nervous.

"Enough."

"That's reassuring—" A finger glided off my cheek.

"Don't," I snapped at the darkness to my right. "Touch me."

"I didn't," Roth replied.

"It wasn't you."

"Oh." His grip tightened on my hand. "Would you think less of me if I admitted I'm kind of creeped out?"

"Yes."

"Wow."

"I'm kidding." The edge of my braid lifted. I snatched it free with my other hand. "If any more of you pervy ghosts lay a hand on me, I will end your existence."

"Do I want to know what's happening?" Cayman's voice came from somewhere.

A high-pitched giggle that sounded neither male nor female answered, and then the air around Roth and I shifted again, as if it were parting as we crossed the gym.

"None of them are approaching me for help," I said after a moment. "Which I would think they would do if they wanted out of here."

"One would think," Roth murmured, coming to a stop. "Cayman?"

"Working on the door now. It's sealed—" Metal ground together and then gave way. "There we go."

Dim light poured in, thank baby llamas everywhere—*oh, no*. This had *nope* written all over it.

A narrow ledge and a set of steps were in front of us, but they weren't unoccupied.

Dead people.

There were dead people lining the steps, pressed to the wall. Dozens of them. I'd never seen anything like it. They stared at us as we came in, their faces all wrong. Some showed whatever had killed them. Bullet wounds. Missing cheeks. Skulls. Bruises and bloat. Deformities. Others showed no visible sign of injury, but they smiled at us, reeking of pure evil. I looked up, and my heart nearly stopped.

They swarmed the ceiling like cockroaches, clamoring and crawling over one another. There wasn't a bare space.

"Can you see?" Roth asked.

"Unfortunately." I pulled my hand free. "You don't want to know."

"I do." Cayman walked through a ghost that didn't have much left of its head. It spun, hissing at him before it rose to the ceiling, crawling over the others crowded there.

"No. You do not." I stepped around one who blew a kiss in my direction. "We should hurry."

And that's what we did.

Racing down the steps, I tried not to look at them, but some stepped out, whispering too low and fast for me to catch what they were saying. Others reached for me.

Halfway down, I recognized one of the ghosts. It was the woman in the dark service uniform, but she looked...

different. Color had leached from her skin, the shadows on her face making her eyes seem like black empty sockets. Her jaw extended, gaping opening into something inhuman and twisted.

She howled.

Roth whipped around. "What the Hell?"

"You heard that?" I eased around the woman, whose face was stretched beyond human possibility.

"Pretty sure everyone in a one-mile radius heard that," Cayman commented. "And I got to say, I am feeling some wicked bad vibes."

"I don't understand. They're all… I don't know. They're all bad." My heart thumped. "Sam said they were trapped, but…"

"Shadow People." Roth jerked his hand around his face like he'd walked into a cobweb. It wasn't. It was the hair from a young woman hanging upside down from the ceiling. "Could've got to them. Corrupted them."

That… God, that was terrible, and we should've gotten in here earlier, taken the risk, because these people…

We came to the end of the staircase, and the smell of rust and rot increased as we walked into a room. Flickering fluorescent light cast shadows along rows of wide lockers. Doors were ripped off, benches toppled over. I looked around, realizing we must be in the old locker rooms, where the Nightcrawlers had been…incubating.

There were no ghosts in here.

Cayman walked through an archway into another opening while Roth stood near me.

Something occurred to me. I reached out and pressed a hand against the bare brick wall.

The wall vibrated under my palm, and a heartbeat later, a golden glow washed over the walls and ceiling and then disappeared, revealing what Roth had suspected we'd find that day in the tunnel.

The entire school was full of angelic wards. "This trapped them here." I pulled my hand away. The wards remained. "Those people could've been good. Just needed help crossing over. They could've even been spirits, because some of them weren't in their death states, but they all looked *wrong*."

I had no idea if Shadow People could do that, but as I looked back at the stairwell, I accepted what I'd known the moment I saw the ghosts and spirits. "They'll all about to become wraiths, and…"

"It's too late." Roth said what I didn't want to. "Ghosts and spirits are the soul exposed. It's more vulnerable in death, when decisions and actions become permanent. It's like they're all infected, and it's incurable."

Heaviness settled in my heart as I tore my gaze from the stairwell. There was no one left here to save.

"Guys?" Cayman's voice rang out from the other side of the wall. "You're going to want to see this."

Roth and I exchanged looks before walking toward the opening. "This is where the Lilin was born, sort of in a nest. It's the old showers."

We stepped into a bare room, and I could make out Cayman kneeling. "What's up?" Roth asked.

"Found something. A hole. There's light down there." He rocked back. "No way down other than to jump, but looks to be about ten feet. Was this here before?"

"No." Roth edged around the eight-by-eight opening. "This is new."

"Should we check it out?"

It took me a moment to realize Cayman was speaking to me. I nodded. "I think we have to."

"All right." Cayman rose. "Meet you down there." He jumped, and after a moment, he signaled the okay.

I went next. My landing sent a poof of dirt and dust into the air. Coughing, I stepped aside so Roth wouldn't land on me when he came through the hole a few seconds later. As the dust cloud settled, my vision adjusted to my surroundings.

It was brighter down here, lit by several spaced-out halogen lights on raised tripods and torches that jutted out of earthen walls.

That was a fire hazard if I'd ever seen one.

The place was a man-made cavern of sorts, opening into a larger space where the ceiling was far higher than the hole we'd jumped through. Piles of rocks and mounds of dirt were stacked and pressed to the walls. Several tunnels branched off, and I suspected at least one must lead to the tunnels we'd been in outside the school. But my attention was snagged by what was situated toward the back of the cavern..

Pale white rocks were stacked on top of one another, forming a six-foot-tall archway. The opening wasn't empty. At first, it looked like a blank space, but as I stared, I realized that the area wasn't stagnant. It moved in a slow churning motion, and every few seconds, a sliver of white whipped through like lighting.

"Is this what I think it is?" Cayman approached the crudely made arch.

Roth came down the center of the cavern. "If you're thinking it's a portal, then you'd be correct."

My breath caught as my gaze bounced from him to the archway. "That's a portal?"

"Yes," he answered.

I'd heard of them but never seen one before. I didn't imagine many had.

"It's limestone." Cayman stepped around it, nearing one of the tunnels. "And you guys discovered there are ley lines through here?"

Realizing Zayne must've filled him in, I nodded. "There's an actual hub in or around this area, where several of them connect."

"Damn," Roth murmured. "With the limestone and the ley line, that makes this one Hell of a conductor for power."

"Limestone is like a sponge, soaking in energy all around it, both man-made and electromagnetic, even kinetic and thermal energy. Everything that's happened in this school? The Lilin being born? All the teenage angst? Those ghosts out there? It's all feeding this thing." Cayman moved closer to the side. "And pair that with the energy line it's sitting on? This portal could be something we've never seen before."

"Like...like a portal to another dimension?"

Roth grinned at me. "Possible. The portals we use look nothing like this."

"This is what they're hiding in here." Cayman cocked his head.

"Then we need to destroy it," I said. "Right? Because whatever it's leading to is probably something Earth ending."

"You can't just destroy a portal," Cayman explained, and

I thought about Zayne's plans. "At least, not by conventional means. Hitting something like this with explosives could make it go up like a nuclear bomb."

"Jesus," I whispered. There went blowing up the school.

Cayman reached out as if to touch it, and I wasn't sure that was a good idea. My gaze shifted to the tunnel directly behind him. The shadows looked different there, thicker.

They moved.

Dammit!

"Cayman!" I shouted. "Behind—"

Too late.

A shadow peeled itself away from the tunnel, moving fast. Cayman spun, but it was already on him.

A Shadow Person.

Without warning, Cayman flew into the air, all the way to the ceiling of the cavern, which was much higher in the middle. At least twenty or thirty feet. He was flipped like a pizza, feet snagged by the shadow.

"Wow." Roth's head tipped back.

"You can see that?" I asked. "What's holding him—well, swinging him?"

"Yep."

Huh. Demons could see Shadow People. Made me wonder if Wardens could, too.

"What the Hell?" Cayman yelled as the SP swung him to and fro. "Man, I'm going to hurl. I'm going to vomit up that marsala."

Roth laughed.

"It's not funny!" he shouted as he swung like a pendulum.

Shaking my head, I stepped forward. "Drop him now!"

The shadow only swung him harder.

"Don't think that authoritative command worked," Roth commented.

"Nope." I sighed. "Put him down! Right now."

Cayman lifted his hands. "Wait—"

The Shadow Person let go, and Cayman plummeted to the ground like a rock.

Whoops.

The demon twisted at the last second and landed on his feet with a curse. "That was rude."

The shadow came down like a ball, unfurling to its full height in front of the archway. The thing looked like a combination of black smoke and shadow with the exception of its eyes. They were bloodred, like burning coals.

I tapped into my *grace* and let it out. The corners of my vision turned white as the whitish-gold fire swirled down my arm, flowing to my hand. Against my palm, the handle that formed was a familiar comfort. The blade erupted from sparks and flames.

The shadow rushed me. I stepped forward, slicing through the midsection of the demonic essence. The shadow folded into itself, collapsing into nothing but wisps of smoke, obliterated for all eternity.

A scratching, scurrying noise like tiny claws rushing over stone drew my gaze back to the tunnel. The shadows in there pulsed and shifted—

Tiny ratlike creatures poured out. Dozens of them, rushing toward us on hind legs, their snouts sniffing at the air.

"LUDs!" Roth exclaimed. "These are LUDs."

I could've gone my entire life without ever seeing them. They really did look like miniature Ravers.

Then the darkness from the tunnel shifted once more. Thick inky tendrils licked out over the earthen walls and seeped across the dirt-packed floor like oil. The mass pulled away and then exploded into a horde of Shadow People pouring into the cavern.

"Holy smokes." I lifted the sword. "You guys take care of the LUDs and I'll get these creepy things."

"Deal." Roth kicked one of the LUDs, sending it flying into the opposite wall.

I caught the first shadow at the shoulders and had spun and jabbed the sword into the midsection of a second before the first had even evaporated. I straightened, swinging the sword through the shoulders of another. Sweat dampened my brow within seconds. It was like playing Whac-a-Mole. Another replaced the one cut down.

"Dammit," Roth growled as he tossed a dead LUD aside. "Nightcrawlers."

I spared a quick glance at the tunnel the shadows had come from. There were many, all of them a bulky, monstrous mass of swirling skin the color of moonstone, horns, and teeth and claws that carried a toxic venom that could paralyze an elephant.

A shadow grabbed my left arm, its touch burning. Swallowing a yelp, I jumped back and brought the sword down. Surrounded, I could only hope that Roth and Cayman could handle the Nightcrawlers until I got to them.

I cleaved through the shadows, knowing the sooner I ended their existence the better. The circle decreased by half, and beyond them I saw Roth and Cayman, now in their demonic forms, their skins like polished onyx and wings as wide as they were tall. For a moment, I was caught by the striking similarity in appearance between Wardens and Upper Level demons—both appeared as if they could've been descendants of angels.

Twisting, I took down another shadow with a quick slice just as one of the Nightcrawlers swiped out, nearly catching Cayman along the back as he faced off with another.

I cursed as I darted forward, jumping over one of those damn LUDs. My approach wasn't stealthy. The demon spun toward me and clawed at my head. I dipped low and then sprang up behind the Nightcrawler, drawing the sword up with me. The fire cut through bone and tissue like it was paper. The demon erupted into flames, leaving behind nothing but ash.

"Thanks," Cayman gasped, snapping the neck of another Nightcrawler.

I nodded as I rushed toward a Shadow Person creeping up behind Roth. As I lifted my sword, I felt coldness dance along my neck and settle between my shoulders.

"He's here!" I yelled, taking down the shadow.

And then there he was, strolling out of the tunnel like he was taking a walk in the park, his white-blond hair a stark contrast against the gloom.

"Bambi!" Roth shouted, calling for his familiar. "Off!"

Nothing happened.

Sulien chuckled as he strode forward. "You'll find that the wards will prevent your familiars from making an appearance."

Hell.

That was unforeseen, but I didn't have the time to dwell on that development. I lowered my sword, standing with my feet shoulder width apart. "Nice of you to join us."

"I like to make an entrance." His *grace* roared to life as Cayman started toward him, the deadly spear sparking white fire tinged in blue. He pointed it at Cayman's chest. "I would not take one more step."

"Back off, Cayman." I started forward. "I got this."

For a moment, I didn't think Cayman was going to listen, but he lifted off the ground, snatching up a LUD and throwing it like a beanbag at a nearby Nightcrawler.

"Are you sure you got this, darlin'?" Sulien asked.

"What did I tell you about calling me that? And yeah," I said, stepping back and slicing through the Shadow Person that appeared in my central vision. "I got this."

"You're right where I wanted you, though," Sulien said. "Did you think about that?"

The final Shadow Person went up in a ripple of smoke. "Are you just going to stand there?" I demanded of Sulien. "Afraid to fight?"

"No." He dipped his chin as he crossed his chest with the spear. "I'm waiting."

Taking shallow breaths, I gave the cavern a quick scan. I saw no more Shadow People or Nightcrawlers. There were still a few LUDs running around and chattering. "Waiting for—"

A horn blared, the sound so deafening and otherworldly I knew it could be the sign of only one thing.

"Roth! Cayman!" I shouted. "Get out of here. Now!"

The two demons froze as the remaining LUDs scattered

toward the tunnels. Pinpricks of light appeared, like stars coming out for the night. They grew and spread rapidly, connecting. Golden-white light flashed across the ceiling, charging the air with power and momentarily blinding me. I stumbled back as it pulsed and pulled away from the ceiling. Iridescent light dripped and sparked, forming a funnel of dazzling brightness. My *grace* throbbed in response to the heavenly glow.

Holy crap.

An angel was coming, and it wouldn't matter that Roth and Cayman were on Team Stop the End of the World.

"Too late." Sulien laughed, his spear collapsing into ash. "Unless they want to reenact what happens when insects fly into bug zappers."

Refocusing on Sulien, I lifted the sword. "You're in so much trouble now."

"You think?" he asked, and lifted a brow.

My step faltered as I prepared to strike him. His actions didn't make sense. He'd reined back his *grace*, and why would he do that when an angel was coming? Angels could be jerks, but they were good, and Sulien was obviously—

The floor rattled and the walls shook. The entire world seemed to tremble. Stacked rocks toppled and hit the packed dirt. Roth rose, his wings spinning him out of the path. He came back down a few feet behind me as Cayman remained crouched, amber eyes glowing like coals.

The trumpet sounded once more, causing my brain to feel like it was bouncing around in my skull. I lost my grasp on my *grace* and my sword collapsed.

In the center of the light, the form of a man took shape.

He was tall, nearly seven feet, and as he stepped out of the column, I saw that he wore billowing white pants, his chest bare and skin so luminous and ever shifting, he was neither white nor brown and yet somehow every shade in existence. Just like my father.

But this was not my father.

That much I knew.

He strode forward, his back to the stone archway and the churning static-filled center. From the amount of power he was throwing off, he was definitely an archangel.

Sulien didn't cower or run. He remained where he stood. Waiting.

"What an entrance," Roth murmured. "Wonder what he's compensating for."

The archangel lifted his hand and flicked his wrist, and then Roth and Cayman were both suspended like an invisible hand had snatched them up. They flew through the air and crashed into the rocks and boulders. Both went down, shifting in and out of their forms, landing in the mess of rocks, arms and legs strewn at awkward angles.

Oh God, they didn't move.

My head snapped toward the archangel as he came to stand behind Sulien, placing his hand on the Trueborn's shoulder.

"My son," he spoke, his voice soft and warm, as if it were full of sunlight. "What have you brought me?"

"The blood of Michael." Sulien smirked. "And two demons. They were unexpected."

A dawning sense of horror woke inside me as the archangel turned his head toward me, eyes pure orbs of white. He stepped around the Trueborn—around his *son*—his lip curling on one side as he looked me up and down.

"The child of Michael," he spoke. "I was expecting someone more…impressive."

I blinked.

"But then again, Michael hasn't taken any real interest in you, now, has he, child?" he continued. "I should not be surprised."

Okay.

That was rude.

"Who in the Hell are you?" I demanded.

"I am the Gospel and the Truth. I appeared to Daniel to explain his visions, and I stood beside your father and defended the people against the Fallen and other nations. I am the Saint that appeared before Zechariah and Mary, predicting the births of John the Baptist and Jesus. I am the archangel who delivered Truth and Knowledge to Muhammad." His wings lifted and spread out behind him, and there… there was something wrong with them. Inky veins streaked through the white, leaking what looked like tar. "I am Gabriel, the Harbinger."

40

Shock rolled through me, feeling like I'd been thrust un-expectedly into freezing water as I stared at *the* archangel Gabriel.

"You look surprised." His lips curved into a smile.

Instinct demanded I take a step back, but I held myself in place. "I don't understand. You're Gabriel."

"Pretty sure he's aware of who he is, darlin'." Sulien looked over to where Roth and Cayman were.

I barely heard the Trueborn. "How could it be you?"

"How could it be me killing Wardens? Demons?" One whitish-blond brow rose. "Because it was me. My son kept an eye on things—an eye on you—but it was me."

I couldn't believe what I was hearing. It had nothing to do with being wrong about Sulien and everything to do with the fact the Harbinger was *Gabriel*, one of the most powerful angels—one of the first to ever be created. But it suddenly made too much sense. The angelic wards and weapons. The ruined video feeds. It seemed so obvious, it was almost painful, but even I couldn't understand how an archangel could work with witches and demons and kill not only Wardens but innocent humans.

"Ask me," he coaxed. "Ask me why."

"Why?"

His smile grew. "I'm going to change the world. That's what all of this is about. What all of this has been about." He gestured toward the archway. "The souls of the deceased. This portal." He paused. "Misha. You. I'm going to change the world for the better."

All I could do was stare.

His wings lowered, their tips nearly touching the ground. "Man never should have received the gift God bestowed upon him. They've never been deserving of such a blessing as eternity. That is what a soul grants a human—an eternity of peace or terror, their choice, but eternity nonetheless. But a soul…it does so much more. That is how one loves. That is how one hates. It is mankind's essence, and man was never deserving to know such glory."

"How… Who can say that man could never be deserving?"

"How could man be deserving of the ability to love and to hate and to *feel* when His first creations—us, His ever faithful and most deserving, the ones who defend His glory and spread His word—never were?"

"Because…you're angels? And you're not human?" I was so confused. *So* confused.

"We have auras. We have a pure essence." He looked at

me, those all-white eyes beyond creepy. "But we do not have souls."

He turned slightly, looking to where Sulien was eyeing the demons, and then to the ceiling. "God has done everything to protect man. Given them life and joy and love. Purpose. The ability to create. Raised the Fallen to watch over them, and given them souls as reward. Has done everything to ensure that, when they leave this mortal coil, they find peace. Even those who sin can find forgiveness, and only the most evil and the most unforgivable face judgment. That will change. Mankind as we know it is at its end. Many of us warned God this day would come. There was no stopping this."

"I don't understand what you're getting at." I tried to keep an eye on Sulien as he nudged Cayman with his boot. "God—"

"God has believed in man, and man has betrayed God. What have they done since creation? What have they done with the gift of life and eternity? They made war and created famine and disease. They brought death to their own doors, welcoming it in. They judge as if they are worthy of doing so. They worship false idols who preach what they want to hear and not the gospel. They use the name of God and the Son as vindication for their hatred and their fear." Gabriel tilted his head, his voice smooth and soft. "There has not been one minute in the course of human history that mankind has not made war upon itself. Not an hour when they do not take another life. Not a day they do not hurt one another with words or deeds. Not a week that they do not strip this land of everything God has given it to offer. Not a month where weapons created to destroy life do not pass from hand to hand, leaving nothing but blood and despair behind."

Gabriel's smile disappeared. "This world that once was a gift has become a revolting curse in which people are judged by their skin or who they love and not by their deeds. Those who are most vulnerable and in need are the most ignored or vilified. If the Son were alive today, He would be scorned and feared, and *that* is what mankind has done. Children kill children. Mothers and fathers murder their young. Strangers kill strangers by the dozens, and—the worst sin of all—it is often done in the name of who is Holy. That is what man has done since creation."

Okay. He kind of had a point there. Mankind could be pretty terrible. "Not everyone is like that, though."

"Does it matter when it takes only a small part of decay to rot and destroy the entire foundation?"

"Yes. It matters. Because while there are terrible people out there, there are many more who are good—"

"But are they? Truly? No one can cast a stone, and yet that is all man does."

"No." I shook my head. "You're wrong."

"You say that, with your limited experience, when I've had thousands of years of watching man aspire to nothing? Watching man become so obsessed with the material and the fallacy of power that they will sell their own sons and betray their own countries to make a profit? Time and time again, I've witnessed entire nations fall and the ones birthed out of the ashes follow the same path as the ones before them. You think *you* know better?"

"I know enough to know you're making broad—like, huge—generalizations."

"Tell me, what festers in that human soul of yours? The need to make the world better? The desire to protect? Or is it consumed with carnal needs? Is it full of anger over his betrayal... Misha's?"

I sucked in a sharp breath.

"It was I who came to him. I who was able to sway him and from whom he learned the truth. He knew what needed to be done to rectify this, and while you might have ended his life, you did more damage to yourself than you could have ever done to him. Your heartache. Your rage. It was your ruin. Your human soul is corrupt."

The same words Sulien had spoken carried a different weight now. There was a heaviness of truth, but it was more than that. "Humans are complicated. *I'm* complicated, capable of caring and of wanting multiple conflicting things. Those things do not necessarily corrupt."

"You've killed without guilt."

He had me there.

"You've broken rules." He stepped toward. "You, like the human side of you, are capable only of destruction. Man treats life like it means nothing but flesh and bone. Therefore it will no longer mean anything more."

My stomach hollowed. "So, God wants this? Wants the end of the world?"

Gabriel smirked. "God no longer wants anything."

"What does that even mean?"

"It means that the infallible has failed, and I can no longer stand by and do nothing. I will not stand by. There will be a new God as this Earth is cleansed and only the truly righteous will remain until they, too, cease to exist and none will be left when all is said and done. This beautiful Earth will return to how it was meant to be."

I exhaled roughly. "And that God is you?"

"Don't sound so dismissive, child. If I have learned anything watching over *humans*," he said, sneering at the word, "it is that they will follow and believe just about anything as long as it's easy."

Well, yet again, he had a point. "I don't think ending the world is easy."

"It is when you don't know it's happening until it's too late."

I stilled.

Gabriel chuckled and the sound was beautiful, like rolling waves. "I will undo both Heaven and Earth, and no one will know until it's too late, until nothing can be done. Then God will know that the words of the messenger were true."

He sounded...insane.

Like, if he was some random person on the street, someone would call the police. But since he was an archangel, he also sounded downright scary.

"With this portal, I will open a rift between Earth and Heaven, and a being born of true evil and the souls who belong in Hell will enter Heaven," he said, a dreamy look settling over his features. "Evil will spread like a cancer, infecting every realm. God and the spheres of all the classes will be forced to permanently close the gates to protect the souls there. Heaven will fall during the Transfiguration."

Oh my God.

"Then, every human that dies will no longer be able to

enter Heaven." His smile returned, a thing of pure joy. "Life on Earth will be rendered pointless as those trapped souls become wraiths or are lured into Hell to be tortured and fed upon. There will no longer be a need for demons to remain hidden since angels and God can no longer interfere. With only Wardens and humans left, Hell will reap this Earth."

Horror swamped me. "Why? Why would you want to do that? To billions of people. To Heaven?"

"Why?" he shouted, causing a bolt of fear to pierce my chest. Sulien whipped around. "*Why?* Have you not been listening? Mankind does not deserve what they've been given, what they've been promised! God has failed by refusing to hear the truth! I've been shunned because I dared to speak up! Because I dared to *question*. No longer have I been sent to spread the gospel or to lead. I've been relegated to the lowest spheres. Me! The voice of God! His evermost faithful!"

"You want to end Earth and Heaven because you got fired from being God's hype machine?" I was dumbfounded.

"You know nothing about loyalty." His chest rose and fell with deep, heavy breaths.

I thought of Thierry and Matthew and Jada. I thought of Nicolai and Danika, and all the Wardens in DC. I thought of Roth, the Crown Prince of Hell, and Layla, and Cayman. I thought of Zayne, and I shook my head. "I know what loyalty is. It is *you* who has no idea."

"And it will be you who helps me complete my plan. How does that feel?"

"How do you think I'm going to help you?"

"During the Transfiguration, this area will be charged with power—the kind that can create that rift. With my blood and the blood of Michael, the gateway to Heaven will open," he explained. "Since Michael knows better than to risk being caught on Earth, your blood will do just fine."

Summoning my *grace*, I let it take hold, and as the Sword of Michael formed, he smiled. "I'm partial to my blood, so no thank you."

The archangel dipped his chin. "Silly girl. It was no request."

41

Gabriel came at me, his arm extending as a blinding golden light flowed down it. A sword with a semicircular blade formed.

It was much, *much* larger than mine.

There wasn't a moment to think about the fact I was about to battle an archangel. All I could do was fight, and hope that Roth and Cayman stayed down.

I blocked his blow, rattled by the impact and unprepared for his strength. The one hit nearly knocked me down. I swung my sword toward his chest. He blocked it with one swipe, forcing me back a step. I attacked, sweeping for his legs, but he anticipated the move. I spun, but he was faster. Our swords connected, spitting sparks and hissing. I pushed and then stumbled forward as the archangel disappeared and reappeared a few feet in front of me.

"That's not fair," I said.

"Life never is."

I charged him, and he met my attack, throwing me back like I was nothing more than a paper sack. On and on we went, circling and attacking. He met each blow with his own shattering strength and moved faster than I could. Each time I blocked him, I felt the blow through every atom of my body.

Even with the bond, exhaustion was beginning to peck away at me, making my arms feel heavier and my swings slower. The sparks from our connecting blows spit into the air as the repeated impact jarred my bones. Sweat dripped down my temples as I feinted to the right, arcing my sword. Gabriel slammed his down, knocking me back.

"Stop," he urged, not out of breath. Not even remotely tired. "You've never trained for this. Your father failed you."

He was right, and the truth sent anger pounding through me. I'd trained with daggers and in hand-to-hand combat. But when it came to sword fighting, all I had was instinct.

"It's not enough," he said, and my startled gaze fixed to his. "You're intelligent enough to have come to that conclusion." I blocked his next brutal swing, but it nearly caused my sword to collapse. "You were trained to deny your nature. I trained my son to embrace his."

"Looks like that worked out well." I gritted my teeth as I darted left and kicked out, catching Gabriel in the leg. It was about as helpful as kicking a wall, based on the way he arched his brow.

"Considering you're mere minutes from losing control of your *grace* while he is over there checking his Picture Book, I'd say it has worked out quite well for him."

I faltered. "Picture Book?"

"Instagram," Sulien corrected. "It's Instagram, Dad."

I blinked.

"Whatever," Gabriel muttered, his bare foot slamming into my midsection, knocking the air from my lungs.

"You...you don't even know what Instagram is?" I gasped through the pain. "And you think you're going to end the world?"

His lips peeled back in a sneer.

My arms shook as I leveled the sword in front of me, trying to keep distance between us. "I bet you think Snapchat is called Picture Talkie."

Sulien snorted. "Actually, he thought Snapchat meant snapping your fingers when you talked."

"Really?" I spared the Trueborn a brief glance.

"Yep." Sulien slipped his phone into his pocket. "But you're still getting your ass kicked."

"At least I don't call Instagram Picture Book," I retorted.

Gabriel's all-white eyes pulsed. "I am bored with this. You cannot win. You will never win. Submit."

"Oh, well, when you ask that nicely, it sucks having to say no."

"So be it."

I blocked his thrust, but he moved to my side before I could track what he was doing. His elbow caught my chin, snapping my head back. I stumbled, regained my footing and struck out with my sword, arms trembling as his blade connected with mine. He spun into my peripheral vision once more, but this time I was expecting his attack. Jumping back, I turned—

His fist slammed into my cheek, and pain exploded along my ribs as he landed another blow. My legs folded before I could stop them. My control over my *grace* was lost as I caught myself before my head slammed into the dirt. Panic unfurled in the pit of my stomach as I struggled to sit up. I pushed it down, knowing I couldn't give in to it.

"You are nothing but a worthless, selfish human the moment you lose control of your *grace*." Gabriel stood above me. "You are weak. Corrupt. Defiled. You are *nothing*."

The little ball of warmth inside me pulsed, and I silently cursed, knowing that Zayne had to have felt the burst of panic. He couldn't come down here. He *couldn't*. I needed to get control of the situation.

I had to.

"You are not worthy of what God gifted you. Just like the rest of the humans," Gabriel went on as I slid my hand to my hip, my fingers unhooking the dagger sheathed there. "You took the purity of a soul and the honor of free will and threw them away."

I rose to my knees, lifting my head as I felt blood trickle out of the corner of my mouth. "I didn't throw away anything."

"You're wrong. No human soul, not even my son's, is clean or worthy of saving."

"Wow." My fingers tightened on the hilt of the dagger. "Father of the year right here."

"At least I'll be there when he dies," he said. "Will Michael be able to say the same?"

"Probably not," I admitted. "But I don't care."

Surprise rolled over Gabriel's face, and I saw my window of opportunity. My chance to gain the upper hand and get the Hell out of here, with Roth and Cayman, somehow.

Shooting to my feet, I slammed the dagger deep into Gabriel's chest. I knew it wouldn't kill him, but it had to hurt. It had to—

The archangel looked down at his chest. "That stung."

I jerked the dagger out, eyes widening in disbelief as I saw no blood—

I didn't see the blow coming.

Gabriel backhanded me, sending me down to the dirt. Stars sparked in my vision. My ears rang. He grabbed my wrist, snatching the dagger from my hand.

"That was embarrassing," he said, tossing it to the ground. "You're nothing but a flawed waste of *grace*, Trinity. Give it up. I can make the next couple of weeks peaceful for you, or I can make them a constant waking nightmare. It is your choice."

When he let go of my hand, I fell back. My gaze blanked out on me for a moment.

Get up.

"In the end, you're nothing but flesh and bone," he said. "Dying from the day you were born."

Get up.

"It's all rather revolting, how the human race aids in its own decay."

Get up.

"Your rage. Your selfishness. Your basic human emotions. All of it corrupts what should never have been given to humans."

The bond in my chest burned, and I knew Zayne was coming. He was close. Too close.

Get up.

Get up before he gets here.

"You're right. I am flesh. I am flawed. I am selfish, but I am also *grace*." I spat out a mouthful of blood, and from the rage and the ruin, I rose onto my feet. "I have heavenly fire in my blood. I have a human *soul*, and that is something you will *never* have."

The archangel drew back.

"That's it, isn't it? *That's* why you hate God. That's why you want to destroy everything. It's not to make it better. It's not to end suffering, you lunatic. All of this is because you don't have a soul." I laughed, stumbling backward, summoning my *grace*. It sputtered and then arrived, the handle almost too heavy for me to hold. "You're a walking cliché, and you dare to insult the aspirations of humans?"

"You know nothing." He stalked forward, and I saw Roth sit up in his human form. Sulien pushed off the wall.

"You forgot to add 'Jon Snow' at the end of that statement."

He halted, head cocked. "What?"

I swung, aiming for the largest part of him. My *grace* could and would kill him. I would end this, because it was my duty.

Gabriel grabbed my right arm just above my elbow and twisted. The crack was so sudden, so shocking, that there was a brief second where I felt nothing. And then I screamed. The red-hot shock of pain fried my senses. I lost my *grace*. The sword collapsed in on itself as I tried to breathe through the pain.

His foot connected with my shin, snapping the bone there, and I couldn't even scream as I hit the ground on one knee, couldn't even breathe around the fire that seemed to engulf my entire leg. He gripped me by the scruff of my neck and lifted me. I clutched at his arm with my good hand and kicked out as I saw Sulien grab Roth.

It happened in a matter of heartbeats. Seconds. Brutal, unending seconds when I realized I couldn't defeat an archangel. This was never a battle I could win, and in the distant part of my mind that functioned above the pain, I wondered if my father had known that and sent me out for the slaughter.

Roth would die.

So would Cayman.

I'd be taken, and the world as we knew it would end, and maybe my father and God didn't care about what would happen. Their attempts to save humankind were half-assed if they'd thought I could do this, and maybe…maybe God had washed *His* proverbial hands of the whole mess.

If not, how did they think I could defeat an archangel?

Gabriel slammed me into the ground with the force of a fall from a building.

Bones shattered *everywhere*.

Legs.

Arms.

Ribs.

I saw something white jutting from my leg as my vision winked in and out. Pain came in a flash of bright light. A thousand nerves tried to fire all at once, attempting to send communications from my brain to my arms and legs, to my pelvis and ribs and spine. My body jerked as something went *loose* inside. I couldn't move my legs. The terror that poured through me filled my veins with icy slush. I struggled to get air into my lungs, but they felt wrong, as if they couldn't inflate.

"I need you alive, at least for a little while longer," he said.

Sure didn't feel like he needed that. "Is it because you find me...endearing and lovable?" I rasped words that sounded off, as if half the letters couldn't be pronounced.

Gabriel knelt beside me, his cruelly beautiful face blurring in and out. "More like I need your blood hot when it flows. I told you I could make this easy and peaceful. I would've let you have your heart's desire. You would've enjoyed what time you had left, but you chose this fate. To suffer. So stupidly human."

Blood spewed from my mouth as I coughed and my breath wheezed. "You...talk a lot."

"I was the voice of God." Gabriel's hand folded over my throat. Air immediately cut off. He lifted me, my feet dangling several feet above the ground and my body loose like a pile of rags. "The messenger of His Faith and Glory, but I am now the Harbinger, and I will usher in a new era. Retribution will be pain with the cleansing power of blood, and as Heaven crumbles into itself, those who remain will have a new God."

"She's right. You do talk too much."

Gabriel turned toward the source of the voice. I managed to turn my head only half an inch, if that, but enough that I could see Roth.

"And you know what?" Roth said, standing without Sulien. His arm hung oddly, but he was standing. "You sound an awful lot like someone I know. Does this sound familiar? 'I will ascend into Heaven, I will exalt my throne above the stars of God; I will sit also upon the mount of the congregation, in the sides of the north; I will ascend above the heights of the clouds; I will be like the most High.'"

"Do not compare me to *him*," Gabriel growled.

"Wouldn't think of it," Roth replied. "It would be an insult to the *Shining One*."

Several things happened at once. Gabriel let out a roar that shook the world as he threw out his arm. Something must've left his hand, because I heard Roth grunt and hit the ground, laughing—he was *laughing*. Gabriel's sneer faded.

"Idiot," gasped Roth. "Egotistical idiot. I hope it eases you to know that you were right."

"You will be here for the death of your son."

My gasp at the sound of Zayne's voice was swallowed in Gabriel's shout as he turned again.

Zayne stood behind Gabriel, his arm around Sulien's neck as the Trueborn struggled, his *grace* flaring from his right arm, forming a spear that could kill Zayne even if he hadn't been weakened. A different kind of fear crowded me.

But Zayne was fast, so incredibly fast as he gripped the side of the Trueborn's head and twisted.

Gabriel screamed, his rage thundering through the cavern like an earthquake as Zayne dropped the Trueborn and then shot forward, slamming into the archangel, breaking Gabriel's hold on my throat. I started to fall, but Zayne caught me. The burst of pain from his embrace threatened to drag me under, and I must have blacked out, because the next thing I knew I was lying on my back and Zayne was rising in front of me, his wings stretched out on either side of him.

And I saw him.

Numerous nicks and grooves scarred his back, and his wings didn't look right. One hung at an odd angle, and below the left wing, there was a deep cut, exposing bone and tissue. That wound was…

Oh God.

How had that happened to him? How had he been wounded? He just got here. He just…

Summoning everything I had left in me, I managed to shift onto my side. I sat up, but pain screamed through my body. My cheek smacked onto the ground. I managed to lift my chin, seeking Roth. He had to get Zayne out of here. Had to get him away from Gabriel. I yelled for the demon prince, but only a croak came out. Something was wrong with my throat.

"You will not live to regret that," Gabriel warned.

"I'm going to rip you limb from limb," Zayne snarled. "And then I will burn your body right next to his."

"I was waiting for this moment." Gabriel's tone was smug— too smug. Warnings went off. "I knew you'd come."

There was a gasping sound, and Zayne took a step back, his wings lifting and then falling. Roth shouted.

"Do you now know why Trueborns and their Protectors are forbidden to be together?" Gabriel's voice was a whisper that carried in the wind that began to pick up inside the chamber. "Love clouds judgment. It is a weakness that can be exploited."

I tried to see what was happening, but I could no longer lift my head.

"Bitterness and hate will fester and grow inside her, just as it did with Sulien and with those who came before her. She will gladly spill her own blood against a God that could be so cruel." Gabriel's voice was everywhere, inside and out, vibrating in my broken ribs. "You took my son, but you have given me a daughter in return."

There was a ripple of golden heated light, and then silence.

"Zayne," Roth called out. "My man…"

I saw Zayne's legs crumple and fold. He went down on his knees, his back to me. I tried to say his name. His hand moved to his front, to his chest. He grunted as his body jerked.

A dagger fell to the ground.

My dagger.

Then he, too, fell.

Zayne landed next to me, on his back and broken wing. Why would he fall like that? I didn't understand what was happening, why Roth was suddenly there beside Zayne. The demon was shouting for someone—for Cayman and then Layla, trying to hold Zayne down, but Zayne pushed Roth off and rolled onto his side facing me.

I saw his chest—I saw the wound over his heart and the blood that gushed with every heartbeat.

"No," I whispered, a great horror sinking its claws into me. "Zayne…"

"It's okay," he said, and blood leaked from the corner of his mouth.

I tried to lift my arm, and all I managed was a twitch that made it feel like I'd been run over by a dump truck. Panic rose like a cyclone as I tried to reach for him again. Suddenly, Roth was behind me. He scooped me up and laid me down so I was right next to Zayne. "You can't. No. Please, God, no. *Zayne, please…*"

Roth carefully took my hand, placing it on Zayne's cheek. The movement hurt, but I didn't care. His granitelike skin was too cool. It wasn't right at all. My fingers moved, trying to rub heat back into his skin. Those pale wolf eyes were open, but they... There was no light in them. His chest wasn't moving. It was still. He was still. I didn't understand, didn't want to. I rubbed his skin, kept rubbing his skin, even as it stopped feeling real.

"Trinity," Roth began, voice all wrong. He rocked back, hands dropping to his knees, and then he looked away, rising to his feet. He staggered a step, hands lifting to his hair as he bent over. "He's—"

"No. *No.*" I searched Zayne's face. "Zayne?"

The only answer was the bond wrenching deep inside me, as if it were a cord stretched too tight. It snapped free as a keening wail tore through the air, ripped from my very soul. I no longer felt the bond.

And then I no longer felt anything.

42

Hell wasn't just being trapped in a broken body. Hell was being unable to escape soul-deep grief while trapped. I thought I'd experienced the worst possible loss with my mother, and then with Misha, but I'd been wrong. Not that their losses were any less devastating. This was...different and it was too much.

This was like purgatory.

Over the course of several hours that turned into several days, I learned I could heal from any wound as long as it wasn't fatal. Broken bones knitted back together and popped into joints they'd been ripped from. Torn flesh stitched back together without the aid of needle and thread, something I hadn't known was possible and apparently neither had Matthew, who'd stitched many of my wounds in the past. Now I understood why Jasmine had been so surprised by the head wound I'd received that night in the tunnel. Severed veins and nerves reconnected, bringing back sensation to places that had long gone numb.

The process was painful.

Slipping out of consciousness only when it became too much and I needed to escape the burning pins and needles along my limbs as blood flow returned, I was awake for most of the healing. I was awake when Layla sat down beside me with tears streaming from her eyes and told me that Zayne was gone.

A part of me had known that already, and she didn't need to go into detail. Too much time had already passed. When Wardens died, their bodies went through the same process a human body did, except it happened much faster. Within a day, there'd be only bones left, and it had been many days. Zayne was gone. His laugh and the smile that never failed to cause my stomach and heart to do strange, wonderful things. His wry sense of humor and his kindness that set him apart from everyone I knew. His intelligence and unending loyalty. His fierce protectiveness that had been apparent before we'd been bonded, something that had annoyed me as much as it had strengthened me. His body and bones and beautiful face… All of it gone before I even regained consciousness.

I screamed.

I screamed when I looked around the room and didn't see his spirit or ghost, stuck in the horrible place of being both relieved and devastated.

I screamed until my voice gave out and my throat was on fire. I screamed until I could no longer make a sound. I screamed until I thought of the senator and finally, truly understood how deep of a cut this kind of pain could make.

How it could lead a person to do anything, utterly anything, to bring their loved one back.

I screamed, realizing that my decision to hold him back, to keep him outside, might have led to his death just as much as falling in love with him had, maybe even more. That it had felt wrong, and I should've known, should not have tried to convince myself that what was right could feel wrong. I'd never know whether the outcome would've been different if he'd gone in with us, or if that would've resulted in an earlier death.

I screamed until it became too much, until there was a sharp sting along my arm and then there was nothing but darkness until I awoke again, only to realize that purgatory was being trapped with grief and sorrow and anger.

Gabriel had been right about one thing. I *was* bitter and vengeful. I wanted retribution against the archangel and even God for creating a rule that had ultimately weakened Zayne, but I wanted Zayne back more, and there had to be a way. This couldn't be it. I refused to accept it. I couldn't. Not when I thought of how he'd said he'd go to the ends of the Earth to find me if I was taken. How he'd sworn he'd stop at nothing to get me back, even from the clutches of death.

The pain of my bones and skin repairing themselves became a fuel. Bringing Zayne back was all I could think about. I didn't talk to Roth or Layla when they checked on me, not after they'd told me that Zayne was gone. I didn't even talk to Peanut when he ghosted in and out of the room.

I planned.

I planned, as day turned to night once more and the stars Zayne had thoughtfully plastered to the ceiling started to glow softly. Constellation Zayne. My heart shattered all over again. Tears welled, but they didn't fall. I didn't think it was possible to cry anymore. The well was empty. Just like my chest, where the bond had once resided, but it was slowly filling back up with a storm of emotions. Some hot. Some ice-cold. I knew, as I stared at those stars, that I was no longer the same. The fight had broken me. The pain had shifted me. Zayne's death had reshaped me.

And my plans breathed the life into me. I just needed my body to get on board.

A soft nudge at my arm drew my gaze. I was greeted with a flicker of a pink tongue.

I had no idea why Bambi was in bed with me, stretched out and pressed against my side like a dog, but when I'd woken earlier and found her there, I hadn't freaked out.

Drawing in a shallow breath, I lifted my fingers on my left hand. They were stiff and achy. I tried to move my arm. A flare of pain danced across my shoulder, but it was nothing like before. I bent my arm at the elbow, wincing as the freshly healed joint ground together, and placed my hand on Bambi's diamond-shaped head. Her tongue gave me another wave and her mouth opened, like she was smiling as she laid her head on my stomach.

Her scales were smooth and yet rough around the edges. I traced them idly, and Bambi seemed to love the attention. Whenever my fingers stilled, she bumped my hand.

After a little while, I could move my leg, bending the right and then the left.

Some time later, the door cracked open and Layla popped her head in. "You're awake."

"I…" Wincing, I cleared my throat. My voice was still hoarse. "I am."

"Up for company?"

Not particularly, but we needed to talk. There was Gabriel and his batshit-crazy plans that someone had to deal with. And then there were my plans. "Where's…Roth?"

"He's here. Let me get him, and you something to drink." She dipped out and returned a few minutes later with a large glass and the demon prince in tow.

As he came closer, I thought he looked different, as if he'd aged a decade. It was his eyes. A weariness was there that hadn't been before. Peanut followed, lingering by the foot of the bed as he stared at the snake.

"I'm not getting any closer," he said.

Bambi tilted her head toward him, wiggling her tongue in his direction. She could see him. Interesting.

Layla sat beside me. "This is ginger ale. I thought it would be good on your stomach."

"Thanks." I lifted my head and started to sit up, but Layla held the cup to my mouth, preventing too much movement. I drank greedily even though it burned the back of my throat.

"I see someone has been keeping you company." Roth leaned against the wall, ankles crossed.

"Yeah, she has." I let my head fall back against the pillow. "Is Cayman…okay?"

"He's fine," he answered.

"Good." I cleared my throat. "We need…to talk about Gabriel."

"We don't have to." Layla placed the glass on the night-stand, next to my mother's book. "Not right now."

"We do," I said. Bambi nudged my hand, and I returned to petting her head. "Has anything happened?"

Layla shook her head as she started twisting the pale strands of her hair.

"I've been...patrolling." Roth said the last word like it was a foreign language. "With everything that happened, I..."

He didn't finish, but I thought I knew what he'd been about to say. That he needed to be doing something.

"Gabriel hasn't been spotted. No Wardens have been killed," Layla continued, staring at Roth. "We did manage to get the school closed."

"How?"

"I went back the next night, started a small fire that might have done some intensive damage to the classrooms." Roth grinned.

Smart idea, since all those ghosts were evil to their core. No human should step foot in that school. "What about Stacey and her diploma?"

"They're finishing the rest of the summer classes at another school." Layla looked at Bambi, who seemed to be purring. Like a cat. "She wanted to be here, but she's..."

Layla didn't need to finish. I already knew. Stacey was hurting. That I could understand.

"I think I took out most of the Shadow People." I got to the point of this conversation as I watched Peanut eye the snake. "The ghosts are still there, and I guess Gabriel will bring more Shadow People in. I don't know why, but Gabriel needs me alive. At least until the Transfiguration."

"We have a little under a month before the Transfiguration," Roth said, folding his arms over his chest. "A couple

weeks until we either find a way to stop Gabriel or the beginning of the end kicks off."

I closed my eyes. "I can't…stop him."

"Trinnie," Peanut said. "Don't say that. You can."

"I can't." I answered him without Layla and Roth realizing. "He's an archangel. You saw what he's capable of. Even
with the angel spikes, we'd have to get close to him. *I* would
have to get close to him. He's impossible to beat." Opening
my eyes, I stared up at the stars. It was hard admitting this,
knowing I was no longer the top of the food chain, but it was
the truth. "At least, by myself I can't. I'm not bonded anymore, and I doubt my father will bond me to another Warden. It's too much of a risk if Gabriel senses him and decides
to use his blood instead of mine. I'm not weak, but I'm not
as strong as I was when I was bonded. Even then, I couldn't
beat an archangel alone."

"So, we need to find a way to weaken or trap him," Layla
suggested. "There has to be something."

"There is," Roth said. "I know of one thing that can take
down an archangel."

My gaze shifted to him. "What is it? Another archangel?
Obviously none of them want to get involved. My father
didn't even—" I pressed my lips together, wincing as my jaw
ached. "They're not stepping in. It's up to me."

"I'm not talking about any of those self-righteous and seriously unhelpful bastards who created their own little home-
grown terrorist." His amber eyes glowed. "I'm talking about
the one being who'd love nothing more than to take down
one of his brethren."

Layla twisted at her waist, understanding creeping into her

pale face. "You can't be thinking what I'm thinking you're thinking."

"I'm not just thinking it," he said. "I'm planning it, shortie."

"Lucifer," I whispered. "You're talking about Lucifer."

"Holy gumdrops," Peanut whispered.

Roth's smile was pure violence. "I'm not just talking about Lucifer. I'm talking about releasing him. All we have to do is convince him, and I don't think that'll be hard."

"But he can't walk Earth in his true form," Layla reasoned as I eased back against the pillow. "If he does, it forces the biblical Apocalypse into play. God would never allow it."

"Call me crazy, but I doubt God is okay with Gabriel attempting to give Heaven an STD," Roth argued. "If Heaven closes its gates, no souls can enter. Those who die will be trapped on Earth. They will either turn wraith or, worse yet, be dragged into Hell and corrupted. Beyond that, there'd be no point in anything. Life would essentially cease upon death. And death will happen at a rate we've never seen before, because with the angels locked away, there's nothing stopping demons except Wardens. Earth would become Hell."

Gabriel had said as much.

"But why would Lucifer want to stop that?" Layla demanded. "Sounds like a great time for him."

"Because it's not his idea," Roth said. "If Gabriel and Bael succeed? His ego will take a blow I'm not sure he could survive. There's only space for one Hell and one ruler of Hell. His throne room is lined with the heads of demons who thought they could take over."

Was it disturbing that I sort of wanted to see his throne room?

Probably.

"So, we're stuck between one possible Armageddon and another possible Armageddon?" Layla sat back.

"Pretty much." He nodded. "Either we sit back and wait until Earth goes to Hell—"

"Or we bring Hell to Earth," she finished. "You think you can convince him?"

"Pretty confident." He rubbed his fingers under his chin. "I just need to talk to him and hope he's in a good mood."

Layla laughed, but it was that slightly crazed-sounding kind of laugh.

"Do it," I said, spine straightening even though it caused immense pain. Bambi lifted her head, eyeing me like she didn't think sitting up was a wise idea. "Talk to Lucifer. Convince him. But there's something else I want."

"Anything," Roth swore, and I doubted that was something he did a lot. Perfect.

"I want Zayne," I said.

"Trinity," Layla whispered. "He's—"

"I know where he is. I know that he's gone. I want him back." My heart started pounding, Zayne's voice so painfully real in my thoughts that I sucked in a sharp, brittle breath. *There'd be nothing that would stop me.* "I *will* get him back."

Roth came to the bed and sat. His familiar wiggled on the other side of me. "Trinity, if I could do that, I would. I would do it for both of you. I swear it, but I cannot. No one—"

"Not true." I met his amber gaze. "Grim can. And before I do a damn thing for my father or for the human race, I want Zayne. I want him back, alive, and I don't care how selfish that makes me, but he deserves to be here, with me." My voice cracked, and Roth lowered his gaze. "I deserve that, and the damn Grim Reaper will give him back to me. Tell me where to find him or how to reach him."

Layla closed her eyes for a long moment and then she asked, "Have you seen him since you woke up?"

"No."

"Does that mean he's crossed over?" she asked.

"It could mean that," I answered. "But Zayne said even death wouldn't stop him. He wouldn't have crossed over."

You know that's not always true, whispered a stupid voice of reason.

People died unexpectedly all the time—people who still had plans and loved ones. While alive, people fully believed they'd come back if they could, but most of the time people *changed* when they entered the light. Their desires and needs remained, but they crossed into the great beyond, and whatever that was reshaped them.

But Zayne hadn't come back, even as a spirit, and I fully believed that if he had crossed over, he would have, even if it was to make sure I was okay.

"But what if he has crossed over," Layla said quietly. "What if he's found peace? Happiness?"

My gaze sharpened on her as my chest hollowed.

"What if he's really okay? And he's waiting for you when it's your time." Tears filled her eyes. "Is it okay to take him from that?"

No.

Yes.

A knot lodged in the back of my throat. What if he was at— *No.* I couldn't let myself think that. I wanted him back too much. I couldn't do this without him. I just couldn't.

"He would want to come back to me," I said. "I don't think

he's crossed over." The knot expanded, pushing out painful words. "I never got to tell him I love him. I should've told him that, but I didn't and his last words to me were that it was okay—" My voice cracked as I clamped my mouth shut. It took several seconds before I could speak again. "I will get him back."

"Trin," Peanut whispered, and I looked over at him. "Think about what you're saying. About what you're planning to do."

"I have thought about this," I told him and then looked to Roth. "It's *all* I have thought about. I know what it means."

It wouldn't be easy.

It would be damn near impossible, and I had no idea if Zayne would return to me as a Warden or as my Protector, but that would be a bridge we'd cross together.

Because I would succeed. Gabriel had been wrong. Rage and ruin had not corrupted me. They *powered* me. I would do anything, give up anything, to make Zayne's return happen. *Anything.* Because we'd promised each other forever, and we would have that, one way or another.

Slowly, Roth lifted his gaze to mine and then, after an eternity, he nodded. "I will tell you how to find him."

And he did.

43

It was a surprisingly cool day for July as I walked the worn dirt path of Rock Creek Park, thick clouds shielding the glare of the evening sun. Sunglasses were still perched on my nose, but I wouldn't need them much longer. Night was about to fall.

Two days had passed since I'd woken up, and each step I took was still painful and stiff, but the fact that I was able to walk after having nearly every bone in my body broken only a handful of days ago was nothing short of a miracle.

So was the fact that I'd been able to escape Layla and Roth, who seemed to have moved in to the apartment, and the never-ending flow of Wardens. They'd been updated by either Roth or Layla, and whenever any of them were there, the somberness was as heavy and suffocating as a coarse blanket.

Everyone was still in shock. Everyone was still grieving the loss of…Zayne. And I think all of them were worried

Gabriel might make a grab for me. While I was recovering, it would be as easy as him walking into the apartment and picking me up.

But even if I were fully healed, it wouldn't be much harder.

Swallowing a sigh, I shuffled along as people jogged past, their sneakers kicking up puffs of dirt. The only reason I'd been able to sneak out was because Roth and Layla had left to speak to Lucifer, leaving Cayman in charge of watching me.

Within five minutes, the demon had seemingly passed out on the couch, but as I'd snuck out, I'd wondered if he was really asleep, or if he was giving me a chance to escape.

I needed to get out of the apartment, away from the wintermint smell that lingered in the bathroom and on the pillowcases I refused to change. I needed to see the real stars, and not the ones on my ceiling—the ones that belonged to Zayne. I needed fresh air, and I needed to get my sore muscles and bones in working order, because sooner rather than later, Gabriel would come for me, and I planned on putting up a fight with or without the aid of one very scary, very powerful evil archangel.

So, I'd pulled on my big-girl pants, ordered an Uber and almost gotten into the wrong car, but I made it to the park by myself. I did it, and God, that felt like a big step.

I kept walking and came upon the bench where Zayne and I had sat the day I'd gone to the coven with Roth. Chest heavy and aching, I made my way to it and took a seat, wincing as my tailbone protested the action. For some reason, the sucker hurt more than anything else.

People strolling past sent concerned looks in my direction once I removed my sunglasses and hooked them in the front of my shirt. I knew I looked like I'd survived a car accident or a death match with a gorilla. Barely. Bones had fused back together. Torn muscles had stitched themselves, and ripped skin had healed, but I was covered in purplish-blue and some angry red bruises that were slow to fade. Gabriel's hand had left marks around my neck. My left cheek was swollen and discolored. Both eyes were swollen with dark greenish-blue smudges under them, and they were bloodshot.

I'd thought the Uber driver was going to take me to the hospital or to the police after getting a good look at me.

Shadows grew around me, and park lights came on as night slowly crept in. Fewer and fewer people passed me, until there was no one else, and then—only then—did I look up at the night sky.

There were no stars.

I didn't know if the sky was empty because it was still over-cast, or if whatever damage Gabriel had done to my body had somehow accelerated the failing of my eyes. Knowing my luck, it was probably the latter.

Closing my eyes, I thought about something I'd avoided for the past two days, something Layla had said. Zayne still hadn't come to me as a ghost or a spirit, and I didn't know if that meant he had crossed over and was adjusting to…well, to *paradise*, and he was doing what Layla had said—waiting for me when it was my time.

Roth had told me what I needed to do to summon the Angel of Death, since I couldn't go to Hell or to Heaven to speak with him. I'd have to get the *Lesser Key*, which was currently at the Warden compound. I doubted they'd just hand that over, so I probably needed one more day before I was ready to force Nicolai to do something he most likely would not want to do. I would summon Grim and I would get Zayne back, but...

Tears spilled from my eyes, wetting my cheeks. How I could still cry was beyond me. I'd thought that well was drained dry, but I was wrong. The tears fell, even when I closed my eyes. Crying was a weakness I couldn't afford right now, especially since I felt like I was so close to tipping over a razor-sharp edge.

But what if Zayne really was at peace? What if he was safe and happy? What if he had the eternity that he very much deserved? How could I... How could I take that from him? Even if Gabriel succeeded in bringing on the apocalypse, Zayne would be safe. The gates of Heaven would close, and maybe it wouldn't crumble into itself like Gabriel claimed. I couldn't imagine God allowing all those souls and the angels to perish. God would *have* to step in before then, and while I'd never see him again, Zayne would be safe.

Could I be that selfish, to bring him back to *this*? To a place where he could die once again fighting Gabriel, to protect a world that would never know all that he'd sacrificed for it? And if we failed to stop Gabriel, there'd be no eternity, no peace or paradise. We'd be stuck in the human plane, where we'd turn into wraiths or be dragged to Hell.

Opening my eyes, I dragged my hands under my cheeks and stared at the sky. Two days ago, I would've said yes, I was that selfish. A week ago, I would've said the same thing... but now?

I loved Zayne with every fiber of my being, with every

breath I took and with every beat of my heart. I didn't know if I could do that to him.

And I didn't know how I could do any of this without him.

I stared at the night sky, wishing for some sign, for something that would tell me what to do, what was right—

A pinprick of light appeared, and I blinked, thinking my eyes were messing with me. But the glow remained, growing brighter and more intense as it raced across the sky. Twisting at the waist, I ignored the pain as I watched the white streak of light disappear beyond the trees, farther than my eyes could track.

Was that…a falling star?

Heart thumping, I turned back around. Had I just seen an actual falling star? A hoarse laugh scratched my throat. Was that the sign I'd been asking for?

If so, what in the Hell did that even mean?

I could interpret that to mean yes, I should summon Grim and possibly rip Zayne away from peace and happiness. Or it could mean that Zayne was okay, just like he'd told me, and that he was watching over me. Or it could mean absolutely nothing at all. I shook my head. No, it had to mean something. I dragged in a deep breath…and every muscle in my body tensed.

I smelled… I smelled snow and winter, fresh and minty.

I smelled *wintermint*.

My pulse kicked up as I reached down, gripping the edge of the bench. My head turned in the direction Zayne had come from the last time I'd been here, but the path was empty, as far as I could see.

Was I experiencing wishful smelling?

Easing my grip on the bench, I'd started to stand, when I felt it. A strange, shivery warmth that danced along the nape of my neck and between my shoulders. A breeze glided from behind me, lifting strands of my hair, and I was surrounded in wintermint.

The warmth spread from my neck down my back, and I sensed I was no longer alone. Someone or something was here, and I knew… I knew Heaven smelled like what you desired most.

My lips parted as I slowly stood, bones and muscles protesting, and turned around, closing my eyes because I was too afraid to look, to discover nothing but darkness existed there, and maybe, just maybe, I was losing a little of my mind. Trembling, I opened my eyes, and I couldn't breathe, couldn't speak or think beyond what I saw.

Zayne.

It was him, his blond hair loose and falling against cheeks and brushing broad, bare shoulders. It was his full lips I'd kissed and loved, and his broad chest that rose and fell rapidly…but those were not his eyes that stared back at me.

These eyes were a shade of blue so vibrant and so clear, they made Warden eyes seem pale and lifeless in comparison. They were the color of the sky at twilight.

And it wasn't his skin.

Where his skin had looked like it had been kissed by the sun, it now carried a faint luminous golden glow. Not like a spirit, because he was blood and bone, but he was…he was *shining*, and my heart was pounding fast.

"Trin," he said, and the tremors turned to full-body shakes at the sound of his voice—*his* voice. It was him, the way he said my name, it was *him*, and he was alive and breathing and I didn't care how. I didn't care why. He was alive, and—

Zayne's shoulders moved, straightening, and something white and golden swept into the air and spread out on either side of him, nearly ten feet wide.

My mouth dropped open.

Wings.

They were wings.

Not Warden wings.

Even with my eyes, I could tell these were *feathered*. They were white and thick with streaks of gold laced throughout, and those gold veins glowed with Heavenly fire, with *grace*.

They were angelic wings.

Zayne was an *angel*.

★ ★ ★ ★ ★

Acknowledgments

I want to thank Natashya Wilson and the amazing team at Inkyard Press for being as excited as me to dive back into the world of demons and gargoyles and angels. Thank you to my agent Kevan Lyon, who helped make this series possible, to my publicist Kristin Dwyer for going above and beyond the call of duty and to Stephanie Brown for making sure I'm actually getting writing done. Thank you to Jen Fisher, who read the original version of this and didn't kill me. Thank you to Malissa Coy, Hannah McBride, Val, Jessica, Krista, Katie, Happy, Sarah, Jessica Bird (who just really loves my puppy), Mike, KA, Liz, Jillian, Lesa, Drew, Wendy, Corrine, Tijan and many, many amazing authors whose books I've read and loved.

A special thanks to all the Stormies who blew me away with the Can You Still See the Stars at Night? campaign to raise awareness about retinitis pigmentosa. I am incredibly honored to have such a thoughtful, awe-inspiring group of readers. You all blew me away, and I will forever be grateful and humbled.

Thank you to the JLAnders for being your fun, llama-loving selves, and to every reader who has picked up this book. You are the reason I'm able to write and tell these stories.

21982319551739